外國人
天天在用
上班族萬用
E-mail 大全

我必須老實説,我沒有在美國學過經營學或經濟學,我學的是新聞學。不過,2000 年歸國以來,我寫的商務信件比任何人都還要多。原因很簡單,僅僅是因為我英文好,親朋好友就都來拜託我幫忙寫,在出口螢幕的公司工作的朋友、進口布料加工再出口的後輩,甚至是在國內龍頭 S 電子公司擔任理事的前輩們,都拜託過我寫英文信件。當然,一開始受託時,只是給了幾句建言,但後來漸漸地,經常變成由我代筆。

國人寫英文信件的習慣

幫忙寫各種商務信件時,可以發現國人寫英文信時的一些專屬的傾向。

第一,容易感到煩躁的傾向。手邊雖然有幾本關於英文信件的書籍,但還是感覺煩躁,即使試著下筆去寫,也寫不出符合狀況的信件。

第二,速戰速決的傾向。即便寫了信件,也因為個性太急,沒有在發信前再次檢查內容、文法。舉我的知音 UCLA 經營學系教授的例子來說,儘管他是美國大學的教授,每次要寄信給我時,一定會再三檢查才寄出。何況是以外語來學英文的我們,不更應該要仔細檢查嗎?

第三,結論寫得不簡潔、過於冗長、天花亂墜的傾向。其實,信件只要簡潔寫出 3~4 句重點就可以了。不過,國人寫的英文信,很多人光是打招呼就 3~4 句了。英文母語人士寫的信,打招呼只有一句,而且最重要的句子,會放在前面開頭的地方。我們則是相反,從小習慣了將結論放在最後面,自然將信件開頭寫得冗長。務必要記住,在當今商務繁忙的時代,商務信件要寫得簡短且點到重點就可以了。

簡單來説,寫商務英語信件時,只要注意以下三點即可。

1. 簡單明瞭。
2. 重要的句子放在前面。
3. 發信之前從頭到尾再檢查一次。

商務人士專屬的英語信件字典

我在 2010 年奔波於商務環境時，便決定為國內商務人士打造一本專屬的商務英語書。

後來我將商務信件整理、分析，歷經了數個月。透過訪查和調查，為要在忙碌的 21 世紀商務環境中生存的上班族，選出了最常使用的 154 個情境、770 篇信件，收錄各狀況中可以實際使用的內容。現在，不必再找好幾本書，東拼西湊內容，只要善用這本書，並替換其中的單字，就可以完成信件了。

以下簡單介紹一下《外國人天天在用上班族萬用 E-mail 大全》這本書的基本架構：

✉ **sample 1**

Dear [Mr.Admas]

My name is Sam Jones. I'm looking for business partners in the Los Angeles area, and Jim Lewis mentioned you. I'm putting together a proposal for a new partnership. So far, I've got several big names on board. I'd love to tell you more about it. Let me know when you're available.

I look forward to talking to you.

Sam
- - - - - - -

我的名字是薩姆・瓊斯。我正在尋找洛杉磯地區的商業夥伴，而吉姆・路易斯提起過您。我正在彙整一項新合夥關係的提案。目前為止，我已經有幾位重要人選就定位。我希望讓您知道更多訊息。請讓我知道您什麼時候有空。我期待與您交談。

look for 尋找～ area 地區 mention 提及 put together 整理，彙整 proposal 提議 several 一些 a big name 一位大人物 on board 已正式登陸，就定位

Try It! 可以替換的字詞

payroll managers 薪資管理師

foreign retail executives 外國零售主管

market analysts 市場分析師

trade experts 貿易專家

organizational structure experts 組織結構專家

以上是本書第一封信件內容。您可以將灰底標示的部分，替換成符合您狀況的敘述（右邊的字詞可供您參考），就可以寫出一封可用於實際狀況中的商務書信。《外國人天天在用上班族萬用 E-mail 大全》收錄了 154 個實際商務狀況，而且每一篇 sample 中都會有 1~2 句以明顯顏色標示的實用佳句，熟悉這些佳句的好處是，您可以將它們運用在其他主題或狀況中，然後再搭配每一則篇短書信旁提供的 5 個可

供替換的關鍵字詞 List，訓練讓您用字遣詞更加豐富。

　　本書不收錄冗長的長篇大論，以最容易閱讀也最容易上手的方式編排，讓你能夠快速找到自己在不同場合所需要用到的各種篇章與實用佳句，輕鬆迅速地為自己量身訂做出一封正確無誤的英文 E-mail。

　　另外，英文商務書信都會有一些制式的語句，特別是信件一開頭的禮貌用語或問候語，以及書信結尾的致謝或祝福語。簡單列舉整理如下：

▲ 開頭的制式語句
1.　I'm writing to... 我寫這封信（的目的）是～
2.　I'm writing to let you know that... 我寫這封信（的目的）是要讓您知道～
3.　I just wanted to... 在此我想 ～／我只是想～
4.　I wanted to drop you a line and ask you to... 我寫這封信是想拜託您～
5.　I hope that this email finds you well. 展信愉快。
6.　I hope everything is going well for you. 展信愉快。／但願您一切順利。
7.　I hope you are doing well. 願您一切安好。
8.　Greetings from...　～（寫信的一方）向您問候！
9.　I hope business is good at your end. 但願貴公司營運一切順利。
10. I have a quick question. 我有個小問題想問一下。
11. This is just a quick note to let you know that... 這封信只是個簡短通知，要讓您知道～

▲ 結尾的制式語句
1.　Thanks for your attention/concern. 感謝您的關注。
2.　Thanks for your interest. 感謝您表達興趣。
3.　Thanks for your business. 承蒙光顧，不勝感激。
4.　Thanks for your time. 感謝您花時間看完。
5.　Let me know if you have any questions. 請讓我知道您是否有任何疑問。
6.　I look forward to hearing from you. 期待您的佳音。
7.　Sorry for any inconveniences. 造成任何不便，深表歉意。
8.　Talk to you soon. 下次再聊。
9.　Regards, / Best regards, / Warm regards, / Kind regards,（私人書信中，顯示與收

信人親密或私下的關係）謹致問候／致上最高的問候／致上溫暖的問候／致上
親切的問候

10. Sincerely yours, / Yours truly / Yours faithfully（對朋友或平輩）謹啟
11. Respectfully (yours),（對長輩或上司）敬請道安
12. Best Wishes, 並候近安
13. Cheers! 玩得愉快！／再見！

　　衷心期待透過這本書，能為各位的英語信件的書寫能力帶來根本性的變化，並
藉由符合目的的信件寫作，帶來職場上的成功。最後，在此書編輯的期間，提供許
多幫助的何次長等人，真的很感謝你們。

白善燁

感謝以下協助完成本書者

何俊英 LG 電子 MC 事業本部 PM 組次長
林奎男 Zespri 韓國總部常務
車元民 三源金屬海外營業部組長
陳宏碩 Arirang TV 事業部長、慶熙大學經營系兼任教授
李志潤 商務英文專任講師
李泰華 大明休閒產業海外行銷部長

朴仁育 韓華海外事業部組長
車尚禹 CJ 食品海外行銷部科長
崔潤泰 Remote 海外營業部部長
柳勝元 高麗大學經營學系教授
李尚真 CJ&M 事業本部組長
金成憲 NHN 事業本部海外服務經理

Contents

Contents

Contents

Part 2 商務以外場合

Case
以 case 來區分「主題」，也就是商務書信中各種可能的情境，每一個 case 底下都有數封書信範例。

Sample 信件
在每一個 case 或「主題」中，精心挑選商場上最常用的情境範例。在這些範例（sample）信件中，注意在此場合、狀況中必備的句子，我們以顏色為您特別標記出來。

Try It! 可以替換的字詞
每一篇 sample 中的必備句子，都會挑選出 1～2 個字詞（以灰底標示），每一個字詞提供 5 個可以替換的字詞，這些字詞大部分是同義字詞，或可能適合您狀況需要的字詞。您可以試著邊想像狀況，邊進行練習。

活用本書範例，
可擴大 200% 的
運用範圍

Consult 尋找 從本書網羅的 770 個商務往來狀況的範例，一般情況中，都可以從中找出自己需要的狀況。

Copy 複製 從不同 case 或主題中，找到符合自己的範例，並練習將重點字詞做適當的替換。

Practice 練習 每一篇範本（sample）中的顏色標示句子，都是商場上那樣的場合中最常使用的慣用語句，讀者更能充分瞭解各語句適用的時機和情境，寫出並說出最專業、最道地的商務英文。

Apply 運用 即使範例信件不完全符合自己的狀況，您也能在同一 case 的其它信件中，找出適合自己使用的句子，並整理出適合自己在各種商務交談或會議等的場合中要說的話。

Part 1

商務往來

介紹 & 邀請 Introductions & Invitation

Case 01 介紹自己 Introducing Myself ▲

✉ sample 1

Dear [Mr.Admas]

My name is Sam Jones. I'm looking for business partners in the Los Angeles area, and Jim Lewis mentioned you. I'm putting together a proposal for a new partnership. So far, I've got several big names on board. I'd love to tell you more about it. Let me know when you're available.

I look forward to talking to you.

Sam

我的名字是薩姆・瓊斯。我正在找尋洛杉磯地區的商業夥伴，而吉姆・路易斯提起過您。我正在彙整一項新合夥關係的提案。目前為止，我已經有幾位重要人選就定位。我希望讓您知道更多訊息。請讓我知道您什麼時候有空。我期待與您交談。

look for 尋找～　area 地區　mention 提及　put together 整理，彙整　proposal 提議　several 一些　a big name 一位大人物　on board 已正式登陸，就定位

✉ sample 2

[Mr.Jones]

I'm writing to introduce myself. My name is Joe Smith and I'm in charge of marketing at Kia. I'm going to be in town next week and I'm interested in meeting with you to discuss cooperating on a promotion. Let me know if you'd be interested.

Thanks,

Joe

我寫這封信的目的是想自我引薦。我的名字是喬・史密斯，我負責的是 Kia 的行銷業務。我打算下週到市區一趟，且希望能和您見上一面，討論一個合作推廣的案子。如果您有興趣的話，請讓我知道。感謝。

be in charge of 負責～　marketing 行銷　be interested in 對～感興趣　discuss 討論　promotion 促銷，推廣

✉ sample 3

Dear [_____]

My name is Robert Paris. Brian Johnson gave me your email address. I'm writing to tell you a little about my operation with a view to doing business together in the future. Let me know if you'd like to hear a little about what we do.

Thanks,

- - - - - - - -

我是羅伯‧巴瑞斯。布萊恩‧強森給了我你的電子郵件位址。我這封信的目的是想告訴您關於我公司營運的一些事情，以期在未來能夠一起發展業務。如果您想了解一點我們所從事的工作，請與我聯繫。謝謝。

> email address 電子郵件位址　operation 公司營運　in the future 在未來　a little about 關於～的一點事情　with a view to 為了～

Try It！可以替換的字詞

company 公司

work 工作

personnel team 人力團隊

market research skills 市場研究能力

economics expertise
經濟專長

✉ sample 4

Dear [_____]

My name is Bill Wilson. I'm writing to tell you a little about my company and the work we do. We've been in the textile industry for ten years and we have a respectable amount of the market share. I'm interested in discussing a possible partnership with you. Would you be available to meet?

I look forward to hearing from you.

- - - - - - - -

我是比爾‧威爾遜。我這封信的目的是想告訴您一點關於我的公司以及我們的業務。我們在紡織業已有十年之久，且擁有令人滿意的市佔率。我想和您討論彼此合作的可能性。我們可以見面談談嗎？我期待您的回覆。

> textile 紡織品　industry 產業　respectable 名聲好的，體面的　amount 數量　market share 市佔率　possible 有可能的　available 可行的

Try It！可以替換的字詞

personal moving business
個人運輸業

small engine repair business
小型引擎維修業

recycled plastics industry
再生塑料產業

smartphone repair business
智慧型手機維修業

dental instrument industry
牙科儀器產業

✉ sample 5

Dear [＿＿＿＿＿＿]

My name is Bill Smith and I'm ❶the president of Smith International. We are a ❷computer hardware distributor. I'd like to talk with you about what we might be able to do for your company. We're building a client base in your region and would like to add you to it. Let me know when a convenient time to speak would be.

Thanks,

－－－－－－－

Try It！可以替換的字詞

❶ the vice president 副總裁

the C.E.O. 執行長

the chief operating officer 營運長

the vice president of sales 銷售副總

the owner 老闆

❷ personnel management consulting firm
人事管理諮詢公司

tax accounting team 稅務會計團隊

fine silk supplier 高級絲綢供應商

rechargeable battery distributor
充電電池經銷商

lawn tractor distributor 割草機經銷商

我的名字是比爾·史密斯，我是「史密斯國際」的總裁。我們是一家電腦硬體經銷商。我想和你談談，我們可以為您的公司做些什麼服務。我們將在您的所在地區建立客戶群，並且希望您的公司是其中之一。請讓我知道方便與您詳談的時間。謝謝。

president 總裁　distributor 經銷商　be able to 能夠～　client base 客戶群　region 地區
add 加入　convenient 方便的

向別人介紹我的老闆 Introducing My Boss to Others ▲

✉ sample 6

Dear _____

I'd like to introduce you to Mr. Kim, the CEO of our company. I'm copying him in on this email so that you two can talk directly about the proposal. Mr. Kim is briefed on our progress so far, so you can jump right in. Let me know if you need anything from me.

Thanks,

Try It! 可以替換的字詞

chair of the board 董事會主席
chief recruitment officer 首席招募主管
leading development researcher
首席發展研究員
underwriter 核保人
investments manager 投資經理人

- - - - - - - -

我想向您介紹我們公司的執行長金先生。我會把這封電子郵件的副本寄給他，以便您可以直接和他討論這項提案。金先生聽過我們到目前為止的進展簡報，所以你將可以直接參與。如果您需要更多資訊，請讓我知道。謝謝。

introduce 介紹 copy A in on B 給 A 寄發 B 的副本 proposal 提案 brief 向～做簡報 progress 進度 so far 迄今 jump right in 直接參與（機會等）

✉ sample 7

Hi, _____

I'm writing to introduce you to Fred Johnson, vice president of sales for our company. He'll be making the final decisions on the agreement, so I thought I should put you two in touch. I've CC'd him on this email, so feel free to contact him with any concerns you might have.

Take care,

Try It! 可以替換的字詞

new product 新產品
final price 最終價
deal 交易
product line 產品系列
contract 合約

- - - - - - - -

我這封信的目的是要向您引介我們公司的銷售副總裁，弗雷德‧強森。他是這份合約的最終決策者，所以我想應該讓您二位取得聯繫。我已將這封電子郵件 C.C. 給他，所以如果您有任何疑問，請儘管與他聯繫。珍重。

sale 銷售，業務 agreement 協議，合約 put... in touch 使～取得聯繫
CC 電子郵件副本（carbon copy）

✉ sample 8

Dear _____

Now that we've had **❶a couple of** meetings, I thought you should contact my boss, Sue Jones. She manages our **❷foreign accounts office**. I reported to her on your account and she likes to have direct contact with our clients. She'll be emailing you later today.

Thanks,

- - - - - - - -

由於我們已經舉行了幾次會議，我想你應該已和我的老闆蘇瓊斯取得聯繫。她管理我們的外國客戶營運處。我向她報告關於您的事情，且她想直接與我們的客戶聯繫。今天晚些時候她會發郵件給你。謝謝。

a couple of 一些　boss 老闆　foreign 國外的　report 報告　direct 直接的

✉ sample 9

_____

I'd like to get you in contact with Jerry Lee. He's director of marketing for our Seoul office, and he's overseeing the account. He'll be able to address any concerns you have. His email is jlee@kia.com.

Thanks,

- - - - - - - -

我想讓您與李傑瑞取得聯繫。他是我們首爾辦事處的行銷總監，他負責監管客戶處。他將能夠解決您的任何疑慮。他的電子郵件是 jlee@kia.com。謝謝。

director 主管　oversee 監督　account 帳戶，交易，客戶　address 解決，處理　concern 關切，疑慮

✉ sample 10

Dear _____

Min Hwan Han is the sales director for our office and I'd like to introduce him to you so that you have someone to contact any larger concerns about products and service. Mr. Han is eager to ensure your satisfaction, so feel free to contact him if you have any issues.

Thanks,

- - - - - - - -

Try It! 可以替換的字詞

talk with 與～談談

meet (with) 與～會面

email 寄電子郵件給～

communicate with 與～溝通

ask advice 尋求建議

韓敏煥是我們公司的業務總監，我想將他介紹給您認識，以便您如有任何關於產品和服務等更重大的問題，有人可以連繫。韓先生很希望您會滿意，所以如果您有任何問題，儘管與他聯繫。謝謝。

sales director 業務總監　service 服務，業務　be eager to 渴望～　ensure 確保　satisfaction 滿意
issue 議題，問題

介紹我的公司 Introducing My Company ▲

sample 11

Dear ⬚

I'm writing to tell you a little about my company, Miller and Associates. We are a full-service consulting firm, and we've been operating since 1998. Our client list includes some of the biggest names in a variety of industries. Attached is a brochure outlining our services. I look forward to hearing from you in the future.

Thank you for your time.

Try It!可以替換的字詞

accounting 會計
tax 稅務
business law 商事法
human resources 人力資源
business streamlining 企業精簡

- - - - - - - -

我寫這封信的目的是想跟您介紹我的公司 Miller and Associates。我們是一家全方位服務的顧問公司，且本公司已自 1998 年營運至今。我們的客戶名單包括各產業中的一些知名企業。隨附一本概述我們服務的小冊子。我期待未來能夠得到您的回覆。感謝您花時間看完這封信。

full-service 全方位服務的　consulting firm 顧問公司　operate 營運　big name 大人物，知名企業
since 自～以來　brochure 小冊子

✉ sample 12

Dear ⬚

My name is Joan Smith and I'm writing to tell you a little bit about my company, JS Inc. We supply textiles to both the fashion industry and the furniture industry. We've been in business for twenty years and we have an extensive client list. I'd like to talk with you about doing business together.

I hope to hear from you.

Try It!可以替換的字詞

printers 印表機
environmental sustainability items
環境可持續發展能力項目
information storage devices
資訊儲存設備
wood products 木製品
recycled plastics 再生塑料

- - - - - - - -

我是喬安‧史密斯，我寫這封信的目的是想讓您了解關於我公司 JS Inc 的一點事情。我們提供紡織品給時裝業及家俱業者。我們在這一行已經二十年了，而且擁有廣大的客戶群。我想和您談談一起合作生意的可能性。期待您的回覆。

supply 提供　textile 紡織品　furniture 家俱　be in business 在營運中　extensive 廣泛的

✉ sample 13

Dear (_____)

My name is Robert Pollard. I'm the president and founder of Pollard Exports. I've been in the ❶export game for over a decade, and I've been quite successful in building relationships with overseas firms. I'm always looking to expand my ❷network of suppliers and I'd love to talk with you about working with us.

I look forward to hearing from you.

- - - - - - - -

Try It！可以替換的字詞

❶import 進口
trade 貿易
manufacturing 製造業
international marketing 國際行銷
international trade 國際貿易

❷lineup 陣容
cooperation 合作
complex 集團
group 群體
system 系統

我是羅伯特‧波拉德。我是「波拉德出口」的總裁暨創辦人。我在出口業已十多年，並且已成功地與一些海外公司建立關係。我一直致力於擴大我的供應商網絡，而且我很樂意與您討論我們的合作事宜。我期待著您的回音。

founder 創辦人　export 出口　game 行業，職業　decade 十年　successful 成功的　expand 擴大

✉ sample 14

Dear (_____)

I'm writing to introduce myself and my firm. My name is Jeffery Golden and I'm the marketing director for Design-Tech Software. We've been in the software business for the last 15 years and have carved out a niche in the database management industry. I'd like to get a chance to talk to you about our product line. Feel free to contact me if you are interested.

Sincerely,

- - - - - - - -

Try It！可以替換的字詞

company 公司
business 公司，企業
enterprise 企業
team 團隊
office 營業處

我寫這封信的目的是要介紹我自己和我的公司。我的名字是傑佛瑞‧戈登，我是 Design-Tech Software 的行銷總監。過去 15 年來，我們一直從事軟體業務，並在資料庫管理行業上，已佔有一席之地。我希望有機會與您討論我們的系列產品。如果您有興趣，請儘管與我聯繫。謹啟。

carve out 開拓～　niche 利基（市場），地位　Sincerely (yours) 真摯地祝福；謹啟（信的結尾語）

✉ sample 15

Dear [_____]

My name is Joshua Jefferson. I'm sales director at Smith Tech. We are the premier supplier of ❶computer hardware for corporations in North America. Attached is a brochure outlining some of our more successful products and presenting some ❷testimonials from our satisfied customers. Let me know if you'd be available to discuss how we could work together.

Thank you for your time.

- - - - - - - -

我是約書亞‧傑佛遜。我是 Smith Tech 的業務總監。我們是許多北美地區公司的首要電腦硬體供應商。隨附一本小冊子,其中概括介紹我們比較受歡迎的產品,以及來自我們感到滿意的客戶 — 他們的見證。請讓我知道我們彼此是否有機會可以討論合作的可能。感謝您花時間看完這封信。

premier 首要的　corporation 公司　present 呈現　testimonial 見證,推薦書　satisfied 感到滿意的 customer 顧客

介紹產品目錄 Introducing a Catalog Interests ▲

✉ sample 16

Dear ⌐‾‾‾‾‾⌐

I hope you are doing well. This is our 2019 catalogue. It's got our whole line for the coming year along with the new pricing. If you have any questions, feel free to get in touch with me.

Thanks,

- - - - - - - -

Try It！可以替換的字詞

new prices 新的價格

new quantities 新的數量

new payment methods 新的付款方式

new shipping prices 新的運費

several new items that you may be interested in
一些您可能感興趣的新品項

但願您你一切順利。這是我們 2019 年的產品目錄，其中包括我們未來這一年的全部產品系列，還有新的定價。如果您有任何問題，請隨時與我聯繫。謝謝。

whole 全部的　coming year 未來這一年　along with 與～一起　pricing 定價
get in touch with 與～取得聯繫

✉ sample 17

Dear ⌐‾‾‾‾‾⌐

It's that time of year again! I'm sending out our new catalogue to all of our clients. When you have a second, take some time to look it over and familiarize yourself with the new line of products and the changes in price and availability. Call me if you have any questions.

Thanks,

- - - - - - - -

Try It！可以替換的字詞

color 顏色

price and quantity 價格和數量

quality 品質

product details 產品細節

design 設計

每年的這個時刻又到了！我在此寄出我們的新目錄給我們所有客戶。要是您有空的話，請花點時間瀏覽並了解一下新的產品系列，以及價格與可提供之產品的改變。如您有任何問題，請與我聯繫。謝謝。

second 一點點時間　look... over 瀏覽～　familiarize 使熟悉　change 變化
availability 可利用性，可得性

✉ sample 18

Dear (..........)

Attached is our new textiles catalogue for the fall. We've added several new products that I think you'll be interested. When you get a chance, look over the new additions and let me know what you're interested in.

Thanks,

- - - - - - - -

附件是我們今年秋季新的紡織品目錄。我們已經新增幾項我認為您會感興趣的新產品。當你有機會翻閱時，請瀏覽一下這些新增的項目，並讓我知道你對什麼感興趣。謝謝。

attached 附件的，附上的　textile 紡織品　fall 秋天　several 一些　chance 機會　addition 新增項目

✉ sample 19

Dear (..........)

I'm sending you our catalogue so that you can get a sense of what we offer. You can look it over and see if anything meets your needs. We have an extensive inventory, so I'm quite certain you'll find what you're looking for.

Thanks,

- - - - - - -

我寄給您我們的目錄，以便讓您了解我們提供的東西。你可以看看是否有什麼是符合您的需求。我們有多種產品的存貨，所以我相信您會找到您正在找尋的東西。謝謝。

extensive 大量的　inventory 庫存（品）　certain 確信的

✉ sample 20

Hi , ┌──────────┐

I hope business is good at your end. Attached is our 2015-10 product catalogue. I thought you'd like to see what we're offering. Please take a look at it and let me know if you have any questions about what you see.

Thanks,

- - - - - - - -

祝您生意興隆。附件是我們的 2015 年 10 月的產品目錄。我認為你會想看看我們提供的內容。請過目，如果您對於所見到的有任何問題，請聯繫我們。謝謝。

at your end 貴方，你那一邊　catalogue 目錄　offer 提供　take a look 看一下

✉ sample 21

Hi, ⌐ ¬

We're setting up a series of meetings here in Taiwan with many of our partner companies. We'd like to involve you as well. We think meeting face-to-face and showing you our production facilities will really improve communication. Let me know if you think it will work for your schedule.

I hope to hear from you soon.

- - - - - - - -

Try It！可以替換的字詞

our production line 我們的生產線

our entire manufacturing process
我們整個製造過程

the way we do business
我們營運的方式

our methods of manufacturing
我們的製造方法

how we've streamlined our processes
我們如何精簡流程

我們將在台灣這邊與我們的許多夥伴企業舉辦一連串會議。我們也希望貴公司可以參與。我們認為面對面的會談以及向您展示我們的生產設施，將可真正地促進彼此溝通。如果您認為您的時程安排許可的話，請讓我知道。希望盡快能獲得您的消息。

set up 舉辦～ partner 合作／商業夥伴 involve 包含 as well 同樣，也 production 生產 facility 設施 improve 增進 communication 溝通，交流

✉ sample 22

⌐ ¬

What would you think about coming out to Taiwan for some meetings? We'd like to get your input on some of the projects we're working on. Let me know if you'd be available next month.

Thanks,

- - - - - - - -

Try It！可以替換的字詞

our new ideas 我們的新主意

a few things we are planning
我們計畫中的一些事情

new prototypes we are working on
我們正在研究的新樣品

our long-term goals 我們的長期目標

our short-term projects
我們的短期計畫

對於前來台灣參加幾場會議，您覺得如何呢？對於我們正在進行的一些專案計畫，我們希望得到您的意見。請讓我知道您下個月是否有空。謝謝。

input 提供的意見 project 專案，計畫 work on 進行～

✉ sample 23

Try It!可以替換的字詞

I'm writing to extend an invitation. I'd really love to get you over here for a meeting. We'd like to show you our operation and have some meetings about a possible partnership. What does your schedule look like?

Talk to you soon,

- - - - - - - -

for dinner and a conversation
（為了）吃頓晚餐及商談

to talk numbers （為了）談談價錢

to discuss a great opportunity
（為了）討論一個很好的機會

to move forward with what we've discussed
（為了）繼續我們先前的討論

to talk more formally
（為了）進行更正式的商討

我寫這封信是想邀請您。我誠摯希望您可以來這裡參加一場會議。我們希望讓您來看看我們的營運狀況，並一起開會談談可能的合作。您的時程表可否允許呢？希望很快可以一起商談。

extend 給予　invitation 邀請（函）　partnership 合作關係　look like　看起來像是～

✉ sample 24

Try It!可以替換的字詞

I'd like to invite you and your team out to Taiwan next month. We've had a few teleconferences, but I think it's time that we had a face-to-face meeting. Would you be available to fly out? Let me know and we can begin preparations.

Thank you,

- - - - - - - -

discussion in person 面對面的討論

gathering with our executives
與我們的主管一起會面

dinner and talk in person
一起共進晚餐及面會

formal proposal in person
親自正式提案

meeting between our two groups
我們雙方之間的會談

我想邀請您及您的團隊下個月前來台灣一趟。我們已舉行過數次電話會議，但我認為是時候進行面對面的會議了。您是否可以搭機前來呢？請知會我一聲，以便我們可以開始做準備。謝謝。

invite 邀請　teleconference 電訊／電話會議　face-to-face 面對面的　preparation 準備工作

✉ sample 25

We're going to be having a series of meetings ❶next month, and we'd really like you to be involved. If your schedule permits it, would you like to fly out and meet with us? I think it would be ❷quite productive. Let me know what you think.

Thanks,

- - - - - - - -

❶ next January 明年一月

in a few weeks 數周之後

next year 明年

starting March 1 三月一日起

early in the summer 初夏時

❷ beneficial to both of us
對於我們雙方皆有益處

very useful 很有用的

a wonderful partnership
一個很美好的合作關係

a smart business move
一項聰明的商業行為

a good opportunity for us
對我們而言的一個好機會

我們將在下個月舉行一系列會議，我們真的希望您能參加。如果您時間上允許的話，您可以搭機前來與我們見面嗎？我想這場會議會讓您覺得很有收穫的。請讓我知道你的想法。謝謝。

a series of 一系列的～　be involved 參與　fly out 搭飛機出訪　productive 富有成效的

接受邀請 Accepting an Invitation ▲

✉ sample 26

Hi , ┌┈┈┈┈┈┐

My schedule is **pretty flexible** next month, so I think I can clear out a few days. If you could just send me the schedule with as much detail about the agenda, I'll make my travel arrangements.

I look forward to seeing you.

- - - - - - - -

下個月我的行程相當彈性，所以我想我可以空出幾天時間。如果您可以發給我時間表及詳細議程內容，我將進行差旅的安排準備。我期待著與您見面。

pretty 相當地　flexible 靈活的　clear out 清空，清除　as much 同樣地　detail 細節　agenda 議程
travel 旅遊　arrangement 安排，準備

Try It ! 可以替換的字詞

fairly open 有很多空檔的
clear （時間上）未作安排的
easy to work with 很容易安排事情
open to change 可隨時更改
rather open 還算有空檔的

✉ sample 27

Hi , ┌┈┈┈┈┈┐

I think coming out to Taiwan would be a ❶**great idea**. Let me check my schedule and we can start talking about possible dates. I can also prepare ❷**a presentation** about some of the new business ventures we're involved in.

I'll contact you soon.

- - - - - - - -

Try It ! 可以替換的字詞

❶ fantastic thing 很棒的事情
wonderful opportunity 很好的機會
good starting point 好的開始
wise decision 明智的決定
smart move 明智之舉

❷ a slideshow 一個幻燈片秀
an agenda 一項議程
an outline 一份摘要
details 細節
costs 費用

我想，前往台灣是個好主意。我查看一下我的行程表，然後我們可以開始討論可能的日期。我也可以準備一份關於我們參與一些新創事業的介紹。我會盡快與您聯繫。

check 查看　date 日期　presentation 介紹　venture 風險投資事業　contact 聯繫

✉ sample 28

Dear [_____]

I'm happy to accept your invitation. I think it would be beneficial to both of our companies if we get together. Let me know what your schedule is like.

Thank you,

- - - - - - - -

我很高興接受你的邀請。我認為如果我們一起合作，對於我們雙方公司而言都有好處。請讓我知道您的行程安排。謝謝。

accept 接受　beneficial 有益的　both 雙方　get together 在一起（合作）

Try It! 可以替換的字詞

a smart thing 一件聰明的事
profitable 有利可圖的
a benefit 一大好處
helpful 有幫助的
useful 有用的

✉ sample 29

Dear [_____]

Thank you for your invitation. I think I can fit a trip to Taiwan into my schedule next month. I'd like to bring ❶a few of my people along so we can all get a sense of your operation there. Would this be acceptable?

I look forward to ❷hearing from you.

- - - - - - - -

Try It! 可以替換的字詞

❶my players 我的團隊成員
some of my assistants 我的幾位助理
my secretaries 我的祕書們
some financial partners 一些金融夥伴
my chief operations controller 我的營運總監

❷your quick reply 您的儘速回應
your response 您的回應
your decision 您的決定
your return letter 您的回信
your answer 您的答案

感謝您的邀請。我想我下個月可以將訪台納入行程表中。我想帶幾位下屬一起過去，這樣我們都可以了解您那裡的營運狀況。這樣可以嗎？我期待您的回音。

fit... in 將～排入　bring... along 帶著～一起　sense 意義，觀念

✉ sample 30

Try It! 可以替換的字詞

Coming to Taiwan sounds like a great idea. I think seeing your operation in action will help us meet your needs more efficiently. We can work out the details this week.

I look forward to seeing you in Korea!

the timeline 時間表

the agenda 議程

the dates and times 日期和時間

our schedules 我們的行程表

when would be a good time
恰當的時機

- - - - - - - -

去台灣一趟聽起來是個好主意。我認為看到您營運中的狀況，將有助於我們更有效率地滿足您的需求。我們可以在本週擬定好細節。我期待著到台灣與您見面！

sound like 聽起來像是～　in action 在營運中　meet one's need 滿足某人的需求
efficiently 有效率地　work out 做出，解決

sample 31

Dear [   ]

Thank you so much for the kind invitation. Unfortunately, I can't make it out to Taiwan next month. This quarter is just too busy for us. I hope we can work out something early next year.

Thanks,

- - - - - - - -

非常感謝您的盛情邀約。不巧的是，我下個月沒辦法到台灣。我們這一季太忙了。我希望明年初我們能夠排除萬難。謝謝。

> quarter 季度　busy 忙碌的　work out 制定出，圓滿解決～　early next year 明年初

Try It！可以替換的字詞

decide 決定
schedule 排定
try 嘗試
pencil in 暫定（人或事）
arrange 安排，準備

sample 32

Hi, [   ]

Unfortunately, my schedule is ❶full for all of next month. We've got a ❷product roll-out we're preparing for so I'm not able to travel. Maybe farther down the line I'll be able to make it.

Thanks for thinking of me.

- - - - - - - -

Try It！可以替換的字詞

❶ booked 有預訂的
unavailable 不可行的，沒空的
completely filled 毫無空缺的
not flexible 沒有調整空間的
entirely full 全滿的

❷ new department opening
新部門開張
new C.E.O. joining our company
新執行長到任
new prototype 新的樣式
full publicity agenda 滿檔的宣傳工作
new marketing campaign
新的行銷活動

不巧的是，我下個月的行程已滿。我們正為產品推出作準備，所以我無法抽身前往。也許再過一段時間我就能夠過去一趟。感謝您考慮到我。

> unfortunately 不幸地　full 充滿的　product 產品　roll-out（新產品的）發布　farther 再往前的
> make it 成功，做得到

✉ sample 33

I'm afraid I can't make it to Taiwan for at least the next few months. We have too many accounts that need constant attention, so I can't spare any time for travel. I hope my schedule clears up this summer so that we can arrange something.

Thanks,

- - - - - - - -

至少接下來的幾個月內，我恐怕都沒辦法到台灣去。我們有太多客戶必須不斷照料，所以我無法挪出離開工作崗位的時間。我希望今年夏天，我可以在行程表中排出一點時間，以便我們可以做些安排。謝謝。

at least 至少 account 客戶，帳目，報表 constant 持續的 attention 關注 spare 騰出（時間、人手） arrange 整理；布置；安排；籌備

✉ sample 34

Hi ,

Thanks for wanting to involve us in ❶the conference. We'd like to send someone out, but unfortunately we can't spare anyone. We're a little shorthanded at the moment, and everyone we've got is busy ❷on an account. If things change, I'll let you know.

Thanks,

- - - - - - - -

感謝您邀請我們參加這場會議。我們想要派人過去，但不巧的是，我們沒有人有時間。我們現正處於人力短缺的狀態。所有人都有自己的事情要忙。如果事情有變化，我會讓您知道。謝謝。

conference（正式）會議 sent out 派出 shorthanded 人手不足的 at the moment 此刻，目前

✉ sample 35

Dear [_____]

I think it makes sense for us to come out to Taiwan, but I'm afraid our office is just too ❶backlogged right now. We've got a lot of products to ship out, and there's ❷no end in sight. Maybe we can work something out down the line.

Thanks for understanding.

- - - - - - - -

Try It ! 可以替換的字詞

❶ full of tasks 工作滿檔

overwhelmed 忙翻天了

shorthanded 人手不足的

busy with clients 忙於處理客戶的事情

backed up with orders
有太多訂單要處理

❷ no possibility of it ending
沒有結束的可能性

no end near 短期內看不到盡頭

not a chance we'll finish soon
不太可能很快就會結束

no chance we'll be done by next week
到下週都還無法結束

not a possibility of ending by the end of the month
到月底前都還不太可能結束

我認為我們確實應該到台灣去一趟，但恐怕我們公司現在還有太多工作待處理。我們有許多產品要運送出去，而且目前還看不到盡頭。也許之後我們會有機會去。感謝您的理解。

make sense to ～是明智的做法　office 辦公室，公司　backlogged 積壓很多工作的　product 產品
ship 運送　in sight 在視線範圍內　down the line 未來，稍後

詢價、估價 & 議價 Inquiry, Estimates & Price

Case 01 對產品進行大致上的詢問 Making General Inquiries About a Product ▲

✉ sample 36

Dear [____]

I'm writing to get some information about item #4689 in your catalogue. I'd like to see some more details concerning what colors and sizes are available. I'd also like to know about availability. If you could please get this information to me ASAP, I would greatly appreciate it.

Thank you for your time.

- - - - - - - -

我寫這封信的目的是想要詢問您目錄中產品編號 #4689 的資訊。關於現有的顏色和尺寸，我想了解更多細節部分。我還想知道目前是否有貨。要是您能夠盡快提供這些資料給我，我會感激不盡。謝謝您花時間看這封信。

availability 可用性　ASAP 盡快地 (= as soon as possible)　greatly 非常地　appreciate 感激

✉ sample 37

Dear [____]

Could you send me a description of the T-23 monitor? I see it listed in the catalogue, but I'd like a little more information about performance and compatibility. I'd also like to see some screen captures that demonstrate resolution.

Thanks,

- - - - - - - -

可以請您寄給我一份關於 T-23 監視器的簡介嗎？我在您目錄中看到這個型號，但我想要了解更多關於其性能和相容性的資訊。我還想看到顯示其解析度的螢幕截圖。謝謝。

description 說明　list 列入名單／簿中　performance 性能　compatibility 相容（性）　demonstrate 示範
resolution 解析度

✉ sample 38

Try It！可以替換的字詞

Could I get some information on your new product line?
I see that the new catalogue has a few additions, but I
can't really tell what new features are offered. So you
have a more detailed product description?

Thanks,

monitor line 顯示器系列

laptop availability 筆記型電腦存貨

keyboard products 鍵盤產品

flatscreen monitors 平面顯示器

product support 產品支援

- - - - - - - -

可以給我您新產品系列的相關資訊嗎？我看到那份新目錄中有一些新增的產品，但不了解有什麼新的
功能。那麼您有更詳細的產品說明嗎？謝謝。

Addition 新增項目 tell 辨別 feature 功能，特點

✉ sample 39

Try It！可以替換的字詞

My company is in the process of choosing a supplier
and we're considering using your operation. Could you
give us an overview of your product line, including price
and availability? You can email me with the information
anytime.

Thanks for your attention.

quantities 數量

shipping prices 運費價格

dimensions (especially depth)
尺寸（尤其是深度）

compatibility 相容性

quality of the items 這些品項的品質

- - - - - - - -

我公司正在進行徵選供應商的程序，且我們正考慮與貴公司合作。能否請您給我您產品系列的簡介，
包括價格和可供貨情況？您可以隨時寄給我相關資訊的電子郵件。感謝您的關注。

choose 選擇 supplier 供應商 consider 考慮 operation 運作（狀況） overview 概述
include 包含

Try It！可以**替換的字詞**

I'd like to get some information from you. We're looking for **networking routers** for an office situation, and I see that you've got a pretty wide range. Could you give me a rundown on the prices and specifications along with any recommendations you might have?

Thanks,

- - - - - - - -

new USB ports 新的 USB 埠
compatible keyboards 相容的鍵盤
routers and splitters 路由器和分歧器
LCD handheld devices
LCD 手持式裝置
processors 處理器

我想向您索取一些資訊。我們正因辦公室用途在找尋網絡路由器，而且我知道您的產品種類非常廣泛。您能否給我我價格和規格的簡介，以及您可能提出的任何建議？謝謝。

situation 情況　range 系列，範圍　rundown 簡要說明，概述　specification 規格　along with 和～一起
recommendation 推薦

詢問價格 Inquiring About Price ▲

✉ **sample 41**

Dear ⌐ ⌐

I'm writing to request pricing information for item #4689 in your catalogue. I'd like to get the current price per unit as well as any bulk discounts you offer. We're trying to make our final decisions on which product to go with, and we'd appreciate a prompt reply.

Thanks,

- - - - - - - -

我寫這封信是想詢問您目錄中 #4689 的價格資訊。我想知道目前每單位的價格，以及您提供任何大量購買的折扣。我們將對於選擇哪一樣產品做出最終決定。如您能儘快回覆，我們將會非常感激。謝謝。

> **Try It！可以替換的字詞**
>
> education 教育
> college 大學
> multiple-line 多項產品系列
> large order 大批訂單
> nonprofit 非營利組織（集團）

> request 要求　current 現在的　per 每～　unit（成品）一個，單位，設備　A as well as B　A以及B
> bulk 大量，大宗　discount 折扣，優惠　decision 決定　prompt 迅速的　reply 回覆

✉ **sample 42**

Dear ⌐ ⌐

Could I get the current price for the W-234 network cable? I can't seem to find it listed on your website, and we're trying to prepare a rather large order. If there's a bulk discount, I'd like to get that too.

Thanks,

- - - - - - - -

我可以詢問目前 W-234 網路線的價格嗎？我似乎無法在您的網站上找到它，我們正在努力為一件大訂單做籌備。如果有大量購買的優惠，我也想了解相關資訊。感謝。

> **Try It！可以替換的字詞**
>
> graphics card 顯示卡
> wireless mouse 無線滑鼠
> motherboard 主機板
> speakers 喇叭
> optical disk drive 光碟機

> website 網站　prepare 準備　rather 相當，頗　order 訂單

✉ sample 43

Dear _____

I was wondering if you could help me out. I'm preparing my 2019 budget and I'd like to get the most accurate price information I can. Could you send me the most current prices for your product line? I'd appreciate it greatly.

Thanks,

- - - - - - - -

我想知道你是否可以幫我個忙。我正在規劃我 2019 年的預算，所以我想盡可能了解最準確的價格資訊。可否請您寄給我您系列產品的最新價格資料？非常感謝您。謝謝。

wonder 想知道　budget 預算　accurate 精確的

✉ sample 44

Dear _____

What is the price for product #662? For some reason it doesn't appear on your current price list. I'm going to be placing an order soon, and I need the exact price in order to get it approved.

Thanks for your prompt attention.

- - - - - - - -

編號 #662 的產品的價格為何？不知何故，它不在您目前的價目表中。我就快要下訂單了，因此我需要確切的價格，才能申請批准。感謝您即時的關注。

reason 原因　appear 出現　place an order 下訂單　exact 確切的　approve 批准　attention 關注

✉ sample **45**

Dear ┌┈┈┈┈┈┈┐

Could you help me out with some price information? I'm trying to do some comparisons between various suppliers and I don't seem to have current numbers for your product line. I'd love to get that from you if possible.

Thanks,

- - - - - - - -

可以請您協助提供給我一些價格訊息嗎？我正要找幾家供應商做些比較，而且我似乎沒有貴公司目前產品系列的價位。可以的話，請您提供資訊給我。謝謝。

help... out 給予～幫助　comparison 比較　various 各種的　supplier 供應商
numbers（價格的）數字資訊

Try It！可以替換的字詞

inventions 發明品

operating system software 作業系統軟體

Blu-ray DVD players 藍光 DVD 播放機

Webcams 網路攝影機

digital scanners 數位掃瞄機

詢價之回覆 Responding to Price Inquiries ▲

✉ sample 46

Dear [_____]

Thanks for your interest. Attached is the most current price listing for item #4689. It contains both unit price and bulk pricing. Notice that there is a 5% discount for every hundred ordered up to 400. Let me know if you have any questions.

Thanks again,

Try It! 可以替換的字詞

over 500, with a maximum discount of 50%
數量超過 500，最高折扣 50%

up to 300 到 300

with a maximum of a 20% discount
最高 20% 的折扣

500 and up 500 個以上

over 100, up to 15% off
超過 100 個，最高可享 15% 折扣

感謝您（對本產品）的興趣。附件是品項 #4689 的最新價格清單。它包含單價和批量價格。請注意，訂單數量達 400 個的話，每 100 個可享 5% 的折扣。有任何疑問的話，請讓我知道。再次感謝您。

interest 興趣　contain 包含　unit（商品、組織、機構等的）單位　bulk 大量　pricing 定價
notice 注意　discount 折扣

✉ sample 47

Dear [_____]

Thanks for getting in touch with me. The W-234 currently runs 12.99 per unit. We offer a 5% discount on orders of 50 or more. Let me know when you're ready to order and I can expedite the process for you.

Thanks,

Try It! 可以替換的字詞

each 每一（個、件）

per box 每盒

per dozen 每一打

per pair 每一對

for 100 一百（個、件）

感謝您與我聯繫。W-234 現在每單位售價是 12.99 美元。訂購滿 50 個以上的話，我們提供 5% 的折扣。要是您準備要訂購時，請讓我知道，我會儘速安排處理。謝謝。

get in touch with... 與～取得聯繫　currently 現在　run（數量、數字等）大體是～
be ready to... 準備要～　expedite 加速　process 過程，處理

✉ sample 48

Dear [_____]

Attached is our **①current** price list. As you can see, we've **②reduced** prices on a number of items. Let me know if you have any questions or if you are ready to place an order.

Thanks,

- - - - - - - -

Try It! 可以替換的字詞

①most recent 最新的

latest 最新的

most up-to-date 最新的

annual 年度的

yearly 一年一度的

②lowered 降低

cut 調降

chopped 砍，削減

slashed 大幅度削減

dropped 使下降

附件是我們目前的價目表。正如您所看到的，我們已經調降許多產品的價格。如果您有任何疑問，或準備下訂單，請與我聯繫。謝謝。

as you can see 如你所見　reduce 降低　a number of 許多的

✉ sample 49

[_____]

Item #662 currently runs $42.50 per unit. If you have any other questions regarding price, please let me know. Some of our newer offerings haven't yet made it into the catalogue.

Thank you for your interest.

- - - - - - - -

Try It! 可以替換的字詞

concerns 關切，關心的事

requests 要求

queries 詢問

problems 問題

inquiries 詢問

品項 #662 目前每單位的價格是 42.50 美元。如果您對價格還有任何疑問，請讓我知道。我們有一些新產品還沒有編入目錄中。感謝您對本產品的興趣。

regarding ~關於　offering 待售品

✉ sample 50

....

Thanks for your interest. I'm attaching our current price list. Let me know if there are any questions. We can **❶work with you** throughout the order process to ensure that everything goes **❷smoothly**.

Thanks again,

- - - - - - - -

Try It！可以替換的字詞

❶ assist you 協助您

work alongside you 與您協力合作

be there with you 和您一起

support you 支援您

answer all your questions
解答您所有問題

❷ as planned 按計劃地

perfectly 完美地

problem free 毫無問題地

ideally 理想地

without issues 沒有問題地

感謝您表示有興趣。我附上我們目前的價目表。如果有任何問題,請聯繫我。我們會在整個訂單處理流程中與您一起解決問題,以確保一切運作順利。再次感謝。

work with... 與～合作　throughout 在～的整個過程中　process 過程　ensure 確保
smoothly 順利地

請求估價 Requesting Estimates ▲

✉ sample 51

To Whom It May Concern:

I'm writing to request an estimate for your service. We have a job coming up and would like to get some numbers. Attached are the specifics of the job. I would appreciate a rough figure for the work. If you need any further details, feel free to contact me.

Thank you,

- - - - - - -

your support 您的支援服務

your company's assistance 貴公司的協助

your engineering team 您的工程團隊

a few days' work 幾天的努力

your team's abilities 您團隊的專業技能

致相關人士：我寫這封信是想索取您服務的估價。我們即將有一件案子，所以想了解一些價格數字。附件是這個案子的詳細資訊。麻煩給我一個粗估數字，非常感激。如果您需要更多細節部分，請隨時與我聯繫。謝謝。

request 要求　estimate 報價，估價　number（報價的）數字　specifics 詳細資訊　rough 粗略的 figure 數字，數值　further 更進一步的

✉ sample 52

Dear ⸻

I'd like to get an estimate for your consulting service. Let me know what you need to know in order to provide a rough price for us. We'd like to get started as soon as possible.

Thanks,

- - - - - - -

reference 推薦，委託

distribution management 配送管理

inventory control 存貨管控

college recruitment 大學招聘

tax 稅務

我想知道貴公司諮詢服務的估價。請讓我知道您提供粗略報價給我們時，需要了解的事項為何。我們希望可以盡快開始。謝謝。

consulting 諮詢　in order to... 為了〜　provide 提供　get started 開始　as soon as possible 盡快

✉ sample 53

Dear ....

We are in need of a delivery service for a product we are shipping to the U.S. and attached are the **specifics** for the job. Could you put together an estimate for us?

Thanks in advance.

details 細節
particulars 詳細情況
numbers 數字資訊
contracts 合約
facts 事實資訊

我們需要寄送服務。我們有個產品要運送至美國。附件是相關詳細資訊。您能為我們估一下運費嗎？
先跟您說聲謝謝。

be in need of... 需要～ delivery 遞送 ship 運送 put together 整理 in advance 預先

✉ sample 54

Dear ....

I'm writing to get an estimate for your company's services. We used you last year and were **quite happy** with the results. If you are interested in working with us again, let me know and I'll send you the details.

Thanks,

pleased 滿意的
very enthused 非常開心的
overwhelmed 開心至極的
delighted 感到高興的
esteemed 對於～評價很高的

我寫這封信的目的是想索取貴公司的服務估價。我們去年使用過您的服務，而且對於結果非常滿意。
如果您有興趣再次與我們合作，請告知我，我會發送詳細資訊給您。謝謝。

get an estimate 取得估價 quite 相當地 result 結果 be interested in... 對～感興趣

✉ sample 55

Dear [............]

I would like to get an estimate for the attached job. The deadline is November 23, so I'd like to get the process started as soon as possible. Let me know if you need any further information in order to put together a figure.

Thank you,

- - - - - - - -

針對附件所示的工作，我想取得估價資訊。截止日期是 11 月 23 日，所以我想盡快開始處理。請讓我知道您在彙整價格數字時，是否需要任何進一步的資訊。謝謝。

deadline 截止時間　process 過程

Try It！可以替換的字詞

quickly 很快地

soon 即將

next week 下週

shortly 不久之後

very soon 就快，即將

✉ sample 56

Dear _____

Thank you for getting in touch with us. I've looked over the specifications for the job and we've come up with a figure for you. Attached is a breakdown of all of the costs involved. This is a preliminary figure and is subject to change after we've come out to look at the work in person. Let me know if you have any questions.

Thanks,

an early estimate 初步估計

an estimate 估價

a rough guess 粗略估價

a quick ballpark figure
簡單的初估數字

a rough calculation 一個概算金額

- - - - - - - -

感謝您與我們聯繫。我們已經查看過這工作的詳細內容，並為您提供一個數字。附件為所有相關費用的明細。這是一個初估數字，且在我們親自到場檢視概況之後，可能會有所變動。請讓我知道您是否有任何疑問。謝謝。

get in touch with... 與～聯繫　come up with... 提出～　figure（金額的）數字　breakdown 明細（表）
preliminary 初步的　be subject to... 受制於～　look at... 查看～　in person 親自

✉ sample 57

Dear _____

I've received your request for an estimate. Thank you for thinking of us. We'll get the pricing information together for you by the end of the day.

I look forward to working with you.

tomorrow 明天

Friday 星期五

the next business day 下一個工作日

your deadline 您的截止日期

early evening 傍晚

- - - - - - - -

我已經收到您的報價請求。感謝您想到我們。我們將在今天結束之前整理價格資料給您。我期待與您合作。

receive 收到　request 請求　pricing 定價　end 結束　day 日

✉ sample 58

Attached is an estimate for the job. It's itemized in order to give some context to the total figure. Look it over and let me know if it is acceptable.

Thank you for your interest.

- - - - - - - -

附件是有關這工作的報價，以逐項列出的方式呈現，以便您了解全部金額的計算方式。請仔細過目，並讓我知道這金額是否可以接受。感謝您對我們感興趣。

itemize 分項／逐條列述　context 上下文，來龍去脈　total 總共的　acceptable 可以接受的

✉ sample 59

Dear

It's great to hear from you. We'd love the chance to work with you again. Just send me the details about the job and we'll put together some numbers for you.

Thanks,

- - - - - - - -

很高興有您的消息。我們很高興有機會再次與您合作。請寄給我這工作的詳細內容，我們會整理出一些金額數字給您。謝謝。

hear from 得知～的消息或收到～的信　chance 機會

✉ **sample 60**

Dear ⌐‥‥‥‥‥‥¬

Thank you for your interest. In order for us to proceed, I'll need to get some specifics from you. I've attached a form asking for the relevant information. If you could fill this out and get it back to us, we'll get the ball rolling.

I look forward to working with you.

- - - - - - - -

感謝您的關注。為了讓彼此合作能夠繼續進行，我需要您提供一些詳細訊息。我附上一份要求相關資訊的表格。如果您可以填完表格並寄回來給我們，我們會開始著手進行。我期待與您合作。

proceed 繼續　form 表格　relevant 相關的　fill... out 填寫～　get the ball rolling 開始著手進行

Try It！可以替換的字詞

a document 一份文件

an outline 一份摘要

a spreadsheet 一個試算表

a questionnaire 一份問卷

a required contract 一份必要的合約

sample 61

Dear Valued Clients,

Due to market fluctuations and some changes in the availability of certain raw materials, we are being forced to raise our prices by 4%, effective immediately. We always strive to provide the best products at the lowest possible prices, but small price increases are sometimes unavoidable. As always, we value your patronage.

Thank you,

- - - - - - - -

Try It! 可以替換的字詞

uncertainty in the market
市場的不確定性

competitor pricing
競爭對手的價格策略

the economy 經濟狀況

economic factors 經濟因素

the recession 不景氣

致尊貴的客戶：由於市場波動以及特定原物料供應的些許變化，我們不得不將價格提高4％，即日起生效。我們一直致力於盡可能以最低的價格提供最好的產品，但價格些微上漲的情況有時是不可避免的。一如既往，我們珍視您的惠顧。感謝您。

fluctuation 變化　raw material 原料　force 迫使　raise 提高　effective 生效的　strive to... 力求～
increase 增加　unavoidable 不能避免的　value 珍視　patronage 贊助商，惠顧

sample 62

Dear ＿＿＿＿＿

I'm writing to inform you of a small increase in our prices. Periodically it is necessary to adjust our prices to reflect the market. We will continue to offer bulk discounts and repeat customer discounts.

Feel free to call me with any questions.

- - - - - - - -

Try It! 可以替換的字詞

long-time customer 老客戶的

multiple-line 多項產品系列的

multi-year 多年的

occasional special 不定期特惠的

personalized 客製化的

我寫這封信的目的是要通知您，我們小幅調漲了價格。我們必須定期調整價格，以反映市場行情。我們會繼續提供大量訂購以及老顧客專屬折扣。有任何疑問的話，請儘管與我聯繫。

inform 通知　periodically 定期地　it is necessary to... 做～是必要的　adjust 調整　reflect 反映
market 市場　continue 繼續　repeat customer 老顧客

✉ sample 63

Try It！可以替換的字詞

[................]

I wanted to let you know that our prices are set to increase next week. The prices on the current price list will be good through Friday. Starting Monday there will be an across-the-board increase of 1.5%.

Let me know if you have any questions.

- - - - - - - -

go up 上升
rise 上漲
escalate 上升
mushroom 呈蘑菇狀快速升騰
swell 上漲

我想告知您，我們的價格預計下週將調漲。目前價目表上的價格至本週五為止還有效。從下週一開始，價格將全面調漲 1.5%。請讓我知道您是否有任何疑問。

> set 預定的 increase 提高 price list 價目表 good 有效的 through 直到（時間點）
> starting Monday 從星期一開始 across-the-board 全面性的

✉ sample 64

Try It！可以替換的字詞

Dear [................]

Attached is our new price list. You may notice that prices on several items have increased ❶slightly. As always, we work to get the best prices for our partners. However, occasional price increases ❷are unavoidable. We will continue to offer discounts on select items.

Thank you for your understanding.

- - - - - - - -

❶ significantly 顯著地
somewhat 有些
a little 一點點
over last year's prices 超過去年的價格
a tiny amount 少量地

❷ have to happen 必定會發生
are inevitable 無法避免的
must happen 必定會發生
occur periodically 定期地發生
will always occur 總難免會發生

附件是我們新的價目表。您可能會發現有些品項的價格已略微調漲。一如以往，我們致力於為我們的夥伴提供最優惠的價格。然而，偶爾的價格調漲是不可避免的。我們將繼續提供特定商品的優惠折扣。感謝您的理解。

> notice 注意到 slightly 略微地 however 然而 occasional 偶爾的 select 挑選出來的

✉ sample 65

The 2019 catalogue is coming out next week! We're really excited about the new product line. I just wanted to give you a heads-up about the prices. We've been forced to raise prices on several of the more popular brands. It shouldn't cut into your bottom line too much.

Let me know if you have any questions.

Try It！可以替換的字詞

items we offer 我們提供的品項

things we have 我們的產品

products we're showcasing
我們展示的產品

prototypes 樣品

servers we are carrying
我們擁有的伺服器

- - - - - - - -

我們 2019 年的目錄將在下週出爐！我們對於新的產品系列感到非常興奮。我想請您留意一下價格的部分。我們不得已調漲幾個較受歡迎品牌的價格。這應該不會對您的盈虧產生太大的影響。請讓我知道您是否有任何疑問。

heads-up 提前警告，當心　raise 提高　popular 受歡迎的　cut into 削減　bottom line（最終）損益

✉ sample 66

Dear _____

I wanted to **give you a heads-up on** an upcoming price change. We've been forced to bump the price of the G32 up by 2%. It's not a terribly large increase, but I didn't want it to come as a surprise. Let me know if you have any questions.

Thanks,

- - - - - - - -

warn you of 預先通知您～
caution you on 審慎提醒您～
tip you off about 預先告訴您有關～
forewarn you of 預先通知您～
notify you of 通知您～

我想提前通知您一件即將產生的價格變動消息。我們不得不將 G32 的價格提高 2％。雖然這調幅並不大，但希望不會讓您感到吃驚。請讓我知道您是否有任何疑問。謝謝。

upcoming 即將到來的　be forced to 被迫～　bump... up 使（價格、數量等）上漲
by 以～（某個量或程度等）　terribly 相當大地

✉ sample 67

Dear _____

I'm writing to let you know about a price increase on some of our items. The ❶**network routers** that were previously sold for $43 per unit will now cost $46. This price adjustment has been made because of an increase in ❷**manufacturing** costs. Feel free to contact me if you have any questions or concerns.

Thank you.

- - - - - - - -

❶cooling towers 冷卻塔
accelerator boards 加速板
expansion buses 擴充匯流排
graphics adapters 顯示卡
memory sticks （電腦的）記憶棒，記憶卡

❷production 生產
construction 建造
development 開發
fabrication 製造
assembly （機械的）組裝

我寫這封信的目的是要告知您，我們某些商品的價格已調漲。先前每部售價 43 美元的網路路由器，現在調漲為 46 美元。價格調整的原因來自製造成本的增加。如果您有任何問題或疑慮，請隨時與我聯繫。謝謝。

previously 以前　per 每～　because of 由於～　manufacturing 製造的　cost 成本

✉ sample 68

Dear [_____]

From time to time it is necessary for us to adjust the prices of our products in order to respond to the pressures of the market. Therefore, I am writing to inform you that we have raised our prices for the 2019 product line. These new prices will be reflected in the upcoming catalogue. Please feel free to get in touch with me if you have any questions.

Thank you.

- - - - - - - -

我們時而必須調整我們的產品價格，以因應市場的壓力。因此，我寫這封信要告知您，我們已經調漲了 2019 年產品系列的價格。這些新價格將出現在即將發行的產品目錄中。如果您有任何疑問，請隨時與我聯繫。感謝您。

from time to time 不時地　adjust 調整　respond to... 對～作出反應　pressure 壓力　therefore 因此　raise 提高　reflect 反映

✉ sample 69

Dear [_____]

I'm writing to let you know that we've had to make a little price increase to the RX-9. It's a popular item so we've had to make some incentive payments to our manufacturer in order to increase the output. I hope this won't affect your future orders too much. Let me know if you have any questions.

Thanks,

- - - - - - - -

我寫信是為了讓您知道，我們不得不稍微提高 RX-9 的價格。這是一個受歡迎的產品，所以我們不得不支付一些激勵獎金給製造商，來刺激生產量。我希望這不會對您未來的訂單造成太大衝擊。如果您有任何疑問，請與我們聯繫。謝謝。

popular 受歡迎的　incentive 鼓勵性質的　payment 付費，款項　manufacturer 製造商　output 產量　affect 影響

✉ sample 70

Dear _____

I'm writing to inform you that there has been a small price increase on all items. Periodically we have to make such adjustments in order to keep our pricing in line with the market. We continue to be ❶committed to providing our customers with the best deal on the best ❷merchandise. Feel free to contact us with any questions.

Thank you.

– – – – – – – –

Try It！可以替換的字詞

❶ concerned with 關注於～

the best at 善於～

the nation's number one at
在～保持全國第一

many business'option at
成為許多企業的選擇

unwavering at 在～（方面）堅定不移

❷ sports equipment 體育器材

paper supplies 紙類供應品

cleaning products 清潔用品

kitchen utensils 廚具

space heaters 暖氣機

我寫這封信的目的是要通知您，我們所有商品的價格都有小幅調漲。我們必須定期做這樣的調整，以使我們的定價能與市場行情保持一致。我們會繼續致力於提供我們的顧客最好的商品以及最划算的交易。有任何問題，請隨時與我們聯繫。謝謝。

price increase 價格上漲　item 品項，商品　periodically 定期地　adjustment 調整　pricing 定價
in line with... 與～一致　be committed to... 全心投入～　merchandise 商品

回覆漲價通知 Responding to the Price Increase Notice ▲

 sample 71

Hi, [＿＿＿＿]

I just wanted to ask a couple of questions about the price increase. Will the new prices be applied to orders that have already been made? Also, is there any chance of getting one more order in before the increase takes effect? I'd appreciate anything you can do for me.

Thanks,

- - - - - - - -

我想請教幾個關於價格調漲的問題。新的價格是否用於已經下的訂單？另外，在新的價格生效之前，是否還有機會再增加新的訂單？感謝您為我做的一切。謝謝。

Try It！可以替換的字詞

contracts 合約
requests 申請
agreements 協議
deals 交易案
transactions 交易案

> a couple of 一些　apply 申請　already 已經　get... in 新增加，插入～　take effect 生效

 sample 72

Dear [＿＿＿＿]

I'm a little concerned about these new prices. We've been looking around at some other suppliers. Your new prices seem to be a good deal above theirs. Is there any reason for the disparity?

Thanks,

- - - - - - -

我有點想關切一下這些新的價格。我們一直在尋找一些其它的供應商。您的新價格似乎比他們高出許多。請問這樣的差異是否有任何原因？謝謝。

Try It！可以替換的字詞

competitors 競爭對手
other companies 其它公司
of your competition 您的競爭對手中
other options 其它選擇
companies with reasonable price range 價格範圍合理的公司

> be concerned about 關心～　a good deal 划算的交易　reason 理由　disparity 差異，不一致

✉ sample 73

Dear [_____]

Thanks for letting me know. I'd like to make some orders this week. Just to confirm, they'll be covered under the old price structure, right? We'd like to get some savings.

Thanks,

- - - - - - - -

謝謝您通知我。我這一週想下一些訂單。只是想確認一下,它們還適用於舊價格,對嗎?我們希望節省一些成本。謝謝。

today 今天
tomorrow 明天
soon 很快地
as quickly as possible 盡快地
by the end of the week 在這個週末之前

confirm 確認　cover 涵蓋,適用於　price 價格　structure 結構　saving 節省

✉ sample 74

[_____]

❶Regarding the new prices, will we still be able to get our bulk discount? I'm trying to plan the next ❷quarter's orders and I want accurate numbers. Please let me know how this will affect us.

Thanks,

- - - - - - - -

❶About 關於～
On the topic of 關於～的話題
Following up on 有關～的後續消息
For 對於～
In regards to 關於～

❷year's 年度的
month's 月的
week's 週的
trimester's 三個月的
semester's 學期的

關於新價格,我們現在還能享有大宗訂購的折扣嗎?我正在計劃下一季的訂單,我想知道確切的數字。請讓我知道這對我們有何影響。謝謝。

regarding 關於～　still 仍然　quarter 一季　accurate 確切的　affect 影響

:.............:

We've been making monthly orders for the last year. Is there any chance that we could be "grandfathered in" under the old pricing scheme? It would really help us out a lot.

Let me know.

- - - - - - - -

five and a half years 五年半	
three years 三年	
several years 數年	
ten quarters 十個季度	
decade 十年	

我們過去一年來每個月都有下訂單。我們是否有機會適用舊有價格方案 — 免適用新價格方案？這確實可以大大地幫助我們。請讓我知道。

monthly 每月的　chance 機會，可能性　grandfather 使～繼續享有既得權利，使～免除適用新規則
scheme 計畫，方案　a lot 很多

要求降價 Asking for a Price Decrease ▲

✉ sample 76

I'm writing to inquire about the flexibility of your current price structure. Is there any chance of getting a slightly lower price per unit? I'd love it if we could get, say 3% off. We're planning on doing a lot of business with you in the future, so any help would be appreciated.

pricing scheme 價格方案

prices 價格

shipping charges 運費

price pyramid 價格金字塔

pricing factors 定價因素

Thanks,

- - - - - - - -

我寫這封信的目的是想詢問您目前價格策略上的議價空間。是否可能稍微降低每單位的價格呢？要是可以給我們，比方說，3％ 的折扣，我們就會願意接受。我們正計劃未來與您們合作多項業務，因此，我們感激任何您能提供的協助。謝謝。

flexibility 靈活性，彈性　slightly 略微地　lower 減價　say 比如説～　off 折扣

✉ sample 77

Dear

I was wondering if we could get a reduction in price on our next order. There'll be more orders over the next several months, and a price break would definitely increase the number of orders we make with you.

lowering 降低

decrease 降低，減少

drop 降低

decline 降低

cut 刪減

Let me know if you can work with us on this.

- - - - - - - -

我想知道我們下次的訂單是否可享有降價優惠。未來幾個月還會有更多訂單，價格調降肯定可以增加我們跟您下訂單的次數。請讓我知道您能否與我們在這件事上合作。

wonder if 想知道是否～　reduction 減價，折扣　definitely 必然　increase 增加

✉ sample 78

I'm looking at the 2019 catalogue and the prices seem a little steep. Is there any room for negotiation? We'd like to make several orders over the next few months and it would help if we could get, say, a 2% break.

Thanks,

- - - - - - - -

我正在看 2019 年的產品型錄，但價格似乎有點高。請問是否有議價空間呢？我們未來幾個月會下幾張訂單，如果我們能夠獲得，比方說，2% 的折扣，將會有所幫助。謝謝。

steep（價格）很高的　room for... ～的空間、餘地　negotiation 談判

✉ sample 79

We're going to be ordering 200 of the T-235 network routers. They're listed at $30 each. Is there any chance we could knock a few dollars off of that? It would really help out a lot and encourage us to use you as a supplier in the future.

Let me know what you can do.

- - - - - - - -

我們將訂購 200 台 T-235 網路路由器。其定價為每單位 30 美元。是否可能給我們便宜幾美元的價格呢？這確實將很有幫助，且能鼓勵我們在未來將貴公司列為合作廠商之一。請讓我知道您的決定如何。

each 每一　knock... off 砍（價格）　encourage 鼓勵～

✉ sample 80

Dear [............]

I'm writing to see if we could discuss a price break on our next order. We have been regular customers for the last few years, and I would like to see about making ❶a deal to ease the price a bit.

Let me know if there is anything ❷you can do.

- - - - - - - -

我寫這封信的目的是想看看，我們下一張訂單是否有降價的討論空間。過去數年來，我們一直是老客戶，因此希望彼此可以協議稍微降價。請讓我知道您的任何決定。

price break （批量訂單的）價格折扣　regular customer 老主顧　would like to 想要～　ease 減輕

回覆降價要求 Responding to the Price Decrease Request ▲

✉ sample 81

As usual, thanks for your business. For a special customer such as you, I think we could come down to 2% on orders of 50 or more. Would that be suitable to you? I hope it takes some budget pressure off of you.

Thanks again,

- - - - - - - -

a committed	一位忠誠的
a valued	一位受重視的
an appreciated	一位令人讚賞的
a respected	一位受敬重的
a prized	一位受重視的

像往常一樣，感謝您的惠顧。對於像您這樣特別的客戶，我想我們可以給 50 件以上的訂單 2% 的折扣。您認為這樣可行嗎？希望這樣可以降低您部分預算上的負擔。再次感謝。

> as usual 像往常一樣　business 交易，往來　such as 諸如～　come down（價格、溫度等）降低；下降　suitable 合適的　take off 拿掉，取下～

✉ sample 82

Dear

Thanks for getting in touch with me. Currently we are unable to make any reductions in price. We value your ❶ loyalty and will certainly keep it in mind going forward. Unfortunately, economic realities are forcing us to hold the prices ❷steady.

Thank you for understanding.

- - - - - - - -

❶faithfulness	忠誠
devotion	忠誠
allegiance	忠貞
reliability	可靠
dependability	可靠
❷firm	穩定的
stable	穩定的
solid	穩固的
fixed	固定的
sturdy	穩健的

感謝您與我聯繫。目前我們無法降低任何品項的價格。我們重視您的忠誠度，並且未來也必定會牢記在心。但遺憾的是，經濟上的現實迫使我們必須保持價格的固定。謝謝您的理解。

> get in touch with 與～取得聯繫　currently 現在，目前　unable 不能夠的　value 重視　loyalty 忠誠度　economic 經濟的　reality 現實　steady 穩定的，不變的

✉ sample 83

I think we can do something for you. While we can't cut as much as 2%, I can manage a 1.5% break. We value our relationship with you and really want to keep you around. Let me know if this helps.

Thanks,

- - - - - - - -

我想我們可以為您做點事情。雖然我們不能調降到 2% 這麼多，但我可以設法達到 1.5% 的折扣。我們重視與您的關係，並且確實希望與您維持關係。請讓我知道這對您是否有助益。謝謝。

> while 當，雖然～ 但 cut 刪減 as much as 2% 多達 2% manage 設法做到 break 打斷，打折
> relationship 關係

Try It ! 可以替換的字詞

handle 處理
make 做出
suggest 建議
agree to 同意
offer 提供

✉ sample 84

I think we can definitely ❶help you out with the price on an order as large as 200. We can do $28 per unit. We should be able to do that on ❷subsequent orders of over 100 as well. I hope this helps.

Thanks,

- - - - - - - -

Try It ! 可以替換的字詞

❶ assist you 幫助您
aid you 幫助您
help out 幫到底
work 處理
be flexibile 可通融的

❷ following 接下來的
ensuing 後來的
successive 相繼而來的
later 之後的
future 未來的

我想，訂單數量達 200 單位時，我們絕對可以幫您解決價格的問題。我們可以給您每單位 28 美元。而接下來的訂單量超過 100 單位的話，我們應該也能夠提供同樣的價格。我希望這會有所幫助。謝謝。

> help... out with 幫助～（某人某事） as large as（數量等）多達～ subsequent 接下來的
> as well 同樣地，也

✉ sample 85

Dear ....

We have a rewards program for loyal buyers. Once you reach your 10th order, you get a 5% reduction in price. My records show that you've made 9 orders with us, so after your next, you'll qualify for the break.

As usual, we value your business.

Try It!可以替換的字詞

cherish 珍惜
enjoy 和～感到愉快
appreciate 感謝
respect 重視
treasure 珍視

- - - - - - - -

我們為忠誠的客戶提供獎勵計劃。一旦下單次數達到第 10 次，您的價格將降低 5%。我的記錄顯示，您已經向我們下了 9 張訂單，所以從您的下一張訂單以後，您將有資格獲得優惠折扣。像往常一樣，我們重視與貴公司的往來。

reward 獎勵　loyal buyer 忠實的買家　once 一旦～　reach 達到　record 紀錄　qualify for 有～的資格

業務會議 Business Meeting

Case 01 約定商務會議 Setting Up the Business Meeting ▲

✉ sample 86

Hi, _____

I'm just writing to see if we can get together early next week for a meeting. We've got some reports we'd like to go over with you. Let me know if Tuesday afternoon is okay for you.

Thanks,

- - - - - - -

我寫這封信的目的是想確認能否在下周初一起開個會。我們有幾份報告,想和您一起仔細討論一下。請讓我知道週二下午您是否有空。謝謝。

if 是否~ get together 聚在一起 meeting 會議 report 報告 go over 詳細討論

Try It! 可以替換的字詞

Wednesday morning 週三早上

Monday evening 星期一晚上

Thursday around 11:00
週四十一點左右

late Friday morning 週五早上晚一點

early Tuesday 週二早些時候

✉ sample 87

_____

Would it be possible to schedule a meeting for sometime next week? I'd like to go over some ideas for a promotion. Let me know if you've got an opening.

Thank you,

- - - - - - -

下週是否有可能在某個時間安排一場會議?我想談談宣傳活動的一些想法。請讓我知道您是否有空。謝謝。

would it be possible to...? 有沒有可能~? schedule 將~排入行程表 promotion 推廣,宣傳
opening 空檔,機會

Try It! 可以替換的字詞

an internship 一項實習計畫

a new product line 新系列產品

a future investment opportunity
一個未來的投資機會

our hiring procedures 我們的雇用程序

a new prototype 一件新樣品

✉ sample 88

[_____]

I've got a few questions about the ❶distribution of our products. It's really more in depth than we can talk about by phone or email. Would it be possible to meet? Let me know what your ❷calendar looks like.

Thanks,

– – – – – – – –

❶marketing 行銷
advertising 廣告
promotion 宣傳
delivery 寄送
shipping 運送

❷week looks 週計畫如何
schedule looks 時程表如何
month looks 月計畫如何
Friday afternoon looks
星期五下午如何
Mornings look 早上的時間如何

關於我們產品的分銷，我有幾個問題想請教。比起我們透過電話或電子郵件談論，這會是更深入討論的方式。有沒有可能安排見個面呢？請讓我知道您的時程表是否允許。謝謝。

a few 一些～ distribution 分銷，分配 depth 深度 calendar 日程表，時間表

✉ sample 89

Dear [_____]

I would like to propose a meeting. We have a few proposals we'd like to make. I think we could really benefit from working together. How would next week be?

I look forward to hearing from you.

– – – – – – –

profit 獲益
do well 進展順利
gain 獲得收益取
earn well 收穫頗豐
move forward 繼續往前進

我想提議開個會。我們有一些想提出的建議。我認為我們確實都可以從合作中獲益。下週您覺得怎麼樣？我期待您的回音。

propose 提議 proposal 提案 benefit 獲得利益 together 一起 look forward to 期待～
hear from 收到～的消息

✉ sample 90

Try It！可以替換的字詞

contract 合約

covenant 協議，協定

pact 協約

settlement 協議

deal 約定

I need to talk to you about some changes we'd like to make in our partnership agreement. Is there a day that's good for you next week? I'm traveling for the rest of this week, but my schedule is pretty clear after that.

Thanks,

- - - - - - - -

我必須和您談談我們想在合作協議中更改的一些事項。下週您可否挪出一天出來呢？我這的週末前都還在出差，不過之後我的行程安排上會相當寬鬆。謝謝。

change 更改　partnership 夥伴關係，合作　agreement 協議，契約　travel 出差　rest 其餘的
clear（時程表）有空的

變更商務會議日期 Changing the Business Meeting Date ▲

sample 91

How flexible is the 15th for that meeting? It turns out I'm booked that day. Would the 14th or the 16th work for you? Let me know when you're available.

Sorry for the inconvenience.

unavailable 沒有空的
booked solid 行程滿檔
completely scheduled 行程滿檔
preoccupied 事先有約的
busy 繁忙的

- - - - - - - -

15 日的那場會議是否可以彈性變更呢？事實上那天我已經有約了。14 日或 16 日您可以嗎？請讓我知道您何時有空。不便之處，深表歉意。

> flexible 靈活的，有彈性的　it turns out (that...) 結果，事實上～　booked 已約定好的
> work 可行，沒問題，行得通　available 有空的，（時間上）可配合的　inconvenience 不便

sample 92

I'm afraid I'm going to have to reschedule our meeting next week. Would Thursday work for you instead of Wednesday? If not, I may have to put it off until next week. Sorry if this disrupts your schedule too much.

Thanks,

get-together 聚會
reunion 團聚，重聚
appointment 約定
engagement 約會
discussion 討論

- - - - - - - -

恐怕我必須重新排定我們下週會議的時間了。從週三改到週四的話您可以嗎？如果不行，我可能得延後至下週。要是這樣大大地打亂您的行程安排，真是抱歉。謝謝您。

> reschedule 重新安排（時程表）　instead of 而非～　if not 若非如此，否則　put... off 延遲～
> disrupt 擾亂，使混亂

✉ sample 93

Dear ⌐ ¬

Would it inconvenience you too much if we change the date of next month's meeting from the 23rd to the 25th? I have ❶a client who will only be in town on the 23rd, so I'm trying to ❷accommodate him. Let me know if that will work for you.

Thanks,

- - - - - - - -

Try It！可以替換的字詞

❶ a partner 一位合夥人
a boss 一位老闆
a teammate 一個團隊成員
an old friend 一個老朋友
a fellow researcher 一位研究同事

❷ make time for 為～騰出時間
assist 幫助
be of service to 為～提供服務
find time for 抽出時間給～
reschedule 重新排定行程

如果我們將下個月的會議日期從 23 日改為 25 日，這樣會造成您的不便嗎？我有一位客戶只能在 23 日前來市區拜訪，所以我想配合他的時間。請讓我知道這時間您是否可行。謝謝。

inconvenience 造成～（某人的）不便　date 日期　client 顧客，客戶　accommodate 給～方便，通融

✉ sample 94

⌐ ¬

I was wondering if we could change the date of our meeting next week from Tuesday to Wednesday. I've got a conflict that I didn't foresee, so I'll be out of the office visiting with a client on Tuesday. Let me know if Wednesday will work for you.

Thanks,

- - - - - - -

Try It！可以替換的字詞

a previous meeting
一場早已約好的會議
an unscheduled appointment
一場非預定的約會
a legal issue 一個法律問題
a court requirement 一項出庭要求
a research and development
breakthrough 一項研發上的的突破

我想知道我們是否可以更改下週會議的日期 — 從週二改為週三。我遇到一個先前未預料到的行程衝突，因此週二我會離開辦公室，外出見客戶。請讓我知道週三您是否可行。謝謝。

wonder if... 我想知道是否～　conflict（行程上的）衝突　foresee 預料　be out of office 不在辦公室
visit with 探訪～

✉ sample **95**

If it isn't too much of an inconvenience, I'd like to push our meeting forward a day to Thursday. My Friday has turned out to be a little overbooked. Let me know if that's okay and what time would work for you.

Thanks,

- - - - - - - -

要是不會造成您太大的不便，我想把我們的會議往前推一天到週四。我週五的行程有點太滿了。請讓我知道那樣的話是否可行，以及您什麼時間方便。謝謝。

push forward 往前推　overbooked 行程排得太滿

that works for you 那對您來說可行

that inconveniences you
那對您來說不方便

that works 那樣是可行的

you're okay with that 對您來說是可行的

that's no problem 那是沒問題的

確認商務會議 Confirming the Business Meeting ▲

✉ sample 96

Hi, _____

I'm just writing to confirm the 16th at 2:30 for our meeting. I'll be bringing a couple of people from our office along to introduce to you. Let me know if there are any changes in the schedule.

Looking forward to seeing you,

- - - - - - - -

我寫這封信只是要確認我們會議時間為 16 日的 2:30。我會帶幾位公司同仁一起過去,並介紹給您認識。請讓我知道這樣的時間安排會不會有任何變化。期待與您見面。

> confirm 確認　bring... along 帶來～　a couple of 一些,幾位

Try It!可以替換的字詞

agenda 議程
meeting 會議
time 時間
date and time 日期和時間
plans 計畫

✉ sample 97

Hi, _____

I just wanted to confirm that we're on for the 20th at 10:30. I'm excited about sharing some new ideas. If you have any data you want me to bring, just let me know.

Thanks,

- - - - - - - -

我只是想確認一下,我們的會議時間是 20 日的 10 點 30 分。我很期待可以分享一些新的點子。如果您有任何要我帶過去的資料,儘管告訴我吧。謝謝。

> on 知情的,了解～的　be excited 很興奮的　share 分享　data 資料

Try It!可以替換的字詞

prototypes 原樣,樣品
inventions 發明品
goals 目標
projects 專案
proposals 提案

✉ sample 98

Try It! 可以替換的字詞

I'm writing to confirm our meeting on the 17th at 4:30. I'm looking forward to going over some marketing ideas. By the way, could you bring some samples of the advertising graphics you were telling me about?

Thanks,

advertising 廣告
promotion 宣傳
sales 銷售
public display 公開展示
commercial （電視和廣播的）廣告

- - - - - - - -

我寫這封信是要確認我們 17 日 4:30 的會議。我期待能夠討論一些行銷理念。順道一問，您能否帶些你曾跟我提到過的廣告圖片的樣本嗎？謝謝。

look forward to... 期待～　go over 仔細檢查～　by the way 順道一提　sample 樣品　advertising 廣告　graphic 圖示，圖像

✉ sample 99

Dear

Try It! 可以替換的字詞

I have you down for a meeting on the 25th at 1:30. Is this still good for you? I'll be bringing my ❶companion from the ❷finance team along to share a few ideas. Let me know if there's any problem with the schedule.

Thanks,

❶ fellow investors 投資夥伴
partners 合作夥伴
boss 老闆
colleague 同事
ally 夥伴

❷ international sales 國際銷售
design 設計
general affairs 總務
real estate 不動產
internet relations 網際網路關係事務

- - - - - - - -

我們已約定 25 日 1:30 一起開會。這時間對您而言還是可以嗎？我將帶領我的財經團隊同仁一起過去，分享一些看法。請讓我知道這個時程安排是否有任何問題。謝謝。

down for... 為～（某事）約定好　still 仍然　companion 同事　finance 金融，財務

✉ **sample 100**

Hi, ☐

Are we still on for the 16th at 2:30? I'm looking forward to meeting with you. Let me know if you need to reschedule.

Thanks,

- - - - - - - -

我們約定的時間還是 16 日 2:30 嗎？我很期待與您見面。請讓我知道您是否需要改時間。謝謝。

be on for 知悉，認同～（某事） reschedule 重新安排時間

Try It! 可以替換的字詞

anticipating meeting 期待見面

eager to be meeting 渴望見面

expecting to meet 期待見面

hopeful to be meeting 希望能見面

awaiting to meet 等著要見面

✉ sample 101

I'm terribly sorry, but I'm afraid I'm going to have to cancel the meeting. We've had a bit of a crisis here at the office and everybody is scrambling to take care of it. I'll contact you next week about rescheduling.

Sorry for the inconvenience.

- - - - - - - -

我很抱歉，因為我恐怕必須取消這次會議。我們公司這邊出現了一點危機，每個人都拼命地要處理這件事。我下週會針對改時間的事與您聯繫。造成不便，深表歉意。

Try It！可以替換的字詞
an emergency 一個緊急狀況
a catastrophe 一場大災難
a predicament 一個困境
a disaster 一場災難
an unforeseen circumstance 一個出乎意料的情況

> terribly 非常地　cancel 取消　a bit of 一點點～　crisis 危機　scramble to 一窩蜂地去做～
> take care of 處理～

✉ sample 102

Unfortunately, I will not be able to attend the meeting we had arranged for the 20th of July. Certain business concerns make it unwise for us to enter into any new partnerships. If circumstances change, I will contact you to schedule a new meeting.

Thank you.

- - - - - - - -

真是可惜！我將無法參加我們已經排定 7 月 20 日進行的會議。某些營運上的顧慮使得我們進入任何新的合作關係一事，成為不明智之舉。如果情況有變化，我會與您聯繫，並安排新會議。謝謝。

Try It！可以替換的字詞
new issues 新的問題
financial problems 財務問題
economic factors 經濟因素
partnerships with other corporations 與其它公司合作
expenses 費用

> unfortunately 遺憾地，可惜　attend 出席　arrange 安排　concern 關切之事，顧慮
> unwise 不明智的，愚蠢的　enter into 進入～狀態　partnership 夥伴關係，合作

I hate to do this to you, but I'm going to have to cancel that June 16th meeting. We aren't going to have our products ready for shipment by that date, so we won't be able to make any kind of commitment. I hope this doesn't cause you too much trouble.

Sorry for the confusion.

promise 保證
pledge 保證
assurance 保證
vow 擔保
contract 契約

雖然我很不想這麼做，但我還是得取消 6 月 16 日的會議。我們無法在那日期前做好送貨的準備。所以我們不能答應任何事情。希望這不會造成您太大麻煩。抱歉讓您感到困惑。

hate 不願　have... ready 將～準備好　shipment 裝運，運送　commitment 承諾　cause 造成
trouble 麻煩　confusion 混亂

✉ **sample 104**

Due to unforeseen circumstances, I'm afraid that I will not be able to make the meeting we scheduled for the 16th of June. Please accept my apologies. I will let you know if I am able to reschedule.

Thank you for your patience.

assistance 協助
tolerance 寬容
persistence 堅持
understanding 了解
acceptance 接受

由於出現一些意外狀況，恐怕我無法參加我們預定 6 月 16 日舉行的會議。請接受我的道歉。我會讓您知道我是否能夠重新安排時間。感謝您的耐心。

due to... 由於～　unforeseen 不可預見的　make a meeting 能夠參加會議　accept 接受　apology 道歉
patience 耐心

✉ sample 105

I apologize for doing this, but I'm afraid I'll have to cancel next Friday's meeting. We've got some last-minute changes to make to our new items before we're ready to show it for our potential buyers. I'll let you know when we can reschedule.

Sorry for the inconvenience.

new products 新產品

samples 樣品

product line 產品系列

production process 生產過程

trial products 試用品

- - - - - - - -

我對此感到抱歉，因為我恐怕必須取消下週五的會議。在我們準備將新產品展示給潛在買家看之前，必須進行最後的修改。我會讓您知道我們什麼時候可以重新安排會議時間。抱歉造成您的不便。

apologize 道歉　last-minute 最後一刻的　potential 可能的　buyer 顧客，買家

✉ sample 106

Try It! 可以替換的字詞

put off 使～延期
delay 延遲
push back 往後延
rearrange 重新安排
reschedule 重新排定

If it won't be too much of an inconvenience, I'd like to postpone our meeting. I'm going to be out of town on business until the 16th and I feel like I need a little more time to recover and prepare before we get together.

Let me know if this will work for you.

- - - - - - - -

如果不會造成太大不便，我想延後我們的會議。我將離開本地去出差，一直到 16 日才回來，我想在我們會面之前，我需要多點時間重新調整狀態與準備。請讓我知道這樣對您而言是否可行。

inconvenience 不便　postpone 將～延期　on business 出差　until... 直到～為止　feel like 想要～
recover 恢復

✉ sample 107

Try It! 可以替換的字詞

an issue 一個難題
a setback 一個阻礙
a glitch 一個差錯
a dilemma 一個困境
a troublesome day 一個麻煩的日子

I'm afraid I'm going to need to put off our meeting. Thursday turns out to be a problem for me. Would the following Thursday be okay? Let me know.

Thanks,

- - - - - - - -

恐怕我必須延後我們的會議了。事實上週四對我而言有困難。下週四可以嗎？請讓我知道。謝謝。

turn out 結果是～　following 接著的

✉ sample 108

Due to **❶unexpected circumstances** I will not be able to keep our Tuesday appointment. Would it be possible to reschedule it for later in the week? I'm really looking forward to meeting with you. Let me know what your schedule will allow.

Sorry for **❷the inconvenience.**

- - - - - - - -

由於發生意料之外的狀況，我將無法履行週二的約定。是否有可能重新排約至本週晚些時候呢？我真的很期待跟您見面。請讓我知道您可以的時間。造成不便，深表歉意。

unexpected 料想不到的　keep an appointment 守約　later in the week 本週晚些時候　allow 允許

✉ sample 109

I'm afraid I'm going to have to postpone that meeting on the 16th. We're waiting for some market analysis to come back to us so that we'll be able to show you the numbers you asked for. How would the 20th work for you? I hope this doesn't **disrupt** your schedule too much.

Thanks for understanding,

- - - - - - - -

我恐怕必須延後 16 日的會議。我們正在等待收回市場分析資料，才能夠讓您看到您要求的數據。20 日您可以嗎？我希望這不會太擾亂您的行程安排。感謝您的理解。

analysis 分析　ask for 請求～　disrupt 使混亂

✉ sample 110

I regret that I'm going to have to rearrange our meeting. Events beyond my control have made it necessary for me to be in the office all day on Monday. Would Tuesday or Wednesday work for you? I hope that this doesn't cause you too much trouble.

Thanks for understanding.

Try It！可以替換的字詞

any headaches 任何頭痛的狀況

scheduling conflicts 時間安排上的衝突

any problems 任何問題

major concerns 重大問題

to miss anything 錯過任何事

- - - - - - - -

我很遺憾必須重新排定我們的會議時間。一些我無法掌控的事件，使得我週一整天都必須待在辦公室裡。週二或週三您可以嗎？希望這不會給您帶來太多麻煩。謝謝您的理解。

regret (that...) 對～感到遺憾　rearrange 重新安排　beyond... 超出～（範圍）之外　control 控制
make it necessary for A to... 使得 A 必須～（去做某事）　cause 造成～

sample 111

Dear _____

I'm writing to propose a preliminary meeting. I'd like to get together with you for some brainstorming. I think that our two organizations could really benefit from doing business together. Would you be interested in discussing some possibilities?

I look forward to hearing from you.

- - - - - - - -

我寫這封信的目的是想提出一個籌備會議。我想和您大家一起集思廣益。我認為我們兩個組織確實能夠從合作事業中獲益。您有興趣討論一些可能性嗎？我期待著您的回音。

> propose 提出（建議）　preliminary 初步的，預備的　brainstorming 集思廣益　organization 組織
> benefit from... 從～獲益　possibility 可能性

Try It！可以替換的字詞

groups 團體
institutions 機構
entities 實體
corporations 企業
teams 團隊

 sample 112

Dear _____

Would you be interested in meeting next week in order to start generating some ideas? We're very interested in working with you and I think the first step would be to start brainstorming. Let me know if this sounds good to you.

Thanks,

- - - - - - - -

您是否有興趣在下週會面，並開始構思一些想法呢？我們很有興趣與您合作，而且我認為第一步是大家開始集思廣益。請讓我知道您是否認為這樣的想法可行。謝謝。

> in order to 為了～　generate 產出，創建　step 步驟，階段　sound 聽起來～

Try It！可以替換的字詞

projects 計畫
outcomes 結果
tentative plans 暫定計劃
thoughts 想法
goals 目標

✉ sample 113

Try It!可以替換的字詞

initiate 開始著手於～

quicken 使～加快速度

start 開始

begin 開始

kick off 啟動

I think that in order to jumpstart this project, we should get together and try to come up with some new ideas. I propose we meet next week and throw out some ideas just to see what sounds good. What do you think?

Let me know.

- - - - - - -

我認為，為了啟動這項計畫，我們應該一起試著提出一些新的想法。我提議我們下週會面，並提出一些想法，看看有什麼不錯的主意。您覺得如何？請讓我知道。

jumpstart 啟動，使～前進　come up with 想出～　throw out 拋出，丟出～

✉ sample 114

Try It!可以替換的字詞

meeting 會議

get-together 聚會

summit 高峰會

discussion 討論會

seminar 研討會

I'd like to schedule a brainstorming session with you sometime in the near future. It doesn't need to be too formal; just a way for us to see what kind of projects we might collaborate on. Does this sound good to you?

I look forward to hearing from you.

- - - - - - -

我想在不久的將來，找個時間安排與您進行一場集思廣益的討論會。它不需要太正式，其目的只是要找出我們可能一起合作什麼樣的專案。您覺得如何呢？我期待您的回音。

session 會議　sometime 在（將來或過去）某個時候　near 不遠的　formal 正式的　way 方法
collaborate on 在～方面合作

✉ sample 115

Try It ! 可以替換的字詞

I'm making a proposal of an informal meeting designed to help us generate some business ideas. We like what we've seen of your operation, and I think that we can benefit each other greatly. Why don't we get together next week and talk about some possibilities?

I look forward to hearing from you.

procedure 程序
company 公司
business 營運
enterprise 企業
process 製程

我提議舉行一場非正式會議，目的是幫助我們發想一些商業創意。根據我們所了解您的營運方式，我們相當認同，而且我認為我們雙方可以從合作中受益良多。我們下週會面並討論一些可能性如何？我期待您的回音。

make a proposal 提案，建議　informal 非正式的　designed to... 設計用來～.
help A + 原形動詞 幫助 A～　operation 營運，業務　why don't we...? 我們何不～?

提議舉辦商務會議 Suggesting the Business Meeting ▲

✉ sample 116

Dear [____]

We've got some business ideas we'd like to run past you. I think there are some ways that could be mutually beneficial. Would you like to meet sometime next week to discuss a couple of proposals?

I look forward to hearing from you.

- - - - - - - -

我們有一些營運上的構想，想聽聽您的意見。我認為有一些方法可以讓彼此受益。下週找個時間見面討論一些提案可以嗎？我期待您的回音。

Try It！可以替換的字詞

ideas 想法
goals 目標
suggestions 建議
offers 提議
propositions 建議

business 商業　past 通過～　way 方式　mutually 互相地　beneficial 盈利的　discuss 討論
proposal 提案

✉ sample 117

Dear [____]

We've been following your performance for some time and we like what we've seen. I'd like to propose that we meet to discuss a possible partnership. I think we could both profit each other by doing business together. Let me know if you are open to meeting.

Thanks,

- - - - - - - -

我們已關注貴公司營運成果一段時間了，且對於我們所見感到滿意。我希望我們可以會面開會討論可能的合夥關係。我認為我們一起合作的話，雙方都可以獲得利益。請讓我知道您是否有空可以會面討論。謝謝。

Try It！可以替換的字詞

alliance 結盟
joint venture 合資企業
association 夥伴關係
working relationship 合作關係
collaboration 合作

follow 關注～（發展狀況等）　performance 成效，實績　each other 彼此
open to... 有接受～的可能性（準備接受新的想法、建議等）

✉ sample 118

I think we could both benefit from a face-to-face meeting. I have some figures I'd like to show you that I think you'll find quite interesting. There are going to be a lot of opportunities opening up soon and I'd like to get you involved.

I look forward to hearing from you.

- - - - - - - -

我想我們雙方都可以從一場面對面的會議中有所收穫。我有一些想讓您看看的數據，我認為你會很感興趣的。很快地，會有很多機會等著我們，希望您能參與。我期待您的回音。

face-to-face 面對面的　figure 數值　quite 十分地　opportunity 機會　involved 參與其中的

Try It! 可以替換的字詞

charts 圖表
numbers 數字
data 資料
statistics 統計數據
information 資料

✉ sample 119

Dear _____

I'd like to suggest that we meet next week to discuss the latest ❶sales figures. I think I have some ideas about how to improve your ❷performance. Would you be interested in meeting?

Thanks,

- - - - - - - -

我想建議我們下週開個會，來討論最新的銷售數據。我想我有一些關於提高您工作績效的想法。您有興趣見面討論嗎？謝謝。

suggest 建議　latest 最新的　figure 數值　performance 表現，績效

Try It! 可以替換的字詞

❶ sales projections 銷售預估
marketing outcomes 行銷成果
target profits 目標獲利
net income 淨收入
revenue streams 營收來源

❷ work 工作
operation 營運
workload 工作量
functions 職責
job 工作

✉ sample 120

Dear [＿＿＿＿＿]

My company has put together a new product line and we are looking for overseas **distribution partners**. I'd like to get together with you in order to show you what we're offering and see if your operation would make a good fit with ours. Let me know if you would be amenable to such a meeting.

Thanks,

- - - - - - - -

敝公司已推出新產品系列，且我們正在尋找海外經銷夥伴。為了向您介紹我們提供的產品，我希望可以和您會面，看看彼此是否適合。請讓我知道您是否可接受這樣的一場會面。謝謝。

> put together 整理，彙整　product line 產品系列　overseas 海外的　distribution 分配，分發
> offer 提供　operation 營運　fit 適合，勝任　amenable 肯順從的，可接受的

marketing outlets 行銷通路

suppliers 供應商

outlets 銷售點

markets 市場

collaborators 合作者

✉ **sample 121**

Hi, _____

It was great to talk to you yesterday. Attached are the minutes from the meeting. I think we made some real progress. If you have time, look over the document and let me know what you think the next step should be.

Thanks,

- - - - - - - -

昨天跟您談得很愉快。附件是會議紀錄。我想我們已取得很大的進展。麻煩您再抽空看一下這份文件，並讓我知道您對於下一步應如何進行的想法。謝謝。

attached 附上的　minutes 會議紀錄　progress 進度，進展　look over 把～看一遍　document 文件
step 步驟

✉ **sample 122**

Dear _____

I thought the meeting went really well the other day. I just wanted to make sure we're on the same page with regard to the marketing plan. Below I've outlined what I see as the major decisions we reached. Let me know if I've understood everything correctly.

Thanks,

- - - - - - - -

我認為幾天前的會議進展相當順利。我只是想確定一下，關於行銷計畫的部分，我們的想法步調是一致的。以下是我摘要出我所理解的，作為我們達成的重大決策。請讓我知道我所理解的一切是否皆正確。謝謝。

make sure 確定　on the same page（為了同一目標而）步調一致　with regard to... 與～有關
outline 概括論述　major 主要的　reach a decision 作出決定　correctly 正確地

✉ sample 123

Dear _____

Thanks for putting so much effort into this morning's meeting. I'm attaching the minutes I typed up, including the sales figures from **my presentation**. Let me know if you have any questions or anything you'd like to add.

Thanks,

- - - - - - - -

感謝您為今天上午的會議付出了這麼多努力。我附上我製作的會議記錄，包括我的簡報中的銷售數字。請讓我知道您是否有任何問題，或者有任何想補充的內容。謝謝。

✉ sample 124

Hi, _____

Great meeting last week. The project is really starting to shape up. I've had my secretary type up a report on the **progress** we made at the meeting and I'm attaching it for your perusal. Let me know if you have any inquiries.

Thanks,

- - - - - - - -

上週的會議太棒了。這項專案真的開始有進展了。我已請我的祕書將我們在會議上取得的進展打成一份報告，並附上供您審視。請讓我知道您是否有任何疑問。謝謝。

Dear _____

Thank you for meeting with me last week. It seems the meeting was quite profitable. I've typed up a summary of where I think we stand now and I'm sending it along for you to look over. I look forward to meeting with you again soon.

Thanks,

- - - - - - - -

謝謝您上週和我會面。這場會議真是頗有助益。我已打完一份摘要報告，內容提及我認為我們目前的狀況，在此寄給您詳細過目一下。我期待很快可以再見到您。謝謝。

quite 十分　profitable 有益的　summary 摘要　stand 處於某種狀態　soon 不久

beneficial 有益的
productive 富有成效的
useful 有用的
positive 有建設性的
valuable 有價值的

✉ sample 126

Try It！可以替換的字詞

I thought the meeting was quite useful. I just wanted to ask that you keep the meeting **confidential** for now. We're still not sure which direction we're going to go, so we don't want word to get out yet.

Thanks for understanding.

private 私人的
hush-hush 不可洩漏出去的
classified 列為機密的
off-the-record 不留記錄
secret 祕密的

- - - - - - - -

我認為這場會議相當成功。在此我想要求您將此會議列為機密。我們仍不確定我們將往哪個方向前進，所以我們不希望任何一個字洩露出去。感謝您的理解。

> confidential 機密的，祕密的　for now 目前，當下　direction 方向　word 言語
> get out（消息等）洩露，被說出去

✉ sample 127

Try It！可以替換的字詞

Yesterday's meeting was a real ❶**step forward**. Thanks for all of your hard work. Just a quick note: We aren't quite ready to announce the ❷**partnership**, so I'd appreciate it if you could keep our talks under wraps for the time being. Let me know if you have any questions.

Thanks,

❶ positive one 正面的會議
great experience 很棒的經歷
good step 好的一步
nice time 美好的時光
useful time 有效的時間利用

❷ details 詳細資訊
cooperation 合作
work together 一起合作
outcomes 結果
goals 目標

- - - - - - - -

昨天的會議可說是往前邁出一大步。感謝您辛勤付出的一切。只是要提醒一下：我們還沒真正準備要宣布合夥關係，所以如果您能將我們的談話暫時保密，我會感激不盡。請讓我知道您是否有任何疑問。謝謝。

> forward 往前　note 注意，備註　keep... under wraps 保密～
> for the time being 暫時地（直到事情發生變化為止）

✉ sample 128

Dear ⌐⌐⌐⌐⌐

It was good to see you yesterday. I'm feeling quite
❶confident about the direction things are going.
However, I wanted to remind you that the contents of
the meeting should stay confidential for now. Until we're
ready to send out **❷a press release**, it's our policy to keep
our deals quiet.

Thanks a lot, and I look forward to meeting with you
again soon.

- - - - - - -

很高興昨天與您見面。我對於事情的發展方向充滿信心。不過，我想提醒您，目前會議內容須暫時保密。直到我們準備發布新聞稿為止，我們的策略是保持我們的交易內容不公開。非常感謝，我也期待很快將與您再次會面。

confident 有信心的　remind 提醒　content 內容　send out 發出　press release（官方的）新聞稿
policy 政策

✉ sample 129

Dear ⌐⌐⌐⌐⌐

I wasn't sure if I mentioned this at the meeting yesterday,
but I would appreciate it if you could keep our talk
confidential. We have other partners who need to be
told about our **agreement** before it's made public.

Thanks for understanding.

- - - - - - -

我不確定我是否在昨天的會議上提過這件事，不過如果您能將我們的談話內容保密，我會很感激。在公開之前，我們還會有其它合作夥伴需要知道我們的協議。感謝您的理解。

mention 提及　make... public 使公開

✉ sample 130

Hi, [_____]

I just wanted to send you a quick note to remind you to keep the contents of yesterday's meeting to yourself for now. We don't really want our competitors to get wind of the deal before we're ready to announce.

Thanks,

- - - - - - - -

rivals 競爭者

challengers 競爭者

opposing businesses 競爭公司

adversaries 對手

enemies 敵對者

我在此想發給您一個簡短通知，請您暫且對於昨天會議的內容保密。在我們準備宣布之前，我們不太希望我們的競爭對手得知這筆交易的消息。謝謝。

to oneself 止於（某人）自己　competitor 競爭者　get wind of 得知～的風聲

辦公室溝通 Communication in the Office

Case 01 提早下班 Leaving Work Early ▲

✉ sample 131

Dear _____

I wanted to let you know that I am leaving work early today. My daughter is very ill and it is imperative that I (should)be at the hospital with her. I will be in touch about missed appointments.

Try It！可以替換的字詞

meetings 會議
agenda items 議程項目
work 工作
items 項目
phone calls 電話，來電

我想通知您，我今天會早點下班。我女兒生病了，我必須留在醫院陪伴她。對於無法赴約一事，我會再進行聯繫。

> leave work 離開工作崗位　early 提早　ill 生病的　imperative 必須的　in touch 聯繫　miss 錯過　appointment（正式的）約定，約會

✉ sample 132

Dear _____

I have not been feeling well all week. Today it has reached its worst. I will be leaving the office during the ❶ lunch hour. If there is ❷ an issue please let me know.

Try It！可以替換的字詞

❶ afternoon 下午
evening hours 晚間
late morning 上午晚些時候
scheduled department meeting 預定的部門會議
three o'clock hour 三點鐘左右

❷ a problem 問題
a major concern 重大問題
a trouble 麻煩事情
a predicament 難以解決的事
a difficulty 困難

我這整個星期以來都不太舒服。今天已到達最糟的狀況了。我會在中午休息時間離開辦公室。若有什麼問題請告訴我。

> not feel well 感覺不舒服　reach 到達　worst 最糟的狀況　leave 離開～　during 在～的期間　lunch hour 中午休息時間　issue 問題

✉ sample 133

Dear [_____]

As I told you last week, I have **family** commitments this afternoon. I will not be attending any meetings after two o'clock. I will return in the morning.

- - - - - - - -

Try It ! 可以替換的字詞
personal 個人的
religious 宗教（上）的
academic 學術相關的
private 私人的
medical 醫療（上）的

誠如我上週告訴過您，我今天下午家裡有事。兩點過後我不會出席參加任何會議。我明天早上會回來。

commitment 要事　attend 出席　return 返回

✉ sample 134

Dear [_____]

I am very sick today. Because of that, I am leaving the building immediately. I do not want to infect others with this **cold**. I apologize for any inconveniences.

- - - - - - - -

Try It ! 可以替換的字詞
bug （由病原引起的）小毛病
flu 流感
influenza 感冒
illness 生病
chicken pox 水痘

我今天身體不太舒服。因此，我得馬上離開公司。我不想把感冒傳染給其它同事。帶來任何不便的話，我感到抱歉。

immediately 立刻地　infect 傳染　apologize for... 為～道歉　inconvenience 不便

✉ sample 135

Dear _____

My wife is unable to pick up our children from child care, so I must leave the office a few hours early. Will I be missing anything important? I plan to catch up on missed work this evening.

Try It! 可以替換的字詞

urgent 緊急的

required 需要處理的

of major concern 重大的，要緊的

significant 重要的

critical 重要的

- - - - - - - -

我太太無法去托兒所接小孩，所以我必須提前幾個小時離開辦公室。我會遺漏掉任何重要的事情嗎？我預計今晚會趕緊處理錯過的工作。

unable to... 無法～　pick up（開車去）接（某人）　child care 托兒所，幼兒園　important 重要的
catch up on 補做，迎頭趕上

通知同事表定的會議 Notifying Coworkers of the Scheduled Meeting ▲

✉ sample 136

Dear [　　　　　]

I wanted to let you know about next week's meetings. We will be meeting ❶every afternoon for about three hours. I hope you are able to attend. Your input is ❷extremely valuable.

- - - - - - - -

Try It！可以替換的字詞

❶ each 每一個
almost every 幾乎每一個
every other 每隔一～（天、星期等）
Tuesday 星期二
late 晚些的

❷ highly 相當，高度地
tremendously 非常地
awfully 非常
really 很，非常
particularly 尤其地

我想通知您下週的會議。我們每天下午都要開大約三小時的會。我希望您能夠出席。您給予的意見非常重要。

be able to 能夠～　attend 出席　input（努力等的）投入，提供　extremely 非常地　valuable 有價值的

✉ sample 137

Dear [　　　　　]

It should come as no surprise that we have a meeting next week. The company bosses have determined that we really need to hurry up this production of new cables. I look forward to seeing you there.

- - - - - - - -

Try It！可以替換的字詞

anticipate seeing 期待見到
expect to see 期待見到
will wait to see 期待見到
look ahead to seeing 期待見到
am sure to see 一定會見到

我們下週要開個會，這也不是什麼令人驚訝的事。公司老闆們已決議，我們真的必須加快新電纜生產的腳步。我期待在會議上見到您。

come as no surprise 不是什麼令人驚訝的事　boss 老闆　determine 決定　hurry up... 加快～
production 生產

✉ sample 138

Dear [_____]

As you know, the company has a new meeting ❶schedule. Rather than meeting daily, we plan to meet only once a week for an entire day. This should allow for better ❷brainstorming.

- - - - - - - -

Try It！可以替換的字詞

❶ timeline 時間表
arranged 安排好的
arrangement 安排
list 清單
plan 計畫

❷ development 發展
teamwork 團隊運作
problem solving 問題的解決
suggestions 建議
innovations 創新

如您所知，公司有個新的會議行程。我們預計從每天開會改為一個星期開一次整天的會議。如此對於大家集思廣益，應可獲得更好的成效。

schedule 時間表，計畫表 rather than 而不是～ entire 全部的 allow for 可允許～
brainstorming（每個人提出一些想法，然後決定什麼是最好的）腦力激盪

✉ sample 139

Dear [_____]

Once again, we will be having a company-wide meeting at four o'clock. Does this fit into your schedule? My superiors tell me we all are required to be there.

- - - - - - - -

Try It！可以替換的字詞

work with 對～行得通
mesh with 充分融入～
agree with 符合，與～一致
match 配和～
go with 與～一致

再一次提醒，我們將在四點鐘召開全公司會議。您的時間可以配合嗎？我的主管告訴我，我們所有人都必須參加會議。

fit into 排得進～ superior 上級，主管 be required to 被要求去～

✉ sample 140

Dear ⌐ ̄ ̄ ̄ ̄ ̄¬

Our president wants everyone to attend his semi-annual state-of-the-company address. He plans to tell us where our profits are and what we can do to improve our revenue. I can't wait to see you there.

- - - - - - - -

我們總裁希望每個人都能參加他半年一次的公司營運狀況講座。他計劃將告訴我們，我們應從何獲得利潤，以及我們該如何增加營收。我非常希望見到您出席。

president 總裁　semi-annual 半年一次的　address 演說，講座　profit 利潤　improve 改善
revenue 營收　can't wait to... 等不及想去做某事

Try It！可以替換的字詞

speech 演講
lecture 演說
oration （官方的）演講
discourse 談話
talk 談話

✉ sample 141

Dear ⟨＿＿＿＿＿⟩

The meeting this afternoon went very ❶smoothly. It only lasted an hour and we completely finished the outline for the new product ❷roll-out. I'll get you copies of the PowerPoint later.

- - - - - - -

Try It！可以替換的字詞

❶well 很好地
effortlessly 毫不費勁地
efficiently 有效率地
nicely 很好地
easily 容易地

❷advertising 廣告
marketing strategy 行銷策略
development 發展
packaging 包裝
shipping options 送貨方式

今天下午的會議相當順利。只開了一個小時，我們就徹底完成新產品推出的大綱計畫。我稍後會將 PowerPoint 的副本寄給您。

smoothly 流暢地　last 持續　completely 完全地　finish 完成　outline 大綱，摘要
roll-out（新產品的）推出　copy 複製

✉ sample 142

Dear ⟨＿＿＿＿＿⟩

Can you tell me about the meeting we had today? I had to miss it because of illness. But I'd really like a summary of everything that we went over.

- - - - - - -

Try It！可以替換的字詞

the major points 重點
the strategies 策略
the details 詳細資訊
the whole 全部內容
all 全部的東西

您能夠告訴我，我們今天的會議內容嗎？我因為生病而無法出席。但我真的想要看一下會後的摘要內容。

illness 疾病　summary 摘要　go over... 查看～

✉ sample 143

Dear [_____]

The meeting today was very long and not too ❶ productive. We had ❷an outside agency discuss hiring procedures, but it was nothing we didn't know already. I can tell you more about it over lunch.

- - - - - - - -

Try It！可以替換的字詞

❶ creative 有創造力的
inspiring 鼓舞人心的
fruitful 成果豐碩的
dynamic 有動力的
helpful 有幫助的

❷ an external 一個外部的
a hired 一個雇用的
a partnering 一個合夥的
a human resources 一個人力資源的
a management 一個管理的

今天的會議相當冗長，而且成效並不佳。我們請了一個外部機構來討論聘雇程序，不過盡講些我們都已經知道的事情。我可以在午休時間告訴您更多事情。

productive 富有成效的　agency 代辦處，機構　hiring procedures 聘顧程序

✉ sample 144

Dear [_____]

Are you aware that you missed today's meeting? We discussed globalization of the new cell phone line. My department chair will give you the specifics.

- - - - - - - -

Try It！可以替換的字詞

promotion 促銷
international tracking 國際追蹤
endorsement
（名人上電視的）代言推薦
validation 驗證
testing 測試

您知道您錯過今天的會議了嗎？我們討論過如何讓這支新手機全球化。我的部門主管會提供您細節資訊。

aware 知道的　discuss 討論　globalization 全球化　chair 主席　specifics 具體細節

✉ sample 145

Dear [_____]

This morning's meeting went quickly. Bill was able to summarize his research in just a few minutes. It looks like we'll be coming in under budget. That's great news!

- - - - - - - -

今天早上的會議進行得很快。比爾能夠在短短幾分鐘內概述他的研究成果。看來我們參與的計畫不會超出預算範圍。這真是個好消息！

Try It！可以替換的字詞

right at 正好相當於～

way below 遠低於～

with a positive 以足夠的～

on 根據～

with a minimal 以最低的～

quickly 快速地　summarize 總結　research（學術的）研究　a few 一些　look like... 看起來像～
come in 參與（計畫等）　budget 預算

交代員工任務 **Directing Employees** ▲

✉ sample 146

Dear [_____]

As your boss, it is my responsibility to provide you with daily schedules. Today I need you to finish all your reports from last week. If there is a problem, please let me know. I look forward to seeing them.

- - - - - - - -

身為你的老闆，我有責任提供你每日的行程表。今天我需要你完成上週所有的報告。有問題的話，請讓我知道。我期待看到報告。

responsibility 責任，義務　provide A with B 提供 B 給 A

Try It！可以替換的字詞

task lists 工作清單
agendas 議程
to-do lists 待處理之工作清單
productivity goals 生產力目標
objectives 目標

✉ sample 147

Dear [_____]

Please confirm all your ❶appointments today with me. When you're done with each of them, I want you to summarize them for me. It's important that I stay ❷on top of everything that is going on.

- - - - - - - -

請跟我確認你今天所有的約定事項。當你完成任何一件事時，我希望你讓我知道大略的狀況。重要的是，我必須掌握所有目前事情的狀況。

confirm 確認　appointment（會面的）約定　on top of... 掌握，了解～

Try It！可以替換的字詞

❶phone calls 電話
meetings 會議
agenda items 議程項目
engagements 約定事項
prior arrangements 預定事項

❷focused on 集中管理～
informed of 對～知情
in charge of 掌管著～
up-to-date on 掌握～的最新消息
in the loop with 得知～的最新進度

✉ sample 148

Dear [_____]

With all the ❶changes going on, I need you to continue with ❷quality control today. Our new product line is not very consistent. Any suggestions you have are welcome.

- - - - - - -

Try It！可以替換的字詞

❶ updates 更新事項
transformations 變更的事情
modifications 修正的事項
conversions 轉變
variations 變化

❷ shipping verifications 貨運驗證
personnel oversight 人事監督
product checking 產品檢查
quality assurance 品質保證
safety checks 安全檢查

因為出現這麼多變故，我希望你今天繼續做好品質管控。我們新的產品系列不是很穩定。有任何建議歡迎提出。

continue 繼續　quality control 品質管控　consistent 一致的，恆常的　suggestion 建議

✉ sample 149

Dear [_____]

Please finish all of your telephone interviews today. After that, I'd like your entire department to work on the program reports. We need them done by next week.

- - - - - - -

Try It！可以替換的字詞

billing statements 對帳單
inventory lists 庫存清單
supply chain records 供應鏈記錄
file cabinets 文件櫃
payroll breakdown 薪資明細

請完成今天的所有電訪。然後，我希望你們整個部門一起處理專案報告。我們需要它們在下週之前完成。

entire 全部的　department 部門　work on... 進行，處理～　need A done by... 需要 A 在～之前完成

✉ sample 150

Dear [_____]

Are you aware of your to-do list today? If not, please finish preparing for tomorrow's meeting. I need all PowerPoints looking fantastic. Also, please make copies of the agenda for all those meetings.

Try It！可以替換的字詞

incredible 很棒的

unbelievable 精彩的

awesome 令人驚嘆的

great 極好的

top-of-the-line 上等的

- - - - - - - -

你知道你今天的待辦事項嗎？如果不知道的話，請為明天的會議做好準備。我需要所有的 Power-Points 內容看起來是完美的。另外，請影印所有會議的議程。

be aware of... 知道，了解～　to-do list 待辦事項　fantastic 極好的　make a copy of... 將～影印一份
agenda 議程

產品介紹 & 行銷 Product Introduction & Marketing

✉ sample 151

Dear ⌐⎯⎯⎯⎯⌐

I'm writing to tell you about our latest product, the RX-9. Our product line has always been on the **cutting edge** of the industry, and this newest addition to our offerings is no exception. I've attached a few images and a detailed description of the RX-9. I think you'll like what you see. Let me know if you have any questions.

Thank you for your time.

Try It！可以替換的字詞

progressive side 不斷在進步
revolutionary side 不斷在革新
forward-looking edge 往前進的優勢
advanced side 先進的一方
radical edge 基本的優勢

- - - - - - -

我寫這封信的目的是讓您了解我們的最新產品 RX-9。我們的產品系列在這個產業始終具有絕對的優勢，而這個最新上市的產品也不例外。我附上 RX-9 的圖片和詳細說明。我想您會喜歡您所看到的內容。請讓我知道您是否有任何疑問。感謝您花時間看完這封信。

latest 最新的　on the cutting edge 具有絕對的優勢　addition 增加物　offering 提供的產品
exception 例外

✉ sample 152

Dear ⌐⎯⎯⎯⎯⌐

This email is to let you know about our new RX line of networking hardware. We've worked for the past two years to source the best parts and develop the **best designs**, and the result is the strongest family of networking gear available today. Attached are some images as well as performance specifications. Let me know if you'd like to discuss these top-of-the-line products further.

Thank you.

Try It！可以替換的字詞

lowest cost items 最低成本的品項
most environmentally friendly materials 最環保的材料
cheapest options 最便宜的選擇
longest-lasting parts 最耐久的零件
best options 最好的選擇

- - - - - - -

這封電子郵件旨在通知您有關新的 RX 系列的網路硬體設備。在過去兩年中，我們致力於從特定來源取得最好的零件，並開發最佳設計產品，而成果就是當今最強大的網絡設備家族。附件是一些圖片和性能規格。請讓我知道您是否有意願進一步討論這些最優質的產品。謝謝。

source（從特定來源）取得（商品、零件等）　family 家族系列　gear 設備，齒輪
specification 產品規格　top-of-the-line 頂級的

✉ sample 153

Dear (...........)

I'd like to tell you a little about our newest product, the Smith Tech Portable Photocopier. This innovative new product combines the power and functionality of a copier with the portability necessary with today's traveling businessperson. I've attached a few images and a detailed description of the functions. Let me know if you have any questions.

I look forward to hearing from you.

- - - - - - - -

我想告訴您關於我們最新產品「Smith Tech 攜帶式影印機」的些許資訊。這部創新的產品將影印機的電源與功能性，與其可攜帶性結合在一起，這是當今出差中的商務人士必備的。我附上了一些圖片和功能的詳細說明。請讓我知道您是否有任何疑問。期待您的佳音。

combine A with B 將 A 和 B 結合 functionality 功能性 portability 可攜帶性

✉ sample 154

Dear (...........)

I'm writing to give you a brief description of our newest product, the X-23 flat screen monitor. The X-23 offers the highest resolution for its price range. It also boasts an extraordinarily rugged construction. We think this product is a real game changer and we're looking for partners for overseas distribution. Please take a moment to look over the attached product description and let me know if you'd be interested.

Thank you for your time.

- - - - - - - -

我寫這封信的目的是要向您簡單介紹一下我們的新產品 — X-23 平面顯示器。 X-23 在同一個價格區間的產品中解析度算是最高的。它的另一特色就是在結構上相當堅固耐用。我們認為這項產品會成為同業中的革新產品，且我們正在尋找海外經銷夥伴。請花點時間過目一下隨附的產品說明，並請讓我知道您是否有興趣。感謝您花時間看完這封信。

for one's price range 在某個價格區間 extraordinarily 格外地，非常地 rugged 堅固耐用的
construction 結構

✉ sample 155

Dear _____

I'm happy to give you an advanced look at our new product, the Smith Tech G32. This item will be reaching stores here in Taiwan by the end of the year. The attached images will make it clear that we've put a lot of effort into an ❶innovative design, and the ❷performance numbers below show how efficiently the G32 runs. Let me know if you'd like to discuss working with us on distributing the G32 in your country.

Thank you.

- - - - - - - -

Try It！可以替換的字詞

❶ ground-breaking 開創性的

pioneering 首創的

inventive 有創造力的

original 原創的

new 新的

❷ product reviews 產品評鑑

product performance tests
產品性能測試

details of third-party testing
第三方使用測試之詳細資訊

speed charts 速度圖表

quality control outcomes 品管成效

我很高興帶給您我們新產品 Smith Tech G32 的高級版樣式。這個產品將在今年年底在台灣這邊上市。附件所示的圖片可讓您清楚看見我們在創新設計上下了很大的功夫，且以下性能數字顯示了 G32 的運行效率。讓我知道您是否有意願討論與我們一起在您的所在國家經銷 G32。謝謝。

advanced（技術上）先進的　make it clear that... 使～清楚地被看見　efficiently 有效率地

行銷產品 Marketing the Product ▲

✉ sample 156

Hi, ⬚

I'd like to discuss our marketing plan for the new product. I have a plan I think will reach a wide ❶customer base in a short amount of time. I'd like to hear some of your ❷ideas as well.

Talk to you soon,

- - - - - - - -

Try It！可以替換的字詞

❶ number of people 人數
audience 觀眾
target group 目標群體
viewership 收視率
number of potential buyers
潛在買家數量

❷ brainstorming outcomes
集思廣益的結果
thoughts 想法
opinions 意見
feelings 感覺
views 看法

我想討論一下我們對於這新產品的行銷計畫。我有一個計畫 ─ 我認為可以在很短的時間內觸及廣泛的顧客群。我也想聽聽您的一些想法。期待再聊。

wide 廣大的，廣泛的　customer base 客戶群　amount 量

✉ sample 157

Dear ⬚

We're ready to start planning our marketing campaign for the RX-9. I think we should focus on getting reviews placed in print and Internet publications. I'd also like to discuss holding some events and demonstrations. Let me know what you think.

Thanks,

- - - - - - -

Try It！可以替換的字詞

surveys 意見調查
details 詳細訊息
assessments 評價，估價
appraisals 評價
evaluations 評價，評估

我們已準備好開始規劃我們 RX-9 產品的行銷活動。我認為我們應該以平面媒體與網路刊物上的評論為主。我還想討論舉辦一些活動和展示會的可能性。讓我知道您的想法。謝謝。

focus on 專注於～　review 評論，回顧　publication 發行，出版物　demonstration 展示，演示

✉ sample 158

Try It！可以替換的字詞

I'd like to work on the marketing plan. There are a number of avenues we could pursue, but I think building word of mouth among early adopters is key. To that end, I'd like to plan a few presentations at local computer stores. What do you think?

Thanks,

- - - - - - - -

customers 顧客
purchasers 買家
clients 客戶
buyers 買主
patrons 贊助人

我想擬定行銷計畫。我們有一些可採取的手段，但我認為在初期採用者中建立口碑是關鍵。基於此目的，我想在當地的電腦商店做些產品展示會。您覺得如何呢？謝謝。

> work on 進行，處理～　avenue 手段，途徑　early adopter 初期採用者（產品剛上市時的首批購買者）　key 關鍵的　to that end 為了這個目標　local 當地的

✉ sample 159

Try It！可以替換的字詞

The marketing of the G32 has gone well so far. I think we are ready for the next phase. Now that the name is out there, we should start focusing on getting the message out about the low price. Any ideas on how to go about that?

Let me know what you think.

- - - - - - - -

stage 階段
chapter 重要時期
segment 時段
point 時間點
period 時期

到目前為止，G32 的行銷進展順利。我想我們已準備好進入下一階段。既然這個品名已經家喻戶曉，我們應該開始將重心放在低價的訊息。關於如何進行，您有任何想法嗎？請讓我知道您的想法。

> phase 階段　now that... 既然～　get out 公布（消息等）　go about 著手處理～

✉ sample 160

Dear ⬚

How are things going on the marketing end? I saw the ads you placed in *The New Yorker*. Have you had much response from them? I think if they've been successful, we should consider expanding the campaign to other publications. Let me know what you think.

Thanks,

- - - - - - - -

行銷這方面做得如何呢？我看到您在《New Yorker》上刊登的廣告。您獲得眾多回響了嗎？我認為如果有不錯的反應，我們應該考慮將該活動擴展到其他出版物。請讓我知道您的想法。謝謝。

end 部分，方面　response 反應　expand 擴大　publication 出版物

詢問產品廣告相關事項 Inquiring About Product Advertisement ▲

✉ sample 161

Dear _____

I'd like to place an ad in the next issue of *The New Yorker*. I want to get my product in front of an audience that perfectly matches your demographic. Please send me pricing information for all ad sizes.

Thank you.

- - - - - - -

Try It！可以替換的字詞

businesses 公司
an executive 一位公司主管
a business leader 一位企業領袖
a decision-maker 一位決策者
a mind 一個念頭

我想在下一期《New Yorker》上刊登一則廣告。我想讓我的產品讓您認為會來購買的顧客群看到。請寄給我所有廣告規格的價格資訊。謝謝。

place an ad 刊登一則廣告　issue 刊物（如雜誌等）　in front of... 在～前面　audience 觀眾
perfectly 完美地　match 符合　demographic 人口統計　pricing 定價

✉ sample 162

Dear _____

I'm writing to ❶inquire about ad pricing on your ❷radio station. I would like the full range of lengths, schedules, and frequency. I'd also like to see any demographic information you have for your various programs.

Thanks,

- - - - - - -

Try It！可以替換的字詞

❶question 提問
ask 詢問
query 查詢
request information 請求訊息
see if you can tell me
請問您是否能告訴我

❷television station 電視台
webpage 網頁
newspaper 報紙
AM radio channel AM 廣播頻道
satellite radio station 衛星廣播電台

我寫這封信的目的是想詢問你們廣播電台的廣告價格。我想了解關於廣告長度、時間表和播放頻率的完整資訊。我也想知道您各個節目的聽眾人數。謝謝。

radio station 廣播電台　a full range of... 各種各樣的～　length 長度　frequency 頻率
various 多種類的

✉ sample 163

Dear [_____]

I would like to discuss the possibility of advertising in your publication. Could you put together a package with the relevant information regarding price and format? I'd like to be able to place an ad by the end of the month.

I look forward to hearing from you.

- - - - - - - -

我想討論一下在您的出版品中刊登廣告的可能性。您能否將有關價格和格式的相關資訊彙總起來？我想在本月底前刊登廣告。期待您的佳音。

advertise 打廣告　publication 出版物　package（有關聯的）一組事物　relevant 相關的
regarding 關於～　format 格式

Try It！可以替換的字詞

a file 一個檔案

a report 一份報告

a profile 一份檔案介紹

a summary 一份摘要

details 詳細訊息

✉ sample 164

Dear [_____]

I'm trying to plan my advertising budget for the next ❶quarter and I need updated information from all of my ❷sources. Could I get the full range of your ad rates? This would really help me plan my ad buying.

Thank you.

- - - - - - - -

我正在計畫下一季度的廣告預算，且我需要來自各方的最新資訊。您能提供我廣告費率的完整資訊嗎？這對我購買廣告確實會有幫助。感謝您。

budget 預算　quarter 一季　update 更新　source 資訊、資料來源　ad rate 廣告費率

Try It！可以替換的字詞

❶month 月

year 年

half year 半年

season 季

few months 幾個月

❷informants 情報提供者

suppliers 供貨商

marketers 經銷商

connections 固定客群

followers 追隨者

✉ sample 165

Dear ⸝⸝⸝⸝⸝⸝⸝

I'm writing to get some information from you about placing some ads. I'm looking for ads in a variety of media and I know your company specializes in organizing such campaigns. Perhaps we can meet next week so that you can give me a rundown on the possibilities.

Thanks,

- - - - - - - -

我寫這封信的目的是想請您提供一些廣告刊登的資訊。我正在找尋各種媒體的廣告方案，且我知道貴公司專門經營此類業務。也許我們可以約下週見面，以便您可以針對各種可能性跟我作個介紹。謝謝。

Try It！可以替換的字詞

operations 業務
things 事物
methods 方法
ventures 事業
undertakings 承攬之業務

a variety of... 各種各樣的～ media 媒體 specialize in... 專攻，擅長於～
organize 安排，使～有條理 campaign 活動 rundown 概述，簡要報告

Case 04　保證產品的品質 Guaranteeing Product Quality ▲

✉ sample 166

Try It！可以替換的字詞

better 更好的
greater 更好的
higher quality 更高品質的
more advanced 更先進的
high-class 優等的

I just wanted to write and tell you that I can personally vouch for the quality of this product. It really is remarkable. I am sure that you won't find a **superior** product on the market today. If you decide to go with us, you're getting the top of the line.

Talk to you soon,

- - - - - - - -

我寫這封信的目的是想告訴您，我個人可以向您保證這項產品的品質。它確實是令人稱羨的。我相信您在目前的市場上，找不到比這個產品更好的了。如果您決定選擇我們，您就會獲得這個系列中最佳的產品。期待再聊。

vouch for 為～擔保　remarkable 出眾的，非凡的　be sure 很有信心的　superior 高級的
go with... 贊同，選擇～

✉ sample 167

Try It！可以替換的字詞

characteristics 特點
value 價值
worth 價值
excellence 卓越
details 詳細資訊

As you're making your final decisions about which supplier to go with, I'd like you to keep in mind that we stand behind the **quality** of our products one hundred percent. I can guarantee that you won't have any of the reliability issues that often plague other companies' products.

Let me know if you have any questions.

- - - - - - - -

當您最終決定選擇哪一家供應商時，我希望您牢記，我們百分百保證我們產品的品質。我可以保證，您不會遇到其它公司產品經常遭遇的任何信賴度問題。請讓我知道您是否有任何疑問。

keep in mind... 牢記～　stand behind... 支持，保證～　reliability issues 信賴度問題　plague 煩困擾

✉ sample 168

Regarding your questions about the quality of the Smith Tech 75 monitor, I can tell you that there isn't another model on the market that has a better track record. If you look at the number or returns we've received, you'll see that our customers are satisfied. If you need any other assurances, how about this: I'm using a ST-75 right now!

Thanks,

- - - - - - - -

關於您對於 Smith Tech 75 顯示器品質的詢問，我可以告訴您，市場上沒有其它比這款產品表現更好的型號。如果您有看見我們獲得的營收數字，您會發現我們的客戶是感到滿意的。如果你需要其他見證，那這道訊息如何？我目前正在使用 ST-75 型號！謝謝。

> regarding... 關於～ track record 追蹤紀錄 return 收入 satisfied 感到滿意的 assurance 保證

✉ sample 169

Dear ⬚

Global Electronics Tech stands behind each and every item we produce. I can guarantee that you will not have any complaints about the quality of the products you choose to purchase from us. Look around online and you'll find countless five-star reviews of our appliances. You can buy with confidence.

Let me know if you have any questions.

- - - - - - -

Global Electronics Tech 公司為我們製造的所有產品作後盾。我可以保證，您不會對於選擇從我們這裡購買的產品品質有所抱怨。您可以上網看看，您會發現有不計其數的、對於我們產品的五星評論。請放心購買。請讓我知道您是否有任何疑問。

> complaint 抱怨 countless 不計其數的 five-star 五星級的 appliance 設備

✉ sample 170

Dear _____

Every MC Soft product is manufactured to our **exacting** specifications, and then thoroughly tested before bearing the MC Soft logo. We take quality assurance very seriously, so you can rest assured that our products are reliable and durable.

Let me know if you would like more information.

MC Soft 的每一項產品都依照我們嚴格要求的規範製造，並且進行全面測試，然後才會貼上 MC Soft 的標識。我們的品保相當嚴謹，因此您可以放心，我們的產品可靠耐用。請讓我知道您是否有需要更多資訊。

manufacture 製造　exacting 嚴格要求的　thoroughly 徹底地　bear 印有，標上
quality assurance 品質保證　seriously 認真地　reliable 可靠的　durable 耐用的

✉ sample 171

Attached is a document detailing the RX-9. Regarding the warranty, I'd like to add a few things. The warranty covers all repairs for two years. ❶Damages caused by the owner and factory defects are both covered ❷equally. I don't think you can get a better deal than that. Let me know if you have any questions.

Thanks,

- - - - - - - -

Try It！可以替換的字詞

❶ Harm 損壞
Scratches 刮傷
Destruction 毀壞
Impairments 損壞
Dings and dents 凹痕部分

❷ by us 由我們
uniformly 一致地
evenly 平均地
similarly 同樣地
in the same way 以相同的方式

附件是詳述 RX-9 的一份文件。關於產品保證的部分，我想補充幾點說明。這項保固涵蓋兩年期間中的所有維修項目。持有者造成的損壞及出廠瑕疵均在此保固範圍內。我認為您不可能獲得比這更好的價位了。請讓我知道您是否有任何疑問。謝謝。

> detail 詳細說明　warranty 保固　cover 包含，適用於～　repair 修理　damage 損壞　owner 持有人
> factory 工廠　defec 瑕疵　equally 同等地

✉ sample 172

I just wanted to let you know that the printer's extended warranty covers two years or 500,000 printouts. That means you can breathe easily and not have to worry about repair costs. We're confident that you won't have any problems.

Thanks,

- - - - - - - -

Try It！可以替換的字詞

relax 放輕鬆
calm down 安心，保持鎮定
loosen up 放鬆一下
reduce your stress 減輕您的壓力
not worry 不擔心

我在此想告知您，這部影印機的延長保固期為兩年，或是五十萬張的保證印量。這意味著，您可以鬆一口氣，無需擔心維修費用。我們有信心您不會有任何問題。謝謝。

> extended 延長的　printout（電腦等的）印出資料　breathe 呼吸　easily 輕易地　cost 費用
> confident 有信心的

✉ **sample 173**

In regard to your questions about the warranty, the G23 does indeed carry a lifetime warranty. If you have any problems (not including those caused by the user) we offer full-service repairs. I hope this sets aside any fears you have about buying the G23.

Thanks,

- - - - - - - -

關於您對於保固的提問，G23 確實擁有終生保固。如果您有任何問題（不包括使用者造成的損壞），我們提供全方位的維修服務。我希望這樣的說明可以解除您對於購買 G23 的憂慮。謝謝。

in regard to 關於～　indeed 的確　lifetime 終生的　set aside 將～擱置一邊，不理會～　fear 擔憂

Try It！可以替換的字詞

the full gamut of 全方位的
an array of 一系列的
all possible types of 所有可能類型的
any imaginable 任何想像得到的
all 一切的

✉ **sample 174**

The product warranty covers any problems you may have for five years. Usually, a product of this kind carries a three-year warranty, so I hope you can see the level of confidence we have in the product.

Thanks,

- - - - - - - -

本產品保固涵蓋您五年內可能遇到的任何問題。通常來說，這類產品的保固期為三年，所以我希望您能了解我們於對本產品是充滿自信的。謝謝。

carry（保固等）具有～效益　confidence 信心　level 水平

Try It！可以替換的字詞

shields you from 保護您免於承受～
deals with 處理～
takes care of 處理～
insures 保證～
will fix 將解決～
will pay for 將為～支付

✉ sample 175

┌─────────────────┐
└─ ─ ─ ─ ─ ─ ─ ─ ─┘

I just wanted to remind you that the warranty for the Smith Tech 3023 is quite robust. We offer full repairs on any damage incurred in the first two years, and after that we offer a deeply discounted service. Let me know if you have any questions.

Thanks,

- - - - - - - -

heavily 充分地
greatly 大大地
seriously 極度地
profoundly 很大程度地
much 很大地

我只是想提醒您，Smith Tech 3023 的保固非常完善。對於頭兩年內發生的任何損壞，我們提供全面的維修。而之後，我們會提供相當優惠的折扣服務。請讓我知道您是否有任何疑問。謝謝。

remind 提醒　robust 堅固耐用的　incurred 招致的　deeply 深度地　discounted 折扣的

產品發表 & 簡報 Presentation

✉ sample 176

Dear _____

When we spoke at the conference last week about our 2019 product line, you indicated that you might be interested. Could we pick a date for us to come out and do a quick presentation to ❶preview the ❷line? Let me know when works for you.

Thanks,

- - - - - - - -

Try It！可以替換的字詞

❶ showcase 展示
sketch 概要說明
give you an impression of 讓您有～的印象
provide details about
提供～的細節
answer any questions you may have
about 回答您可能遇到的任何問題

❷ production 生產過程
pieces 產品
inventory 存貨
range of goods 產品系列
equipment 設備

上週在會議中我們談到 2019 年的產品系列時，您表示可能感興趣。我們可以挑一個日期，一起出來做一個簡報，並預覽一下產品系列嗎？讓我知道您什麼時間方便。謝謝。

conference（大型的）會議　product line 產品系列　pick 挑選　quick 短時間的　preview 預覽

✉ sample 177

Dear _____

We'd like to come and present our services to you. How does your calendar look next month? If you could find an afternoon one day, we could do a presentation for you and your staff.

Thank you for your attention.

- - - - - - - -

Try It！可以替換的字詞

quick overview 簡短介紹
general summary 總結
catalog synopsis 目錄摘要
personal outline 個人概述
brief PowerPoint presentation
簡短的 PowerPoint 介紹

我們想過來向您介紹我們的服務項目。下個月您可以安排個時間嗎？如果您可以找一天下午，我可以為您和您的員工們做個介紹。感謝您的關注。

present 展示　find 找出　do a presentation 做一個簡短介紹　staff 員工

✉ sample 178

Dear [...........]

I'm writing to see about a date for our presentation. When we spoke last, you indicated that you'd be interested in learning more about our product line. What day would be good for us to come and show you a little bit about what we do?

I hope to hear from you.

- - - - - - - -

我寫這封信的目的是要確認我們發表會的日期。我們上次在商討時，您提到會想了解更多我們產品系列的訊息。哪一天我們可以過去一趟，向您簡單說明我們所做的產品呢？期待您的佳音。

Try It！可以替換的字詞

product family 產品系列

line of home painting kits 家庭繪畫工具包系列

complete array of camping needs 完整的露營必需品系列

office computing solutions 辦公室電腦運算解決方案

catalog of goods 產品目錄

> indicate 指出（評論等）　learn 了解　a little bit 一點兒的

✉ sample 179

Dear [...........]

You mentioned the other day that you were interested in seeing our presentation. What date would be good for you? We have quite a bit of flexibility, so why don't you check your calendar and let us know what date works for you.

Thank you,

- - - - - - - -

您前幾天提到，您有興趣看一下我們的產品介紹。您哪一天方便呢？我們的時間相當彈性，所以何不看一下您的行事曆，並讓我們知道您哪個日期方面。謝謝。

Try It！可以替換的字詞

open time 有空的時間

free space in our calendar 我們行事曆中可利用的時間

options for scheduling 可安排的選項

flux with our presentation times 我們做展示的彈性時間

options 選項

> mention　提及　quite a bit of 相當多的～　flexibility 靈活性　why don't you... ~? 你為什麼不～？

✉ sample **180**

Dear [_____]

I'm writing to schedule **❶**a date for us to come and give you a presentation of our product. We'd like to ask for a couple of hours of your time to take you through the details and show you what we have **❷**to offer. You won't be disappointed. Let me know what your calendar looks like.

I look forward to hearing from you.

- - - - - - - -

Try It！可以替換的字詞

❶a moment 某個時候

an opportunity 一個機會

a small window of time 一小段時間

a chance 一個機會

a place, date, and time
一個地點、日期、時間

❷that may spark your interest
可能引起你興趣的

that could be of great benefit to you
可能對您而言是有很大利益的

that is right up your alley
正和您胃口的

that could change your business forever
可能永遠改變貴公司的

that fits your needs 符合您需求的

我寫這封信的目的是想為彼此敲定一個日期，然後做個產品介紹。我們想請您花幾個小時的時間，讓我們帶您了解詳細的資訊，並向您展示我們提供的產品。你不會感到失望的。請讓我知道您方便的時間。期待您的佳音。

schedule 將～排入行程表　date 日期　a couple of... 一些～　be disappointed 感到失望的

通知發表的時間 Giving a Notice About the Presentation ▲

✉ sample 181

Dear 〔⋯⋯〕

I just wanted to let you know that we'll be giving a presentation of our new product line on the 25th of September. I hope you can be there. We have some really exciting new items to present. Please RSVP by the 15th so we know to expect you.

Thanks,

- - - - - - - -

Try It! 可以替換的字詞

thrilling 令人驚奇的
stimulating 激發興趣的
electrifying 令人振奮的
stirring 令人激昂的
exhilarating 令人嘆為觀止的

在此我想通知您，我們將在 9 月 25 日發表我們新的產品系列。我希望您能前來。我們有一些相當令人振奮的新產品要發表。請在 15 日之前回覆告知，以便我們能夠恭候您的駕到！謝謝。

exciting 令人興奮的　RSVP 敬請回覆

✉ sample 182

Dear 〔⋯⋯〕

It was good seeing you at the ❶conference last week. I just wanted to tell you about a presentation we'll be giving at the end of the month. It's an overview of some ❷innovative new services we'll be offering. I've attached an invitation. I hope you can make it!

Thanks,

- - - - - - - -

Try It! 可以替換的字詞

❶ event 盛事
symposium 學術論壇
colloquium 學術討論會
company-wide picnic 全公司野餐活動
working lunch 工作午餐

❷ groundbreaking 開創性的
original 原創性的
stunning 驚人的
dazzling 耀眼的
striking 引人注目的

很高興在上週的會議中見到您。在此我想告知您，我們將在本月底進行一場發表會。在會上我們將大略介紹一些我們將提供的創新服務項目。我已附上一份邀請函。希望您能參加！謝謝。

conference（大型）會議　give a presentation 發表一場展示活動　overview 概述　innovative 創新的
invitation 邀請函　make it 出席

✉ sample 183

Dear ⬚⬚⬚⬚⬚⬚

We are excited to announce that we'll be giving a presentation next week at the Sheraton Inn in New York. We'll be demonstrating a number of new products. Afterwards there will be a chance to meet and discuss partnership opportunities.

I hope to see you there.

- - - - - - - -

我們很高興宣布，我們將於下週在紐約喜來登酒店舉行一場產品說明會。我們將展示一些新產品。之後，我們會有機會見面，並討論合作的機會。希望能在現場見到您。

demonstrate 說明，示範 a number of 一些 afterwards 後來，隨後 partnership 合夥關係
opportunity 機會

Try It！可以替換的字詞

new 新的
budding 開始發展的
potential 潛在的
latent 潛在的
impending 即將到來的

✉ sample 184

Dear ⬚⬚⬚⬚⬚⬚

I hope everything is going well with you. Next week we're giving a presentation in which we will outline some exciting new projects we're working on. It'll be a great chance to learn about some new business opportunities. Let me know if you can make it.

Thanks,

- - - - - - - -

展信愉快。下週我們將進行一場產品展示，期間我們將概略介紹一些我們正在進行的、令人興奮的新專案。這會是個了解一些新商機的絕佳機會。請讓我知道您是否能夠到場。謝謝。

outline 簡要說明或介紹 work on... 著手進行～

Try It！可以替換的字詞

delineate 詳細說明
sketch out 簡要描述
run through 稍微帶過
draft 粗略描述
summarize 概括說明

✉ sample 185

Dear _____

We've been working on a new service that we're really excited about. We'll be unveiling it at a presentation on the 26th. I hope you can come out and hear a little about what we've been doing. Drop me an email if you can make it.

Thanks,

- - - - - - - -

Try It！可以替換的字詞

promoting 宣傳

first previewing 首次發表

introducing 介紹

publicizing 宣傳

marketing it for the first time
首次宣傳

我們一直在進行一項新的服務，我們對此感到相當興奮。我們將於 26 日在一場展示會中揭示這項服務。希望您能前來聽聽我們一直在做的事情。如果您能參加，請發一封電子郵件給我。謝謝。

unveil 揭露　drop 寫、寄（信等）　email 電子郵件

✉ sample 186

Dear [＿＿＿＿＿]

I have you down to attend our presentation, originally scheduled for the 25th. Unfortunately, one of our presenters had a minor ❶medical emergency, and so won't be able to do the presentation until the 30th. Let me know if you can make it. I'm sorry if this causes you ❷too much inconvenience.

Thank you for your understanding.

- - - - - - - -

Try It！可以替換的字詞

❶home 家庭的
family 家庭的
children 孩子
legal 法律上的
pet 寵物的

❷too great 太大的
an excess 過度的
overwhelming 難以忍受的
overly much 過度的
unneeded 不必要的

我已邀請您參加我們的展示會，原定於 25 日舉行。不幸的是，我們的一位發表人遇到一個輕微的醫療緊急情況，因此我們要到 30 日才能進行這場展示。如果您能參加，請讓我知道。如果這會給您帶來太多不便，我很抱歉。謝謝您的理解。

down to 列入～（名單） originally 本來 scheduled 預定的 medical 醫療的 emergency 緊急情況 cause 造成

✉ sample 187

[＿＿＿＿＿]

We've had a bit of a scheduling snafu, so I'm afraid we're going to have to change the date of the presentation from the 15th to the 16th. I hope you are still able to make it. Let me know if it's going to be a problem.

Thanks,

- - - - - - - -

Try It！可以替換的字詞

issue 問題
problem 問題
barrier 障礙
snag 意料不到的障礙
setback 挫折

我們遇到一點行程上的問題，所以很抱歉我們不得不將發表日期從 15 日改到 16 日。我希望您仍然能夠參加。請讓我知道這樣的更改是否會有問題。謝謝。

a bit of 一點點～ snafu 混亂情況 be able to... 能夠～

✉ sample 188

Due to unforeseen circumstances, we've been forced to change the date of the presentation from the 25th to the 26th. I hope this doesn't inconvenience you too much. We look forward to seeing you there.

Thank you for your patience.

- - - - - - - -

由於不可預知的情況，我們被迫將發表日期從 25 日改為 26 日。我希望這不會給你帶來太多不便。我們期待在那裡見到您。感謝您的耐心。

due to... 由於～　unforeseen 不可預見的　circumstance 情況　force 迫使　inconvenience 造成～不便

✉ sample 189

Dear

I'm looking forward to seeing you at next month's presentation. Unfortunately, due to a last-minute scheduling problem, we are going to have to change the date. The original date of the 17th was not going to work for several of the attendees. Instead, we'll be moving the presentation to the 18th. I hope it is still possible for you to attend.

Thank you for your understanding.

- - - - - - - -

我期待在下個月的發表會中見到您。不幸的是，由於在最後一刻出現行程上的衝突，我們不得不更改日期。有些與會者無法在原本 17 號這個日期出席。因此，我們打算將發表會改至 18 號。我希望您仍可能出席。謝謝您的理解。

last-minute 最後一刻的　attendee 與會者

✉ sample 190

┌──────────┐
└ ─ ─ ─ ─ ─ ┘

We're really excited about the presentation next week. Unfortunately, we're going to have to move the date back a day. Instead of the 10th, it'll now be held on the 11th. I hope this doesn't ❶prevent you from ❷ participating. If you have any problems, give me a call.

Sorry for the inconvenience.

- - - - - - - -

Try It! 可以替換的字詞

❶ preclude 妨礙
forbid 阻礙
stop 使～無法
withhold 抑制
keep 阻止

❷ attending 參加
partaking 參與
joining us in this venture
參與我們這份事業
involving yourself 把您自己算在內
sharing 一同參與

我們真的相當期待下週的展示會。遺憾的是，我們必須將這日期往後延一天。現在將改到 11 號舉行，而不是 10 號。希望這不會讓您無法出席。如果您有任何問題，請電話聯繫我。造成不便，深表歉意。

unfortunately 遺憾地　move the date back 把日期往後挪　instead of 而不是～　hold舉行
prevent A from... 使 A 無法～　participate 參與

✉ sample 191

Dear ⌐ ⌐

I hope this isn't too much of an issue, but would it be possible to change the presentation time from 1:00 to 2:00? It turns out I've got a meeting scheduled for noon and I'm not sure how long it's going to ❶run. Let me know if that ❷works for you.

Thanks,

- - - - - - -

Try It！可以替換的字詞

❶ last 持續
carry on 繼續
endure 持續
keep going 繼續
take 耗費（時間等）

❷ is acceptable 是可以接受的
is alright for you 對您來說是可行的
is satisfactory 是令人滿意的
is up to par 是合乎標準的
is tolerable 是可以容忍的

我希望這不會造成大問題，可以將發表的時間從 1:00 改為 2:00 嗎？事情是這樣的，我中午有安排一場會議，且我不知道這會議會開多久。請讓我知道這對您是否可行。謝謝。

issue 問題　turn out 結果是～　scheduled for 已排定～　noon 中午　run（活動等）進行

✉ sample 192

Dear ⌐ ⌐

We've had a **slight** schedule change, so the presentation on Monday will be starting at 10:30 instead of 11:00. That also means that we'll be done by 11:30 instead of 12:00. I hope this doesn't cause you any problems.

Thanks,

- - - - - - -

Try It！可以替換的字詞

minor 次要的
small 少量的
little 一點點的
tiny 極小的
trivial 瑣碎的

我們的行程表有點小變化。星期一的發表會將在 10:30 開始，而不是 11:00。也就是說，我們會在 11:30 結束，而不是 12:00。我希望這不會給你帶來任何問題。謝謝。

slight 輕微的　instead of 而不是～　cause 造成～

✉ sample 193

Dear [............]

I have a **❶quick** request. Could we move Monday's presentation from 9:00 to 10:00? I have a conflict in my schedule that I'm trying to **❷resolve**. It would help a lot if I could bump the presentation forward an hour.

Let me know if that works for you.

- - - - - - - -

Try It！可以替換的字詞

❶ rapid 緊急的
speedy 急速的
short 唐突的
brief 簡短的
concise 簡要的

❷ figure out 解決
determine what to do about
對於～決定要做什麼
settle 解決
make go away 讓～消失
work out 解決

我有個緊急的請求。我們可以將周一的發表會時間，從 9:00 改到 10:00 嗎？我的行程表出現一點衝突，而我正試圖解決中。如果我可以將發表會時間往後延一個小時，那將會有很大的幫助。請讓我知道這對您是否可行。

quick 緊急的　request 請求　move 移動　conflict 衝突　resolve 解決　bump 挪開，移走　forward 往前

✉ sample 194

Dear [............]

There has been a small change in the schedule of the presentation. We will be beginning an hour later than planned due to **a conflict** in the availability of the conference room. This means that we will be starting at 4:00 instead of 3:00. Please adjust your schedule accordingly.

Thank you for your understanding.

- - - - - - - -

Try It！可以替換的字詞

a disagreement 意見不同
an argument 爭論
a clash 衝突
a variance 歧見
a dispute 爭議

這場發表會在行程上出現一點小變化。由於會議室使用出現衝突，我們開會時間將比原先預定延後一小時。也就是說，我們開始時間是 4:00，而不是 3:00。因此，請調整您的行程表。感謝您的理解。

due to 由於～　availability 可利用性　adjust 調整　accordingly 因此

✉ sample 195

┌ ─ ─ ─ ─ ─ ─ ┐
└ ─ ─ ─ ─ ─ ─ ┘

We're going to have to move the presentation back an hour. Unfortunately, there was a mix-up with the hotel conference center so the room won't be available until 3:00. I hope that doesn't cause you any problems.

Thanks,

- - - - - - - -

我們必須將這場發表會延後一小時。不巧的是，酒店會議中心出現一點狀況，會議室要一直等到下午三點才能使用。我希望這不會造成你任何問題。謝謝。

move... back 將～往後移動　mix-up 混亂　available 可用的　not... unitl 直到（時間點）～才能～

取消產品發表會 Canceling the Presentation ▲

✉ sample 196

I'm afraid we're going to have to **cancel** next week's presentation. It turns out one of our sales reps is going to be traveling and won't be available. We'll try to reschedule somewhere down the line. I hope this doesn't cause you too much trouble.

Sorry for the inconvenience.

Try It！可以替換的字詞

call off 取消
put off 將～延後
stop 停止
terminate planning of 終止～的計畫
not hold 不舉辦

- - - - - - - -

恐怕我們必須取消下週的發表會了。事實上，我們的一位業務代表要去出差而無法參與。之後我們會重新安排時間。我希望這不會給你帶來太多麻煩。很抱歉帶來不便。

cancel 取消　turn out... 結果～　sales rep 業務代表　travel 出差　reschedule 重新排定時間
down the line 之後，日後

✉ sample 197

Dear

Due to some unexpected problems, I'm sorry to inform you that the presentation scheduled for March 23rd has been cancelled. Thank you for your interest in our products. We will let you know as soon as we are able to reschedule.

Thank you.

Try It！可以替換的字詞

Because of 由於～
Since there were 因為有～
As there are 因為～
For the reason of 基於～的原因
In response to 為因應～

- - - - - - - -

由於一些意料之外的問題，我很遺憾地要通知您，原定 3 月 23 日的說明會已取消。感謝您對我們產品感興趣。一旦能夠重新安排時間時，我們會立刻通知您。謝謝。

unexpected 意料不到的　inform... that 通知～（某人某事）　scheduled for 預定～的　interest 興趣
as soon as 一旦，只要～

✉ sample **198**

Dear ⌐ ¬

The presentation we had planned for next Thursday has been canceled. Certain issues came up which make it inadvisable for us to take on any new partners at the present time. We hope to be able to invite you to a presentation further down the line.

Thank you for your understanding.

- - - - - - -

我們計畫下週四舉行的發表會已取消。一些特定問題的出現，使得我們目前不宜接受任何新的合作夥伴。不過未來我們仍希望能夠邀請您參加一場發表會。謝謝您的理解。

certain 特定的　issue 問題　come up 出現　inadvisable 不宜的　take on 招收，取得
at the present time 目前

✉ sample **199**

Dear ⌐ ¬

Thanks for your interest in our company. Unfortunately, the presentation scheduled for next week has been called off. There were several scheduling conflicts that we were not able to work around. We will try to find a date further down the line and reschedule.

Thank you very much for your understanding.

- - - - - - -

感謝您對我們公司感興趣。不幸的是，原定下週舉行的發表會已經取消。出現了一些行程安排上的衝突，而我們尚無法著手處理。之後我們會試著找個日期並重新安排時間。非常感謝您的理解。

call off 取消～　conflict 衝突　work around 開始處理（問題等）

✉ sample 200

Dear ⬚⬚⬚⬚⬚⬚

I'm afraid we need to call off next week's presentation. We've had to make some last-minute changes in our product line, so we won't be ready to unveil it until later in the quarter. I'll get in touch with you soon to explain in more detail.

Sorry for any inconveniences.

- - - - - - - -

恐怕我們必須取消下週的發表會。我們必須針對我們的產品系列進行最後一刻的修正，因此我們只能在本季稍後才會準備發表。我會盡快與您聯繫並說明細節部分。造成任何不便，深表歉意。

unveil 揭露，發表　quarter 季度　get in touch 取得聯繫

Try It！可以替換的字詞

introduce 介紹

show 展出

reveal 揭示

disclose 公開

tell you about 告訴您關於～

要求準備發表會要用的設備
Asking for Preparing for the Presentation Facilities ▲

✉ sample 201

Hi, _____

I'm just writing to discuss next week's presentation. We're going to need a conference room with a seating capacity of 20, an overhead projector, and access to a WiFi network. Let me know if any of this will be a problem.

I appreciate all of your help.

- - - - - - - -

我寫這封信的目的是要討論下週的發表會。我們需要一個可容納 20 人座位的會議室、一部高架投影機,並可提供 WiFi 上網。請讓我知道這部分是否有任何問題。感謝您一切的協助。

> conference room 會議室　seating 座位　capacity 容量　overhead projector 高架投影機
> access 取得(的管道或方式)　WiFi (Wireless Fidelity) 無線網路技術

Try It！可以替換的字詞

presentation room 簡報室
waiting room 等候室
meeting room 會議室
board room 董事會辦公室
large rectangular room
大型的長方形會議室

✉ sample 202

_____

For next week's presentation, we'll need a ❶good-sized meeting room, say a seating capacity of 20+. Also, could you check to see that we have enough electrical outlets? I know it sounds ❷crazy, but at our last presentation, we couldn't plug in our laptop!

Thanks for the help.

- - - - - - - -

為了下週的發表會,我們將需要一個大型的會議室,例如可容納 20 人以上空間的地方。另外,可以請您看一下我們是否有足夠的電源插座嗎?我知道這聽起來很荒謬,不過在我們上次發表會上,就發生我們的筆電無法接上電源的情況!感謝協助。

> good-sized 相當大的　enough 足夠的　electrical outlet 電源插座　plug in 將～插上電源
> laptop 筆記型電腦

Try It！可以替換的字詞

❶ decently-sized 尺寸合適的
modestly-sized 適當大小的
respectably-sized 大小適當的
fairly large 相當大的
regular 一般規格的

❷ odd 古怪的
bizarre 不尋常的
unwise 愚蠢的
senseless 愚昧的
outlandish 異乎尋常的

✉ sample 203

Dear [   ]

I'm excited about the presentation next month. I just wanted to confirm with you that the **facilities** will be ready for us. We'll need a room big enough for the number of people we're expecting to attend. We also need access to the Internet for a portion of the presentation.

Please let me know if any of this will be a problem.

- - - - - - - -

我對於下個月的發表會感到相當興奮。我在此想跟您確認我們要用的設施會準備妥當。我們需要一個足夠大的會議室，以容納我們預計會來參加的人數。我們還需要可以上網的設備 — 發表會一部份內容需要。請讓我知道這部分是否有任何問題。

facility 設施　ready 準備好的　big enough for 對於～足夠大　the number of ～的數量　portion 部分

✉ sample 204

Dear [   ]

I'm looking forward to the presentation. Could you check and make sure that the room is **ready for us**? I need a whiteboard in addition to a projector. If you have any trouble getting those things together, let me know.

Thanks,

- - - - - - - -

我相當期待這場說明會的到來。您能檢查並確認我們要用的會議室是否準備妥當呢？除投影機外，我還需要一塊白板。如果您在準備這些東西時遇到任何問題，請讓我知道。謝謝。

check 檢查　make sure 確定　whiteboard 白板　in addition to 除了～　projector 投影機　trouble 麻煩

✉ sample 205

Dear _____

I'm writing to check on the facilities for our presentation next Wednesday. Could you confirm that we will have the use of one of your larger conference rooms for the entire morning? We will be arriving early, so I'd like to be able to set up before the attendees arrive.

Thank you for your help.

- - - - - - - -

我寫這封信的目的是想確認我們下週三發表會所需要的設施。您可以確認貴單位較大間的會議室可以讓我們使用一整個上午嗎？我們會提早抵達，所以我希望可以在與會者到達之前安頓好。謝謝您的幫助。

check on 檢查～ larger 較大的 entire 整個的 set up 做好準備 attendee 與會者

Try It！可以替換的字詞

clientele 客戶

potential customers 潛在顧客

paying participants 付費的參與者

members 會員們

donors and partakers 捐助者及參與者

簽訂合約 & 協商 Contract & Negotiation

Case 01 | 開價、出價 Making an Offer ▲

✉ sample 206

Dear _____

We've looked over your proposal and run some numbers on future profitability. We're ready to make you an offer of $5,000 per unit. This is our bottom-line offer, so I hope it's acceptable to you. Get in touch with me after you've had a chance to discuss it with your people.

I look forward to hearing from you.

- - - - - - - -

Try It! 可以替換的字詞

Return via certified mail a response
以掛號信件回覆

Please let me know your decision
請讓我知道您的決定

We can talk more about this
我們可以進一步談這件事

There will be more to discuss
還有更多要討論的

I will await your response
我會等候您的回覆

我們已大致看過您的提案,並針對未來的獲利能力做出一些估算。我們準備給您的報價是每單位 5,000 美元。這是我們的報價底線,所以我希望這是您能夠接受的。在您有機會與您的員工討論這件事之後,請與我聯繫。期待您的佳音。

look over 粗略查看~ proposal 提案 profitability 獲利能力 make you an offer of 向您提出一份~的報價 bottom-line 底線的 acceptable 可以接受的 get in touch with 與~取得聯繫

✉ sample 207

_____

Attached is a preliminary offer. This isn't a hard number. We're willing to negotiate, but I think it's a good starting place. Let me know how your people feel about it.

Thanks,

- - - - - - - -

Try It! 可以替換的字詞

an initial 初步的

a starting 最初的

an introductory 最初的

a pilot 開始的

our first 我們首度的

附件是一份初步報價。這不是一個沒有商量餘地的價格。我們願意商討,但我想這會是一個很好的開始。請讓我知道您的人員對此有何看法。謝謝。

preliminary 初步的 offer 報價 be willing to 願意~ negotiate 協商 starting place 起點

✉ sample 208

Dear [_____]

We've got an offer ready for you. I'm attaching the ❶ details. I think it's a ❷reasonable price, and I hope you find it so too. Let me know what you think.

Thanks,

- - - - - - - -

Try It！可以替換的字詞

❶facts 實際資料

numbers 數字

account summary 會計資料匯總

summarization 概要

basics 基本資訊

❷just 公正的

rational 合理的

non-discriminatory 無差別待遇的

fair 公平的

flexible 彈性的

我們已準備好一個報價給您。我附上了明細。我認為這是一個合理的價格，我希望您也能夠認同。讓我知道您的想法。謝謝。

get... ready 將～準備好　details 詳細資訊　reasonable 合理的

✉ sample 209

Dear [_____]

Here is our final offer. I think for the services you'd be providing, it's fair. Take some time to think it over and let us know if you want to go forward.

Thanks,

- - - - - - - -

Try It！可以替換的字詞

lowest possible 盡可能最低的

concluding 最後的

definitive 明確的

irrevocable 不可改變的

absolute best 絕對最好的

這是我們的最終報價。我認為，對於您可能提供的服務，這是合理的價格。請花點時間考慮一下，並讓我們知道您是否有意願進行下一步。謝謝。

final 最終的　take time 花點時間　think... over 思考一番～　go forward 前進

✉ sample 210

Dear _____

We've come to a decision on our offer. I don't think your **asking price** is unreasonable, but in the current economic climate, we think we can get a better deal elsewhere, so we're offering 10% less. Let me know if this is acceptable to you.

I look forward to working with you.

- - - - - - - -

我們對於報價金額已做出了決定。我不認為您要求的價格是不合理的，但在當前的經濟形勢下，我們認為應該還有一個更好的交易價格，所以我們願意再降 10%。請讓我知道這樣您是否可以接受。我期待與您合作。

come to a decision 做出一項決定　unreasonable 不合理的　current 現在的　climate 氣候，情勢
deal 交易（價）　elsewhere 別處　less 較少的　acceptable 可接受的

提出一項合約條款 Offering a Contract Condition ▲

✉ sample 211

Dear [_____]

I'd like to add a **❶condition** to the contract. It's something the main office is insisting on. The addendum is attached, so take a look at it and see if it would be acceptable **❷on your end.**

Thanks,

- - - - - - -

Try It！可以替換的字詞

❶ stipulation 條款
provision 條款
proviso 但書，附帶條件
term 條款
rider 附加條款

❷ with your people 對於您的人員來説
to you 對您而言
to your superiors 對於您的上司
with those around you
對於您周遭的人
within your research team
在您的研究團隊中

我想在這份合約中添加一項條款。這是我們總部所堅持的。附件是要追加的部分，因此，請您過目一下，看您這邊是否可以接受。謝謝。

main office 總部，總公司 insist on 堅持，堅決要求 addendum 附錄，附加條款
on your end 在您這一方

✉ sample 212

[_____]

Attached is a condition we'd like to put in the contract. It's a fairly standard clause, but we feel like it needs to be there to protect us from any trouble further down the road. Let me know if you object.

Thanks,

- - - - - - -

Try It！可以替換的字詞

fine print （合約的）細則
agreement 協議
bargain 協議，交易
written mutual understanding
書面相互理解
company-wide treaty 全公司合約

附件是我們想要放在合約中的條款。儘管這是個絕對標準的條款，但我們覺得它存在的必要性壓於讓雙方未來免於遭受任何麻煩。請讓我知道您是否有異議。謝謝。

fairly 相當地 clause 條款，條文 protect A from B 保護 A 免受 B down the road 將來的某個時候
object 反對

✉ sample 213

Dear [_____]

If it's not **too late in the game**, I'd like to add one last condition to the contract. I don't think it's a deal breaker. I've attached the wording. Look it over and tell me if it's going to be a problem.

Thanks,

倘若目前還不會太遲，我想在合約中添加一項最後的條款。我不認為這是違約條款。該條款內容如附件所示。請過目一下，並讓我知道這是否會是個問題。謝謝。

game（商業中的）領域 deal breaker 違約款 wording 措詞，用字

Try It！可以替換的字詞

beyond the point of no-return 過了無法重新來過的階段

overly late 太遲了

behind schedule 進度落後的

too delayed 延遲太久的

too overdue 過期太久了的

✉ sample 214

Dear [_____]

We have a condition we'd like to put in the contract. It basically states that we won't be held liable for damages incurred during shipment. We don't want to bear ❶the responsibility for the shipping company's ❷errors. Let me know if you think that's fair.

Thanks,

Try It！可以替換的字詞

❶ all blame 所有責任

the entire brunt 全部責任

complete liability 完全的責任

total accountability 全部的責任

whole guilt 全部的罪過

❷ slip-ups 疏忽，閃失

blunders 疏忽

miscalculations 錯估形勢

boo-boos 愚蠢的錯誤

faults 失誤

我們有一項條款想放進這份合約中。基本上它要陳述的是，我們對於貨物運輸過程中遭受損壞不承擔任何責任。我們不想承擔運輸公司犯錯的責任。請讓我知道您是否認為這是合理的。謝謝。

basically 基本上 state 陳述 hold liable for... 對～負責 damage 損壞 incur 招致
bear the responsibility 承擔責任 error 錯誤

✉ sample 215

Dear _____

In order to keep the contract fair to both of our sides, I'd like to add one condition. It simply states that if either party fails to meet the terms within a reasonable time, the contract is null and void. Let me know if you're okay with that.

Thanks,

- - - - - - - -

evenhanded 公平的
balanced 平衡的
impartial 不偏私的
stable 穩定的
not biased 不偏袒任一方的

為了確保這份合約對我們雙方是公平的，我想新增一項條款。它只是陳述，如果任何一方在一個合理時間內無法遵循這些條款，則這份合約視同無效。請讓我知道您是否同意。謝謝。

in order to 為了～　side 方面　simply 只是　state 說明　party 一方　meet the terms 遵循這些條款　reasonable 合理的，正確的　null 無效的　void 失效的

✉ sample 216

I know it's a little late in the game, but we'd like to make a couple of changes to the contract ❶terms. They're ❷ minor changes, so they shouldn't throw a wrench in what we've agreed to so far. **Let me know if we can do it.**

Thanks,

- - - - - - - -

❶ details 細節
vocabulary 語彙
terminology 專業術語
expressions 表達用語
language 語言

❷ tiny 極小
not big 不大的
petty 瑣碎的
minor-league 次要的
inconsequential 不是那麼重要的

我知道目前來說有點晚了，但我們想針對合約條款做些修改。因為是次要的變更，應不會破壞我們迄今為止達成的協議。 請讓我知道我們是否可以這麼做。謝謝。

a couple of 一些　term 條款，條文　minor 次要的　throw a wrench 阻礙，破壞　agreed 同意
so far 目前為止

✉ sample 217

I'm working on getting my **bosses** to sign off on this contract, and there's one final change they'd like to make. I don't think it's too major of an issue. I've attached a new version with slightly different terms. Take a look at it and let me know what you think.

Thanks,

- - - - - - - -

lawyers 律師
financiers 金融專家
backers 贊助者
analysts 分析師
legal team 法律團隊

我正努力讓我的老闆們簽字批准這份合約，而他們想做出最後一項更正。我不認為這是個大問題。我附上新版本的合約，其中有些條款稍作修正。請過目，並讓我知道您的想法。謝謝。

work on 著手處理～　get A to... 使 A 去做某事　boss 老闆　sign off 做結束，簽結　major 主要的
slightly 些微地

✉ sample 218

Dear ....

I hope everything is going well. I wanted to run a change in the terms of the contract past you. We would like to extend the deadline for delivery by one month. This would give us a little more flexibility. Let me know if you'd be okay with that.

Thanks,

- - - - - - - -

Try It！可以替換的字詞

propose 提議
put forward 提出
hint at 提出
advise 建議
offer 提出

但願一切順利。我想告知您這份合約中的一些條款要做修正。我們希望將交貨期限延長一個月。這會給我們更多的彈性空間。請讓我知道那是否對您來說是 O.K. 的。謝謝。

run a change 做出一項變更　extend 延長　deadline 截止時間　delivery 交付，送達　flexibility 彈性

✉ sample 219

Dear ....

I've been looking over the contract, and there's a ❶change I'd like to make to the terms. I'm a little uncomfortable with the liability waiver. I've attached ❷a new version of the contract. Let me know if the change is acceptable to you.

Thanks,

- - - - - - - -

Try It！可以替換的字詞

❶ modification 修改
small adjustment 小調整
tiny amendment 小修正
slight variation 些微變更
minor alteration 次要的修改

❷ a revised edition 一個修訂版
a completed version 一個完整版
an updated file 一份更新檔案
a restructured version
一個重新架構的版本
a fixed edition 一份修訂版

我已經看過合約內容，我想針對某些條款做些修改。我不太認同責任豁免這部分。我附上新版的合約。請讓我知道您是否可接受這項修正。謝謝。

look over 查看～　uncomfortable 不舒服的　liability 責任　waiver 豁免　acceptable 可以接受的

✉ sample 220

We have a little problem with the contract. We've done some calculations, and I don't think the percentage that the contract guarantees is quite high enough to meet our production costs. I've attached an amended version with a different number. Let me know if you'd be amenable to the change.

Thanks,

我們對於合約有一點小問題。我們已做了一些估算，而我不認為合約中保證的百分比足以滿足我們的生產成本。我附上不同金額數字的修正版本。請讓我知道您是否可以接受這項變更。謝謝。

calculation 估算　percentage 百分比　guarantee 擔保，保證　production cost 生產成本
amended 修正的　amenable 願意接受的

✉ sample 221

Dear ⌐⌐⌐⌐⌐

I'd like to open negotiation on the deal. I'm attaching some ❶numbers we think are fair. Have your ❷people take a look at them and let me know what you think. I look forward to reaching an agreement with you soon.

Thanks,

- - - - - - - -

Try It！可以替換的字詞

❶ values 價格，價值
estimates 估算值
guesses 估算數值
proposals 提案
figures 數字

❷ support crew 支援人員
investors 投資人
shareholders 股東
depositors 存戶
entire staff 全體員工

我想就這筆交易開始協商。我附上一些我們認為公平的金額數字。請您的人員過目一下，並讓我知道您的想法。我期待很快可以與您達成協議。謝謝。

open negotiation 開始協商　have A take a look 讓 A 過目　reach an agreement 達成共識，達成協議

✉ sample 222

Dear ⌐⌐⌐⌐⌐

I'm excited about moving forward toward an agreement. I've put together some terms that represent our starting position. In the attached document, you'll find both a dollar amount and a time frame. Take some time to look it over, and let me know what you think.

I look forward to hearing from you.

- - - - - - - -

Try It！可以替換的字詞

a valuable position 一個珍貴的地步
a joint agreement 一份聯合協議
a new contract 一份新合約
a new beginning 一個新的開始
this wonderful prospect 這美好的前景

我很高興即將達成協議。我已經將一些條款彙整完畢，這代表我們的初始立場。在附帶的文檔中，您可以看到金額及時間範圍。請花點時間看一下，並讓我知道您的想法。期待您的回音。

put together 彙整～　represent 代表　position 立場，地步　both A and B A 和B 兩者都
time frame 時間範圍

✉ sample 223

Dear [_____]

I'm happy to be working with you on this deal. Hopefully we can get through the negotiation process quickly and painlessly. Would you like to put together some numbers for us to start from? I've attached all of the product documentation so that you'll have the information you need to make an offer.

I look forward to hearing from you.

我很高興能與您合作這個案子。希望我們能夠快速且輕鬆地完成協商過程。可以請您為我們整理一些彼此可以開始商討的數字嗎？我已附上所有產品文件，以便您取得用來報價的資訊。期待您的佳音。

hopefully 希望地　get through 完成，通過～　process 過程　painlessly 輕鬆地

Try It！可以替換的字詞

effortlessly 輕鬆地
smoothly 平順地
fluently 流暢地
with ease 輕鬆自在地
naturally 自然地

✉ sample 224

Dear [_____]

We are ready to begin negotiations on the price for the products. I've put together an offer that I think is fair, and I'd like to put it out there to get the ball rolling. I think $10 per unit is well within the range of what the market will bear. Let me know your thoughts on this.

Thanks,

我們準備開始就這些產品的價格進行商談。我已經整理出一個我認為合理的報價，在此我想提出來，好讓事情能夠繼續進行下去。我認為每單位 10 美元正好落在市場能夠容許的價格範圍內。請讓我知道您對此事的看法。謝謝。

put... out 提出，公開　get the ball rolling 讓事情繼續進行下去　per 每～　unit 單位　range 範圍
bear 容許

Try It！可以替換的字詞

a bid 一個標案
a bargain 一件買賣
our deal 我們的交易案
a good proposition 一個很合理的報價
a nice starting position 一個很好的起點

Dear

I'm looking forward to coming to an agreement with you. I would like to open the negotiation by outlining what we can provide. Attached is a summary of the number of units we have available and the earliest date we can deliver them by. Let me know what you think.

Thank you.

- - - - - - - -

我期待與您達成一項協議。我會概略介紹我們的服務項目，然後藉此開始進行商討。附件是我們現有的單位數字彙整，以及我們可以寄送出去的最早日期。請讓我知道您的想法。謝謝。

> came to an agreement 達成一項協議　would like to 想要～　outline 概述　the number of ～的數字
> earliest 最早的

Try It！可以替換的字詞

a synopsis 一份概要

a précis 一份摘要

a rundown 一份簡要說明

an abridged version 一個簡略版

a summation 一份摘要

✉ sample **226**

Hi, _____

I just wanted to double-check that this is your **❶current** offer. We like the look of it, but I want to make sure I have the right numbers. If you could just write me back to confirm, I think we're ready to **❷move forward**.

Thanks,

- - - - - - - -

Try It！可以替換的字詞

❶ present 現在的
existing 目前的
up-to-date 最新的
most recent 最近的
in-progress 進行中的

❷ advance 前進
move ahead 前進
go forward 前進
run with this 進行這項工作
push onward 往前推進

在此我想再次確認這是您目前的報價金額。這是我可以接受的，但我想確認這些金額數字是否正確。若您可以給我回信確認，我想我們就可以準備繼續進行下去了。謝謝。

double-check 再檢查，再確認　current 目前的　make sure 確認　confirm 確定　move forward 前進

✉ sample **227**

Dear _____

I have a quick question. I understand that $15 per unit is your current request. Is that correct? We're trying to determine if we can move forward with this, but I wanted to confirm that number first. Let me know when you get a chance.

Thanks,

- - - - - - - -

Try It！可以替換的字詞

settle on 決定
ascertain 確定～無疑
clarify 弄清楚
establish 確定
maker certain 確認

我有個小問題想請問一下。據我了解，每單位 15 美元是您目前的要求。是那樣沒錯吧？我們就要決定是否繼續進行這件事，但我想先確認那個數字是正確的。麻煩您有空時再回覆我一下。謝謝。

request 請求　correct 正確的　first 一開始的　when you get a chance 當您有空時

✉ sample 228

Dear ⌐ ⌐

Could I confirm with you that the number below is your
❶final offer? We're ready to make our final decision, and
I want to be sure we're both on the same page. Once I
hear from you, we'll be ready to tell you our ❷answer.

Thanks,

- - - - - - - -

我可以跟您確認，以下的金額數字是您的最終報價嗎？我們準備要做最後的決定了，所以我想確認我們的想法是一致的。一旦我收到您的回覆，我們會準備好告訴您我們的答案。謝謝。

below 下方的　on the same page （基於相同目標而）具有共識的，看法一致的　answer 答案

✉ sample 229

Dear ⌐ ⌐

I'd like to **double-check** that you've agreed to raise your
offer by 5%. We're happy with that number, but I wasn't
sure if you'd fully agreed to it yet. Let me know if we're
on the same page.

Thank you.

- - - - - - - -

我想再次確認，您已同意提高 5% 的出價。我們對那數字很滿意，不過我還不確定您是否完全同意這數字。請讓我知道我們的看法是否是一致的。謝謝。

raise 提高　fully 完全地　yet 然而

✉ sample 230

Dear [_____]

After our last meeting, I wasn't certain if I had a firm offer from you. Was $10 per unit acceptable to you? If so, we're ready to move forward with the deal. Let me know as soon as you can.

Thanks,

- - - - - - - -

經過我們上次會議之後，我不確定您給我的報價是否是確定的。每單位 10 美元是您可以接受的嗎？倘若如此，我們就要準備繼續進行這項交易案。請盡快回覆我。謝謝。

not certain if 不確定是否～ firm 肯定的 acceptable 可接受的 as soon as you can 盡快

Try It！可以替換的字詞

a concrete bid 一個具體的出價金額

a definitive proposal 一項明確的提案

an unchangeable agreement
一份不會更改的協議

a fixed deal 一個確定的交易案

a certain compromise
一個明確的折衷方案

拒絕對方公司的出價 Rejecting the Other Company's Offer of Money ▲

✉ sample 231

I'm afraid we aren't going to be able to ❶accept your offer. We just can't go quite that low. I hope we can do business together ❷in the future.

Thanks,

- - - - - - - -

Try It! 可以替換的字詞

❶ receive 接受
take on 接受
consent to 同意
say yes to 同意
work with 認為～可行

❷ in the years to come 在未來幾年內
in the days and months ahead 在未來的日子裡
within the year 在這一年之內
shortly 不久之後
someday soon 不久之後的某一天

恐怕我們無法接受您的出價。我們沒辦法接受這麼低的價格。我希望將來能夠共同開展業務。謝謝。

accept 接受　offer 出價（金額）quite 相當地　that low 那麼低　do business 做生意
in the future 在未來

✉ sample 232

Dear

I received your offer and talked it over with my partners. I'm afraid we can't agree to your terms. The market price for our product is simply higher than what you're willing to pay. I hope you understand.

Thank you.

- - - - - - - -

Try It! 可以替換的字詞

current price 現價
demand 需求
price per share 股價
economic value 經濟價值
market value 市價

我收到您的報價，並且已和我的合作夥伴討論過。恐怕我們無法同意您的條件。我們產品的市場價格正好高於您願意支付的價格。希望你您能夠明白。謝謝您

talk... over 討論～　market price 市場價格　simply（為了強調某句話）只是，就是　higher 更高
be willing to... 願意去～（做某事）

✉ sample 233

Dear _____

I think we've done everything we can to reach an agreement, but I'm afraid we won't be able to accept your offer. The ❶economic conditions are such that it just wouldn't be ❷feasible for us to go that low. I hope you understand.

I look forward to doing business with you again.

- - - - - - - -

我想我們已盡一切努力要達成協議，但恐怕我們無法接受您提出的價格。由於現今的經濟狀況如此，對們無法接受那麼低的價格。希望您能明白。期望可以與您再合作。

economic 經濟上的　condition 情況　such that 如此以致於～　feasible 行得通的

✉ sample 234

Dear _____

Unfortunately, we just can't agree to the terms of your offer. I understand your position, but we can't go quite that low. If you reconsider down the road, let me know and we'll work something out.

Sorry it didn't work out this time.

- - - - - - - -

很遺憾的是，我們無法同意您提出的條件。我了解您的情況，但是我們無法接受這麼低的價格。如果未來您可以重新考慮，請讓我知道，屆時我們可以找到合作的方案。未能合作成功，深表遺憾。

agree to 同意～　position 立場　reconsider 重新考慮　down the road 將來的某個時候
work out 解決，想出～（解決辦法等）

✉ sample 235

Dear [_____]

I've looked over your offer, and I'm afraid I'm going to have to pass. The numbers just don't work out for us in the long run. I hope we're able to do business in the future, but this deal doesn't seem meant to be.

Thanks,

– – – – – – – –

Try It！可以替換的字詞

say no 說不

move on to our next vendor
找尋我們下一個供應商

withhold from going with you
退出與您的合作關係

stop our negotiations
停止我們的商談

refuse this contract 拒絕這份合約

我已看過您的報價，但恐怕要讓它成為遺珠之憾了。我們最後決定，這個金額數字是並不可行的。我希望我們在未來仍有合作機會，這次似乎無法達成交易了。謝謝。

pass 忽略　in the long run 在最後　meant to be 意味著～

結束協商 Wrapping Up the Negotiation ▲

✉ sample 236

I think that covers just about everything. We're ready ❶to sign! I'll have a ❷courier bring over the final contracts and we can wrap this up. It's been a pleasure doing business with you.

Thanks,

- - - - - - - -

Try It!可以替換的字詞

❶ to give you our signature
給你我們的簽名

to commit 做出承諾

and willing to become partners
並願意成為合作夥伴

to go first into this deal
先進行這筆交易

to give this our all
投入我們一切的心力

❷ bike messenger 自行車快遞員

delivery service 快遞服務

carrier 送信人

secretary 秘書

dispatch rider 快遞員

我想一切都沒問題了。我們準備好要簽字了！我會派一位快遞將最終版合約送過去，然後我們就可以簽訂了。很高興與您一起做生意。謝謝。

courier 送貨員，快遞員　wrap... up 完成～　It's been a pleasure ~ing 很高興～

✉ sample 237

We're happy with the terms you're offering and we're ready to sign off on those last minor changes. This has been a great experience. Not all trades go down this smoothly.

Thanks,

- - - - - - - -

Try It!可以替換的字詞

transactions 交易

exchanges 交流

partnerships 合夥關係

business discussions 商務洽談

one-on-one negotiations 一對一協商

我們對您提供的條件感到滿意，而且我們準備簽，正式同意最後的細微修正。這是一次很棒的經驗。並非所有交易都會像這次這麼順利進行。謝謝。

sign off on 正式批准／同意～　minor 細微的　experience 經驗

✉ **sample 238**

Dear ⌐‾‾‾‾‾‾⌐

Your latest offer looks ❶acceptable to us. I'm happy to say that we're ready to move forward. We've signed the contract and we're sending it over to you for countersign. Thanks for ❷a smooth negotiation.

Talk to you soon.

- - - - - - - -

Try It!可以替換的字詞

❶ suitable 合適的

good enough 足夠好的

up to par 合乎標準的

better than before 比以前更好的

wonderful 極好的

❷ an effortless 毫不費力的

an easy 順利的

a time-saving 節省時間的

a cost-effective 有成本效益的

a perfectly acceptable
完全可以接受的

您最新報價看來是我們能夠接受的。我很高興地說，我們準備要繼續邁進了。我們已經簽了合約，並且我們將合約送過去給您簽名確認。協商非常順利，在此致上謝意。期待再聊

latest 最新的　countersign 副署，確認同意　smooth 流暢的，順利的

✉ **sample 239**

Dear ⌐‾‾‾‾‾‾⌐

We've gone over all of the fine print, and I think that about wraps it up. We can meet tomorrow and sign the contracts. Thank you for your hard work on this deal.

I look forward to seeing you.

- - - - - - - -

Try It!可以替換的字詞

details 詳細內容

minutiae 細節

finer points 細則

contract details and numbers
合約細節和數字

particular speed bumps
特定的障礙

我們已經仔細看過所有細則部分，而且我想這樣大概就可以結束了。我們可以明天見面並簽合約。感謝您在此次交易中的辛勞。我期待與您見面。

go over 仔細查看～　fine print（合約等的）限制性質的細則　hard work 辛勞

✉ sample 240

Try It! 可以替換的字詞

get great feedback 獲得很棒的反饋

get promoted 獲得升遷

enjoy the fruits of labor
享受付出的成果

get praise 得到好評

benefit 獲益

Dear ⸎⸎⸎⸎⸎⸎⸎

I think we've got ourselves a deal. We think your offer is fair, and we're ready to move ahead. I think we're both going to **advance** from this agreement.

Thanks for all of your hard work.

- - - - - - - -

我想我們已經達成了協議。我們認為您的報價是公平的，且我們已準備好繼續前進。我認為我們雙方都可以一起執行這項協議。感謝您的辛勞。

get oneself a deal 達成一項協議 advance 前推

簽訂合約 Signing a Contract ▲

✉ sample 241

Dear _____

Attached is the signed contract. I think that's the last thing you need from me, so I hope we can expect delivery of the product by the 18th. Let me know if there are any problems.

Thanks,

- - - - - - - -

附件是已簽字的合約。我想這是我最後要給您的文件了。所以我希望我們所預期的交貨日期是不晚於 18 日。請讓我知道您是否有任何問題。謝謝。

Try It！可以替換的字詞

final paper 最終文件

most important thing 最重要的事

only paperwork 唯一的文件

authorization 授權許可

formal approval 正式批准

> signed 已簽字的　contract 合約　expect 期望，期待　delivery 交貨

✉ sample 242

Dear _____

I've signed the contract for the purchase of 200 multi-function printers. Attached is a scan of the contract. The hard copy is in the mail and should reach you within 48 hours. After you receive the contract, let's begin discussing delivery.

I look forward to hearing from you.

- - - - - - - -

我已簽署這份購買 200 台多功能印表機的合約。附件是這份合約的掃描檔案。紙本資料已透過郵件寄送，您將在 48 小時內收到。您收到合約後，我們就開始討論交貨事宜。期待您的回音。

Try It！可以替換的字詞

delivery options 配送方式

receiving our goods 收到我們的貨品

shipment 裝運

shipping preference 偏好的運送方式

sending the printers 運送印表機

> purchase 購買　multi-function 多功能的　hard copy 紙本　in the mail 已郵遞寄送　reach 到達

✉ sample 243

Dear [ ]

Now that we've ❶agreed on everything, it looks like the only thing left is to sign on the dotted line, and I've done that! The contract has been ❷signed and I sent it to you this afternoon. You should receive it in the next couple of days. Let me know if you don't get it.

Thanks,

- - - - - - - -

既然我們已同意一切事項了，看來剩下唯一要做的就是在虛線上簽字了，我已經簽過了！合約已簽畢，我今天下午已寄出給您。幾天內您應該會收到。如果沒有收到，請讓我知道。謝謝。

now that 既然～　agree on 同意～　look like 看起來像是～　left 剩下的
sign on the dotted line 在虛線上簽名　receive 接收　couple of 幾個，一些～

✉ sample 244

Dear [ ]

I've received the signed contract from you and I've countersigned it. It will go out with today's mail and you should get a copy within a couple of days. Once that's squared away, we can proceed with the transaction.

Thanks,

- - - - - - - -

我已收到您簽字了的合約，而我也回簽完畢。今天就將它郵寄出去，您應可於數日之內收到一份。待您收到之後，我們就可以繼續這項交易了。謝謝。

countersign 副署，回簽（確認）　copy 副本　square away 將～準備就緒　proceed with 繼續進行～
transaction 交易

✉ sample 245

Dear _____

Attached is the contract for the purchase of the furniture. You can print it out and sign it and then send me a hard copy in the mail. When we've got the paperwork out of the way, we'll begin delivery of your order.

Thanks,

- - - - - - - -

official papers 正式文件

forms 表格（文件）

formalities 正式的資料

signings 已簽之文件

signatures and fine print
簽字與附屬細則

附件是購買家具的合約。您可以將其印出並簽名，然後將紙本寄一份給我。當我們完成紙本文書作業之後，我們會開始處理您的訂單與交貨。謝謝。

fabric 編織品　print... out 將～列印出來　get... out of the way 處理（困難的事情），將～解決掉
paperwork 文書作業

商品訂購 Product Order

Case 01 詢問新產品 Inquiring About New Products ▲

✉ sample 246

Dear _____

I'm writing to request some information on your new product, the RX-9. I think it may meet my company's needs, but I need some more details on price and warranty. Could you send me a rundown of all the specifications?

Thanks,

- - - - - - - -

我寫這封信目的是想索取您的新產品 RX-9 的一些資訊。我認為它可能符合我公司的需求，但我需要更多關於價格和保固方面的詳細資訊。您可否寄給我所有規格的概要嗎？謝謝。

> request 請求　meet one's needs 滿足某人的需求　warranty 保固　rundown 概要說明
> specifications 規格

Try It! 可以替換的字詞

data 數據
particulars 個別資訊
facts 論據
reviews 評論
detailed itemization 詳細分項說明

✉ sample 247

Dear _____

Could I get some information on your new laptop? I'm interested in making a bulk purchase in the future, and I think your product may be right for my company. I'd like to know a little about the performance of the processor.

Thanks for your time.

- - - - - - - -

我可以索取您最新筆電的一些資訊嗎？我想未來我會大量購買，我認為您的產品可能適合我公司使用。我想了解一下處理器的性能。謝謝您的寶貴時間。

> laptop 筆記型電腦　bulk purchase 大量採購　performance （機器等的）性能
> processor【電腦】處理器

Try It! 可以替換的字詞

portable storage devices
行動儲存裝置
tablet PC 平板電腦
smartphone 智慧型手機
MP3 player MP3 播放器
DVD burner DVD 燒錄機

✉ sample 248

Dear [_____]

I'm writing to ask about the G23. Could you send me a general description of its functions and dimensions? My office is in need of new printers, and I think the G23 could be the one for us. Any materials would be appreciated.

Thank you for your help.

- - - - - - - -

我寫這封信的目的是想詢問有關 G23 的資訊。您能寄給我其功能和尺寸的整體說明嗎？我公司需要新的印表機，而我認為 G23 可能就是我們需要的款式。任何資料的提供，將不勝感激。感謝您的協助。

general 整體性的　description 說明，描述　dimension尺寸　in need of 需要～　the one 就是這個

✉ sample 249

Dear [_____]

Could I get some information about the new monitor? I'd like to know about screen dimensions and resolution. Also, if you could send me some images, I'd appreciate it.

Thanks,

- - - - - - - -

可以給我這部新顯示器的相關資訊嗎？我想知道螢幕的尺寸和解析度。此外，如果您能發一些圖片給我，我將不勝感激。謝謝。

monitor 顯示器　screen 螢幕　resolution 解析度　image 影像，圖像

✉ sample 250

Dear [_____]

I'd like to get some information about your new
❶product. Could you please send me a ❷brochure with
a rundown on its functionality and speed? I'd also like to
see some images if possible.

Thank you,

- - - - - - -

我想索取一些關於您新產品的資訊。可否請您寄給我一本簡述其功能和速度的小冊子？如果可能的
話，我也想看到一些圖片。謝謝。

brochure 小冊子　functionality 功能性　speed 速度

✉ sample 251

Dear _____

We're looking at your T-23 model monitor as a possible purchase. We're currently building an inventory of hardware and we're making purchases from a number of sources. If you could send us a sample of the T-23, we will be able to decide whether or not it meets our needs. If we like what we see, you can count on a fairly big order.

Thanks,

- - - - - - - -

a small pile	些許的
a roomful	數量很多的
various types	各種類型的
all types	所有類型的
numerous kinds	多種的

我們正在考慮購買您的 T-23 顯示器。我們目前正在建立一份硬體存貨清單，並準備從一些來源處購買。如果您可以寄給我們 T-23 的樣品，我們就能夠確定是否符合我們的需求。如果我們喜歡我們所看到的東西，您可以期待接獲一筆相當大的訂單。謝謝。

inventory（店內的）庫存，存貨　source 來源　meet one's needs 滿足某人的需求　count on 信賴～

✉ sample 252

Dear _____

I'm writing to request a sample of fabric #2365. We are currently making our purchases for fall 2019, and I'm trying to get a large number of samples for us to choose from. If you can get the sample to us within the week, we will consider it for purchase.

Thank you.

- - - - - - - -

an example	一個樣本
a mock-up	一個樣本
a swatch	一份樣品
a small piece	一小塊
a square	一（大）塊

我寫這封信的目的是想索取一個 #2365 織物的樣品。我們目前正為 2019 年秋季進行採購，而我現在正要蒐集大量的樣品，以供我們選擇。如果您可以在一週內給我們樣品，我們會考慮購買。謝謝。

fabric 織物　a large number of 大量的　consider 考慮

✉ sample 253

Dear _____

Would it be possible to send us a sample of the G32? We need to **❶get our hands on it** before we decide whether or not we want to **❷distribute** it. It certainly looks good on paper. If it meets our expectations, we plan on ordering a good number of units.

Thanks,

- - - - - - -

Try It！可以替換的字詞

❶ feel its intricacies 查看細節內容

play around with it
試試使用的感覺

truly know its details
確切了解其細節

fully analyze it 徹底進行分析

completely understand it
完全理解它

❷ supply 供給

disseminate 散播

provide 提供

list 將～列入清單

deliver 遞送

是否可以將 G32 的樣品寄給我們呢？在我們決定分銷該產品之前，我們必須對它好好檢視一番。該產品在紙本上看起來確實很棒。如果符合我們的期望，我們計畫將大量訂購。謝謝。

> get one's hands on... 好好了解一下～ whether or not 是否～ a good number of... 很多的～

✉ sample 254

Dear _____

I would like to request that a sample network router be shipped to our offices in New York. We are interested in becoming a distributor of the router. In order to make our final decision, we need to get a good look at the actual product. Let me know if this **is possible** and I will provide you with a shipping address.

Thank you for your time.

- - - - - - -

Try It！可以替換的字詞

can be accomplished 可以被完成

would even work 甚至是可行的

is promising 是有可能的

is likely 是有可能的

is doable 是可行的

我想請您寄送一個網路路由器樣品到我們紐約的辦公室。我們有興趣成為這款路由器的經銷商。為了做出最終決定，我們必須仔細檢視一下實際產品。請讓我知道這樣是否可行，然後我會提供您運送地址。謝謝您的寶貴時間。

> router 路由器 distributor 經銷商 actual 實際的 shipping address 運送地址

✉ sample 255

Try It!可以替換的字詞

Dear ⸚⸚⸚⸚⸚⸚⸚

I'm writing to request a sample of the T-III. My ❶company is interested in making a sizable order, but we need to get our hands on the product before ❷committing to a purchase. Below is the address to ship it to.

Thanks,

- - - - - - -

❶advertising agency 廣告代理商

home-shopping network
家庭購物網

sales associate team 銷售助理團隊

college 大學

municipality 市府當局

❷obligating to 對於～負有責任義務

binding ourselves to 承諾要～

requiring we go with you for
我們有必要和您一起去～

insisting on 堅持～

knowing we need this for
知道我們需要這東西用來～

我寫這封信的目的是想要索取 T-III 的樣品。蔽公司有興趣下一筆大訂單，但我們需要先看到產品的實體，才會能承諾購買。以下是寄送的地址。謝謝。

sizable 可觀的，非常大的 commit to 承諾～

通知有意願購買 Informing of the Intent to Purchase ▲

✉ sample 256

Dear _____

I'd like to go ahead and purchase the product. If you could send me an invoice, I'll arrange for payment. Let me know if you need any other information from me.

Thanks,

- - - - - - - -

Try It！可以替換的字詞

a bill 一張帳單
a statement 一張結帳單
a proof of purchase 一張購買證明
a bill of lading 一張提貨單
an account summary 一張帳目摘要

我想繼續進行並購買這項產品。麻煩您先將發票寄給我，我會安排付款事宜。如果您需要我提供任何其他資訊，請讓我知道。謝謝。

go ahead （按計劃）繼續進行 purchase 購買 invoice 發票，發貨單 arrange 安排 payment 付款

✉ sample 257

Dear _____

Thank you for your patience in answering all of my questions about the G32 monitor. ❶I'm convinced it's the ❷right product for my company, so I'd like to go ahead and make a purchase. I'd like to order 450 at the price we discussed.

Thanks again for all of your help.

- - - - - - -

Try It！可以替換的字詞

❶ Undoubtedly, 毫無疑問地，
It's clear to me that 我很清楚了解～
I believe 我相信～
Without question, 毫無疑問地，
You have proven 您已證明～

❷ proper 適合的
correct 正確的
precise 確切的
exact 精確的
just-right 正合適的

感謝您耐心回答 G32 顯示器的所有問題。我確信這是適合我公司的產品，所以我想繼續進行並購買這東西。我想以我們討論出來的價格訂購 450 件。再次感謝您的協助。

patience 耐心 be convinced 深信的 right 對的 at the price 以此價格

✉ sample 258

Dear ⌐‾‾‾‾‾¬

We've compared your prices and the quality of your product with other suppliers in the market and we've decided you offer the best deal. We're ready to go forward with the purchase. I'd like to arrange for 300 units to be shipped to our warehouses in New York. I believe we agreed on $450 per unit?

I look forward to completing this transaction with you.

Try It！可以替換的字詞

around the country 在全國各地

in our city 在我們的城市中

in the state 在這個州內

around the globe 在全球各地

we know 我們所認識的

- - - - - - -

我們已經將您的價格和產品品質與市場上其他供應商的進行比較，並確定您提供的價格是最優惠的。我們已準備好要進行採購。我想預訂 300 個單位，運送至我們在紐約的倉庫。我相信彼此都同意每單位 450 美元的價格吧？期待與您完成此交易。

compare A with B 比較 A 和 B　suppliers 供應商　warehouse 倉庫，大型零售店　complete 完成
transaction 交易

✉ sample 259

Dear ⌐‾‾‾‾‾¬

I'd like to go ahead and make an initial order of 20 units of product #1205. Please send me an invoice for the total amount including shipping and insurance. I'll arrange for payment as soon as the delivery has been finished.

Thank you.

Try It！可以替換的字詞

including freight and handling
包括運送和搬運費

in duplicate 一式兩份

by email 以電子郵件

as soon as possible 盡快

and send a copy to my secretary
並將副本寄給我秘書

- - - - - - -

我想繼續進行，並首訂 20 件 ＃1205 的產品。請寄給我一張總金額的發票，包括運費和保險。交貨完成後我會盡快安排付款事宜。謝謝。

initial 最初的　total amount 總金額　insurance 保險

✉ **sample 260**

Dear [_____]

I'm writing to let you know that we've decided to purchase the iPhone cases we **discussed** (model #1532). We'd like to start with an order of 500 units. I can arrange payment once you've provided me with an invoice.

Thank you.

- - - - - - - - - - - -

我寫這封信是要讓您知道，我們已經決定購買我們討論過的 iPhone 外殼（型號 #1532）。我們要先訂購 500 個。一旦您提供發票給我時，我就可以安排付款事宜。謝謝。

purchase 購買　provide A with B 提供 B 物給 A

✉ sample 261

Dear ┌──────────┐

I'd like to place an order for 50 of the RX-9s. We'll be paying by credit card. The account number and expiration date are below. We'd like the express shipping option, which should get the order to us by the 14th. Let me know if there are any problems.

Thanks,

- - - - - - - -

我想訂購 50 個 RX-9。我們會以信用卡付款。卡號和有效日期如下。我們要選擇速遞方式，可以讓我們在14日之前收到訂貨。請讓我知道是否有任何問題。

cheapest 最便宜的
fastest 最快的
overnight 隔夜就到的
certified 有公信力的
courier 送遞急件的

place an order 下訂單　credit card 信用卡　account number 帳號　expiration date 截止日期
express 快速的，快遞的　option 選項

✉ sample 262

Dear ┌──────────┐

We're ready to make an order. We want 150 units of the X51. We'll make payment as soon as you confirm the order. Let me know what I need to do to expedite the shipping process.

Thanks,

- - - - - - - -

我們已經準備好要下訂單了。我們想要 150 個 X51。我們會在您確認訂單後立即付款。讓我知道我還需要做什麼，以加快運送過程。謝謝。

authenticate 驗收
substantiate 證實
double-check 複核
verify 核對
endorse 批註

make an order 下訂單　unit（成品的）單件，單位　make payment 支付　expedite 加快處理

✉ sample 263

Dear [..........]

I'd like to place an order for 200 bolts of fabric #2342. Ideally, we would like to receive the order by the 18th of this month. Let me know if that would be possible. We will **arrange** payment once you have confirmed the order.

Thank you,

- - - - - - - -

我想訂購 200 匹 #2342 的織品。理想情況下，我們希望在本月 18 日之前收到此批訂貨。請讓我知道這樣是否可行。一旦您確認訂單後，我們將安排付款。謝謝。

bolt（棉布等的）一匹 ideally 理想地 arrange payment 安排付款

Try It！可以替換的字詞

organize 整理
stop by for 停下來處理～
send a courier for 以快遞寄送～
discuss 討論
talk about 談論

✉ sample 264

Dear [..........]

I'm writing to place an order. We would like 400 units of item #523. What is the earliest we can expect shipment? Also, let me know if there is a **price break** for this bulk order.

Thanks,

- - - - - - - -

我寫這封信是要跟您訂貨。我們想要 400 件 #523 的商品。我們可以預期最快什麼時候出貨？如果您對這張大訂單有提供折扣，也請告知我們。謝謝。

would like 想要～ earliest 最早的時間 expect 期待 shipment 運輸，運送
price break（大訂單的）降價空間 bulk order 大量訂貨，大訂單

Try It！可以替換的字詞

discount 折扣
markdown 減價
lowering of the total price 降低總價
free shipping option 免運費選項
reduced shipping fee 減免運費

✉ sample 265

Dear [_____]

Could we get 100 of the G32 monitors? We'd like the express delivery option on those. That means we can expect delivery within two weeks, right? Let me know if you need any more information.

Thanks,

- - - - - - - -

我們可以訂購 100 台 G32 顯示器嗎？我們想以快遞的方式交付。也就是說，我們可以預期在兩週內收到貨，對吧？請讓我知道您是否需要更多其他資訊。謝謝。

option 選項　within 在～之內

Try It！可以替換的字詞

specifications 規格

specific data 特定資料

personal data 個人資料

shipping information 送貨資訊

payment information 付款資訊

✉ sample 266

Dear [⋯⋯⋯⋯]

I'm writing to let you know that I haven't **received** the product I ordered last Monday. **We were expecting delivery within three days. Could you look into this for me?**

Thanks,

- - - - - - - -

我寫這封信是想告訴你，我尚未收到上週一訂購的產品。原先我們預期的到貨時間是三天內。您可以幫我深入了解一下嗎？謝謝。

> delivery 送達，交付　look into 深入了解～

✉ sample 267

Dear [⋯⋯⋯⋯]

I'm writing because I have yet to receive the order I placed two weeks ago. Is it possible that it was lost in transit? Please check your ❶records and find out if it was sent out. It's ❷urgent that I receive the product by the end of the week.

Thank you for your prompt attention.

- - - - - - - -

我寫這封信的原因是，我尚未收到我兩週前訂購的貨品。是否有可能在轉運過程中丟失了？請檢查您的紀錄，看是否已發貨。我必須在這週末之前收到產品。感謝您的迅速回應。

> have yet to do... 還沒去做～　order 訂單，訂購的商品　in transit 在轉運過程中　find out 找出～
> urgent 緊急的　by the end of the week 在這週末之前

✉ sample 268

Dear _____

The product I ordered last week (order #23465) was supposed to have been shipped by Friday. It is Thursday and I still have seen no sign of delivery. Do you have a tracking number? If so, please send it to me.

Thank you for your attention in this matter.

- - - - - - - -

我上週訂購的產品（訂單編號＃23465）原訂在星期五前發貨。今天是星期四了，我仍未看到到貨的訊息。你有追蹤號碼嗎？如果有的話，請寄給我。感謝您對此事的關注。

be supposed to 應該～　sign 徵象　tracking number 追蹤號碼　matter 事件

✉ sample 269

Dear _____

I'm writing to inquire as to the whereabouts of the order I placed last week. I expected it to arrive on Tuesday, but it still isn't here. Could you please find out what the hold-up is and get back to me as soon as possible?

Thank you.

- - - - - - - -

我寫封信的目的是想詢問我上週訂貨的下落。我預計它會在星期二到貨，但還沒收到。可否請您找出延誤的原因，並儘快回覆我呢？謝謝。

as to 關於～　whereabouts 行蹤，下落　arrive 到達　hold-up 延誤，耽誤　get back to... 回覆～
as soon as possible 盡快

✉ sample 270

Dear _____

I'm writing regarding delivery of my order (#143554). I had understood that the express shipping option would be used in getting it to me, but if that were the case, it should have arrived days ago. Could you please ascertain what has happened to the shipment and get back to me?

Thank you for your attention.

- - - - - - - -

我寫這封信的目的是想了解關於我訂單（＃143554）運送的狀況。我知道寄送給我的方式是速運，但就此看來，它應該在幾天前就到貨。可否請您查明這批貨發生了什麼事並回覆我呢？謝謝您的關注。

regarding 關於～　express shipping 速運　option 選項　case 狀況　ascertain 確認，查明　shipment 貨運

Try It！可以替換的字詞

check 確認
determine 確定
establish 證實
learn 了解
discover 找到

✉ sample 271

┌╌╌╌╌╌╌┐
└╌╌╌╌╌╌┘

I'm afraid I'm going to have to cancel our order. We simply can't have such ❶unreliable shipping. In a ❷fast-paced business such as ours, fast turnaround time is essential.

Thanks.

- - - - - - -

Try It!可以替換的字詞

❶ unpredictable 不可預測的
erratic 不穩定的
fly-by-night 不可靠的
undependable 不可信賴的
untrustworthy 不值得信賴的

❷ speedy 講求速度的
constantly moving 不斷變化的
expedited 加速進行的
quick 迅速的
hurried 急切的

恐怕我不得不取消訂單了。我們根本無法接受如此不能信任的運輸方式。在我們這種快節奏的運作中，快速的整備時間至關重要。謝謝。

cancel 取消 unreliable 不能信任的 fast-paced 步調快速的 such as 諸如～
turnaround time 周轉時間、整備時間

✉ sample 272

Dear ┌╌╌╌╌╌╌┐
     └╌╌╌╌╌╌┘

Unfortunately, we are going to have to cancel our order. It turns out that we will not need the 200 units. I hope this isn't too much of an inconvenience. Please credit our account for the full amount.

Thank you for your understanding.

- - - - - - -

Try It!可以替換的字詞

refill our account with
將～匯回我們的帳戶
pay back 將～（金額等）退回
repay 償還
refund 退還～（款項）
reimburse 償還

不幸的是，我們必須取消訂單。事實上我們不需要這 200 單位的產品。我希望這不會造成太多不便。請將全部的貨款匯回我們的帳戶。謝謝您的理解。

turn out 結果是～ inconvenience 不便 credit 匯回～（賬戶） account 帳戶 full amount 全部金額

✉ sample 273

Dear _____

Due to unforeseen circumstances, I'm afraid we must cancel our order at this time. We may be able to reorder down the line if our situation changes. I'm sorry for any inconvenience this may cause you.

Thank you for your attention in this matter.

- - - - - - - -

由於不可預見的情況，恐怕我們必須在此時取消訂單。如果之後我們的狀況有所改變，我們可能會重新下訂單。對於此舉可能給您帶來的任何不便，我深表歉意。感謝您對此事的關注。

> unforeseen 不可預見的　circumstance 狀況　reorder 再訂購　situation 情況　change 變化
> attention 關注　matter 事件

Try It！可以替換的字詞

I'm sorry that 我很抱歉～

sadly 遺憾的是～

unfortunately 不幸的是～

regrettably 遺憾的是～

we are sorry to say 我們很遺憾必須説～

✉ sample 274

Dear _____

I'm writing to cancel our order (#2355). To be honest, we were able to find another supplier offering a much better deal. I hope we can work with you again in the future, but for now business realities have forced us to go in another direction.

Thank you.

- - - - - - - -

我寫這封信的目的是想取消我們的訂單（＃2355）。說實話，我們能夠找到另一家提供更優惠價格的供應商。我希望我們在未來能再次與您合作，但目前來說，商場上的現實迫使我們必須朝著另一個方向前進。謝謝。

> to be honest 坦白説　supplier 供應商　deal 交易，買賣　for now 目前　reality 現實　force 迫使
> direction 方向

Try It！可以替換的字詞

expectations 預期事件

actualities 現實

truths 事實

markets 市場

happenings 發生的事件

Try It! 可以替換的字詞

an issue 問題
a concern 憂慮
an alarm 警訊
a distress 苦惱
an anxiety 焦慮

This email is to notify you that we are canceling order #22333. Our inventory needs have changed, so we no longer need the product we ordered. Since this is within 24 hours of placing the order, I assume that this will not be a problem. Let me know if you have any questions.

Thank you.

- - - - - - - -

此封電子郵件旨在通知您,我們想要取消 #22333 的訂單。我們的庫存需求有所改變,因此我們不再需要這些已經下訂的產品。由於這是在下訂單後的 24 小時內,我想這不會造成問題。請讓我知道您是否有任何疑問。謝謝。

notify 通知　inventory 庫存,(管理中的)庫存品　need 需要,有~必要性　no longer 不再
assume(想當然地)認為,假定

取消訂購 ② Canceling the Order ② ▲

✉ sample 276

Hi, [_____]

I'm afraid I'm going to have to cancel the order. My boss has decided to go with another product, but he failed to let me know! I hope we can do business in the future. Sorry for wasting your time.

Thanks,

- - - - - - - -

恐怕我要取消這次訂購了。我的老闆已決定使用其他產品，但他沒有讓我知道！我希望我們將來還能有業務往來。抱歉浪費您的時間了。謝謝。

Try It！可以替換的字詞

try 試用
invest in 把錢投入
order 訂購
purchase 購買
choose 選擇

> cancel 取消　boss 老闆　go with 選擇～　fail to 未能～　do business 做生意　waste 浪費

✉ sample 277

Dear [_____]

I'm writing to inform you that I am canceling my order (#62346). Our current needs have unexpectedly changed, so we will no longer be in need of your product. I apologize for any inconvenience this causes. Please credit our account for the full amount of the order.

Thank you.

- - - - - - - -

我寫這封信的目的是想通知您，我將取消我的訂單（＃62346）。我們目前的需求狀況出乎意料地發生了變化，因此我們不再需要您的產品。如因此給您帶來任何不便，我深表歉意。請將該筆訂單匯款全額退回我們的帳戶。謝謝您。

Try It！可以替換的字詞

need 需要
want 想要
desire 渴望要
have a use for 需要
require 對～有需求

> inform...that 通知～（某人某事）　current 當前的　unexpectedly 出乎意料地　no longer 不再
> in need of 需要～　credit 把～歸於　account 帳戶　full amount 全部金額

✉ sample 278

Dear [............]

Unfortunately, I'm going to have to cancel the order I made yesterday. After I had made the order, I realized that I had made an inventory mistake, and that we do not currently need to replenish our supply. I'm sorry for inconveniencing you. If you could please cancel the order and credit our account, I would greatly appreciate it.

Thank you.

- - - - - - - -

不幸的是，我要取消昨天下的訂單了。在我下單後，我發現我在盤點時出了差錯，因此我們目前不需要補充用品。很抱歉給您帶來不便。麻煩您取消訂單並將款項匯回我們的帳戶，不勝感激。謝謝。

realize 了解 inventory 存貨清單，盤點 currently 現在 replenish 把～再備足
supply 供給，供應（品） inconvenience 造成～不便 greatly 非常地

Try It! 可以替換的字詞

a counting 一個會計上的
a clerical 一個文書的
a minor 一個次要的
a major 一個主要的
a supply 一個用品上的

✉ sample 279

Dear [............]

It looks like I'm not going to need that last order after all. I thought that my retail partners had sold a much larger volume than they had. I'm sorry to back out on you, but I'm going to have to cancel the order.

Thanks for understanding.

- - - - - - - -

看來我應該不需要那最後一筆訂單了。我原以為我的零售伙伴們銷量會遠超過其庫存量。我很抱歉未能對您允諾，但我不得不取消這筆訂單。謝謝您的理解。

after all 終究 retail 零售的 much 大量的 volume（生產、交易等的）量
back out 退出（協議、計劃等）

Try It! 可以替換的字詞

advertised 廣告
vended 出售
traded 交易
retailed 零售
wholesaled 批發

✉ sample 280

Dear _____

I'm writing to cancel order #61616. Our inventory needs have unexpectedly changed, so we will no longer need your product. As this cancellation falls within the 24-hour time limit, I assume this will not be a trouble. Please refund the full amount.

Thank you.

- - - - - - - -

我寫這封信的目的是想取消 #61616 的訂單。我們的庫存需求意外地出現變數，因此我們不再需要您的產品。由於取消時間在 24 小時的限期內，我想這不會帶來麻煩。請退回全部款項。謝謝。

change 改變　cancellation 取消　fall 在～（一個特定的時期或時間）　within 在～範圍內
time limit 期限，時間限制　assume（想當然地）認為

Try It! 可以替換的字詞

grace period 寬限期

return frame 退訂期限

boundary 限期

cutoff point 截止時間

time constraint 時間限制

推薦類似產品 Recommending a Similar Product ▲

✉ sample 281

Dear ⸺⸺⸺

I'm afraid the product you ❶ordered is out of stock. It's quite popular and it may be several weeks before it's available. I'd like to recommend the RL-10. It's ❷virtually identical to the RX-9, and it's slightly cheaper. If you'd like, I can have that shipped to you by the end of the week. Let me know what you want to do.

Sorry for the inconvenience.

- - - - - - - -

我很抱歉您所下訂的產品正缺貨中。這項產品非常受歡迎，且需要再過幾週才會有貨。我想推薦 RL-10。它幾乎與 RX-9 相同，而且便宜一點。如果您要的話，我們可以在本週末之前出貨給您。不知您意下如何。帶來不便，深表歉意。

out of stock 缺貨　recommend 推薦　virtually 實際上　identical to... 與～相同　slightly 稍微地　cheaper 較便宜的

✉ sample 282

Dear ⸺⸺⸺

There has been an issue with your order. Unfortunately, the product you placed an order for has been discontinued. We do have another version, produced by another company, in the same style and color. Would you like us to send that out to you? Let me know if you need any more information.

Thank you.

- - - - - - - -

您的訂單出現了問題。很遺憾告訴您，您所訂的產品已經停產。我們還有另一款，是由另一家公司生產的，有相同的款式和顏色。要不要我們寄這款給您呢？若您需要更多資訊，請讓我知道。謝謝。

discontinue 中斷　version 版本，款式　produce 生產

✉ sample 283

Dear _____

Due to a surge in ❶demand, the item you requested is currently unavailable. However, I can recommend another product that fulfills the same need. The G33 monitor has the same resolution and screen size and is available in the same range of colors. Let me know if you'd like to ❷substitute it for your original order.

Thank you.

- - - - - - - -

由於需求激增，您訂購的產品目前無法供應。不過，我可以推薦另一款可以滿足您相同需求的產品。G33 顯示器具有相同的解析度及螢幕尺寸，而且也有多種顏色可供選擇。請讓我知道您是否有意願用這產品取代您原來的訂購。謝謝。

surge 激增，猛衝　demand 需求　fulfill 滿足　need 需求　resolution 解析度
substitute A for B 用 A 代替 B　original 原本的

✉ sample 284

Dear _____

I'm writing regarding your order of 7/23/18. It appears that the pattern of fabric that you ordered is no longer available from our suppliers. Below are links to a few alternative fabrics with similar patterns. Take a look at them and let me know if one of them might be acceptable to you.

I'm sorry for any inconvenience.

- - - - - - - -

這封信是關於您 2018 年 7 月 23 日的訂單。我們的供應商不再供應您所訂的布料樣式。以下是一些具有類似樣式的布料連結網址。請看一下，並讓我知道您是否中意其中任何一件。造成任何不便，深表歉意。

regarding 關於～　It appears that 目前看似～　pattern 圖案　fabric 布料　no longer 不再
alternative 替代的　similar 類似的　acceptable 可以接受的

✉ sample 285

Dear ┌----------┐

In our last conversation you expressed interest in the V-2 model MP3 player. Unfortunately, the V-2 is on back order for the foreseeable future. There is another MP3 player with the same features (and a slightly lower price) that we do have in stock. Attached are a description and some images. Let me know if you'd be interested in ordering it.

I look forward to hearing from you.

Try It! 可以替換的字詞

extras 額外功能

options 功能選項

add-ons 附加功能

characteristics 特色

optional extras 選擇性附加功能

- - - - - - - -

在我們上次談話中，您表示對於 V-2 型 MP3 播放器感興趣。不幸的是，在可預見的未來中，V-2 是會缺貨的。但目前有現貨的是另一款具有相同功能（且價格略低）的 MP3 播放器。隨附一份說明書和幾張圖片。請讓我知道您是否有興趣訂購。期待您的佳音。

express 表達　back order 缺貨，延期交貨　foreseeable 可預見的　in stock 有現貨的，有庫存的 description 描述，說明

運送與交貨 Shipping & Delivery

要求寄送方式 Requesting Delivery Option ▲

✉ sample 286

I'd like to arrange for delivery of the product. Do you offer overnight shipping? We need to get this as soon as possible. Let me know the earliest you can ship it.

Thanks,

- - - - - - - -

Try It！可以替換的字詞

express 速遞的
nonstop 直達的
prompt 快速的
next-day 隔日送達的
two-day 兩天的

我想安排這項產品的交貨事宜。你提供通宵速遞的服務嗎？我們必須盡快拿到產品。請讓我知道您最早什麼時候可以出貨。謝謝。

> arrange for 為～作安排　overnight 整夜 的　as soon as possible 盡快　the earliest 最早的

✉ sample 287

Dear

I'm writing to request my order to be delivered via DHL. We have a standing account with them, so I'd like to apply the shipping costs there. Below is the account number to bill. Let me know if you have any questions.

Thank you.

- - - - - - - -

Try It！可以替換的字詞

a permanent 恆常的
a long-term 長期的
an established 固定的
a stable 穩定的
a long-lasting 持久的

我寫這封信是想要求我訂購的產品透過 DHL 運送。我們彼此有長期的客戶關係，所以我會在那邊支付運費。以下是報帳用的帳號。請讓我知道您是否有任何疑問。謝謝。

> request A to-V 要求 A（～去做某事）　via 經由～　standing 常設的　apply 使適用　shipping cost 運費
> account number 客戶編號（分配給重要客戶、公司等的字母和數字等號碼，以便在記帳過程中作帳）
> bill 給～開帳單

✉ sample 288

Dear ⌜‥‥‥‥‥⌝

Regarding delivery of my order, would it be possible to use an express option? I would like to receive the product by the end of the week. Let me know whether this can be done and what the cost would be.

Thank you for your attention.

- - - - - - - -

關於我訂購的產品運送方式，可否選擇速遞？我想在本週末前收到產品。請讓我知道這是否可行以及運費金額。謝謝你的關注。

regarding 關於～ possible 可能的 express 快速的 whether 是否～ attention 關注

✉ sample 289

Dear ⌜‥‥‥‥‥⌝

I'm writing to request that my order be shipped. I know that we had discussed the pick-up option, but I think it will be more cost-effective for us to go with a shipping company. Let me know what information you need from me to have the order delivered.

Thank you.

- - - - - - - -

我寫這封信的目的是想要求我訂購的產品進行運送。我知道我們討論過用小貨車運送的方式，但我認為選擇貨運公司會更節省成本。關於運貨部分，請讓我知道我這邊還需要提供您什麼樣的資訊。謝謝您。

request that 要求～ pick-up 小貨車運送 cost-effective 節省成本的 go with 選擇～
have ~ delivered 將～（貨品等）寄送

✉ sample 290

Dear [＿＿＿＿＿]

I would like to have my order shipped to Los Angeles if possible. I would like to have it shipped via ground in order to minimize costs. I do not have a strict deadline so it's fine if it takes a little longer. Let me know what my options are and we will make the necessary arrangements.

Thank you.

我想將我訂購的產品寄送到洛杉磯 ─ 如果可能的話。我想以陸運方式運送，以將成本壓至最低。我沒有一定要在哪一天送達，所以多花一點時間無所謂。請讓我知道我有哪些選擇方式，以便我們進行必要的安排。謝謝。

if possible 如果可能的話　ground 陸路的　in order to 為了～　minimize 將～降至最低　strict 嚴格的 deadline 截止日期　if it takes a little longer 如果需要花更多時間　arrangement 安排

詢問交貨日期 **Requesting Delivery Date**   ▲

sample 291

Dear _____

I'm writing to enquire as to the delivery date for my order (#6164). My plans for ❶distributing the product will depend upon when I receive it, so please give me as ❷accurate a date as possible.

Thank you for your help.

- - - - - - - -

Try It！可以替換的字詞

❶ giving out 分發
allocating 分配
sharing 分配
dispensing 配發
allotting 分配

❷ precise 精確的
correct 正確的
exact 準確的
true 真實的
perfect 絕對正確的

我寫這封信是想詢問我訂單（＃6164）的交貨日期。我產品分銷的計畫取決於我何時收到它們，所以請盡可能準確地給我一個日期。謝謝您的幫助。

enquire 詢問，打聽　as to 關於～　delivery 交貨　distribute 分銷　depend upon 取決於～ accurate 準確的

✉ sample 292

Dear _____

I would like to get a date for delivery of my recent order. I know that a precise date cannot always be given, but I would appreciate the closest estimation you can make. It would help me greatly to have this information.

I appreciate your assistance in this matter.

- - - - - - - -

Try It！可以替換的字詞

guess 推測
estimate 估價
approximation 概算
educated guess 據理的推測
ballpark figure 粗略數字

我想知道我最近訂單的交貨日期。我知道有時候確切日期是難以得知的，但如果您能告訴我最接近的的預估時間，我將不勝感激。能獲得這消息對我來說會很有幫助。感謝您對此事的幫助。

not always 並不總是～　appreciate 感激　closest 最接近的　estimation 估計，預計　assistance 幫助

✉ sample 293

Dear ⸻

Would it be possible to find out the delivery date for my order? It shipped earlier in the week and I was not given a tracking number. If you could get this information for me, I would really appreciate it.

Thank you.

- - - - - - - -

是否可能查詢一下我訂單的交貨日期呢？送貨時間是在本週稍早時，但我沒有收到貨件追蹤號碼。要是您幫我取得這項資訊，我會非常感激。謝謝您。

find out 找出～　ship 裝運，運送　tracking number （貨物）追蹤號碼

Try It！可以替換的字詞

goods 貨品
items 品項
products 產品
computer equipment 電腦設備
office supplies 辦公用品

✉ sample 294

Dear ⸻

I'm writing to see if you can give me the delivery date for my most recent order. I'd like to be able to plan my week around receipt of the products. If you could let me know, I'd be grateful.

Thank you for your help.

- - - - - - - -

我寫這封信的目的是想請問您，能否告知我最近一筆訂單的交貨日期。我希望能夠大約在收到產品的時候，排定我一週的行程。如果您能讓我知道，我將不勝感激。謝謝您的幫助。

see if 看看是否～　be able to 能夠～　receipt 收到　let me know 讓我知道

Try It！可以替換的字詞

indebted 感激的
obliged 感激的
thankful 感謝的
appreciative 感謝的
more than glad 非常高興

✉ sample 295

Dear _____

Is there any chance that I could get the delivery date for my order from you? I can't seem to see it anywhere on the invoice or in our previous correspondence. I'd appreciate getting this information as soon as possible.

Thank you.

- - - - - - - -

Try It！可以替換的字詞

emails 電子郵件
messages 訊息
discussions 討論
posts 貼文
communications 溝通，交流

我是否可能從您這邊獲知我訂單的交貨日期呢？我似乎無法在這張發票，或是我們之前的通信中看到這道訊息。若能讓我盡快收到這項訊息，我會非常感激。謝謝您。

chance 機會　anywhere 在任何地方　invoice 發票，送貨單　previous 以前的　correspondence 通信

要求準時交貨 Requesting Timely Delivery on Time ▲

✉ sample 296

Dear _____

I'm writing to ask you to ensure that my order is delivered on time. I have had some issues with other suppliers being late with deliveries, and I want to confirm that October 25th will be the date on which my order arrives. I'm sorry to be so insistent, but it is really quite important.

Thank you for your attention in this matter.

Try It！可以替換的字詞

obsessive 執念的
paranoid 偏執的
worried 擔心的
adamant 堅定的
assertive 果斷的

- - - - - - - -

我寫這封信的目的是想麻煩您確認我的訂單準時到貨。我與其他供應商曾有一些交貨延遲的問題，所以我想確認我的訂貨是否可於 10 月 25 日到貨。我很抱歉如此急迫要求，但這非常重要。感謝您對此事的關注。

> ensure 確保　on time 準時　supplier 供應商　confirm 確認　insistent 堅持的，急切的

✉ sample 297

Dear _____

I just wanted to remind you that delivery for my order should be made on the 3rd of November. It is important that I receive the shipment no later than the 3rd. I will be arranging for the order to be broken up and shipped to other distributors, so timing is essential. Let me know if there are any problems.

Thank you for your assistance.

Try It！可以替換的字詞

timeliness 及時
promptness 及時性
coordination 配合
scheduling 行程安排
time management 時間管理

- - - - - - - -

我只是想提醒您，我的訂貨應於 11 月 3 日送達。重要的是，不能在 3 號之後才收到貨。我得安排細分這批訂貨，並送給其他經銷商，因此時間點相當重要。請讓我知道是否有任何問題。謝謝您的協助。

> remind 提醒　shipment 貨品　no later than... 不遲於～　arrange 安排　break up 細分，拆開～
> distributor 經銷商

✉ sample 298

Dear _____

I'm getting in touch with you to ask that you do everything in your power to ensure that my product arrives here in New York on time. I know that there can sometimes be unforeseen difficulties in meeting deadlines, but it is quite important that this particular shipment be delivered before the 4th.

I appreciate your help in this.

- - - - - - - -

我聯繫您的目的是想拜託您盡一切力量，確保我的產品準時送達紐約這邊。我知道在趕上期限前，有時會遇到一些無法預知的困難，但是這件貨物務必在 4 號前送達。感謝您對此事的協助。

> get in touch 取得聯繫　unforeseen 未能預見的　deadlines 截止日期

Try It！可以替換的字詞

unwelcome 討人厭的
unexpected 料想不到的
surprising 意外的
startling 令人吃驚的
out-of-the-blue
突如其來的，出人意料的

✉ sample 299

Dear _____

I hope everything is going well at your end. I just wanted to touch base and make sure that delivery of my most recent order is on schedule. It's really important that I receive the shipment on time, so I'd appreciate it if you could give this order a little extra attention.

Thanks for the help,

- - - - - - - -

我希望您那邊的事情一切順利。我跟您聯繫是想確定我最近訂貨是否會按照預定時間交付。我如期收到貨品這件事情非常重要，所以如果您可以再多關注一下這張訂單的進度，我會非常感激。謝謝幫助。

> go well 進展順利　at your end 在您那一方，貴方　touch base 聯繫，聯絡　make sure 確定
> on schedule 按預定時間

Try It！可以替換的字詞

consideration 考慮，關心
notice 注意
thought 關心
awareness 警覺性
time 時間

✉ sample 300

Dear [ ]

I'm writing to ask for your help in ensuring the punctual delivery of my order. In the past there have been some delays in shipping, and I really need this order to be here on time. If you can help make sure everything goes according to schedule, I would really appreciate.

Thanks,

- - - - - - - -

Try It!可以替換的字詞

goes off as planned 按計劃進行
runs on track 穩定持續進行中
is perfect 是完美的
runs smoothly 進行順利
sticks to the agenda 照表操課

我寫這封信是想請求您協助確認我的訂單可以準時交付。在過去，運貨都會出現一些延誤狀況，但我這次訂貨一定得準時送達。要是您能協助確認一切依照預定行程進行，我會非常感激。謝謝。

punctual 準時的　in the past 在過去　according to 依照～

產品配送通知 Product Shipment Notification ▲

✉ sample 301

Dear [............]

I've arranged to have the product sent out today. It'll be shipped overnight, so you can expect it by tomorrow at the end of business. Let me know if for some reason it doesn't arrive.

Thanks,

- - - - - - - -

今天我已安排出貨，將在隔日送達，因此您預計可以在明天下班前收到。如因某些原因貨品沒有送達，請讓我知道。謝謝。

> arrange 安排　overnight 整夜的，夜間的　expect 預計　at the end of business 下班時
> for some reason 基於於某種原因

Try It！可以替換的字詞

appear 出現
come 到達
get delivered 送到
turn up 出現
get there 送到那裡

✉ sample 302

Dear [............]

❶Below is the tracking number for your order, which was shipped this morning. It should arrive within the next five to seven days. If you have any questions or concerns, please feel free to ❷reach out to me.

Thank you for your business.

- - - - - - - -

以下是您訂單的（貨品），這筆訂單已於今天上午配送。它應該在會五至七天內到達。如果您有任何問題或疑慮，請儘管與我聯繫。感謝您的惠顧。

> tracking number 追蹤號碼　within... 在～範圍內　five to seven days 五至七天　concern 關心的事
> feel free to 隨時，儘管　reach out to... 請別人幫忙

Try It！可以替換的字詞

❶Following 以下的
What follows 下列所述的
Attached 隨附的
At the bottom of this letter 在這封信的最後
Enclosed 附上的

❷reach 聯繫上
contact 聯絡
return a call to（未接獲而）回電話給～
buzz 給～（某人）打電話
send for 派人來（聯繫我）

✉ sample 303

Dear _____

I am happy to inform you that your product has been shipped on schedule. You should be receiving it on the 31st. If for any reason it doesn't appear, please get in touch with me.

It's a pleasure doing business with you.

- - - - - - - -

我很高興通知您，您的產品已按照預定行程進行裝運。您應可於 31 日收到。如果因任何原因而無法到貨，請與我聯繫。與您合作非常愉快。

inform 通知　on schedule 按照行程　for any reason 因任何原因　appear 出現
get in touch with 與～取得聯繫

✉ sample 304

Dear _____

I'm writing to notify you that your order has been shipped. You can expect delivery by the end of the week. If you have any problems, please feel free to contact me.

Thank you.

- - - - - - - -

我寫這封信是想通知您，您的訂單已發貨。預計您可於本週末前收到。如果您有任何問題，請儘管與我聯繫。謝謝。

notify 通知　order 訂單，訂貨　expect 預期　delivery 遞送

✉ sample 305

Dear _____

Below you will find the tracking number for your items, that were shipped **this morning**. As you opted for express delivery, you can expect to receive them within the next 48 hours. If there should be any delays, please don't hesitate to contact me.

Thank you.

- - - - - - - -

以下您可以看到今天早上您訂貨的裝運追蹤號碼。由於您選擇以快遞寄送，應可於 48 小時內到貨。如果有任何延誤狀況，請儘管與我聯繫。謝謝。

opt for 選擇～　express delivery 快遞　delay 延誤　hesitate 猶豫

last night 昨晚

earlier today 今天早些時候

yesterday 昨天

at noon today 今天中午

one hour ago 一個小時之前

確認配送狀況 Confirming Shipment ▲

✉ sample 306

Dear [_____]

I have the shipping information you are asking for. It appears we sent three **boxes** of product to you on Tuesday of last week. Can you double-check that you have not received it yet? If not, we may be able to resend them.

We always value your business.

- - - - - - - -

Try It ! 可以替換的字詞

pallets（裝卸、搬運貨物用的）貨板
different sets 不同的套組
crates（可搬運的）條板箱
truckloads 一貨車的運量
specific samples 特定樣品

我有您要的貨運資訊，上面顯示我們上週二寄送三箱產品給您。你可否再次確認是否尚未收到？果真如此，我們會再重新寄送給您。我們一向重視與貴公司的往來。

it appears (that...) 看起來～　double-check 再檢查一遍　yet 還沒～　resend 再寄

✉ sample 307

Dear [_____]

Can you update me on my **items**? Have they been shipped yet? My company really needs them by Thursday. Please send me tracking information if you have that.

Thank you for your attention.

- - - - - - - -

Try It ! 可以替換的字詞

orders 訂單
containers 貨櫃
things 東西
electronics 電子產品
cables 電纜

您能告訴我關於我品項的最新狀況如何嗎？已經進行裝運了嗎？週四前，貨必須送達我們公司才行。請將貨運追蹤資訊寄給我 — 如果您有的話。感謝您的關注。

update 給予～最新資訊　item 品項　track 追蹤

✉ sample 308

Dear 〔⋯⋯⋯⋯〕

We are unable to provide tracking information about your shipment at this time. I will be able to get that to you by the end of the day tomorrow. If this is an inconvenience I apologize.

Thank you for your understanding.

Try It！可以替換的字詞

sometime 某個時間點

early 早些時候

late 晚一點

the middle of ～的中午

noon 中午

- - - - - - - -

目前我們無法提供您貨物寄送的追蹤資訊。我明天結束之前可以給您消息。若造成您任何不便，深表歉意。謝謝您的理解。

> be unable to 無法～　shipment 裝貨，運送，貨物　inconvenience 不便　apologize 道歉 understanding 理解，諒解

✉ sample 309

Dear 〔⋯⋯⋯⋯〕

I'd like to tell you that I sent your papers via certified mail this morning. The postal agency tells me that you will receive them tomorrow. I will check to see that you have gotten them.

Sincerely

Try It！可以替換的字詞

documents 文件

articles 物件

records 檔案紀錄

certificates 證書

deeds（產權的）契約

- - - - - - - -

我想讓您知道今天早上我已經用掛號寄出您的文件。郵政機構告訴我，您明天就會收到。我會確認您是否已收到。此致。

> via 經由～　certified mail 掛號郵件　postal agency 郵政機構　check to see that 檢查以確認～

✉ sample 310

Dear ┌──────────┐

Our company shipped out your products this morning. You should receive them next week. If you don't have them by Friday, please let me know and we will look into it.

Thank you.

- - - - - - - -

我們公司今天早上將您的產品寄出了。您應該下週就會收到。如果您週五前沒有收到，請告訴我，我們會對此深入了解。謝謝。

> ship out（用船、飛機、貨車等）運送　receive 收到　by... 在～（截止時間）之前
> look into 深入了解～

詢問送貨延遲的狀況 Inquiring About Delivery Delay ▲

✉ sample 311

It's been three days and we still haven't received the shipment. Do you have any idea what's ❶causing the delay? We really need to get this by the weekend, so please let me know ❷what's going on.

Thanks,

- - - - - - - -

Try It！可以替換的字詞

❶ the reason for ～的原因
the origin of ～的起源
the root of ～的根源
the basis for ～的依據
the justification for ～的理由

❷ your thoughts 您的想法
your ideas 您的主意
any changes you can make
您可以做的任何改變
any updates 任何最新資訊
what your team has decided
您的團隊決定的事

已經三天了，我們仍未收到貨。您知道造成延誤的原因為何嗎？事實上我們必須在週末前拿到這批貨，所以請讓我知道目前狀況如何。謝謝。

It's been three days 已經三天了　shipment 貨物，裝載，運輸　cause 造成　delay 延遲

✉ sample 312

Dear ⬚

I'm afraid we have a little problem. As you know, I chose express delivery for my order, which should have guaranteed delivery within 48 hours. Unfortunately, three days have passed, and it still has not been delivered. Please get in touch with me ASAP so that we can resolve this problem.

Thank you.

- - - - - - - -

Try It！可以替換的字詞

I wanted to notify you that
我想通知您～
I'm upset that 我對於～感到不悅
I'm unhappy that 我對於～很不高興
I'm concerned that 我很擔心～
I'm worried because 我很擔心，因為～

我恐怕我們遇到一點問題了。如您所知，我選擇以快遞方式運送我的訂貨，這本應保證可以 48 小時內到貨。不幸的是，三天過去了，貨還是沒到。請盡快與我聯繫，以便我們可以解決此問題。謝謝。

express delivery 快遞　guarantee 保證　get in touch with 聯繫～　ASAP 盡快　resolve 解決

sample 313

Dear ....

In your previous email you gave the delivery date for my order as the 31st. It is now the 3rd, and I still have not received it. Could you please find out what happened and get back to me?

I appreciate your assistance in this matter.

- - - - - - - -

在您之前發送的電子郵件中，您表示我訂貨的運送日期為 31 號。現在已經是 3 號了，但我仍未收到。可以請您能查明發生什麼事，並給我回覆嗎？感謝您對此事的幫助。

> previous 先前的　find out 查明～，找出～　happen 發生　get back to... 再和～聯繫
> assistance 協助，幫助　matter 事件

Try It！可以替換的字詞

with this problem 對於這個問題
with the delay 對於這次的延遲
in a timely manner 及時地
and patience 以及耐心
and hard work 以及辛勞

sample 314

Dear ....

It seems that there has been some problem with the shipping of my order. I expected delivery by the end of last week, but it is now Wednesday and it still has not arrived. Would you be so kind as to look into it for me? I would appreciate it very much.

Thank you.

- - - - - - - -

我訂單的運送似乎出了一點問題。我預計這批貨上週結束前就會到，但現在是星期三了，卻仍未到貨。您可以好心幫我看一下怎麼回事嗎？我會非常感激的。謝謝。

> It seems that 似乎～　expect 期望　kind 仁慈的　so A as to 如 A 一般地去做～

Try It！可以替換的字詞

helpful enough 全力幫助
cooperative enough 樂易幫助
supportive enough 全力支援
ready to lend a hand 準備伸出援助之手
nice enough 相當好心的

✉ sample 315

Dear [_____]

I'm writing to enquire about the whereabouts of my order. I received an email with a tracking number ten days ago. However, the tracking information has not been updated in several days, and I still have not received my order. Could you please investigate it for me?

Thank you.

- - - - - - - -

我寫這封信是想詢問我訂貨的下落。十天前我收到了一封附有追蹤號碼的電子郵件。但是，追蹤資訊已數日沒有更新了，我仍然沒有收到我的訂貨。您能幫我調查一下嗎？謝謝。

enquire 詢問（= inquire） whereabouts 下落，蹤跡 track 追蹤～ several 幾個的 investigate 調查

Try It！可以替換的字詞

explore what is going on
探究發生了什麼

probe the situation 探查該情況

examine it 檢查它

study the situation 研究該情況

inquire into this problem
調查這個問題

✉ sample 316

I'm writing to let you know that we still haven't received the order yet. It's vital that we get it by the end of business Friday. Please see that the order is expedited.

Thanks for your prompt attention.

- - - - - - - -

我寫這封信是要讓您知道，我們仍未收到訂貨。我們週五下班前得收到貨，這很重要。請加速處理這筆訂單。感謝您即刻關注。

order 訂單，訂貨　vital 不可取代的，重要的　expedite 加速　prompt 即刻的　attention 注意

✉ sample 317

Dear ⌐ ⌐

We are a little ❶concerned about not having received a tracking number yet. If the shipment is not sent out now, there will be no ❷hope of us receiving it by the 13th. Please do what you can to get the order shipped as soon as possible.

Thank you.

- - - - - - - -

我們尚未收到訂貨追蹤號碼，感到有點擔心。如果現在都還沒出貨，我們就沒有希望在 13 號之前收到訂貨。請盡您所能盡速處理這筆訂貨。

concerned 擔心的　tracking number 追蹤號碼　shipment 裝貨，運送，貨物
be no hope of 沒有希望可以～

✉ sample 318

Dear _____

I see that our order has still not been shipped. It's essential that we receive the order by the 24th of the month. Please do whatever is necessary to make delivery promptly.

Thank you for your attention.

我發現我們的訂單仍未出貨。我們必須在本月 24 日之前收到訂貨。請採取一切必要措施，盡快交貨。感謝您的關注。

essential 必要的，非常重要的　whatever 無論如何　delivery 交貨，遞送，交付　promptly 即時地

Try It！可以替換的字詞

punctually 按時地
at the appointed time 在約定的時間
rapidly 迅速地
without delay 沒有延誤地
speedily 迅速地

✉ sample 319

Dear _____

We're on a bit of a tight schedule, so it's imperative that we receive our order on time. Please take whatever steps are necessary to get our shipment out today. I'm sure you understand that delays on this order will affect our decisions on which supplier to use on future orders.

Thank you.

我們的行程有點緊迫，因此我們一定得準時收到訂貨。請採取一切必要措施，在今天出我們的貨。我相信您了解，這批訂貨的延誤會影響到未來我們訂貨時，採用哪家供應商的決定。謝謝您。

tight 緊迫的　imperative 迫切的，絕對必要的　take steps 採取步驟　delay 延遲　affect 影響

Try It！可以替換的字詞

strict 緊迫的
stringent 迫切的
harsh 嚴格的
firm 不可變更的
severe 艱難的

✉ sample 320

Dear ⸢⸤⸥⸤⸥⸤⸣

We're getting a little worried about our last order. We need to accept delivery by the 20th in order to have the products ready for sale. If there is a problem, please tell us what we can do to help facilitate delivery. We're counting on you for this order.

Thanks for your help.

- - - - - - - -

我們對於最後一筆訂貨有點擔心。我們必須在 20 號前收到貨物來備好產品以出售。如果有問題，請告訴我們，我們可以做什麼以利於交貨。我們信賴您可以處理好這筆訂單。謝謝您的幫助。

accept 收到　have... ready for sale 將～準備好以待售　facilitate 有利於～　count on 指望～

Try It！可以替換的字詞

get the product moving
繼續處理這產品相關事宜

us receive our order 我們收到訂貨

obtain our products 拿到我們的產品

get the ball rolling 使事情有效解決

get things moving 讓事情有所進展

✉ sample 321

Dear ....

I'm terribly sorry for the ❶delay in shipping. We've had a lot of ❷turnover at our warehouse recently, and unfortunately this has caused a backlog of orders. We'll have your product shipped by the end of business tomorrow.

Thanks for understanding,

- - - - - - - -

Try It！可以替換的字詞

❶ stoppage 堵塞
wait 耽擱
hold-up 延誤
postponement 延遲
suspension 中止

❷ personnel issues 人事問題
firings and hirings 解雇和雇用
new hires 新進員工
accidents 事故
management issues 管理問題

對於交貨的延誤，我感到非常抱歉。我們最近倉庫人員有很大的異動，且不幸的是，導致訂單積壓的情況。我們將在明天下班前將您的產品出貨。感謝您的理解。

terribly 非常地　delay 延誤　turnover 人員變動　warehouse 倉庫，大賣場之類的倉庫　recently 最近　backlog 積壓，停滯

✉ sample 322

Dear ....

Unfortunately, we've had a problem with our shipping company and this has resulted in a delay in the delivery of your order. Please accept my apologies for this trouble. We are working to expedite shipment.

Thank you for your patience in this matter.

- - - - - - - -

Try It！可以替換的字詞

hassle 困擾
bothersome experience 麻煩的經歷
occurrence 發生的事
inconvenience 不便
disturbance 混亂

不幸的是，我們和運輸公司間有點問題，而這導致訂單交付延遲。請接受我為此麻煩事件的致歉。我們正在努力加快運送中。感謝您對此事的耐心等待。

result in 導致～　accept 接受　apology 道歉　trouble 棘手的問題　expedite 加速　patience 耐心

✉ sample 323

Dear _____

I'm sorry to inform you that there has been a delay in the shipment of your order. Because of a clerical error in our inventory control software, we have had to transfer part of your order from another warehouse. This delay should be brief. Please contact me with any concerns.

Thank you for your patience.

- - - - - - - -

我很抱歉要通知您，您訂單的出貨延遲了。由於我們庫存控制軟體中一個文書的錯誤，您訂貨的一部分，我們不得不從另一倉庫來出貨。此延遲問題很快就會得到解決。如有任何疑慮，請與我聯繫。謝謝您的耐心等待。

inform... that 通知～（某人某事） clerical 文書上的 error 失誤 control 管理，控制 transfer 轉移 contact 聯繫～

✉ sample 324

Dear _____

I'm writing to let you know that there will be a slight delay in shipping of your order (#23452). We always strive to deliver all of our customers' orders with as much speed and efficiency as possible, but from time to time an unforeseeable circumstance arises, which slows down the process. Please accept my apologies for any inconvenience this causes.

Let me know if you have any questions.

- - - - - - - -

我寫這封信是為了讓您知道您的訂單（＃23452）發貨時間會略有延遲。我們始終致力於以最快的速度和最佳的效率，交付所有客戶的訂貨，但有時會出現不可預期的情況，讓這流程速度變慢。如造成任何不便，請接受我的致歉。請讓我知道您是否有任何疑問。

slight 輕微的 strive to 努力於～ deliver 遞送 as much A as possible 盡可能如 A 地 efficiency 效率 from time to time 有時候 arise 出現 cause 導致

✉ sample 325

Dear _____

I'm sorry there has been a delay in shipment. Unforeseen circumstances have interfered with our ability to get our orders out on time. We know that time is an important factor in your business and we will work to fix the situation.

Thank you for your understanding.

- - - - - - - -

對於出貨的延遲，我表示歉意。無法預期的情況使得我們無法準時將我們訂單處理完成。我們知道時間在您的行業中是一項重要條件，我們將努力改善這樣的狀況。謝謝您的理解。

---

remedy 補救
clear up 解決
resolve 解決
deal with 處理
make better 改善

---

unforeseen 無法預期的　circumstance 情況　interfere with 妨礙～　ability 能力　factor 因素

✉ sample **326**

Dear _____

I apologize that you received the ❶wrong order. There was a mix-up at the warehouse, and I'm afraid your order was confused with that of another ❷customer. We'll get the correct product to you as soon as possible.

Thanks for your patience.

- - - - - - - -

我很抱歉您收到的貨是誤送的。倉庫方面出了點差錯，恐怕是把您的訂貨與另一位顧客戶的搞混了。我們會盡快將正確的產品交付給您。謝謝您的耐心等候。

wrong 錯誤的，不對的　mix-up 混淆　warehouse 倉庫，倉庫，大賣場之類的倉庫
be confused with 與～混淆了

✉ sample **327**

Dear _____

I'm sorry about the problem with your order. We've investigated the matter and found that we mistakenly sent your order. We have sent out the correct order and we have arranged for pick up of the incorrect order. Please accept my apologies for the inconvenience.

Thank you.

- - - - - - - -

對於您訂單的問題，我感到抱歉。我們調查過這件事，且發現我們將您的訂貨送錯了。我們已送出正確的訂貨，且已安排拿回誤送的貨品。給您帶來不便，請接受我的道歉。謝謝。

investigate 調查　matter 事件　mistakenly 錯誤地　correct 正確的　arrange 安排　incorrect 錯誤的

✉ sample 328

Dear [_____]

I'm writing to apologize for the mix-up in your order. Although we strive to provide the ❶best products and the ❷most efficient delivery, we occasionally make mistakes. I'm sorry that you were inconvenienced. Please be assured that we will not let this happen again.

Thank you for your understanding.

- - - - - - -

Try It! 可以替換的字詞

❶ most excellent 最優的
top 頂級的
perfect 完美的
preeminent 卓越的
superlative 最高級的

❷ fastest 最快的
market's best 市場上最佳的
most secure 最安全的
most top-notch 最頂尖的
best 最好的

我寫這封信的目的是，對於弄錯您訂單一事，表示歉意。雖然我們一直努力提供最好的產品及最有效率的送貨方式，但我們偶爾還是會出差錯。給您帶來的不便，我們深表歉意。請放心我們不會再讓這種情況發生了。謝謝您的理解。

strive 努力　efficient 有效率的　inconvenience 不便　assure 向～保證，擔保

✉ sample 329

Dear [_____]

I'm terribly sorry about the recent confusion. The model numbers for the product you ordered and the one you received only differ by one number and one of our warehouse employees erred in preparing the shipment. I hope this oversight did not cause you too much trouble. We have resolved the situation and your correct order is on its way.

Thank you.

- - - - - - -

Try It! 可以替換的字詞

organizing 整理
setting up 設定
making 處理
arranging 安排
getting ready 做準備

對於最近的混亂情勢，我深表歉意。您訂購的產品型號和您收到的貨品型號只差一個數字，而我們一名倉庫人員在準備出貨時出了錯。我希望這次的疏忽不會給您帶來太大麻煩。我們已經將這狀況解決了，正確的訂貨已在路上了。謝謝您。

confusion 混亂　differ 不同　err 出錯　oversight 疏忽　be on its way 正在路上

✉ sample 330

Dear `⌐ ⌐ ⌐ ⌐ ⌐`

I'm sorry for the error in your recent order. Due to a clerical error, we prepared the wrong product for shipment. We have taken steps to remedy the mistake, and you can expect delivery of the correct product within the next week. Let me know if you have any other problems.

Thank you.

- - - - - - - -

我很抱歉將您最近的訂單弄錯了。由於文書上的錯誤，造成我們運送出去的產品是錯誤的。我們已採取一些步驟，以彌補錯誤，預計您可以在下週內收到正確的產品。如果您有任何其他問題，請告訴我。謝謝。

due to 由於～ clerical 文書（人員）的 take steps 採取步驟 remedy 補救

Try It！可以替換的字詞

cure 補救，解決

sort out 解決（問題等）

analyze and fix 分析和修正

repair and prevent 修正和預防

correct 糾正

付款 Payment

✉ sample 331

Dear _____

I hate to be difficult about this, but the invoice you sent is missing your ❶payee ID number. It's the six digit number you were given when we made the order from you. If you could resend the document with the number included, I'll be able to ❷expedite payment.

Thanks,

Try It! 可以替換的字詞

❶ customer number 顧客編號
contact information 聯絡資訊
order number 訂單編號
personal ID number 個人的身份證號碼
tax identification number
納稅人識別號碼

❷ speed up 加速
hurry 加快
advance 推進
send 寄送
get you 給您

我很不想這麼麻煩，只是您寄來發票少了您的收款人辨識號碼，也就是我們在您下訂單時，給您的六位數字。麻煩您重新發送這份文件，並附帶這個號碼，我才能加速付款程序。謝謝。

difficult 困難的　invoice 發票，出貨單　payee 收款人，領款人　six digit number 六位數字
payment 付款

✉ sample 332

Dear _____

I'm working on getting your payment to you, and I just noticed that your invoice doesn't seem to have a mailing address. I'll need that in order to send the check out. Once I receive it, you'll get your payment.

Thank you.

Try It! 可以替換的字詞

shipping 送貨
transport 運送
distribution 配送
delivery 遞送
home 住家

我正在處理您的付款事宜，而我發現您的發票上似乎沒有郵寄地址。我將需要那項資訊以將支票寄出。我一收到之後，您就會收到這筆款項。謝謝。

notice 注意到　mailing 郵寄　address 地址　check 支票

✉ sample 333

Dear [_____]

I'm trying to get your payment together, but the invoice you sent isn't itemized. Unfortunately, our accounting office requires all invoices to be itemized. If you could just break down the amount into each of the individual services, we will get a check out to you as soon as possible.

Thanks,

- - - - - - - -

我正試圖整理您的款項，但您寄來的發票上沒有逐項列出的資訊。不幸的是，我們的會計室要求所有發票都應逐條列出項目。煩請您將這筆金額詳細列每一筆服務項目，我們才能夠盡快開出支票給您。謝謝。

legitimate 合理的
detailed enough 足夠詳細的
listed out properly 正確列出的
giving me enough information
給我足夠的信息
providing me sufficient data
提供我足夠數據的

itemize 逐項列出　accounting 會計，財政上的　office 辦公室，公司　require 要求
break down A into B 將 A 細分為 B　individual 個別的　get... out 開出～　check 支票

✉ sample 334

Dear [_____]

I have received your invoice. However, it seems to be missing your Tax Identification Number. In order to make payment we have to include this number in our paperwork. If you get that to me, I'll get your money to you.

Thank you.

- - - - - - - -

我收到您的發票了。然而，它上面似乎缺了您的稅務識別號碼。我們的文件中必須包含這個數字，才能夠付款。麻煩您提供給我，我才能夠付錢給您。謝謝。

Try It！可以替換的字詞

funds 款項
cash 現金
payment 款項
required deposit 所需的押金
financial requirements 帳務上的要求

seems to 似乎～　Tax Identification Number 稅務識別號碼　paperwork 文書（工作）

✉ sample 335

Dear _____

I received your invoice. The amount I have in my ❶files differs from yours by about a ❷hundred dollars. Do you think you could double-check your invoice and resend it? I'll double-check my math as well.

Thank you.

- - - - - - - -

Try It！可以替換的字詞

❶ records 紀錄
invoice 發票
documents 文件
reports 報告
system 系統

❷ thousand 千
couple 幾個的
few 少數的
few hundred 幾百的
handful of 少數的

我收到您的發票了。我的檔案中的總金額與您的金額有大約一百美元的差距。可以請您重複確認您的發票並再寄給我一次嗎？我也會重複確認我的數字。謝謝。

amount 金額　differ from 與～不同　about 關於　double-check 重複確認　resend 重寄　math 計算 as well 也

請求延後付款 Requesting Delayed Payment ▲

✉ sample 336

Dear [_____]

Regarding our outstanding account, would it be possible to arrange for payment ❶at a later date? We are having some ❷logistical problems in getting the funds released. Would it be acceptable to you if we sent payment next week?

I hope this isn't too much of an inconvenience.

- - - - - - -

Try It！可以替換的字詞

❶ in a couple days 過幾天之後
in one week 一個星期之後
in precisely 3 days 就在 3 天之後
tomorrow 明天
at the weekend 在這週末

❷ statistical 統計上的
bookkeeping 記帳的
logging 登錄的
backlog 儲備金
computing 計算上的

關於我們的未結帳目，是否可以安排晚一點付款？我們在資金調度上出了一點問題。若是下週才支付款項，您是否可以接受？我希望這不會給您帶來太多不便。

regarding 關於～ outstanding 帳款未清的 account 帳目，帳單 at a later date 在一個較晚的日期 logistical 運籌上的，物流方面的 fund 資金 release 放款，撥款

✉ sample 337

Dear [_____]

I'm writing to see if it would be possible to delay payment for another week. We've had some cash flow issues that have disrupted our usual conscientious settling of accounts. Let me know if this is acceptable to you.

Thank you for your patience.

- - - - - - -

Try It！可以替換的字詞

careful 小心的
double-verified 重複驗證的
diligent 勤奮的
assiduous 勤勉的
meticulous 一絲不苟的

我寫這封信是想看看是否有可能將付款日期再延後一周。我們遇到了一點現金流的問題，使得我們平時嚴謹的作賬出了點亂子。請讓我知道您是否可以接受。感謝您的耐心。

it would be possible to... 是否有可能～ cash flow 現金流 disrupt 擾亂 usual 平時的 conscientious 謹慎，嚴格的

✉ sample 338

Dear ....

I am working to arrange payment for my most recent order, but I've run into a few problems. Would it be okay if I sent payment a little late? I understand that it is important to make prompt payment, but I've had a few unforeseeable issues. Let me know if this will be a problem.

Thank you.

- - - - - - - -

我正在安排我最近這筆訂單的付款事宜，但卻遇到了一些問題。是否可以讓我晚一點付款呢？我了解快速付款是很重要的事，但我遇到一些不可預見的問題。讓我知道這樣是否會是個問題。謝謝。

recent 最近的　run into 陷入，遭遇（棘手問題）　prompt 迅速的　unforeseeable 預料不到的

✉ sample 339

Dear ....

I'm writing to request a little more time in arranging payment for your services. I am aware that this is an inconvenience for you, but I hope that you will be lenient in this situation. I've run into a few problems that have made it difficult to meet my obligations immediately. I would appreciate your understanding in this.

Thank you.

- - - - - - - -

我寫封信是想請求給我們再多一點時間，以安排為您的服務付款。我可以了解這會帶給您不便，但我希望您對於這樣的處境可以寬容些。我遇到一些問題，使得我很難立即如期償付我的款項。我很感激您對此事的理解。謝謝您。

be aware that... 意識到～　inconvenience 不便　lenient 寬容的　situation 情況　meet 符合　obligation 義務　immediately 立即

✉ sample 340

Dear _____

I know that my payment is a little **overdue**, but I was wondering if I could impose upon you for a few more days. I'm expecting a large payment myself, and once I've received it, I will be able to remit payment to you. Let me know if that works for you.

I'm sorry for the inconvenience.

- - - - - - - -

我知道我的付款有點逾期了，但我想知道您是否可以再多寬限我幾天的時間。我自己也在等一大筆款項，且一旦收到之後，我就可以匯款給您。請讓我知道這對您是否是可行。抱歉給您帶來不便。

overdue 逾期的　wonder if 想知道是否～　impose upon 造成～（某人）的負擔　remit 匯款

Try It！可以替換的字詞

past due 逾期的
in arrears 拖欠的
unpaid 未繳納的
outstanding 未付的
behind schedule 進度落後的

匯款通知 Informing of Payment Sent ▲

✉ sample 341

Dear _____

I'm writing to let you know that payment will be ❶sent out today. ❷I'm sorry for the delay. You can expect to receive payment within two business days.

Thank you for your understanding.

- - - - - - - -

❶ delivered 遞送

dispatched 發送

mailed 郵寄

sent off 寄出

given to a delivery service
交給快遞服務公司

❷ I sincerely apologize
我真心致上歉意

It pains me 讓我感到痛苦

I cannot express enough sorrow
我再怎麼表示遺憾都不夠

I'm regretful 我很遺憾

I'm sad 我很難過

我寫這封信是為了通知您，貨款將於今日寄出。對於延誤一事我很抱歉。您可以預期在兩個工作日內收到款項。謝謝您的理解。

payment 貨款　delay 延誤　expect to 預期～　within ～ 在～之內　business day 工作日

✉ sample 342

Dear _____

I just wanted to inform you that payment has been sent. You should receive it in the next three to five business days. I apologize for the lateness of my payment.

Thank you for your patience.

- - - - - - - -

tardiness 延遲

delay 延遲

unpunctuality 不守時

belatedness 延遲

slowness 緩慢

我在此想通知您貨款已經送出。您應可於接下來的三到五個工作日內收到。我為付款的延遲表示歉意。感謝您的耐心等待。

next 接下來的，未來的　three to five 三到五　lateness 延遲　patience 耐心

✉ sample 343

Dear _____

I have arranged for payment to be sent. You should receive **notification** of an electronic payment within the hour. I appreciate your patience in this matter.

Thank you.

- - - - - - - -

我已安排匯款事宜。您應該在這一小時內會收到電子支付通知。感謝您對此事的耐心等待。謝謝您。

> arrange for 為～做安排　notification 通知　electronic payment 電子支付
> within the hour 在這一小時內　matter 事件

Try It！可以替換的字詞

word 消息

a text message notifying you
一道給您的通知簡訊

an email notice 一封電子郵件通知

confirmation 確認

a voice mail 一則語音信箱

✉ sample 344

Dear _____

I've received your email regarding payment. There has been an oversight **at my office** and payment was not sent. I apologize for the delay. I have arranged for payment to be made by the end of business today.

Thank you for your patience.

- - - - - - - -

我已收到您有關貨款的電子郵件。我辦公室內出現一點差錯，未能將帳款送出。我為此延誤致上歉意。我已經安排在今天營業結束前付款。謝謝您的耐心等待。

> regarding 關於～　oversight 疏忽　by the end of business 在營業結束前

Try It！可以替換的字詞

here 在這裡

on our end 在我們這邊

within these walls 在我們裡面

at my company 在我的公司

in my business 在我的公司

✉ sample 345

Dear [_____]

I'm writing to inform you that I have sent payment in the form of a certified check to cover the outstanding amount on my account. I apologize for having been so slow in paying. It will not happen in the future.

Thank you for your understanding.

Try It！可以替換的字詞

ever again 再一次地

to you again 再一次對您

beyond this point 多過這一次

when I make purchases again
當我再次購買時

as long as I am your customer
只要我是您的顧客時

我寫這封信是為了通知您，我已經寄了一張保付支票給您，以支付我帳目中的未結餘額。我很抱歉這麼慢付款。未來不會再發生。謝謝您的理解。

form 形式　certified check 保付支票　cover 以支付～（費用）　outstanding 未付的　amount 金額
account 帳目

✉ sample 346

Dear 〔　　　〕

I'm sorry to hear that you are having trouble meeting your obligations. However, we really must ❶insist on prompt payment. Please ❷remit payment within the week.

Thank you for understanding.

Try It ! 可以替換的字詞	
❶ require 需要	
force 強制	
coerce 強制	
impose 強制	
demand 需要	
❷ send 寄送	
wire 電匯	
submit 提交	
tender 支付	
present 提交	

很遺憾聽到您無法履行義務。但我們必須堅持盡速付款。請在本週之內匯款。謝謝您的理解。

> sorry to hear that 很遺憾聽到～　trouble 麻煩　obligation 義務　insist on 堅持～　prompt 迅速的
> remit 匯款

✉ sample 347

Dear 〔　　　〕

I understand that there are sometimes difficulties in making payment. Thank you for being upfront about it. We can wait another week, but it is essential that we receive payment at that time.

Thank you.

Try It ! 可以替換的字詞	
vital 重要的	
key 重要的	
chief 最重要的	
central 重要的	
non-negotiable 無商量餘地的	

我了解有時會遇到付款方面的難題。感謝您對此事的坦率。我們可以再等一週，但我們必須在那時候收到款項。謝謝。

> difficulty 困難　upfront 坦率的　essential 必要的

✉ sample 348

Dear _____

It is very important for our company to receive payment on time so that we can meet our own expenses and obligations. How much more time do you need? It would be better if we agreed upon a date for payment. Please let me know.

Thank you.

- - - - - - - -

對我們公司來說，準時收款是非常重要的，如此才能支付我們的開銷和債務。您還需要多少時間？付款日期如果能經過雙方同意會更好。請讓我知道。謝謝您。

meet an expense 支付開銷　need 需要　agree upon 同意～

✉ sample 349

Dear _____

I understand that you are having difficulties, but we really must ask that payment be made as soon as possible. We can grant you at most two more days. Then we will need to settle this matter.

Thank you for your prompt response.

- - - - - - - -

我了解您遇到了困難，但我們確實必須請您盡快付款。我們最多可以再給您兩天。然後我們必須解決這問題。謝謝您的快速回應。

grant 給予　at most 至多，充其量　two more days 多兩天　settle 解決　matter 問題　response 回應

┌ ─ ─ ─ ─ ─ ─ ┐

I'm sorry to hear about your difficulties. I understand your situation and we'll do our best to work with you. I'll talk to you in a few days and we can **arrange** a transfer of the funds for immediate payment.

Thanks,

- - - - - - - -

我很遺憾聽到您的困難。我了解您的情況,我們會盡力與您合作。我過幾天會跟您談談,並且我們可以安排這些資金的轉帳,以便立即付款。謝謝。

difficulty 困難　arrange 準備,安排　transfer 轉移,轉帳　fund 資金　immediate 立即的

Try It!可以替換的字詞

set up 準備
place 安排
coordinate 協調
make plans for 為～制定計畫
orchestrate 精心安排

催收帳款 Enforcing Payment

Case 01 催收帳款 **Enforcing Payment** ▲

✉ sample 351

Dear _____

I'm writing to remind you that your account is not currently in good standing. Please remit payment as soon as possible. All payments are due upon receipt of the order.

Thank you for your prompt attention in this matter.

- - - - - - - -

我寫這封信是為了提醒您，目前您的帳戶信用狀況不良。請盡快匯款。所有款項都應在收到訂單後立即繳付。感謝您及時關注這件事上。

> **Try It！可以替換的字詞**
>
> tell you again 再告知您
> warn you 警告您
> repeat 再說一次
> jog your memory 喚起您的記憶
> caution you 請您注意

> remind 提醒　account 帳戶，帳目　currently 目前　standing 聲望，信譽　remit 匯款
> due 應支付的　upon receipt of 在收到～時　prompt 迅速的，即時的

✉ sample 352

Dear _____

You are a valued customer of Smith Technology. Being flexible in our ability to satisfy your needs is important to us. I do want to remind you, however, that your payment for order #12360 is past due. I would appreciate it if you could forward payment for this order as soon as possible.

Thank you for your time.

- - - - - - - -

貴公司是史密斯科技的重要客戶。在我們能力範圍內彈性地滿足您的需求，對我們來說是非常重要。不過，我確實想提醒您，您＃12360 訂單的付款已過期。如果您能盡快匯出此訂單的帳款，我將不勝感激。謝謝您的寶貴時間。

> **Try It！可以替換的字詞**
>
> a long-time 一個長期以來的
> a senior 一位資深的
> a treasured 一位受到重視的
> a major 一位主要的
> the most important 最重要的

> valued 受到重視的　flexible 彈性的　ability 能力　satisfy 滿足　need 需求

✉ sample 353

Dear _____

My records show that there is an outstanding balance on your account. In order for your account to be in good standing, we need to receive payment. If you have already sent payment, please disregard this notice.

Thank you.

- - - - - - - -

Try It ! 可以替換的字詞

pristine 原始的
proper 適當的
first-rate 最上等的
quality 優質的
noble 高等的

我的紀錄顯示您的帳戶中有筆未結餘額。為了讓您的帳戶保持優良信譽狀態。我們必須收到付款才行。如果您已經付款，請忽略此通知。謝謝。

record 記錄 outstanding 未清帳款 balance 餘額 already 已經 disregard 忽略 notice 通知

✉ sample 354

Dear _____

I'm writing to enquire about the delay in payment for order #61246. Payment was due on 8/23/18, but we have still not received it. If there has been ❶some miscommunication, please contact me to ❷remedy it. If not, please remit payment at your earliest convenience.

Thank you for your prompt attention.

- - - - - - - -

Try It ! 可以替換的字詞

❶a mistake 一個錯誤
confusing information 令人困惑的訊息
a wrongful discussion 不當的討論結果
an error 一個錯誤
a miscalculation 計算錯誤

❷discuss it 討論它
talk over the details again
再次談論細節
set up a face-to-face meeting
進行面對面的會談
discuss proper procedures
討論適當的程序
resolve the issue 解決此問題

我寫這封信是要詢問關於訂單＃61246 的延遲付款問題。付款截止日為 2018 年 8 月 23 日，但我們仍未收到。如果有什麼溝通上的錯誤，請聯繫我以作更正。如果沒有，請務必盡速匯款。感謝您的及時關注。

enquire 詢問 miscommunication 溝通錯誤 remedy 補正 at your earliest convenience 請您務必盡速

✉ sample 355

Dear [............]

I hope that this email finds you well. I'm writing to check on the status of your payment for order #23566. As you know, all payments are **❶due** upon receipt of **❷shipment**. If you have any problems with your order, please feel free to contact me. If not, please remit payment.

Thank you for your attention.

- - - - - - - -

Try It！可以替換的字詞

❶ owed 應支付的

expected 預期的

scheduled 排定的

looked-for 預期的

anticipated 預料中的

❷ the batch 這批貨

the load 這批貨

the order 這批訂貨

the consignment 此次交付之貨物

your goods 您的貨品

展信愉快。我寫這封信是想確認您 #23566 訂單的付款狀況。如您所知，所有款項應於收到貨品後支付。如果您對您的訂單有任何問題，請隨時與我聯繫。如果沒有，請匯款。感謝您的關注。

check 確認　status 狀況　due 應支付的　upon receipt of 一旦收到～　contact 聯繫　remit 匯款

✉ sample 356

Dear [_____]

This email is ❶a second reminder that your payment has still not been received. While we try to ❷be flexible with our customers, we must insist that payment be made by the end of tomorrow.

Thank you for your quick response.

- - - - - - -

Try It！可以替換的字詞

❶ another 另一次的
a double 再次的
an additional 額外的
a new 新的
an added 新增的

❷ deal easily 輕鬆交易
have elastic dealings
有彈性的交易
be accommodating 迎合的
be nonrigid 不嚴格的
allow variable situations
允許各種情況

此封電子郵件是第二次提醒您，我們尚未收到您的付款。雖然我們一直試著彈性處理與我們客戶的關係，但我們必須堅持明天結束之前付款。感謝您的快速回覆。

reminder 提醒信 flexible 彈性的 customer 客戶 insist 堅持 payment 付款 response 回覆

✉ sample 357

Dear [_____]

I'm writing regarding your payment for order #12360. As I stated in my previous email of 8/30/18, your payment is past due. Please take steps to remedy this situation.

Thank you.

- - - - - - -

Try It！可以替換的字詞

said 說過
demanded 要求
hinted 示意
claimed 要求
asserted 聲明

我寫這封信與您＃12360 的訂單帳款有關。正如我先前在 2018 年 8 月 30 日的電子郵件中所述，您的付款已逾期。請採取（必要）措施處理這樣的狀況。謝謝。

regarding 關於～ state 陳述，聲明 previous 先前的 due 期限已到的，應支付的
take steps 採取步驟 remedy 補救 situation 情況

✉ sample **358**

Dear ⌐ ‥ ¬

I'm writing again because we still have not received payment for order #61246. It is very important that you contact us to arrange payment immediately. If payment has not been received by the end of the week, your account will be frozen.

Thank you for your quick response.

我再度寫信的原因是，我們尚未收到您訂單 #61246 的付款。請您務必與我們聯繫，以立即處理付款事宜。如果本週末之前尚未收到付款，您的帳戶將被凍結。感謝您的迅速回覆。

arrange 安排，準備　immediately 立即　account 帳單，帳戶，帳目　frozen 凍結的

✉ sample **359**

Dear ⌐ ‥ ¬

I wish to inform you that your account with Smith Technology is currently not in good standing. This email constitutes your second notice for payment. If there are extenuating circumstances surrounding the delay in payment, please contact me as soon as possible so that we can find a solution.

Thank you for your prompt attention in this matter.

我想通知您，您在史密斯科技的帳戶目前信譽不佳。這封電子郵件是給您的第二次付款通知。如果延遲付款原因是情有可原的，請盡快與我聯繫，以便我們找到解決方案。感謝您對此事的及時關注。

constitute 構成　surrounding 環繞著～　extenuate 情有可原的，有助於減輕～　circumstance 情況 solution 解決辦法

✉ sample 360

Dear [_____]

I'd like to tell you about the payment for your most recent order with us (#23566). When I wrote you on 8/25/15, we had not received payment. It is now two weeks later and we still have not received payment. Please make arrangements to have the full balance of your account paid as soon as possible.

Thank you.

- - - - - - - -

我想通知您，您最近的訂單（＃23566）款項的問題。我在 2015 年 8 月 25 日的郵件中提到過，我們還沒收到貨款。而現在又過了兩個星期了，我們仍然沒有收到貨款。請盡快安排支付帳單上的全部餘額。謝謝。

recent 最近的　balance 餘額

Try It! 可以替換的字詞

amount 金額
surplus 餘額
remainder 結餘
tally 帳目
quantity 數額

✉ sample 361

Dear ⌐ ⌐

This is your final notice. Your payment is more than 30 days overdue. If we have not received payment within the next 24 hours, we will turn your account over to a collection agency.

Thank you for your cooperation.

- - - - - - -

這是給您的最後通知信。您的付款已逾期超過 30 天。如果我們在接下來的 24 小時內未收到貨款，我們會將您這筆帳轉給催收機構。謝謝您的合作。

final 最後的　notice 通知　overdue 逾期的　within 在～範圍內　collection agency 欠款催收公司

✉ sample 362

Dear ⌐ ⌐

This email is our final notice for payment of order #12360. Payment must be received by the end of the week or we will resort to legal remedies to recover our payment. Please take the appropriate steps immediately to avoid serious consequences.

Thank you for your understanding.

- - - - - - -

這封電子郵件是我們對於訂單＃12360 的付款最後通知。請務必在本週末之前完成付款，否則我們將訴諸於法律上的補救措施，以收回我們的帳款。請立即採取適當措施，以避免嚴重後果。謝謝您的理解。

resort to 訴諸於～　legal 法律的　remedy 補救措施　recover 拿回，收回　appropriate 適當的 immediately 立即　avoid 避免　consequence 後果

✉ sample 363

Dear [_____]

It is with great concern that I write yet again to enquire after your payment for order #61246. We try to be as patient as possible with our customers, but there is a limit to how long we can wait. That limit is quickly approaching. This email is our last notice. Please pay right away.

Thank you.

- - - - - - - -

帶著相當關切之心，我再次寫信想詢問您訂單 #61246 的帳款。我們盡可能以耐心來對待客戶，但我們可以等待的時間有限。而這個限度正逼近中。此電子郵件是我們的最後通知。請立即付款。謝謝您。

with concern 關切地　enquire 詢問　quickly 迅速地　approaching 接近中的　right away 立即，馬上

Try It！可以替換的字詞

immediately 立即
right now 立即
without delay 沒有延誤地
at once 立即
straight away 馬上

✉ sample 364

Dear [_____]

Our attempts to determine the reasons behind your late payment have not succeeded. Your account is now over one month past due. This is our final notice regarding payment. The next step will be to involve a collection agency. Please arrange for payment immediately.

Regards

- - - - - - - -

我們一直無法確定您延遲付款的原因。您這筆帳已逾期一個月。這是我們最後一次的付款通知。接下來將由代催款機構介入此事。請立即安排付款。致上問候。

determine 推定　reason 原因　succeed 成功　involve 使介入

Try It！可以替換的字詞

ascertain 確認
establish 確定
find out 查出
uncover 揭露
reveal 揭露

✉ sample 365

Dear ──────────

Payment for your order has still not been received, and it has now been over six weeks since you took delivery. This is the third email concerning this issue. If payment is not received within the week, additional steps will be taken to solve the problem. This is our ultimatum on this payment.

I am looking forward hearing from you soon.

- - - - - - - -

remedy 補救
eliminate 去除
get rid of 排除
eradicate 根絕
square 修正

我們仍未收到您訂單的付款，而且自您收到訂貨以來已超過六週。這是有關此問題的第三封電子郵件了。如果本週內未收到付款，我們將採取其他措施來解決問題。這是我們對這筆付款的最後通知，期待您的快速回覆。

order 訂單　delivery 交貨，貨品　concerning 關於～　additional 另外的　solve 解決
ultimatum 最後通牒

要求回覆 Requesting a Reply ▲

✉ sample 366

Dear [_____]

I have sent three emails regarding your past due account. Please reply to this email so that we can arrange for payment. We are willing to work with you to resolve the situation, but you must write us immediately.

I hope to hear from you.

- - - - - - - -

Try It！可以替換的字詞

phone 打電話給～
email 寄發電子郵件給～
fax 傳真給～
contact 聯繫～
call 打電話給～

我已經發送了三封關於您應收賬戶款逾期的電子郵件。請回覆此電子郵件，以便我們為付款作安排。我們願意與您一起解決問題，但您必須立即寫信給我們。期待您的回信。

reply 答覆　so that 以便～　be willing to 願意～　resolve 解決

✉ sample 367

Dear [_____]

I still have not heard from you regarding payment. Please contact me as soon as possible so that we can discuss your account. Keeping open the lines of communication is essential.

Thanks.

- - - - - - - -

Try It！可以替換的字詞

Supporting 支持
Retaining 保持
Maintaining 保持
Having open 保持開放
Keeping alive 保持～有效的

我還沒有收到您付款的消息。請盡快與我聯繫，以便我們討論您的帳款。保持溝通管道暢通非常重要。謝謝。

keep A B　保持 B 處於 A 狀態　communication 溝通　essential 必要的

✉ sample 368

Dear ⸂⸃

I'm writing because I'm a little concerned about the lack of response from you. If you are receiving my emails, please respond. We need to find a solution to this issue so that payment can be made and your account can return to good standing.

I am looking forward your response.

我寫這封信是因為對於您沒有回覆而表示一點關切。如果您收到我的電子郵件，請作出回應。我們必須找到此問題的一個解決方案，以便讓您的賬戶回復正常信用狀態，且您的帳戶可以恢復良好的信譽。我期待您的回覆。

> lack 缺乏　response 反應，回應　respond 回覆　issue 問題　solution 解決方案

✉ sample 369

Dear ⸂⸃

It has been over a week since my last email and I still have not heard from you. It is essential that we work together to resolve this problem. There are different options for the arrangement of your payment, but we must communicate if we are to work this out. Please contact me as soon as possible.

Thank you.

自我上一封電子郵件以來已經超過一個星期，我仍然沒有收到您的回覆。我們必須共同努力解決這個問題。您的付款方式還有不同的選擇，但如果我們要解決這個問題，我們必須進行溝通。請盡快與我聯繫。謝謝您。

> over a week 超過一個星期　since... 自～以來　still 仍然　communicate 溝通
> if we are to 如果我們要～

✉ sample 370

Dear ╌╌╌╌╌╌╌

This is the third email I have sent to you in this month and I have yet to get a reply. I'm concerned that our problems concerning payment will escalate if we do not keep the lines of communication open. Please contact me so that we can discuss this issue further.

I'm looking forward hearing from you soon.

- - - - - - - -

這是我這個月發給您的第三封電子郵件，我還沒有收到回覆。我擔心如果我們不保持溝通管道暢通，我們的付款問題會越來越嚴重。請與我聯繫，以便我們進一步討論這個問題。我期待您儘快回覆。

third 第三的　have yet to 還沒有～　reply 回覆　I'm concerned that... 我很擔心～　concerning 關於～
escalate 逐步增強或擴大　further 進一步地

Try It！可以替換的字詞

hear back from you 得到您的回覆

get a response 收到回覆

learn where we stand
了解我們的處境

receive feedback 收到回饋

get an email back 收到回覆的電子郵件

✉ sample 371

Dear ⌐ ⌐

I understand your ❶frustration and I apologize for the delay in payment. The problem has been ❷cleared up at our end, and payment will be made soon. Thank you for being so understanding.

I'm sorry for any inconvenience.

- - - - - - - -

Try It! 可以替換的字詞

❶ aggravation 惱怒
irritation 煩躁
annoyance 煩惱
disappointment 失望
dissatisfaction 不滿

❷ resolved 解決
finished 終止
patched up 處理完成
fixed 解決
repaired 解決

我理解您感到失望，我為延遲付款而道歉。這個問題已經在我們這邊獲得解決了，且款項很快就會撥出。謝謝您的理解。給您帶來不便，深表歉意。

> frustration 懊惱，挫折　apologize for 為～道歉　payment 付款　clear up 解決
> end（雙方或各方的）一邊，一方面　understanding 理解

✉ sample 372

Dear ⌐ ⌐

I'm sorry for the lateness of my payment. We have had some problems in our bookkeeping system. We are in the process of resolving these problems. Once we have sorted out the confusion, payment will be sent.

Thank you for your patience.

- - - - - - - -

Try It! 可以替換的字詞

systems 系統
computer servers 電腦伺服器
spreadsheet programs 電子表格程式
detailing products 詳述產品
secretarial department 秘書處

我對於付款延遲表示歉意。我們的記帳系統出了些問題。我們正在解決這些問題當中。一旦我們將這亂象解決掉，帳款就能寄出。感謝您的耐心等待。

> lateness 延遲　bookkeeping 記帳　in the process of 在～過程中　resolve 解決　once 一旦
> sort out 處理，整理（問題等）　confusion 混亂　patience 耐心

✉ sample 373

Dear ⸻

I received your email concerning my payment. I'm afraid we have had a slight **cash flow** problem, but it should be resolved by the end of the week. I will let you know as soon as payment has been arranged.

Thank you for your understanding.

- - - - - - - -

我收到您關於付款的電子郵件。但恐怕我們有一點現金流的問題,不過本週末之前應可獲得解決。處理完付款事宜之後,我會立即通知您。謝謝您的理解。

concerning 關於～ slight 輕微的 cash flow 現金流轉,資金流動 as soon as 一旦～,就～
arrange 安排 understanding 理解

Try It! 可以替換的字詞

income 收入
returns 盈利
profits 獲利
money 金錢
earnings 營收

✉ sample 374

Dear ⸻

Thank you for your patience with the delay in payment. I assure you that I recognize the importance of **settling my account** with you. I am currently working to resolve the issues that are causing the delay.

Thank you for understanding this.

- - - - - - - -

感謝您對付款延遲的耐心等待。我向您保證,我了解向您結清我的帳款是一件重要的事。目前我正設法解決導致延遲的問題。感謝您理解這一點。

assure 向～保證 recognize 認知 settle one's account 處理或付清某人的帳款 currently 現在
issue 問題 cause 導致

Try It! 可以替換的字詞

investigating what might cause the problems
調查可能導致問題的原因
sorting out the things 解決這些事情
identifying the sources 找出緣由
eliminating any obstacles 清除任何障礙
finding the reasons 找到原因

✉ sample 375

Dear [_____]

I understand your impatience with this situation, but I assure you that I am doing everything that I can to arrange payment. A late paying client on my end has disrupted my cash flow. Once I receive payment, I will have the funds necessary to pay you.

I appreciate your understanding in this.

Try It！可以替換的字詞

the slow response 緩慢的回應

our accounting department
我們的會計部門

our inability to pay 我們無力支付

these circumstances 這些情況

this mess 這個爛攤子

- - - - - - - -

我理解您對這種情況的不耐煩，但我向您保證，我正盡我所能安排付款事宜。我方一名客戶延遲付款，擾亂了我的現金流。一旦我收到付款，我就會有需要付給您的資金。我很感激您對於此事的理解。

impatience 不耐煩　situation 情況　client 客戶　disrupt 擾亂　necessary 必需的

提出索償及客訴 Claim & Complaint

✉ sample 376

Dear ⌐ ⌐

I'm writing to inform you that the product we received from your company yesterday arrived in an unacceptable condition. First of all, the fabric is torn in several places. It looks as if it was damaged during packing. In addition, there were several missing items. We ordered twelve different fabric patterns, but only seven were shipped. Please take steps to remedy this situation immediately.

Thank you.

- - - - - - - -

我寫這封信的目的是想通知您，昨天我們收到來自貴公司的產品時，出現令人無法接受的狀況。首先，有些地方的布料有撕裂情況，看來似乎是在包裝過程中受損。此外，還有幾件遺失的物品。我們訂購十二種不同的布料樣式，但只收到七種。請立即採取措施補救這樣情況。謝謝。

> It looks as if... 看起來好像～　damage 損壞　packing 包裝　in addition 此外　remedy 補救

Try It！可以替換的字詞

sent 被寄送
received 被收到
in the box 寄到的
in the shipment 在這批貨中
came 送到

✉ sample 377

Dear ⌐ ⌐

There is a serious problem with our most recent order. Specifically, it arrived over two weeks late. While we can understand that there are some uncontrollable events that cause delay, two weeks is simply unacceptable. We need assurances that this sort of problem will not happen again.

Thank you for your attention in this matter.

- - - - - - - -

我們最近這筆訂單出現嚴重的問題。具體來說，就是晚了兩個星期才到貨。雖然我們可以理解有一些無法控制的事會導致延誤，但兩個星期是無法接受的。我們需要您保證這類問題不會再發生。感謝您對此事的關注。

> specifically 具體地　uncontrollable 無法控制的　unacceptable 無法接受的　assurance 保證，擔保
> sort 類別

Try It！可以替換的字詞

unmanageable 難控制的
irrepressible 控制不住的
uncontainable 不受控制的
wild 難駕馭的
disorderly 混亂的

✉ sample 378

Dear ┌┄┄┄┄┄┐

There are two major problems with the service we received from your delivery services. First of all, the shipment was not delivered within the time frame promised by your representative. Second of all, the packages were crushed and had obviously been mishandled. Please contact me immediately to discuss these serious problems.

Thank you.

- - - - - - - -

我們已收到您貨運公司送來的貨品，而這批貨有兩個主要問題。首先，貨物未在您業務代表承諾的時間範圍內送到。其次，包裝被壓壞了，顯然是處理不當的問題。請立即與我聯繫，以討論這些嚴重的問題。謝謝。

time frame 截止日期　representative 代表人，業務代表　package 包裝，包裝箱　crush 壓壞，擠壓

✉ sample 379

Dear ┌┄┄┄┄┄┐

I'm writing to ask that you address the serious problems that we have had with your customer service department. When we attempted to discover what had happened to our missing shipment, your representatives treated us dismissively and rudely. If we are to continue to give you our business, we must be able to trust that we will be respected and given assistance when it is required.

Sincerely,

- - - - - - - -

我寫這封信的目的是想要求您解決我們與貴公司客服部之間的嚴重問題。當我們試圖要找出我們貨物遺失的原因時，貴公司客服代表以不屑及粗魯的態度對待我們。如果我們要繼續提供您生意，我們必須能夠相信，在必要時刻我們會獲得尊重與協助。謹此。

customer 顧客　attempt 試圖　discover 發現　shipment 運輸，運送，裝運
dismissively 輕蔑地，不屑一顧地　rudely 無禮地　trust 信任　assistance 協助　respect 尊重

✉ sample 380

Dear [_____]

I'm writing to enumerate the problems we are experiencing with the G32 monitor.

* The power source is not compatible with US wiring ❶standards.
* The resolution is not ❷up to the specifications indicated in the product description.
* The screen size is too small.

Please take steps to address these issues.

Thank you.

- - - - - - - -

我寫這封信的目的是要列舉出我在使用 G32 顯示器時遇到的問題。
* 電源不符合美國的電線標準。
* 解析度未達到產品說明中所指的規格。
* 螢幕尺寸太小。
請設法解決這些問題，謝謝您。

Try It！可以替換的字詞

❶ requirements 要求
necessities 要件
minimums 最小值
averages 均值
accepted values 可接受的數值

❷ meeting 符合
equal to 等於
the same as 與～相同
as high as 與～一樣高
quite equaling 相當於～

enumerate 列舉　power source 電源　compatible 相容的　wiring 接線　standard 標準　resolution 解析度　up to 達到～（數量、程度等）　specification 規格，規範　indicate 指示　description 描述，說明

進行客訴 Making a Complaint ▲

✉ sample 381

Dear ⌐‾‾‾‾⌐

I'm writing to complain about **the delay in delivery of my order.** When I placed my order I was told it would be shipped within a week. It has now been three weeks and I have yet to receive it. Please take steps to remedy this situation as soon as possible.

Thank you for your attention.

- - - - - - - -

我寫這封信的目的是要對我訂貨的延遲交付狀況進行申訴。我在下訂單時,我得到的消息是會在一週內發貨。現在已經過了三週了,我仍未收到。請設法盡快補救此狀況。感謝您的關注。

complain 抱怨,申訴　place an order 下訂單　I was told (that...) 我被告知～　have yet to 還沒～

✉ sample 382

Dear ⌐‾‾‾‾⌐

I would like to register a complaint about the G32 monitors we just received. The resolution on the monitors does not ❶at all match that ❷guaranteed by your sales representative. We made a sizable order based on what we were told. All business transactions are based on the assumption of good-faith dealing. Please address this issue immediately.

Sincerely,

- - - - - - - -

我想對於我們剛收到的 G32 顯示器進行客訴。顯示器的解析度一點也不符合貴公司銷售代表所保證的品質。我們根據所得知的內容下了一張相當大的訂單。所有商業交易都應以誠實交易為基礎。請立即解決此問題。此致。

register 註冊　complaint 客訴　not at all 一點也不　match 使相稱　sizable 相當大的
based on 以～為基礎　on the assumption 在～前提下　good-faith 誠實　dealing 交易

✉ sample 383

Dear _____

I'm writing to express my ❶displeasure at the slowness of the delivery of my last order. We waited a full month for the shipment to arrive. In our business, it is imperative that we be able to receive merchandise in a timely manner so that we can get them to our ❷retail partners. In the future, if we do not receive our orders promptly, we will re-evaluate our relationship.

Thank you for your attention.

- - - - - - - -

Try It ! 可以替換的字詞

❶anger 生氣

discontent 不滿

unhappiness 不快

absolute disapproval 絕對不認同

true dissatisfaction 真正的不滿

❷outlets 通路商

stores 商店

business friends 商界朋友

many supermarkets 眾多超市

merchandising cohorts 經商的同業夥伴

我寫這封信是要針對我上一批訂貨發生交付延遲的狀況表達不滿。我們等了整整一個月貨才到。在我們生意往來上，我們及時收到商品才能夠交給我們的零售夥伴，這是很重要的事。未來，如果我們沒有及時收到訂貨，我們將重新評估我們的關係。感謝您的關注。

displeasure 不滿意　shipment 送貨，裝載　imperative 強制的，必須的　merchandise 商品
retail 零售的

✉ sample 384

Dear _____

I'm going to have to be honest and tell you that I'm a little bothered by the difficulty I've had getting through to customer service. We've had some serious problems with the new X5 monitors, and we have yet to get someone to talk to us about our issues. I don't know what we can do to improve communication, but please try to resolve the problem as soon as possible.

Thanks,

- - - - - - - -

Try It ! 可以替換的字詞

dipswitches 調光開關

joysticks 操縱桿

parallel ports 平行埠

power supplies 電源

network drives 網路驅動器

我必須坦白跟您說，與貴公司客服有溝通上的困難，這讓我有點困擾。我們新買的 X5 顯示器有一些嚴重的問題，但我們仍無法找到任何人可以討論。我不知道我們可以做些什麼來改善溝通，但請盡快解決此問題。謝謝。

bothered 受到困擾的　get through to 使～（某人）理解　customer service 客戶服務　improve 改善

✉ sample 385

Dear ⌐⎯⎯⎯⎯⎯¬

This email is about a problem we have with the textile shipment we received from your company yesterday. Upon opening the order, we realized that a large amount of the fabric had been stained by some kind of thick black liquid. This must have happened during shipping, or at your factory. We will need to return the order and have it replaced. This is quite an inconvenience for us, as I'm sure you can imagine, so please do whatever you can to expedite the process.

Thank you.

- - - - - - - -

這封電子郵件是關於昨天我們收到來自貴公司的紡織品出貨上的問題。打開訂貨後，我們才發現有大量布料被某種濃黑液體染色了。這一定是發生在運輸過程或在您工廠中。我們必須退回訂貨並進行替換。這對我們來說已造成不便，我相信您可以想像得到，所以請您盡力加快這個過程。謝謝。

textile 紡織品　realize 了解　fabric 布料　stain 染汙　factory 工廠　replace 替換　expedite 加快

Try It!可以替換的字詞

plant 工廠
workplace 工作場所
warehouse 倉庫
storage facility 貯藏庫
stockroom 倉庫

回覆客訴 Responding to Complaints ▲

✉ sample 386

Dear _____

I'm terrible sorry about the delay. We have had some recent difficulties with our delivery service. We are currently working to solve the problem and get your product out to you.

I'm sorry to have inconvenienced you.

attemping 設法

trying 嘗試

laboring 努力要

acting 設法

seeking 尋求

- - - - - - - -

我對延遲一事感到非常抱歉。我們最近在運送服務上遇到一些困難。我們目前正設法解決此問題並將您的產品送達。對於給您帶來的不便，我們深表歉意。

terribly 非常　delay 延遲　recent 最近的　delivery 運送，交付　inconvenience 造成～不便

✉ sample 387

Dear _____

I'm terribly sorry if there was a miscommunication regarding the performance and features of the X5. What was the name of the sales representative who gave you the information about the resolution? It is unusual for any misinformation to be given since all of our sales reps work from the same product descriptions. Please let me know where you got your information, and exactly what the discrepancies are.

Thank you.

details 詳細資料

functionalities 功能性

functions 功能

particulars 特點

descriptions 說明書

- - - - - - - -

如果對 X5 的性能和功能有溝通上的不良，我致上十萬分歉意。提供您這項方案訊息的業務代表是哪一位？由於我們所有業務代表都使用相同的產品說明，因此會出現任何錯誤資訊是不尋常的。請告訴我您的資訊是從哪裡獲得的，以及確切的差異何在。謝謝。

performance 性能　feature 功能　since 因為～　sales representative 業務代表（＝sales rep）
unusual 不尋常的　misinformation 錯誤資訊　description 說明　exactly 確切地　discrepancy 差異

✉ sample 388

Dear [_____]

I'm sorry to hear about the delay in receiving your order. We at Smith Technology value our clients greatly and we know that your time is valuable. We will take steps to make sure that your orders are expedited in the future.

Thank you for your business.

- - - - - - - -

很遺憾聽到您太晚收到訂貨的消息。我們史密斯科技非常重視客戶，並且知道您的時間非常寶貴。未來我們會設法確保您的訂單加速處理。謝謝您的光顧。

value 重視　client 客戶　valuable 寶貴的　make sure that 確保～　expedite 加快～

✉ sample 389

Dear [_____]

Thanks for getting in touch with us. I apologize if you feel that you've fallen through the cracks. I've taken over the case personally, so be dealing with me now. If you could write me an email outlining exactly what your problems are, I'll get to work on solving them.

Thanks for your patience.

- - - - - - - -

感謝您與我們聯繫。如果您有被忽略的感覺，我在此表示歉意。我親自接手了這個案子，所以現在您可以找我處理這件事。如果您給我寫一封電子郵件，說明究竟是什麼問題，我會設法解決的。謝謝您的耐心等待。

get in touch 聯絡　apologize 道歉　fall through the crack 未加注意　take over 接手，接管　case 案子　personally 親自　exactly 精確地　get to work (on...) 開始行動～　patience 耐心

✉ sample 390

Dear ⌐ ⌐

I'm terribly sorry to hear that your shipment arrived with damages. Since we insure every shipment, there should be no problem in replacing and reshipping the order. Unfortunately, there will have to be an investigation of the damage before a replacement can be made. This will take between two to four weeks. I apologize for the inconvenience.

Thank you for your patience.

- - - - - - - -

非常遺憾聽到您收到貨物時出現損壞情況。由於我們每批貨物都有投保，因此換貨及重新訂購應該沒有問題。不過，在更換之前我們必須對損壞情況進行調查。這將需要二到四週的時間。給您帶來的不便，我深表歉意。感謝您的耐心等待。

shipment 運送，貨物　damage 損壞　insure 為～投保　there should be no problem 應該不會有問題
replace 更換　investigation 調查　replacement 換貨　two to four weeks 二到四週

✉ sample 391

Dear ⸤⸤⸤⸤⸤⸤⸤⸥

Thank you for your quick response. However, what I need most is not ❶assurances, but rather for my order to arrive promptly. I will expect ❷delivery by the end of the week.

Thank you,

- - - - - - - -

Try It! 可以替換的字詞

❶ pledges 保證
declarations or promises 聲明或承諾
your word 您的片面之詞
an assertion 一份聲明
constant reassurances 不斷的保證

❷ the receipt 收到貨物
to get my goods 拿到我的貨
arrival 送達
distribution 分送
to have my items 收到我的物品

感謝您的快速回覆。不過,我最需要的不是保證,而是我的訂貨要儘速送達。我期待在本週末之前交貨。謝謝。

response 回覆　assurance 保證　not A but rather B 不是 A 而是 B　promptly 及時地
by the end of the week 在這星期結束之前

✉ sample 392

Dear ⸤⸤⸤⸤⸤⸤⸤⸥

Thank you for your quick reply. Other than the slowness of the shipping, we have been very happy with your company. I hope that we can resolve this issue and continue to have a fruitful relationship.

Kind regards,

- - - - - - - -

Try It! 可以替換的字詞

determine 決定
finalize 終止
get to the bottom of 深入深究
put an end to 終結
disentangle 解開

感謝您的快速回覆。除了送貨太慢之外,我們對貴公司非常滿意。我希望我們能夠解決這個問題並繼續保持良好合作關係。致上親切的問候。

slowness 緩慢　other than 而不是〜　resolve 解決　issue 問題　continue 繼續　fruitful 有成果的

✉ sample 393

Dear ....

A two to four week delay before reshipping is absolutely unacceptable. We must have these textiles delivered to our retail outlets by next Friday. Therefore, it is imperative that we remedy this matter immediately. We did not cause this problem, so we should not be made to suffer for it. Please respond as soon as possible.

Regards,

- - - - - - - -

重新裝載延遲了二至四星期的時間，這是完全無法接受的。我們必須在下週五之前將這些紡織品送到我們的零售店。因此，我們必須立即補救這件事。這個問題不是我們所引起，因此不應由我們來承受。請盡快回覆。致上問候。

reshipping 重新運送　absolutely 完全，絕對　unacceptable 令人無法接受的　textile 紡織品，纖維
retail outlet 零售店　therefore 因此　imperative 必須的

✉ sample 394

Dear ....

Thank you for ❶getting back to me so quickly. I'm glad I'm dealing with someone I know well now. Most of our problems concern the power supply of the G32. The ❷surge protector doesn't seem to work properly. Is there something we're missing about installation? If you could go over it with me, we may be able to find the problem.

Thanks,

- - - - - - - -

非常感謝您很快地回覆我。我很高興可以和我現在相當熟識的人打交道。我們大部分問題都與 G32 的電源有關。這個過載斷路器似乎無法正常運作。我們是不是在安裝的部分遺漏了什麼？如果您可以跟我一起查看一下，也許我們能找到問題所在。謝謝。

get back to 再次聯繫～　most of 大多數～　concern 關於～　power supply 電源
surge protector 過載斷路器　installation 安裝　go over 查看～

✉ sample 395

Dear _____

Throughout the order process, we spoke with Gene Davis, who seemed quite confident that the G32 had a resolution of 1600 x 1200. However, the actual resolution is 1280 x 1024. We based our decision to go with your product on his information. If you cannot provide us with monitors of the proper resolution at the agreed upon price, we will have to look elsewhere for a supplier.

Thanks.

Try It！可以替換的字詞

founded our decision on
我們的決定是以～為根據

rooted our decision in
我們的決定是根據～

originated our decision from
我們的決定是源於～

centered our decision on
我們的決定是以～為中心

grounded our decision on
我們的決定是基於～

- - - - - - - -

在整個訂購過程中，我們和 Gene Davis 談過，他似乎非常有信心 G32 的解析度可達 1600×1200。然而，實際解析度為 1280×1024。我們當時選擇你們的產品，是以他給的資訊為依據。如果您無法以約定價格向我們提供適當解析度的顯示器，我們將必須另尋供應商。謝謝。

> throughout 經過整個～過程　confident 有信心的　resolution 解析度　actual 實際的
> base A on B 將 A 以 B 為根據　go with 選擇～　at the agreed upon price 以約定的價格

✉ sample 396

Dear _____

I'm afraid that it has simply been too long of delay for delivery of my order. I'm going to have to ask for a refund. Please credit my account for the full amount and cancel my order.

Thank you for your prompt attention.

- - - - - - -

恐怕我訂單的交貨時間已經延遲太久了。我打算要求退款了。請將全部金額退還到我的帳戶並取消訂單。感謝您的及時關注。

> simply 只是，就是　refund 退款　credit 將錢存入～　full 全部的　prompt 及時的　attention 關注

Try It！可以替換的字詞

money back 退錢

a gift card in return
以一張禮券作為回報

some sort of reimbursement
某種補償方式

a repayment 還款

a settlement 款項結清

✉ sample 397

Dear _____

I'm afraid that the problems with the G32 make it unsuitable for our needs. I'm writing to request a refund for the full amount of the order including shipping. We will arrange for the return of the units. Please credit our account upon receipt of the return shipment.

Thank you.

- - - - - - -

不好意思，由於 G32 的問題，我們認為它不適合我們的需求。我寫這封信是想要求退還訂單的全部金額，包括運費。我們將安排產品的退貨事宜。請在收到退貨後，請將款項匯回我們的帳戶。謝謝。

> unsuitable 不合適的　need 需求　request 要求　including 包括　arrange 處理，安排
> return 退回，退還　unit 一個單位　upon receipt of 在收到～時　shipment 裝運，運貨

Try It！可以替換的字詞

wants 欠缺的東西

wishes 希望

requirements 需求

desires 渴求的東西

requests 要求

✉ sample 398

Dear [_____]

I'm writing to request a refund for our order (#5321). As you know, prompt shipment is essential in our industry. Delivery of this order has taken far too long to arrive, so we have been forced to seek out another supplier. Please see that our account is credited.

Thank you,

- - - - - - - -

我寫這封信的目的是想針對我們的訂單（＃5321）要求退款。如您所知，快速發貨在我們這個行業中相當重要。由於交貨的時間過長，所以我們已被迫尋找另一家供應商。請將我們的退款匯回帳戶。謝謝。

essential 必要的　industry 產業　be forced to 被迫～　seek out 找出　supplier 供應商

✉ sample 399

[_____]

I'm afraid I'm going to have to ask for a refund. We simply haven't been able to get the T2 to work properly and we feel that our customers won't be able to either. We've arranged to have the shipment returned. Please credit our account for the purchase price.

Thank you for your help.

- - - - - - - -

我恐怕必須要求退款。我們根本無法讓 T2 正常運作，我們覺得我們的客戶也無法做到。我們已經安排退貨。請將我們的購買金額匯回我們的帳戶。謝謝您的幫助。

properly 適當地　customer 客戶　not... either 也不～　purchase 購買

✉ sample 400

Dear ⌐⌐⌐⌐⌐⌐⌐

I'm writing to request a full refund for our order. The damages to our shipment were too extensive, and the wait time for redelivery is too long. Therefore, I have no choice but to ask that our payment be returned. I would appreciate it if the refund could be made as soon as possible.

Thank you.

Try It！可以替換的字詞

option 選擇
alternative 選擇
other way 別的方式
nice way 好方法
substitute 替代方法

- - - - - - - -

我寫這封信是想要求我們的訂單全額退款。我們的貨物損壞範圍太大，而重新等待運送的時間太長了。因此，我別無選擇，只能要求退還我們的付款。如果可以盡快退款，我將不勝感激。謝謝。

damage 損壞　extensive 大量的　wait time 等待時間　redelivery 重新運送
have no choice but to... 除了～別無選擇

sample 401

Dear [　　　　]

The product I received was not the one I ❶thought I was getting. I would like to exchange it for item #2346. Would it be possible to do this? Would there be ❷a change in price?

Thank you,

- - - - - - - -

Try It！可以替換的字詞

❶ believed 相信
supposed 認為
reckoned 認為
hoped 希望
understood 了解

❷ a discretion 斟酌（金額）
a difference 不同
an adjustment 調整
a variation 變動
a modification 修正

我收到的產品不是原本我所想要的。我想將這產品換為 #2346 這件。如此的話是否可能？價格是否會有不同？謝謝。

product 產品　exchange A for B 將 A 更換為 B　item 品項，項目　possible 可能的

 sample 402

Dear [　　　　]

I'm writing to see if it would be possible to exchange the fabric I ordered, pattern #23552, for a different one, pattern #23557. We realized upon receiving our order that the shade is darker than it looked in the picture. Please let me know the procedure for doing an exchange.

Thank you,

- - - - - - - -

Try It！可以替換的字詞

lighter 更淺的
deeper 更深的
less vivid 較不鮮艷的
closer to blue 較接近藍色的
more like red 更接近紅色的

我寫這封信是想知道我是否可以將我訂購的布料 — 圖樣 #23552 — 更換為另一種， #23557 這款圖樣。我們收到訂貨後發現，它的色層比圖片中的顏色要暗。請讓我知道換貨的程序。謝謝。

fabric 布料　shade 對比度，色層　procedure 程序　exchange 交換

✉ sample 403

Dear [_____]

I would like to exchange the product I recently ordered from you. The network routers that we ordered are not compatible with the voltage in American electrical outlets. I see that you also sell another model. Could we make an exchange? Let me know what your policy is.

Thank you,

- - - - - - - -

我想更換我最近訂購的產品。我們訂購的網路路由器與美國電源插座的電壓規格不相容。我看到您也賣其他型號。我可以更換嗎？請讓我知道您規定的方式。謝謝。

recently 最近　compatible 相容的　voltage 電壓　electrical outlet 電源插座　policy 規範，政策

Try It！可以替換的字詞

surge protectors 過載保護器
adapter kits 變壓器套件
jigsaws 線鋸
wireless tablets 無線平板電腦
extension cords 延長線

✉ sample 404

Dear [_____]

I think we made a little mistake when we ordered our last shipment of fabric. We intended to order the red plaid, but we mistakenly ordered the red polka dots. We'd like to exchange this order for the one we wanted. Please let me know if this will be possible.

Thanks,

- - - - - - - -

我想我們上一批紡織品訂貨出了一點小差錯。我們打算訂購紅色彩格布，但我們誤訂了紅色波爾卡圓點。我們想將此此訂單換成我們想要的。請讓我知道這是否可行。謝謝。

make a mistake 犯了一個錯誤　orde 訂購　shipment 運輸，運送，裝載　intend 打算　plaid 格子圖案
polka dot 波爾卡圓點

Try It！可以替換的字詞

desired 期望
asked for 要求
ordered 訂購
placed an order for 下～的訂單
are extremely excited to receive
非常高興收到

✉ sample **405**

Dear ┌╌╌╌╌╌╌╌┐

Would it be possible for me to exchange the hard drives I ordered for a different model. I realized when I received them that they are not compatible with the CPUs in the computers that we are assembling. Please let me know as soon as possible whether the exchange will be possible.

Thank you.

----

putting together 將～拼湊在一起
piecing together 拼湊
collecting 收集
gathering 聚集
pulling together 將～聚在一起

我可以將我訂購的硬碟換成其他型號的嗎？我收到貨時，我發現這些硬碟與我們正在組裝的電腦 CPU 不相容。請盡快讓我知道是否可以更換。謝謝。

hard drive 硬碟　assemble 組裝　as soon as possible 盡快地

✉ sample 406

Try It！可以替換的字詞

a working 有用的
an operating 有作用的
a performing 可運作的
an executing 可執行的
a worthy 值得的

Dear ⌐ ̄ ̄ ̄ ̄ ̄⌐

I'm writing to ask that my company be compensated for the time spent as we tried to solve the problem with your product. As you know, we sent our order back four times and were still not able to get a functioning product. We lost a lot of work hours as well as opportunities to use other suppliers and we would like to be compensated. Please call me so we can discuss this issue further.

Thank you for your prompt attention.

- - - - - - - -

由於我們已花時間試圖解決您的產品問題，因此我寫這封信想要求讓我公司得到賠償。如您所知，我們已將訂貨退回四次，但仍無法得到一個功能正常的產品。我們已花費大量的工作時間以及失去和其他供應商配合的機會，所以我們希望有所補償。請打電話給我，以便我們進一步討論這個問題。感謝您的及時關注。

function 機能 A as well as B A 以及 B opportunity 機會 supplier 供應商

✉ sample 407

Try It！可以替換的字詞

negligence 疏忽
lapse 失誤
insufficient service 服務不周
bad assistance 幫不上忙
inadequate support 不當支援

Dear ⌐ ̄ ̄ ̄ ̄ ̄⌐

This is to ask for compensation for the business my company lost due to the late delivery of the order I made from you. Because of the slow shipping, a number of my retail partners chose to go with other distributors for their products. Attached is the amount this poor service has cost my company. Please review it and get in touch with me as soon as possible.

Thank you.

- - - - - - - -

由於您延遲交付我的訂貨，而造成我方丟失業務，因此這封信旨在要求賠償。由於交貨延遲，一些與我們合作的零售夥伴選擇為他們的產品與不同的經銷商合作。附件顯示因服務不佳而造成我方的損失金額。請檢視之，並盡快與我聯繫。謝謝。

due to 由於～ shipping 運送，裝運 a number of 一些 retail 零售 distributor 經銷商 cost 使花費

✉ sample 408

Dear _____

As you know we have not been able to solve the compatibility issues with the hardware we ordered from you. At this point I feel that we are entitled not only to a refund, but also to compensation for the trouble we have gone to trying to make this inferior product work for us. Please contact me to discuss a fair restitution.

Thank you.

- - - - - - - -

如您所知，對於向您訂購的硬體，我們一直無法解決其相容性的問題。由此來看，我認為我們不僅有退款的權利，且可要求賠償，因為我們試圖使用這樣的劣質產品卻造成我們在工作上的問題。請與我聯繫，以討論如何進行公平的賠償。謝謝。

> at this point 在這一點上　be entitled to 有～資格　refund 退款　inferior 品質較差的
> restitution 歸還，賠償

Try It！可以替換的字詞

middle ground 妥協，中間立場
amends 賠償
repayment 歸還款項
return 退款
compensation 補償

✉ sample 409

Dear _____

The problems with the textiles we ordered from your company have caused considerable problems with our business here in Australia. We expected to be able to immediately distribute the products to our stores, but instead we were left with empty shelves. I hate to resort to this, but I'm afraid I must ask for compensation. We are still working on estimating what our losses have been. When we have arrived at a number, we will let you know.

Sincerely,

- - - - - - - -

我們從貴公司訂購的紡織品已經為我們在澳大利亞的業務帶來了相當大的問題。我們希望能夠立即將產品分銷到我們的商店，但反而我們的貨架上空無一物。雖然我不想如此，但恐怕我還是得要求賠償。我們仍在估算我們的損失。當我們算出金額時，我們會讓您知道。謹此。

> considerable 相當大的　distribute 分配　be left with 留下～　resort to 訴諸於～　estimate 估算

Try It！可以替換的字詞

send out 發送
hand out 分發
allocate 配給
give out 分發
issue 發給

✉ sample 410

Dear _____

I'm afraid I have a ❶fairly serious problem. Not only did the part I order not work with my computer, but it caused considerable damage to my CPU. I'm going to have to ask for compensation. The ❷value of my computer is $1200. The machine is now unusable as a direct result of your product.

Thank you for your quick response.

- - - - - - - -

Try It！可以替換的字詞

❶ quite 相當，頗
rather 相當，頗
moderately 相當地
reasonably 正當地
comparatively 相當地

❷ market value 市價
cost 費用，成本
worth 價值
MSRP 建議售價
retail value 零售價

恐怕我要提出一個相當嚴重的問題。我訂購的零件不僅不適用於我的電腦，甚至它對我的 CPU 造成相當大的破壞。所以我將要求賠償。我的電腦價值是 1,200 美元。您的產品直接導致我的電腦無法再使用。謝謝您的快速回覆。

farily 相當地　serious 嚴重的　not only... but (also)... 不僅～而且～　part 零件　damage 破壞
compensation 賠償　unusable 不能使用的　a direct of result 一個直接的結果

✉ sample 411

I still have not received a response concerning the problems I'm having with the product. Whether or not I give you my business again depends on a prompt resolution of these problems. Please respond as quickly as possible to this email.

Sincerely,

- - - - - - - -

Try It!可以替換的字詞

we're experiencing 我們正經歷
occurring 發生
happening 發生
in the works 在運作中
stirring 發生中

針對我對於此產品提出的問題，我仍未收到回覆。我會不會再給您生意，取決於這些問題是否可獲得及時解決。請盡快回覆此電子郵件。謹此。

> response 回覆　concerning 關於～　whether or not 是否～　depend on 取決於～　prompt 迅速的 resolution 解決　quickly 迅速地

✉ sample 412

Dear

This email is to express my exasperation at the lack of a response to my complaints. If we are to continue to do business together, I must know that problems can be resolved and resolved quickly. Please respond as soon as you get this.

- - - - - - - -

Try It!可以替換的字詞

utter fury 相當的憤怒
vexation 惱怒
endless anger 無盡的憤怒
enragement 盛怒
ongoing annoyance 持續的煩惱

這封電子郵件是為了表達對於我投訴無門的憤怒。如果我們要繼續一起合作生意，我必須知道問題可以得到解決，且是迅速解決。收到這封信後，請盡快回覆。

> express 表達　exasperation 惱怒，憤怒　complaint 申訴　do business 做生意　as soon as 盡快

✉ sample 413

Dear (............)

I'm concerned about the lack of **a clear** response to the complaints I made on March 12th. It is absolutely imperative that we resolve this issue as quickly as possible. If you cannot handle the problem, please put me in contact with your supervisor so that we can move forward.

I look forward to hearing from you soon.

Try It! 可以替換的字詞

an apparent 一個明白無誤的

a transparent 一個透明的

a plain 一個清楚的

a simple 一個簡明的

an unambiguous 一個明白的

- - - - - - - -

對於我在 3 月 12 日所做的投訴未能獲得明確的答覆，我在此表達關切。我們絕對必須盡快解決這個問題。如果您無法處理此問題，請讓我與您的主管聯繫，以便我們能繼續進行。我期待很快收到您的回覆。

lack 缺乏，不足　absolutely 絕對地　imperative 必需的　handle 處理
put A in contact with B 讓 A 與 B 聯繫　supervisor 主管，經理

✉ sample 414

Dear (............)

I'm writing in regard to the complaints I expressed in my email of 8/13/18. I have yet to receive a reply, and the problems I explained **remain** unsolved. I urge you to contact me as soon as possible so that we can find a solution to these serious concerns.

I look forward to your prompt reply.

Try It! 可以替換的字詞

are left 處於～（某種狀態）

stand 停留在～（某狀態）

are still 仍然是～

continue to be 持續是～

are staying 持續著～

- - - - - - - -

我寫這封信是關於我在 2018 年 8 月 13 日的電子郵件中表達的不滿。我還沒有收到回覆，且我提出的問題仍未得到解決。我需請求您盡快與我聯繫，以便我們能找到解決這些嚴重問題的方法。期待您的迅速回覆。

in regard to 關於～　remain 仍然～　unsolved 未解決的　urge...to... 呼籲，要求（某人去做某事）
serious concerns 嚴重的問題

✉ sample 415

Dear ⟨_____⟩

I'm not sure if you have been getting my emails. I have written several times in the last week to express impatience at your inability to solve my problem. Please get in touch with me as soon as possible with a solution.

- - - - - - - -

我不確定您是否有收到我的電子郵件。對於您無法解決我的問題，我上週寫過好幾封表達不耐的信。請盡快與我聯繫並提供解決方案。

sure 確定的　several times 好幾次　impatience 不耐　inability 無能　solution 解決辦法

Try It！可以替換的字詞

state 陳述

convey 傳達

put across 說明

suggest 暗示

communicate 傳達

回覆客訴 Responding to Complaints ▲

✉ sample 416

Dear [_____]

We have received your complaints. Please ❶know that we are working ❷hard to solve the problems. We should have everything taken care of by tomorrow.

Thank you very much for your patience.

- - - - - - - -

Try It！可以替換的字詞

❶ be aware 了解～
take solace in the fact
對於～的事實有同感
find peace knowing 放心地去了解
do not question 不要懷疑
believe 相信

❷ diligently 勤奮地
assiduously 不懈地
attentively 專心地
around-the-clock 連續二十四小時地
with everything we have
盡我們一切力量地

我們收到了您的投訴。請了解我們正努力解決問題。明天之前我們應該會把一切都處理好。非常感謝您的耐心等待。

complaint 投訴，抱怨　work hard 努力工作　solve 解決（問題）　take care of 照顧，處置～
by tomorrow 明天前

✉ sample 417

Dear [_____]

I assure you that we understand your complaints, and we are working to find a solution. We will contact you by the end of the day with an update on our efforts. I apologize for the problems and I promise that we are on the case.

- - - - - - -

Try It！可以替換的字詞

grievances 不滿
protests 抗議
moans 委曲
appeals 控訴
objections 異議

我向您保證，我們了解您的不滿。我們正努力尋找解決方案。我們將在本日結束之前與您聯繫，並告知我們的最新進度。我為這些問題道歉，並承諾我們會處理這件事。

assure 保證　solution 解決方案　update 更新，最新消息　efforts 努力　apologize 道歉　promise 承諾
be on the case 正處理這件事中

✉ sample 418

Dear [_____]

I understand your ❶annoyance with the problems you have experienced. Please understand that we are committed to solve your problems as quickly as can ❷ reasonably be expected. We should have the issues you spoke of resolved within the week. I will email you as soon as we've solved the problem.

Thank you for your patience.

- - - - - - -

Try It！可以替換的字詞

❶ limitations 侷限，限度
frustrations 挫折，挫敗
disappointments 失望
continuous questions 持續存在的問題
ongoing irritations 持續的煩躁

❷ sensibly 明智地
rationally 理性地
logically 合乎邏輯地
plausibly 合理地
convincingly 可說服人地

我理解您煩惱著所遇到的問題的。請了解我們一直努力在合理的預期範圍內，盡快解決您的問題。我們應可於一周內解決您所說的問題。一旦問題解決了，我就會給您發電子郵件。感謝您的耐心。

experience 經歷 annoyance 煩惱 be committed to 致力於～
as quickly as reasonably 盡可能在合理範圍內 have A resolved 解決 A 問題 issue 問題

✉ sample 419

Dear [_____]

We have received your complaints and are working to address your concerns. Once we have more information concerning the whereabouts of your order, we will contact you. In the meantime, I ask that you be patient with the process.

Thank you for understanding.

- - - - - - -

Try It！可以替換的字詞

truly request 真懇地請求
yearn 熱切盼望
solicit 懇求
expect 期盼
demand 要求

我們已收到您的投訴，且正努力解決您關切的事。一旦我們得知更多有關您訂單下落的訊息，我們將與您聯繫。與此同時，我拜託求您在此過程中保持耐心。謝謝您的理解。

address 解決 concerns 關心的事，重要的事 once 一旦，一經～ concerning 關於～
whereabouts 行蹤，下落 order 訂單，訂貨 in the meantime 與此同時 patient 耐心的
process 過程，進程

✉ sample 420

Dear [ ]

I understand your frustration. These problems are
❶serious, and we are working to solve them. As soon as
we have ascertained exactly what the **❷malfunction** with
the hardware is, we will make the necessary repairs and
ship you the replacement products. Until then, I can only
ask for your patience.

Thank you.

- - - - - - - -

Try It！可以替換的字詞

❶grave 嚴重的

grim 嚴重的

inexcusable 不可寬恕的

sobering 嚴重的

surely correctable 必然可修正的

❷breakdown 故障

wrong 故障

failure 故障

blip 暫時的問題

error 故障

我理解您的沮喪。這些問題很嚴重，但我們正努力解決中。一旦我們確切查明導致硬體故障的原因，
我們將進行必要的維修並運送替換的產品給您。在那之前，我只能請您耐心等候。謝謝。

ascerntain 確定，弄清 malfunction 故障 repair 維修事項 replacement 替換（品）

✉ sample 421

Dear [............]

I'm happy to inform you that we have solved the problem. Your replacement order has been shipped out and should arrive within the week. I would like to apologize again for the inconvenience.

Thank you for your patience.

- - - - - - - -

Try It！可以替換的字詞

delighted 高興的
elated 興高采烈的
charmed 喜悅的
overjoyed 非常高興的
so very pleased 非常高興的

我很高興可以通知您，我們已經解決了這個問題。您更換的訂貨已運出，應可於一周內到貨。對於給您帶來的不便，我想再次道歉。謝謝您的耐心等待。

inform 通知　ship 運送　within the week 一周內　inconvenience 不便　patience 耐心

✉ sample 422

Dear [............]

I'm writing to let you know that we have found the problem with the hard drive that you ordered. It was ❶ set to operate at the wrong speed. There is a ❷quick fix that will allow you to ensure compatibility with your system. I'm sorry for the difficulties you have had.

Thank you for your understanding.

- - - - - - - -

Try It！可以替換的字詞

❶ arranged 設置的
established 已確立的
regulated 制定的
configured 設定的
programmed 以程式設定的

❷ workaround 解決方法
solution 解決方法
simple mend 簡單修護方式
trouble-free repair 故障排除的維修方式
patch 暫時解決方法

我寫這封信是想讓您知道，我們發現您訂購的硬碟有問題。它的運轉速度設定錯誤。有一個快速解決方案，可以確保它與您的系統相容。對於給您帶來的任何麻煩，我們深表歉意。謝謝您的理解。

set 設定　operate 運轉　quick fix 快速解決方案　allow 容許　ensure 確保　compatibility 相容　difficulty 難題

✉ sample 423

Dear ┄┄┄┄┄

I have good news. We have resolved the problem with the shipping company and they are now **releasing** your order. It should be delivered within the next 48 hours. I appreciate your patience in this matter. I assure you that problems like this are not typical at our company.

Thank you again for your patience.

- - - - - - -

我有好消息。我們已經解決了貨運公司的問題,他們現在正要派送您的訂貨。應該在接下來的 48 小時內到貨。感謝您對此事的耐心等待。我向您們保證,這樣的問題在我們公司並不常見。再次感謝您的耐心等待。

release 派發 order 訂貨 matter 事件 assure 保證 typical 典型的

✉ sample 424

Dear ┄┄┄┄┄

I wanted to let you know that the problems that made it difficult for you to contact our customer service department have been resolved. There was an issue with our phone system. Your calls were being routed to a voice mailbox that is no longer in use. You can be sure that **from now on** you will have no problems contacting us.

Thank you for your patience in this matter.

- - - - - - -

我想告訴您,您難以聯繫我們客戶服務部門的問題已得到解決。我們的電話系統出現問題。您撥打的電話被轉接到已經沒使用的語音信箱。從現在開始可以確定您一定可以聯繫到我們。感謝您對此事的耐心等待。

make it difficult for A to do... 讓 A 很難做～ customer service department 客戶服務部門
route（透過特定路線）轉送 in use 在使用中 from now on 從現在開始

✉ sample 425

Dear ⌐‾‾‾‾‾‾‾¬

I am writing to inform you that we have found a way to address your complaints. We are sending a new shipment to replace the one that was damaged. You should receive it by the end of the week. I apologize for the problems you have encountered. I can personally guarantee you that they are not ❶common at our company and they ❷will not happen again.

Thank you for your generosity.

- - - - - - - -

我寫這封信是想通知您，對於您的投訴，我們已找到解決的方法。我們正要將新的貨品運出，以更換損壞的那件。您應該會在本週末前收到。我為您遭遇的問題表示歉意。我個人可以向您保證，這些問題在我們公司並不常見，也不會再發生。謝謝您的寬宏大量。

address 解決　shipment 運送，裝運　encounter 遭遇　personally 就個人而言　common 常見的

道歉與解釋 Apology & Excuse

Case 01 致上歉意 ① **Making an Apology** ① ▲

sample 426

Dear [   ]

I'm terribly sorry for the delays we've experienced in getting the report to you. I know your time is valuable. We will work to avoid issues like this in the future.

Thank you for your patience.

- - - - - - - -

Try It! 可以替換的字詞

I promise we will improve upon issues
我保證我們會改善問題

Our communications will not be handled
我們的溝通將不會被處理

We will do our best to head off problems
我們會盡力避免

You will not have to experience delays
您不會再遇到延誤狀況

Improvements will be made to interactions
會改善互動方式

對於我們所遇到寄送報告給您的延遲狀況，我感到非常抱歉。我知道您的時間寶貴。未來我們會努力避免出現類似問題。感謝您的耐心等待。

terribly 非常　delay 延遲　report 報告　avoid 避免　issue 問題

sample 427

Dear [   ]

I'm writing to apologize for losing my temper at the meeting. I know that the low sales figures are not your fault. I've been under a lot of pressure lately and I'm afraid I didn't control my emotions very well. I hope you can forgive me.

Regards,

- - - - - - - -

Try It! 可以替換的字詞

stress 壓力
strain 壓力
anxiety 焦慮
burdens 負擔
concerns 擔憂

我寫這封信是要為我在會議上發脾氣而道歉。我知道銷售不佳不是您的錯。我最近承受很大的壓力，很抱歉我沒有能掌控好自己的情緒。我希望您能原諒我。謹此。

apologize 道歉　temper 情緒，性情，脾氣　fault 錯誤　pressure 壓力，壓迫　lately 最近
control 控制　emotion 情緒

✉ sample 428

Dear _____

I'm sorry for the **misunderstanding** last week. I hope you didn't wait for us too long. We had written down the wrong time for the meeting. I know your time is valuable and I'm sorry if we wasted too much of it.

Thanks for your understanding.

- - - - - - - -

對於上週發生的誤解，我感到抱歉。我希望您沒有等我們太久。我們把這場會議的時間寫錯了。我知道您的時間寶貴。如果我們浪費了您太多寶貴時間，我致上歉意。謝謝您的理解。

> misunderstanding 誤會，誤解　wait for 等待～　too long 太久　write down 寫下來～　meeting 會議　waste 浪費

✉ sample 429

Dear _____

I'm truly sorry for the mix-up last week. I really thought that the documents I sent you were the right ones. **Imagine my surprise** when I realized they weren't. I hope I didn't cause you too much trouble.

Thanks for your patience.

- - - - - - - -

真的很抱歉上週搞砸了您的工作。我以為我發送給您的這些文件是正確的。當我得知並非如此時，可以想像我有多驚訝。我希望我沒有造成您太多麻煩。謝謝您的耐心等待。

> mix-up 搞混，搞砸　imagine 想像，猜想　surprise 驚訝　realize 意識到　cause 引起　trouble 麻煩

✉ sample 430

Dear [_____]

I know I really **disturbed** your plans by being late last week. I apologize for causing so much trouble. I really should have double-checked the directions before driving to the meeting site. I won't let it happen again.

Thanks for understanding.

- - - - - - - -

我知道上週的遲到真的擾亂了您的計畫。造成這麼多麻煩，我表示歉意。我確實應該在開車去會議現場前，再次確認方向。我不會再讓這種情況發生。謝謝您的理解。

disrupt 擾亂　plan 計畫　double-check 再次確認　direction 方向

致上歉意 ② Making an Apology ② ▲

✉ sample 431

Dear ⌐⌐⌐⌐⌐

I'm sorry I wasn't able to make it to the meeting on Tuesday. I had a crisis at the office and I wasn't able to get away. I apologize if I've inconvenienced you too much. Let's reschedule for next week.

Thanks for understanding.

- - - - - - - -

抱歉，我週二當天未能出席會議。我在公司遇到了危機，因此無法離開。如果我給您帶來太多不便，我在此致上歉意。我們下週再約時間吧。謝謝理解。

Try It！可以替換的字詞
make an exit 離開
leave 離開
go away 離開
depart 離開
sneak away 悄悄離開

be able to 能夠～ make it to 出席～ crisis 危機 get away 離開～ office 辦公室 apologize 道歉 inconvenience 造成不便 reschedule 重新安排

✉ sample 432

Dear ⌐⌐⌐⌐⌐

I'd like to apologize for the mistake we made on your order last week. Our system is designed to avoid situations like this, but this time something went wrong. It was really inexcusable, and I promise it won't happen again.

Thank you for your patience.

- - - - - - - -

我想為上週處理您訂單時所出的差錯致上歉意。我們系統的設計就是用來在避免這種情況發生，但這次卻出了問題。這確實是不可原諒的，我保證不會再發生這種情況。感謝您的耐心。

Try It！可以替換的字詞
set up 設定
intended 用於，作為
planned 設計為
deliberately constructed 刻意打造為
devised 設計為

mistake 錯誤 be designed to do 被設計用來～ situation 情況 go wrong 出了問題 inexcusable 不可原諒的，不可饒恕的

✉ sample **433**

Dear [..........]

I'm terribly sorry for giving you the wrong time for the meeting yesterday. I could have sworn that I typed 1:00 rather than 10:00. I was so embarrassed when you showed up three hours early. I know that your time is valuable and I never intended to waste it. If there's any way I can make it up to you, please let me know.

I'll talk to you soon.

- - - - - - - -

我非常抱歉昨天給您的會議時間錯誤。我可以發誓我打的時間是 1:00 而不是 10:00。讓您提早三個小時出現，我感到很不好意思。我知道您的時間很寶貴，我從不打算浪費您的時間。如果我能以任何方式彌補您，請告訴我。我會盡快和您談談。

> swear 保證，發誓　type 打字　rather than 而不是～　embarrassed 尷尬的　show up 出現
> valuable 寶貴的　intend to 打算～　waste 浪費　make it up 彌補

✉ sample **434**

Dear [..........]

Please forgive me for my ❶rude behavior yesterday. I've been under a lot of pressure recently, but that is no excuse for not being ❷professional. I didn't mean to raise my voice during the meeting. That was really inexcusable. I hope you can forget about it so that we can have a fresh start.

Thank you for your patience.

- - - - - - -

請原諒我昨天的粗魯行為。我最近承受了很大的壓力，但這不該是表現不夠專業的藉口。我不是故意在會議期間大聲講話。那真的是不可原諒的。我希望您可以不要計較這件事，讓我們有一個新的開始吧。感謝您的耐心。

> rude 粗魯的　behavior 行為　under pressure 在壓力之下　be no excuse for 不能成為～的藉口
> raise 提高

✉ sample 435

Dear [_____]

I'd like to apologize for the errors in the sales report I presented at the meeting yesterday. I know that I under-represented sales of your company's products. That was never my intention. It was my own math mistake in the spreadsheet that led to the problem. I've written to all of the attendees at the meeting to give them the correct numbers. I've cc'd you on that email too. I'll definitely be more careful in the future.

Thanks for understanding.

- - - - - - - -

我想為昨天在會議上發表的銷售報告錯誤道歉。我知道我低估了貴公司的產品銷售情況。那絕非我的本意。導致此問題的原因是，我在這張電子表格程式中的數字計算錯誤。我已經寫信給會議的所有出席者，並已給他們正確的數字。那封電子郵件我也已轉寄副本給您。我將來一定會更加小心。謝謝您的理解。

present 發表 underrepresent 低估；未能完全呈現～ sales 銷售量 lead to 導致～ attendee 與會者 definitely 一定，絕對 cc 轉寄（電子郵件）副本給～

Try It！可以替換的字詞

slides 幻燈片

computer presentation 電腦簡報

data 數據

statistics 統計資料

figures 數字

Case 03

請求寬恕或原諒 ① Making an Excuse ①

sample 436

Sorry, but I can't make it to the dinner party on Saturday evening. I've got my in-laws in town this weekend, so I'll be busy ❶entertaining them. I'll take a ❷rain check though.

Thanks,

\- - - - - - - -

Try It ! 可以替換的字詞

❶ amusing 使歡樂
humoring 迎合
wining and dining 以好酒好菜款待
visiting 拜訪
seeing 照料

❷ time change 時間上的變更
later date 晚些的日期
postponement 延期
delay 延遲
rescheduling 重新安排

對不起，我無法參加星期六晚上的派對。我岳父母這個週末會過來鎮上，所以我得忙著招呼他們。我還是下次再參加好了。謝謝。

dinner party 晚宴　evening 晚上　in-laws 岳父母（或公婆）　entertain 招待
rain check 下次再去，改期

sample 437

Dear

I'm not going to have the proposal finished before Friday. I'm afraid my intern really messed things up by losing half of our files! Once we get the missing information restored, we'll be able to get everything to you.

Sorry for the delay.

\- - - - - - - -

Try It ! 可以替換的字詞

renewed 更新
back 拿回
fixed 修復
reconstructed 重新建檔
re-established 重新建檔

我無法在星期五之前完成這項提案。很抱歉因為我的實習生丟失了一半檔案而把事情搞砸！一旦我們拿回丟失的資料，我們將能夠為您提供一切資訊。抱歉造成延誤了。

proposal 提案　finish 完成　intern 實習生　mess... up 搞砸～　half of 一半～　missing 不見了的
restore 恢復，使復原

✉ sample 438

Try It ! 可以替換的字詞

[_____]

I'm afraid the sales report won't be ready until later in the week. We've had a problem getting this new computer ❶software to work right, so we can't get ❷an accurate set of numbers yet. Once an IT engineer figures it out, we should be in business.

Thanks for your patience.

- - - - - - - -

❶ program 程式
course 課程
agenda 議程
plan 計畫
schedule 進度表

❷ a correct 正確的
a precise 精確的
an exact 準確的
a perfect 分毫不差的
a literal 如實的

我擔心銷售報告要到本週晚些時候才會準備好。我們新的電腦軟體無法正常運作,因此無法獲得一組精確的值。一旦 IT 工程師解決這個問題時,我們就會開始處理。謝謝您的耐心等待。

afraid 害怕,擔心〜 until 直到〜 accurate 精確的 set of 一組 figure...out 解決〜

✉ sample 439

Try It ! 可以替換的字詞

Dear [_____]

I'm going to have to put off the meeting for another day. It turns out we've got some problems at our warehouse that I have to attend to. There always seems to be something delaying us, right? I'm sorry if this is too much of an inconvenience.

Thanks,

- - - - - - - -

obstructing 妨礙
holding up 延誤
impeding 妨礙
hampering 阻礙
drawing out 牽制

我不得不把這場會議往後延一天。事實上,我們的倉庫遇出現了一些我必須負責處理的問題。難免總會有一些事情造成我們工作上的拖延,對吧?如果這造成很大的不便,我致上歉意。謝謝。

have to 不得不〜 put off 推遲〜 another 另外的 turn out 事實證明〜 warehouse 倉庫
attend to 注意,關心 always 總是

✉ sample 440

┌─ ─ ─ ─ ─ ─ ─ ┐
└ ─ ─ ─ ─ ─ ─ ─ ┘

I'm sorry I didn't have the figures ready at the last meeting. We had a computer glitch right as I was about to leave for the meeting and I lost all of my data. I'll get them to you as soon as I recover them.

Thanks for understanding.

- - - - - - - -

對於上次會議中我沒有準備好這些數字，真是抱歉。當我正要出發參加會議時，我們的電腦發生故障了，我遺失了所有數據。我一修復資料就會盡快把數據發送給您。感謝您的理解。

figures 金額，數字　glitch 小故障，失靈　be about to 正要～　lost 丟失　as soon as 盡快～

✉ sample 441

Dear ◻◻◻◻◻

I'm sorry we were not able to address your concerns yesterday. You see, yesterday was a ❶holiday here in Taiwan, so the offices were closed. Sometimes these problems occur when dealing with international ❷trade. I hope the delay was not too long.

Thank you for your patience.

- - - - - - - -

Try It！可以替換的字詞

❶ special day 特別的日子
vacation day 放假日
national day of mourning 國喪日
day off 休假日
government recess 國定假日

❷ companies 公司
partners 合作夥伴
entities 實體
businesses 公司
agencies 代理商

對於昨天我們無法解決您的問題，我在此致上歉意。如您所知，昨天在台灣這邊是休假日，所以公司都休息。有時我們必須處理國際貿易時，就是會出現這樣的問題。我希望不會延遲太久。謝謝您的耐心等待。

address 解決　concern 關心的事　closed 關閉的　occur 發生　international 國際的　trade 貿易，交易

✉ sample 442

Dear ◻◻◻◻◻

Unfortunately, we cannot connect you with our support desk today. Our main technology specialist is out with the flu today, so we are short-staffed. We should be able to get to you tomorrow. I'm sorry for the inconvenience.

Thank you for your understanding.

- - - - - - - -

Try It！可以替換的字詞

internet services 網際網路服務
computer experts 電腦專家
help desk 服務台
computing geniuses 電腦天才
technology crew 技術人員

很遺憾，我們無法讓您與我們的支援服務台取得聯繫。我們主要的技術專家今天罹患流感，所以我們人力短缺。我們明天應該能夠聯繫您。造成不便，深表歉意。謝謝您的理解。

connect 聯繫　support 服務　desk 桌，台　specialist 專家　flu 流感　short-staffed 人力短缺的

✉ sample 443

Dear [............]

I'm sorry about the slow response to your complaints. We have recently undergone a **restructure** of our customer service department, and we are still working out the kinks in the system. Your problems are very important to us, and we will be able to address your concerns very soon.

Thank you very much.

- - - - - - - -

reorganization 改組
streamlining 人力精簡
shuffling 改組
reform 改革
modification 變革

對於我們太晚回應您的投訴，我感到很抱歉。我們最近客戶服務部門進行重組，我們仍在處理這個系統中的關鍵問題。您的問題對我們非常重要，我們很快就能解決您的問題。非常感謝您。

recently 最近　undergo 經歷～　restructure 重組，改組　kink 關鍵問題　very soon 很快地

✉ sample 444

Dear [............]

I'm afraid we're not going to be able to get your order to you by Friday. Unfortunately, there has been a problem with the product, and we've had to recall a number of the units. This should be cleared up soon. When dealing with technology of this **nature**, such issues are unavoidable. Let me assure you that once you do receive the shipment, the quality will be very high.

Thank you for the patience.

kind 種類
sort 類型
type 類型
form 型式
makeup 屬性

我看我們恐怕無法在週五之前交付您的訂貨。因為很不幸，這產品出了一點問題，我們不得不召回一部分。問題應該很快就會獲得解決。當我們在處理這類型技術時，這樣的問題是不可避免的。請讓我向您保證，您收到貨時，會發現產品品質相當棒。謝謝您的耐心等待。

recall 召回，回收　clear up 解決　deal with 處理～　nature 性質，類型　unavoidable 不可避免的
shipment 貨物

✉ sample 445

Dear ⬚⬚⬚⬚⬚

As you know, your order is shipping late, and I just wanted to give you a little explanation. We've had a problem with our delivery company and have had to **①switch to** another. Some of our outstanding orders were carried over, but some were not. Yours was among those that got lost in the **②shuffle**. We've remedied the situation, and I'm sorry if there was too much inconvenience.

Thanks,

- - - - - - - -

Try It！可以替換的字詞

❶ change to 更改為～

go with 選擇

pick 選擇

decide upon 決定

make a hard choice but go to 在難以抉擇後還是得～

❷ switchover 轉換

chaos 混亂

disorder 混亂

pandemonium 混亂（場所）

mess 混亂

如您所知，您訂購的商品已延遲出貨，我正想給您稍微說明一下。我們和配合的貨運公司有一點問題，我們不得不換另一家。我們一些未交付的訂貨已結轉，但有些還沒有。您的訂貨屬於這次變動過程中未被處理的。我們已針對此狀況進行補救，若給您帶來太多不便，我在此深表歉意。謝謝。

order 訂單，訂貨 explanation 說明 switch 轉移 outstanding 未完成的
carry over（產品等）運送轉移 get lost in the shuffle 在此變動中未經處理 remedy 補救

Case 05　化解誤會 Clearing Up Some Misunderstanding ▲

✉ sample 446

Dear [_____],

I think there's been some kind of misunderstanding. I thought we had agreed to meet on Thursday, but in your last email it looked like you were thinking Wednesday. We should **clear this up** before someone ends up wasting time. Let me know when you get a chance.

Thanks,

- - - - - - - -

Try It！可以替換的字詞

fix it 修理它
repair it 修理它
clarify it 澄清這一點
explain it 解釋這件事
spell it out 詳細說明

我認為我們之間有一點誤解。我以為我們已經同意在星期四見面，但在您上一封電子郵件中似乎您認為是星期三見面。我們應該澄清此事，否則會讓人最終落入浪費時間的窘境。請讓我知道您何時有機會（出來見面）。謝謝。

> kind of 有一點～　misunderstanding 誤解　agree 同意　clear... up 澄清，整頓～　before... 在～以前
> end up...（以不好的身份、狀態、境況等）結束

✉ sample 447

Dear [_____],

I think there's been a mix-up **concerning** the payment schedule. Could you give me a call when you get a chance so we can sort it out? I'll be here for the rest of the day.

Regards,

- - - - - - - -

Try It！可以替換的字詞

relating to 關於～
in regard to 關於～
with regard to 關於～
with respect to 關於～
in respect of 關於～

我認為我們在付款時間表上有所誤解。您有空可以給我打個電話嗎？這樣我們才能解決這問題。我今天都會在這裡。致上問候。

> mix-up 混淆　concerning 關於～　payment 付款　schedule 時間表　sort... out 整頓，解決
> the rest of the day 當日剩下的時間

✉ sample 448

Dear [_____]

I think maybe we've had a misunderstanding. You seemed a little upset with me at the last meeting. I hope I haven't done anything to cause you problems. Please let me know so we can clear things up.

Thanks,

- - - - - - - -

我想我們也許有一點誤會。在上次會議上您似乎對我有點不高興。我希望我沒有做了什麼造成您的困擾。請讓我知道，以便我們可以解決問題。謝謝。

seem 似乎～　irritated 被激怒的　last meeting 上次會議　cause 造成～

✉ sample 449

Dear [_____]

I'm afraid we may have had a little miscommunication. I need to have the completed sales reports by Friday so that I can show them to our partners. You mentioned at the meeting that you would have them on Monday. That would be too late. Let me know if you'll have them ready by Friday.

Thanks,

- - - - - - - -

我擔心我們可能有些許的溝通不良。我必須在星期五之前拿到完整的銷售報告，以便我可以拿給我們的合作夥伴們看。您在會議上提到您星期一才會拿到。那會太遲了。請讓我知道您是否能在星期五之前準備好它。謝謝。

completed 完成的　partner 夥伴，共同出資人　mention 提到　late 遲的　sales 銷售　report 報告

✉ sample 450

Dear [_____]

I'm writing to clear up a misunderstanding. I hope you don't think that I spoke to Mr. Lee about the project before clearing it with you. I value your ❶input very much, and I would never bypass you in that way. Rest assured that I will keep you ❷in the loop.

Thank you.

- - - - - - - -

Try It! 可以替換的字詞

❶ suggestions 建議
ideas 想法
contribution 貢獻
thoughts 想法
offers 提議

❷ in the know （比其他人）熟悉內幕的
informed 得到消息的
up to date 獲知最新訊息的
clued in 獲知線索的
aware 知情的

我寫這封信的目的是想澄清誤解。我希望您不要認為我在為您說明那件事之前，已先和李先生談過。我非常重視您提出的意見，我絕不會那樣忽視您的想法。請放心，我會讓您獲知最新資訊。謝謝。

clear A with B 向 B（人）說清楚 A（事）　value 重視　input（訊息和意見的）提出，提供　bypass 繞過，忽視　rest assured that 對於～放心　in the loop 得到最新資訊

解釋生氣的原因 Explaining the Source of Anger ▲

✉ sample 451

I expected to have the contracts on my desk by 5pm yesterday. Frankly, I'm a little irritated that there's been such a big delay. We really need to wrap up this deal. Please try to get everything together by the end of business today.

Try It！可以替換的字詞

finish (up) 結束
end 結束
close 完結
finalize 終結
settle 完成

我預期昨天下午 5 點之前合約會放在我的桌子上。坦白說，出現這麼嚴重的延遲，我有點惱火。我們真的得結束這筆交易了。請在今天下班之前將所有資料整理完畢。

expect 預期　contract 合約　frankly 坦白地　irritated 惱火的　need to 必須～　wrap up 結束～
by the end of business 在辦公時間結束之前

✉ sample 452

I must say I'm a little annoyed. I'm not sure how you managed to confuse the internal sales report with the one intended for our outside partners. It caused me quite a bit of embarrassment. Please try to be more scrupulous in the future.

Try It！可以替換的字詞

sensible 聰明的
careful 小心的
thorough 周密的
conscientious 認真的
reliable 可信賴的

我必須說我有點生氣。我不確定您如何將內部業務報告，與我們外部夥伴的報告混淆。這讓我有點尷尬。未來請試著更加謹慎些。

manage to 設法～　confuse 混淆　internal 內部的　intended 打算中的，預期　embarrassment 尷尬
scrupulous 謹慎的

sample 453

Try It！可以替換的字詞

honest 誠實的
open 開誠的
clear-cut 明確的
simple 坦率的
basic 守本分的

If we're going to work on this project together, we're going to have to be more **straightforward** with each other. You can't bring up new proposals at a meeting with the client when you haven't even spoken to me about them yet. Please have a little more respect for me in the future.

- - - - - - -

如果我們要一起進行這個專案，我們彼此必須更加坦誠相待。當您還沒有和我談過新的提案時，您不能先在會議上向客戶提出。未來請您再多尊重我一點。

work on 進行著～　straightforward 直接的，坦率的　each other 彼此　bring up 提起，談到～
client 客戶　respect 尊重，尊敬

sample 454

Try It！可以替換的字詞

seal 蓋印於
obtain 得到
acquire 取得
fasten 確定
close out 使～成定案

I'm not sure what you were thinking when you decided to skip the meeting yesterday. That was an important point in this project, and I'm a little angry that you didn't realize that. Please understand that we have to do everything right at this stage if we want to **secure** the deal.

- - - - - - -

昨天您決定不參加會議時，我無法理解您的想法。那是這項專案的一個重點，而您沒有意識到這一點，這讓我有點生氣。請理解現階段我們必須做對每一件事情 — 如果我們想要確定這項交易。

sure 確信的　skip 跳過，遺漏　realize 意識到　right 正確地　stage 階段　secure 確定　deal 交易，合約

✉ sample 455

If we are going to work together, I need you to be a little more direct with me. If I had understood you had reservations about the direction the deal was going in, I wouldn't have scheduled a meeting with our distributor. A meeting with someone from an external company is not the time to air our grievances with each other.

we need to understand one another better. 我們必須更加了解彼此。

I need to know where you stand. 我必須知道您的立場為何。

we need to communicate. 我們必須溝通。

I want you to be upfront with me. 我希望您能對我坦白。

I have to have reliable information from you. 我需要您提供可靠的訊息。

如果我們要一起合作，我需要您對我更加坦白點。如果我早知道您對這項交易的方向有所保留，我就不會安排與我們經銷商進行一場會議。與公司以外的人開會，並不是抒發我們彼此間有何不滿的適當時機。

work together 一起工作　reservation（意見上的）保留，異議　direction 方向，趨勢　meeting 會議　distributor 經銷商　air 發表，宣揚　grievance 不滿，牢騷

提問、提議、要求 Inquiry, Suggestion & Request

Case 01　提問 Asking a Question　▲

sample 456

Dear _____

I just had a quick question. Are the sales figures you sent me last week the most recent ones? I'm trying to put together an order and I need the current figures so I can decide how many units I need. I'd appreciate it if you could let me know if these are the latest.

Thanks for the help.

- - - - - - - -

我只是想快速地問個問題。您上週寄給我的銷售數據是最新的嗎？我正試著整理訂單，而我需要目前的數據，以便我可以決定我需要多少單位。如果您能告訴我這些數據是否是最新的，我將不勝感激。謝謝您的幫助。

> **Try It! 可以替換的字詞**
>
> most recent 最新的
> exact ones 確切的數字
> precise values 精確值
> ones I need 我需要的數字
> best to use 最好用的

sales figures 銷售數字　put together 整理，彙整　decide 決定　unit（成品等的）單位，單元

sample 457

Dear _____

There's something I'm not quite clear on. Did you say that the price of the G32 had gone up 2% or 3%? I don't remember what you had told me, and I can't find the original email. Could you let me know as soon as possible?

Thanks,

- - - - - - - -

有件事我不太明瞭。您是說 G32 的價格漲了 2% 還是 3%？我不記得您跟我講過什麼了，我找不到原始的電子郵件。可以請您能盡快告訴我嗎？謝謝。

> **Try It! 可以替換的字詞**
>
> sure about 確定～
> knowledgeable on 了解～
> aware of 得知～的
> keen for 知悉～的
> straight with 清楚明白～

clear 明瞭的　go up（價格）上漲　original 原始的　as soon as possible 盡快

✉ sample 458

Dear _____

I hope you are doing well. I was ❶wondering if I could ❷bother you with a quick question. Is the newest line of textiles you are producing going to be ready for distribution this fall, or in the winter? I'm interested in placing an order soon, and I'd like to know what my options are.

Thank you in advance for your help.

- - - - - - - -

Try It！可以替換的字詞

❶ hoping 期待著

speculating 猜想

questioning 有疑問

probing 探究

suspecting 猜想

❷ take up your time 佔用您的時間

worry you 打擾您

trouble you 麻煩您

disturb you 打擾您

fret you 麻煩您

展信愉快。我想知道是否可以請教一個簡單的問題。您生產的最新紡織品系列是否準備於今年秋天進行分銷，還是在冬天？我很快就會下訂單，我想知道我有什麼樣的選擇。對於您的協助，先說聲謝謝了。

> I was wondering if 我想知道～（是否）　bother 打擾　textile 紡織品　distribution 分銷
> place an order 下訂單　in advance 預先

✉ sample 459

Dear _____

I'm writing to get a little information from you. Would you be able to tell me what shipping service you use for overseas delivery? We have had some problems with our service, so we're looking for alternatives. If you could give me any recommendations, I'd appreciate it.

Thank you.

- - - - - - - -

Try It！可以替換的字詞

others 其它選擇

choices 選擇方案

a new supplier 一個新的供應商

replacements 替代方案

another 另一家

我寫這封信是為了從您這邊取得一些資訊。煩請您告訴我，您在海外派送方面配合的是哪家貨運公司？我們在運貨服務方面出現一些問題，因此我們正在尋找替代方案。如果您能給我任何建議，我會很感激。謝謝。

> overseas delivery 海外派送　alternative 替代方案　recommendation 建議

✉ sample 460

Dear [........................]

I have a question for you. What is the largest number of products you are capable of shipping at one time? We want to make a rather large order from you, and we weren't sure if we would need to break it up into smaller orders. I'd appreciate a quick response on this so that we can plan accordingly.

Thank you for your assistance.

- - - - - - - -

我有一個問題想請問您。您一次能夠運送的產品最大量是多少？我們想跟您下一筆相當大的訂單，但我不確定是否要將它拆為幾個較小的訂單。如您能快速回覆這件事，好讓我們有所計畫，我們會非常感激。謝謝您的幫助。

largest 最大的　capable of 能夠～　one time 一次　rather 相當地，頗　break up 拆開　response 回覆
accordingly 相應地

✉ sample 461

Dear [_____]

I just wanted you to run something. What would you think of hosting a meeting between our companies next month? I think it would be very beneficial for us to have a larger scale conference since we have increased the amount of business we do together. If we coordinate more closely, I think we will both profit. Let me know what you think.

Thanks,

Try It! 可以替換的字詞

holding 舉行
having 進行
getting 舉行
experiencing 進行
trying 嘗試進行

- - - - - - - -

我只是想告知您繼續進行。下個月我們兩家公司舉辦一場會議，您認為呢？我想，舉辦一場大規模會議，對我們雙方都有很大的好處，因為我們一起合作的生意已蒸蒸日上了。如果我們能夠更緊密地協調合作，我認為對雙方都有益。讓我知道您的想法。謝謝。

> run 進行　host 主辦　beneficial 有益的　larger scale 規模更大的　coordinate 協調

✉ sample 462

Dear [_____]

I'd like to throw out an idea and see what you think. I think we could really benefit from making our business relationship more permanent. The one-time deals we've done in the past have been very profitable for both of us. What would you think of entering into a more formal agreement so that we can do such deals on a more regular basis?

Let me know if this sounds reasonable to you.

Try It! 可以替換的字詞

singular transactions 單一交易
exchanges 交易
particular contracts 特殊合約
agreements 協議
one-time pacts 一次性協議

- - - - - - - -

我想提出一個想法，並看看您有何想法。我想，要是我們的業務關係可以更加長久，我們確實可以從中獲益。過去我們經歷過的一次性交易，對我們雙方來說都是很有利潤的。如果可以簽訂一份更正式的協議，以便我們能夠定期進行此類交易，您覺得如何呢？請讓我知道您是否覺得這聽起來很合理。

> permanent 長久的　enter into an agreement 簽訂一份合約　on a regular basis 定期地

✉ sample 463

Dear [_____]

I had an idea I wanted to share with you. Would you be interested in collaborating on a project with me? I think that we really need to have a conference in which ❶ diverse importers meet to network and discuss possible joint ❷ventures. What would you think of trying to organize such a conference with me? Let me know if you have the time and inclination to work with me on this.

I look forward to hearing from you.

- - - - - - - -

我想和您分享我的一個想法。您是否有興趣與我合作一項專案？我認為我們真的需要一起開個正式會議，會議中各進口商可以一起發表並討論可能的合夥事業。您認為和我一起籌辦這樣的一場會議如何？請讓我知道您是否有時間及意願，和我一起進行這項任務。期待您的回音。

share 分享　collaborate 合作　diverse 各種各樣的　importer 進口商　organize 籌辦
inclination 意願，傾向

✉ sample 464

Dear [_____]

I have a proposal for you. Would you be interested in sharing some of your contacts? Since we are not in direct competition with each other, I thought we might be able to benefit from giving each other access to our client lists. I have quite a few contacts that might be in the market for your products, and I'd imagine the same is true of you. Let me know if you think it's a good idea.

Thanks,

- - - - - - - -

我給您一個建議。您是否有興趣分享您的一些聯絡人？因為我們彼此並非是直接競爭的關係，我認為我們可以從透過客戶名單共享而獲益。我有很多聯繫名單，可能會需要使用您的產品，我想您的（對我來說）也是如此。請讓我知道您是否認為這是個好主意。謝謝。

access 使用　quite a few 相當多的　in the market for... 處於～的市場中，對～有需求

✉ sample 465

Dear [_____]

I'm writing with a proposal for you. What would you think of doing a ❶cross promotion with our ❷network routers and your desktop computers. I think we could really benefit each other by offering a package deal. Let me know what you think.

Thanks,

- - - - - - - -

我寫這封信是想給您一個建議。如果將我們的網路路由器與您的桌上型電腦一起進行交叉推廣，您覺得如何呢？我們可以提供一套協議，我想我們確實是可達到互惠互利的。讓我知道您的想法。謝謝。

cross promotion（兩公司的產品之間的）交叉推廣　benefit 受益　offer 提供
package deal 成套協議或交易

提議合作 ② **Proposing to Work Together** ② ▲

✉ sample 466

Dear 〔_____〕

I hope everything is going well with you. I'm writing to see if you'd be interested in ❶collaborating on a project with me. We are trying to create a business directory that would allow easy access to contact information for everyone in the ❷industry. If you would be interested in working on this with me, let me know.

Thanks,

- - - - - - - -

Try It ! 可以替換的字詞

❶ working together 一起工作
joining forces 一起工作
teaming up 合作
working in partnership 合作任務
acting as a team 團隊合作

❷ trade 行業
line of work 行業
occupation 職業
vocation 職業
profession 職業

希望您一切安好。我寫這封信是想詢問您是否有興趣與我合作一個專案。我們正試著建立一份工商人士名冊，可以讓我們輕鬆取得業內人士的連絡資訊。如果您有興趣與我合作這件事，請讓我知道。謝謝。

go well 進展順利　collaborate 合作　directory 名冊，目錄　access 存取

✉ sample 467

Dear 〔_____〕

I'm writing with a proposal for you. I'm trying to put together a marketing plan, and I think it would work best if we partnered with another firm. Your name immediately came to mind. Attached is a detailed proposal. If you have a chance, look it over and see if you are interested.

Let me know if you have any questions.

- - - - - - - -

Try It ! 可以替換的字詞

right away 立刻
at once 立刻
instantly 很快地
instantaneously 即刻
right off 馬上

我寫這封信是想給您一個建議。我正試圖要彙整一個行銷計劃，我認為如果我們與另一家公司合作，會產生最好的效果。而我立刻想到您。附件是一份詳細的提案。您有空的時候，請仔細過目一下，看看是否感興趣。請讓我知道您是否有任何疑問。

put together 彙整　initiative 初步的，創始的　attach 附上　detailed 詳細的　see if... 看看是否～

✉ sample 468

Dear _____

I enjoyed working with you last year, and there's a new project coming up that I thought you might like to be a part of. It's a cross-branding deal for textiles and a fashion label. We would be working together to create a group of products that would be sold from the same catalogue. Let me know if you think this sounds interesting.

I hope to hear from you soon.

- - - - - - - -

去年能夠和您一起工作真的很棒，而現在有個新的專案，我認為你可能會想參與其中。這是紡織品和時尚品牌的跨品牌推廣協議。我們將共同創建一組產品，這些產品將出現在同一個目錄中進行銷售。請讓我知道這是否讓您感興趣。希望很快能有您的消息。

cross 交叉的　branding 品牌打造　label 標籤，商標，標記　create 創建

✉ sample 469

Dear _____

I'm working on a deal with another company, and I've realized that I'm lacking some of the expertise necessary to pull it off. I was wondering if you'd be interested in getting involved. Obviously, we'd split any profits derived from your work. Give me a call and I'll give you more details.

Thanks,

- - - - - - - -

我正在與另一家公司簽訂合約，而且我知道我缺乏一些必要的專業知識來實現這一目標。我想知道您是否有興趣參與其中。當然，我們也會就您參與的部分中去分給您任何的獲利。給我個電話，我會告訴您更多細節。謝謝。

deal 交易，合同，協議　another 另一家　realize 意識到　expertise 專業知識
pull... off（透過努力）實現～　split 分割，分享

✉ sample **470**

Dear ⌐ _ _ _ _ _ ⌐

I've got an interesting project coming up that I think you might profit from getting involved in. We're going to be having ❶some meetings next week about a new marketing initiative and ❷I wondered if you'd like to partner with us. Give me a call and I'll go over the details with you.

I look forward to hearing from you.

- - - - - - - -

Try It！可以替換的字詞

❶a few 些許

several 幾個的

a handful of 少數

a bunch of 一些

one or two 少數幾個

❷I questioned 我想請問

I'm inquiring 我想問一下

I'm seeing 我想知道

I'm finding out 我想了解

I'm asking 我想問一下

我想提出一項有趣的專案，我想您可以從參與中獲益。我們將在下週召開幾場關於新的行銷活動會議，我想知道您是否願意與我們一起合作。給我打個電話，然後我會跟你詳細說明。期待您的回音。

interesting 有趣的　come up 出現　profit 獲益　partner with 與～合夥

拒絕提案 Rejecting the Proposal ▲

✉ sample 471

Try It！可以替換的字詞

Hi, [____]

Thanks for throwing this idea my way. Unfortunately, we've already planned our promotions for 2019, so there isn't really ❶room for any ❷new plans. I'll definitely keep this concept in mind for the future though.

Thanks again for thinking of us.

- - - - - - - -

❶ a place 一個地方
space 一個空間
a provision 一個預備空間
an opportunity 一個機會
flexibility 彈性

❷ proposed 被提出的
suggested 建議的
last-minute 最後一刻的
additional 另外的
potential 潛在的

謝謝你向我提出這個建議。不幸的是，我們已經計劃好 2019 年的促銷活動，所以實在已沒有任何新計畫的空間。不過在未來，我一定會記住這個概念。再次感謝您考慮到我們。

throw 丟擲，傳遞　promotion 促銷，推廣　room 空間，餘地　keep... in mind 將～牢記在心　though 但是，不過

✉ sample 472

Try It！可以替換的字詞

Dear [____]

I think the idea of an industry-wide conference is a great one. However, my schedule is just too full right now for me to take on such a big project. I certainly hope you can find someone to organize it with you. I'd certainly be happy to attend.

Thank you.

- - - - - - - -

agenda 議程，行程表
timetable 時間表
to-do list 待辦事項
personal appointment availability
個人約會可用時間
availability sheet 有空的時間表

我認為辦一場全產業會議的想法很棒。但是，我現在的行程安排太滿，無法承接這樣一個大專案。我當然希望你能另外找到人一起籌組會議。我也當然會樂意參加。謝謝。

industry-wide 全產業的　conference 會議　take on 承接～　organize 籌組　certainly 當然

sample 473

Try It！可以替換的字詞

mantra 規範，真言
rule 常規
guiding principle 指導原則
course of action 行動方針
procedure 常規

I agree that sharing contacts is a good idea. I am afraid it's our company's policy that client lists are strictly confidential. I ran your idea up to my boss, but she wouldn't go for it. Maybe somewhere down the line we can try again.

Thanks,

- - - - - - - -

我同意分享聯絡資訊是一個好主意。但我怕我們公司規定客戶名單是要嚴格保密的。我有把你的想法轉達給我老闆，但她沒有表示同意。也許我們未來會有機會再試一次。謝謝。

contacts 聯絡人　policy 政策　client list 客戶名單　strictly 嚴密地　confidential 機密的
try again 再試一次

sample 474

Try It！可以替換的字詞

suppleness 靈活
elasticity 彈性
give 彈性，靈活性
pliancy 柔軟性
effortlessness 輕鬆自如

Dear

Thanks for expressing such confidence in us. I've been very pleased with the business we've done together in the past, and I hope that there will be more deals in the future. However, it is important for my company to retain the flexibility that an informal relationship grants. In this uncertain economic climate, it's just too risky to enter into binding relationships with other firms.

Thank you for your understanding.

- - - - - - - -

感謝您對我們充滿信心。我對我們過去共同進行的業務感到非常滿意，我希望將來會有更多的往來。但是，對我公司而言，保持非正式關係所賦予的靈活性非常重要。在這種不確定的經濟情勢中，與其他公司建立有約束力的關係，風險太大。謝謝您的理解。

confidence 信心　pleased 對～感到滿意　in the past 在過去　retain 保持　grant 給予
economic climate 經濟情勢　enter into... 進入～狀態，開始從事～　binding 有約束力的　firm 公司

✉ sample **475**

Thanks for reaching out to me. I think your idea is a sound one, but I'm also concerned that trying to organize a company-wide meeting would be too logistically complicated to be worth the trouble. Keeping our meetings small prevents anyone's time from being wasted as well. I hope you understand my point of view on this.

Thanks,

- - - - - - - -

感謝您與我聯繫。我認為您的想法是合理的，但我也擔心，試圖籌辦一次全公司會議將造成後勤作業的複雜性，不值得麻煩行事。舉行小型會議也可免去浪費任何人的時間。我希望您理解我對於這件事的想法。謝謝。

sound 合理的　concerned 擔心的　logistically 在後勤上　worth the trouble 值得麻煩行事
prevent 預防，阻止　being wasted 被浪費　as well 同樣地　point of view 觀點，看法

請求幫忙 Asking Favors

▲

✉ sample 476

Dear _____

How is everything going? I'm writing to ask for a favor. Do you think you could introduce me to Joseph Kim at Smith Technology? I'm trying to build a relationship with his firm, and I thought it would be smoother if we had someone introduce us. If you could help me with this, I'd really appreciate it.

Thanks,

- - - - - - - -

Try It！可以替換的字詞

bridge 橋樑
connection 關係
contact 聯繫
rapport 密切關係
link 關係

近來可好？我寫這封信的目的是想請求協助。您可否把我介紹給史密斯科技的約瑟夫金認識呢？我正努力與他的公司建立關係，如果有人為我們介紹，我認為事情會更順利些。如果您可以幫我這件事，我會非常感激。謝謝。

> ask for a favor 請求幫忙　introduce A to B 介紹 A 給 B　try to 試著～　build a relationship 建立一段關係 smoother 更順暢

✉ sample 477

Dear _____

Could I bother you with a quick favor? Do you think you could look over the attached document and see if the numbers make sense to you? I'm trying to prepare a proposal for your boss, and I want to make sure the data I'm using is good. I'd really appreciate it.

Thanks,

- - - - - - - -

Try It！可以替換的字詞

file 檔案
article 文章
letter 信件
manuscript 手稿
text 文本

不好意思，我可以請您幫個忙嗎？可否請您查看一下附件，看您覺得這些數字是否合理？我正在為您的老闆準備一項提案，我想確保我採用的數據有效的。我真的很感激。謝謝。

> bother 打擾　look over 查看～　make sense 合理　prepare 準備

✉ sample 478

Dear [..............]

I hope everything is going well with you. I was wondering if you could do me a quick favor. Could you contact Bob Howard at ATP Enterprises and find out what they're planning to do with their excess inventory? I've heard that they're trying to liquidate it, and we'd like to get a hold of some of it at a low price. I thought you knew him and maybe you could get the inside track for us.

I appreciate any help you can give me.

希望您一切順利。我想知道您是否可以幫我一個小忙。您能否聯繫 ATP 企業的鮑勃霍華德，並了解他們將計劃如何處理其多餘的庫存？我聽說他們正試圖出清庫存，我們想要以低價買下一部分。我認為既然您認識他，也許您可以讓我們處於有利地位。您的任何協助，我將不勝感激。

wonder 想知道　do... a favor 幫～個忙　excess 過量的　inventory 存貨　liquidate 出清
get a hold of... 得到～　at a low price 以低廉價格　maybe 也許　inside track 內圈，有利的位子

✉ sample 489

Dear [..............]

I'm writing to ask for a little favor. I know that you have done business with Empire State Exporters in New York. We're considering making a deal with them, and I wanted to find out if you had a good experience with them. It would really help to have an objective opinion. Let me know if you can help out.

Thanks,

我寫這封信的目的是想請求一點協助。我知道您和位於紐約的 Empire State Exporters 來往過。我們正考慮與他們簽訂合約，我想知道您過去與他們的往來經驗是否是愉快的。有客觀的意見做參考真的會很有幫助。讓我知道您是否能提供協助。謝謝。

a little favor 一點幫助　consider 考慮　make a deal 做成一筆交易　find out 找出
objective opinion 客觀意見

Dear _____

Could I ask you for a quick favor? I need to have a meeting with some clients in Seoul, and I need the use of a conference room for an afternoon. Do you think you could spare a room for a couple of hours one day next week? I'd owe you one.

Thanks,

- - - - - - - -

a conference 會議
a get-together 聚會
an assembly 大會
a gathering 聚會
a congregation 集會

可以請您幫我個忙嗎？我得在首爾與一些客戶開個會，我需要在下午使用會議室。您下週能否幫我挪出一間會議室，讓我使用幾個小時？我欠您一份人情。謝謝。

client 客戶　conference room 會議室　an afternoon 一個下午　spare 騰出　a couple of hours 幾個小時
owe 欠～

拒絕 &表示遺憾 Rejection & Regret

✉ sample 481

Dear [_____]

Thank you very much for your offer. We are always happy to entertain any reasonable approach from another business. However, the time is not right for us to make a sale at the price you have suggested. Hopefully we will be able to do business sometime in the future.

Thank you.

- - - - - - -

非常感謝您的提議。我們總是歡迎來自其他公司任何合理的請求。但是，現在不是我們根據您建議的價格來販售的適當時機。希望我們將來能夠有生意的往來。謝謝。

Try It！可以替換的字詞

pleased 高興的
glad 高興的
careful 小心的
delighted 高興的
thrilled 興奮的

offer 提議 entertain 接受，準備考慮 reasonable 合理的 approach 接洽，商量 suggest 建議 hopefully 抱持希望地

✉ sample 482

Dear [_____]

I appreciate your taking the time to put together a proposal for a deal. Unfortunately, we are not able to accept the terms. We have already extended ourselves quite a bit this quarter, and we aren't ready to take on any more risk.

Thank you for understanding.

- - - - - - -

感謝您抽出時間來整理一項交易的提案。很遺憾的是，我們無法接受這些條款。本季度我們已經做了很大範圍的擴增，但我們還沒有準備好要承擔更大的風險。謝謝您的理解。

Try It！可以替換的字詞

an offer 提議
an application 申請書
a pitch 計畫
a bid 標案
a plan 計畫

take time 花時間 put together 整理，安排～ accept 接受 term 條款 extend 擴展 quarter 季度 take on 承擔～

✉ sample 483

Dear [_____]

I enjoyed speaking to you on Thursday. You were a very strong candidate for the position. However, we decided to go with someone else who had slightly more experience. We will keep your resume on file in case a suitable position opens up in the future.

Regards,

- - - - - - - -

Try It！可以替換的字詞

job 工作
post 職位
opening 職缺
station 職位
arrangement （職務上的）安排

星期四和您的談話很愉悅。對於這個職位來說您是一個非常優秀的應試者。不過，我們還是決定挑選一位稍微具經驗的人來擔任。我們將保留您的履歷，以便將來有適合您的職缺可以通知您。謹此。

strong（能力）優秀的 candidate 應試者 position 職位，職務 decide to 決定～ go with 選擇～
slightly 稍微地 resume 簡歷 in case... 以防，萬一～

✉ sample 484

Dear [_____]

Thank you for offering your services to our firm. You have an impressive operation and you seem very reliable. However, we do not need your services at this time. We will keep your contact information in case our situation changes.

Thank you again.

- - - - - - - -

Try It！可以替換的字詞

setup 組織
company 公司
firm 公司
business 公司
well-oiled machine 運作良好的機器

感謝您提供服務給我們公司。您良好的營運狀況令人印象深刻，且貴公司似乎是值得信賴的。但是，我們目前暫時不需要您的服務。我們會保留您的聯繫資訊，以備未來我們狀況有所改變。再次感謝您。

service 服務、招待，效勞 impressive 令人印象深刻的 reliable 可信賴的
contact information 聯繫資訊 situation 情況

✉ sample 485

Dear _____

We have considered your proposal, and while we find it quite attractive, we are going to have to decline. The economic situation is simply not right for us at this point. However, we hope that in the future we will find a way to do business together.

Thank you.

- - - - - - - -

我們已經考慮過您的提案，雖然我們覺得它很有吸引力，但我們還是得推辭。以我們此刻的經濟狀況而言，其實不適合。不過，我們希望將來彼此能找到一種可以共同開展業務的方式。謝謝您。

consider 考慮　proposal 提案　attractive 有吸引力的　decline 拒絕　at this point 此刻
find a way do business 找到做生意的方法

Try It！可以替換的字詞

refuse 拒絕

turn you down 拒絕您

reject it 拒絕它

say no 説不

beg off 推辭

斷然拒絕 Rejecting Strongly ▲

✉ sample 486

Dear [............]

We have reviewed your proposal and we do not feel that it would be ❶helpful to us. I do not think that the terms you propose are acceptable at all to a company ❷ operating on our scale. I hope any future proposals are more compatible with the kind of business we do.

Sincerely,

- - - - - - -

Try It！可以替換的字詞

❶ beneficial 有利的
useful 有用的
valuable 有價值的
advantageous 有利的
positive 積極性的

❷ working 營運的
in operation 運作中的
in commission 委託中的
in service 營業中的
in business 營業中的

我們已檢視過您的提案，但我們認為那對我們幫助不大。我不認為您提出的條件，對我們這種規模的公司經營來說是能夠接受的。我希望未來的任何提案，都能夠與我們的商業類型更加一致。感謝。

terms 條件　operate 經營　on our scale 就我們的規模而言　compatible with... 與～一致

✉ sample 487

Dear [............]

I'm afraid I must firmly reject your offer. I know that you are eager to do business with me, but the terms you offer are simply not generous enough. Unless you have a radically different offer to make, I believe this concludes our business together.

Sincerely yours,

- - - - - - -

Try It！可以替換的字詞

drastically 徹底地
fundamentally 根本上地
completely 完全地
totally 全然地
entirely 完全地

恐怕我必須堅定拒絕您的提案了。我知道您引頸企盼與我合作生意，只是您提出的條件不夠大方。除非您有完全不同的提議，否則我想我們這件事就到此為止了。謹啟。

firmly 堅決地　be eager to... 渴望要～　simply 只是，就是　generous 慷慨的，大方的
radically 完全地　conclude 結束，結案

✉ sample 488

Dear [   ]

I have looked over your offer, but I really must pass. The sales figures you use as the basis of your pricing are out of date, and I really don't think the kind of profits you anticipate will materialize. I'm afraid I just don't see any benefit to entering into a deal like this.

Yours truly,

- - - - - - - -

我看過您的報價，但我真的無法接受。這些您用來作為定價基礎的銷售數字已經過時了，我真的不認為您預期的利潤會實現。恐怕我沒辦法看到這樣的交易會有任何好處。感謝。

pass 忽視，略過　sales figure 銷售數據　basis 基礎　pricing 定價　out of date 過時的，老式的
anticipate 預期　materialize 實現

Try It！可以替換的字詞

appear 顯現

come to pass 實現

occur 發生

happen 發生

become visible 可以看得見

✉ sample 489

Dear [   ]

While I appreciate you offered your services to my company, I really must decline. We simply have no need of a freight expediter at this time, and I do not foresee us needing one in the future. Good luck in your future ventures.

Yours sincerely,

- - - - - - - -

雖然我很感謝您為本公司提供您的服務項目，但我真的必須拒絕。我們此時還不需要速運服務，而且我預計未來我們也不會需要這樣的服務。祝您未來的營運順利。謹啟。

while 雖然～　service 服務，業務　decline 拒絕　have no need of 不需要～　freight 貨運
expediter 加速者，促進者　need 需要　foresee 預料

Try It！可以替換的字詞

predict 預料

anticipate 預期

see 認為

imagine 料想

fathom 推測

✉ sample 490

Dear [_____]

Having looked over your offer, I have no choice but to reject it. I understand that you are trying to **❶maximize** your **❷profits**, but your offer doesn't seem to leave room for us to make any profit. I'm afraid we cannot do business on those terms.

Sincerely,

- - - - - - - -

Try It ! 可以替換的字詞

❶ increase 增加
grow 使成長
boost 促進
raise 提升
enlarge 擴大

❷ takings 收入
earnings 獲利
bottom line 盈虧底線
proceeds 收益
income 收入

我看過您的報價之後，我別無選擇，只能推掉它了。我知道您正試著要讓您的利潤最大化，但您的報價似乎沒有為我們留下任何獲利空間。恐怕我們無法按照這些條件和您們做一起合作。感謝。

look over 查看～　have no choice but to... 別無選擇，只能～　reject 拒絕
leave room for A　為 A 留有餘地

拒絕續約之提議 Rejecting an Offer to Extend a Contract ▲

✉ sample 491

Dear ⌐⌐⌐⌐⌐

I'm writing to inform you that we have chosen not to extend the terms of our contract. While we think that the contract was a fair one, we are in the midst of a restructuring of our priorities. We wish to use our resources elsewhere. It has been a pleasure working with you, and we hope to do so again further down the line.

Thank you.

Try It！可以替換的字詞

reorganizing 重組
rebuilding 重建
changing 變更
rethinking 反思
revamping 改造

我寫這封信是想通知您，我們已選擇不延長我們合約的期限。雖然我們認為合約是合理的，但我們正在重新整理我們的優先任務。我們希望將我們的資源用在別的地方。很高興與您合作，我們希望將來能夠再合作。謝謝。

extend 延長　terms 條款　fair 合理的　in the midst of 在～之中　restructuring 重組，改造
priority 優先

✉ sample 492

Dear ⌐⌐⌐⌐⌐

As you know, the period of our contract is set to end next month. After a great deal of ❶consideration, we've decided against extending it. We feel that there are other ❷avenues we prefer to pursue.

Thank you for understanding.

Try It！可以替換的字詞

❶deliberation 深思熟慮
thought 思考
discussion 討論
reflection 反省
contemplation 思索

❷opportunities 機會
directions 方向
leads 管道
chances 機會
prospects 前景

如您所知，我們的合約預計下個月期滿。經過深思熟慮之後，我們決定不再續約。我們認為還有其他管道可以選擇。感謝您的理解。

be set to 預定～　a great deal of 很多的　against 反對～　prefer 較喜歡，寧可選擇　avenue 途徑，方法

✉ sample 493

Dear ⌐⌐⌐⌐⌐

I hope this email finds you well. I'm writing regarding our contract, which is set to expire next month. We have held long meetings about the question of whether or not to renew the agreement, and in the end we have decided against it. Ultimately, we feel that our energies are better spent in another direction. We wish you luck in your future dealings.

Thank you.

- - - - - - - -

展信愉快！我寫這封信是關於我們下個月的合約即將屆滿。我們已就是否續簽合約的問題開了幾次長時間的會議，最後，我們決定不再續約。畢竟，我們認為我們的心力應另作他用。我們祝福您未來生意興隆。謝謝。

> regarding 關於～ expire 過期，期滿 hold a meeting 開會 in the end 在最後
> decide against 決定反對～ agreement 協議 ultimately 最終

✉ sample 494

Dear ⌐⌐⌐⌐⌐

I'm writing to remind you that we've reached the end of our contract with you. I'm afraid we have decided against renewing it. Although there have been some positive numbers, overall we have been disappointed in the profits we have derived from our agreement. Thus, we will be pursuing other options.

Good luck in your future endeavors.

- - - - - - - -

我寫這封信是要提醒您，我們和您簽訂的合約已經到期了。恐怕我們決定不再續約了。雖然有一些正向的數字，但總體而言，我們對於簽定此合約所獲得的利潤感到失望。因此，我們將尋求其他選擇。祝您未來的事業更上一層樓。

> remind... that 提醒～（某人） renew 更新 overall 總體上的 disappointed 感到失望的
> derive... from... 從～得到～

✉ sample 495

Dear _____

The end of our contract has arrived, and I'm afraid we've ❶opted against renewing it. We are happy with the work your company has done with us, but we ❷feel like we can get a better deal elsewhere. I hope that we do find a way to do business together in the future.

Thank you.

- - - - - - - -

我們的合約已經到期了，而且抱歉，我們已經選擇不再續約。我們對於貴公司與我們所合作的事業感到滿意，但我們認為還是可以在別的地方獲得更好的生意。希望我們未來仍有機會一起在生意上合作。謝謝您。

opt 選擇　renew 更新　feel like 想要～　elsewhere 在別處　in the future 在將來

回覆拒絕續約 Responding to Rejection of a Contract Extension ▲

✉ sample 496

Dear (............)

I must say I'm **disappointed** though I can't say that I'm surprised. I know that the market is tight. We would be willing to renegotiate the terms of the contract if you are interested. Call me after you have asked around at other companies, and we can discuss a possible new contract.

I hope to hear from you soon.

- - - - - - - -

disheartened 不高興的
disillusioned 大失所望的
let down 感到失望
upset 感到心煩的
frustrated 有挫折感的

我必須說我很失望，雖然不能說是感到驚訝。我知道市況吃緊。我們仍願意重新協商合約條款 ─ 如果您有興趣的話。在您詢問過其他公司之後再與我聯繫，我們可以討論一份可能的新合約。希望盡快有您的消息。

disappointed 感到失望的　tight 緊張的　be willing to 願意～　negotiate 協商

✉ sample 497

Dear (............)

I understand your ❶decision. Actually, we were a little ❷uncertain as to whether or not to extend the contract, so you have made the decision for us. I hope we can find other ways to work together in the future.

Thank you.

- - - - - - - -

❶ conclusion 最終決定
choice 選擇
resolution 決定
assessment 評估
judgement 判斷

❷ unsure 沒有把握的
doubtful 拿不準的
hesitant 猶豫的
undecided 無法決定的
tentative 遲疑的

我理解您的決定。實際上，我們也不太確定是否要延長合約，所以您為我們做出了決定。我希望我們能在未來找到其他合作方式。謝謝。

as to 關於～　whether or not 是否～　extend 延長　make a decision 做出決定

✉ sample 448

Dear 〔............〕

I'm a little **dumbfounded** by your decision. I felt like we both had a rather profitable year in part because of the work we did together. I hope you'll reconsider and give some thought to renewing. I know that you must make the decision you feel is best for your company, but I do think that you are making a mistake.

I hope to hear from you soon.

- - - - - - - -

對於您的決定我有點驚愕。我覺得我們雙方過去一年都有豐富的收穫，部分來自我們一起合作的事業。我希望您能重新考慮，再想想續約的事。我知道您必須做出您認為最適合您公司的決定，但我認為您做了個錯誤的決定。我希望很快能收到您的回覆。

dumbfound 驚愕失聲的　both 兩者（都）　profitable 有利可圖的　in part 在某種程度上，部份地
reconsider 重新考慮　make a mistake 犯了一個錯誤

✉ sample 499

Dear 〔............〕

I hope I can **dissuade you from** this course of action. We are willing to be flexible in a renegotiation of the terms of the contract. If you feel that you need us to be more generous in order to ensure a profit, we will give a little. Please get in touch with me to discuss renewing.

I look forward to hearing from you.

- - - - - - - -

我希望我能勸阻您採取這一行動。我們願意在重新商議合約條款時給予更多彈性。如果您覺得您需要我們更大方點才能確保獲利，我們會再斟酌。請與我聯繫討論續約。我期待您的回音。

dissuade A from... 勸阻 A 不要～　course of action 行動方針　flexible 有彈性的
renegotiation 重新商議　generous 慷慨的，大方的　ensure 確保

✉ sample 500

Dear ⸺

I understand your position and I respect your decision. Of course, we would like to extend the contract and continue our relationship with you, but if you feel that you are better off moving on, you must do so. I would like to maintain our relationship in the hopes that we can do business down the line.

Thank you.

Try It! 可以替換的字詞

uphold 維持
preserve 保有
keep 保持
continue 持續著（某一狀態）
sustain 維持

- - - - - - - -

我理解您的立場，也尊重您的決定。當然，我們希望延長合約並繼續與您建立關係，但如果您認為不要再繼續下去比較好，那麼就照您的意思吧。但我希望繼續維持我們的關係，希望未來我們還能夠一起合作。謝謝您。

position 立場　respect 尊重　continue 繼續，維持　move on 繼續　be better off ～更好

表達後悔之意 Expressing Regret ▲

✉ sample **501**

Dear ⟨_____⟩

I hope everything is going well at your end. I'm just writing to express my regret at having rejected your offer. I'm afraid I may have acted hastily. If you are willing to discuss it again, I think maybe we can come to an agreement.

Thanks,

- - - - - - - -

但願貴公司營運一切順利。我寫這封信是對於拒絕您的提議，表達後悔之意。我恐怕太過於倉促行事。如果您願意再次討論，我想也許我們可以達成協議。謝謝。

> on your end 在您那一方　express 表示　regret 後悔　hastily 匆忙地，倉促地　be willing to... 願意～
> come to an agreement 達成協議

Try It！可以替換的字詞

too quickly 太快了
hurriedly 匆忙地
at a fast pace 步伐太快
too fast 太快了
on the spur of the moment 一時衝動

✉ sample **502**

Dear ⟨_____⟩

I wanted to contact you to let you know that I regret having turned down your offer of ❶assistance last week. It turned out that you were right about the deal with Smith Technologies. I wasn't able to land the deal because my sales figures weren't high enough. In the future I'll listen more ❷carefully to your advice.

Regards,

- - - - - - - -

我和您聯繫是想告訴您，我很後悔上週拒絕了您的幫助。關於史密斯科技交易案，事實證明您是正確的。由於我的銷售數字不夠高，使得我無法拿到這筆生意。未來，我會更仔細地聽取您的意見。致上問候。

> turn down 拒絕～　It turned out that 結果是～　land the deal 達成協議　sales figures 銷售數字

Try It！可以替換的字詞

❶ help 幫助
aid 幫助
support 支持
backing 支持
sustenance 支持

❷ cautiously 謹慎地
thoroughly 徹底地
warily 謹慎地
closely 仔細地
directly 直接地

✉ sample 503

Dear ⌐ _____ ⌐

I'm writing about the offer that you made last week and that I rejected. Upon further reflection, I regret not taking up on it. Is it too late to change my mind? Let me know.

I hope to hear from you.

- - - - - - - -

我寫這封信是想詢問您上週被我拒絕的那項提議。經過進一步的反思，我很後悔沒有接受它。我現在改變主意是否為時已晚？請讓我知道。希望能夠收到您的回覆。

Try It！可以替換的字詞

the stipulations 規範，規定
the conditions 條款
the requisites 必要條件
the provisos 附帶條件
the language 專門用語

✉ sample 504

Dear ⌐ _____ ⌐

I wanted to express my regret at not having collaborated with you on your last deal. It looks like you had great success. I hope next time I'm wise enough to jump at the opportunity to work with you.

Regards,

- - - - - - - -

對於未能與您在上次的交易案中合作，我想表示遺憾。看起來您（這案子）已相當成功。我希望下次我有足夠的智慧抓住與您合作的機會。感謝。

Try It！可以替換的字詞

grab at 抓住不放
go for 努力求得
accept 接受
take hold of 抓住
take 獲得

✉ sample 505

Dear _____

I seem to have made a mistake when I declined your offer. As you know, prices have plummeted in the last quarter. In retrospect, you really were making a good offer. Call me and we can discuss working out a new deal.

I look forward to hearing from you.

當我拒絕您的提議時，似乎我做錯一件事了。如您所知，上一季的價格大幅下跌。回想起來，您提出的建議非常好。請聯繫我，我們可以討論並敲定一筆新的交易。我期待您的回音。

decline 拒絕　plummet 驟然跌落　quarter 季度　in retrospect 回顧過去　make an offer 提出一個建議
new deal 新的交易

接受 & 同意 Acceptance & Agreement

Case 01 接受對方公司的提案 Accepting Another Company's Proposal ▲

✉ sample 506

Dear [   ]

I'm happy to inform you that we have decided to accept your proposal. I think we can both **❶profit** greatly from doing business together. I will contact you next week so that we can **❷hammer out** the details.

I look forward to working with you.

- - - - - - -

Try It! 可以替換的字詞

❶gain 獲利
benefit 受益
expand 擴產
achieve 獲益
yield 獲得利潤

❷discuss 討論
shape 使具體化
talk about 談論
chat about 聊聊
confirm 確認

我很高興通知您，我們已決定接受您的提案。我認為我們可以經由合夥事業來獲得巨大的利潤。我下週會與您聯繫，屆時我們能夠敲定一些細節部分。我期待與您合作。

accept 接受　profit 獲得利潤　hammer out 解決（問題），設計出　detail 細節

✉ sample 507

Dear [   ]

I am writing to let you know that we've decided to accept your proposal. I think that a cross promotion would result in increased profits for both of our companies. Now that we've agreed to work together, we can meet to plan the first phase.

I'll speak to you soon.

- - - - - - -

Try It! 可以替換的字詞

endorsement
（名人透過電視）廣告代言
sponsorship 贊助
advertisement 廣告
backing 支持
funding 提供資本

我寫這封信是要讓您知道，我們已決定接受您的提案。我認為交叉推廣可使我們雙方公司增加獲利。既然我們現在已經同意合作，我們可以見個面，計劃第一階段的行事。我們再聯繫。

cross promotion（兩公司、產品之間）交叉推廣活動　result in 導致　now that 既然～

✉ sample 508

Dear _____

It is with great pleasure that I accept your proposal. We have run the numbers and come to the conclusion that cooperating on these exports will reduce our costs significantly. Thank you for approaching us. I believe we will both be happy with the results.

Thank you.

- - - - - - - -

我很高興接受您的建議。我們計算過這些數字,並獲得一個結論:在這些出口業務上彼此合作的話,將可顯著降低我們的成本。感謝您與我們聯繫。我相信我們都會對結果感到滿意。謝謝您。

pleasure 高興　come to a conclusion 獲得一個結論　cooperate 合作　export 出口　reduce 降低　srgnificantly 顯著地　approach 聯繫,接近

✉ sample 509

Dear _____

Having given due consideration to your proposal, we have concluded that it is a strong idea that will greatly benefit us. Therefore, we are happy to accept your proposal. I hope that this is the beginning of a long fruitful partnership.

I look forward to speaking with you.

- - - - - - - -

在充分考慮過您的提案後,我們最終認為,這是一個會讓我們雙方受益無窮的好點子。因此,我們很高興接受您的提案。我希望這可以開啟雙方長期且富有成效的合作關係。我期待與您商談。

due 應有的,合適的　consideration 考慮　conclude 結論　benefit 使受益　fruitful 富有成效的

✉ sample 510

Dear _____

We've looked over your proposal, and I think it's **a strong one.** We're ready to move forward with it. Let's meet on Monday to discuss the first step. I think this idea is a real winner.

I'll talk to you soon.

Try It！可以替換的字詞

a well-thought 深思熟慮的

a good 良好的

a helpful 有幫助的

a win-win 雙贏的

an excellent 優秀的

- - - - - - - -

我們已經檢視過您的提案，我認為這是一個很有說服力的提議。我們已準備好繼續進行。我們週一見個面，討論第一步要如何進行吧。我認為這個想法確實會讓我們成為贏家。到時候再聊。

look over 查看～　strong 優秀的，很棒的　ready 準備好的　first step 第一步　winner 獲勝者，贏家

✉ sample 511

Dear ［＿＿＿＿］

I'm thrilled to hear that you've decided to work with us. I agree that there is great ❶potential in this collaboration. I'm looking forward to getting down to business.

I'll speak to you next week.

- - - - - - -

我很高興聽到您決定與我們合作。我認同我們這次的合作有很大的前景。我期待可以開始進行。我們下週再談。

Try It！可以替換的字詞
possibility 可能性
opportunity 機會
future expansion 未來的擴展
profitability 有利可圖
growth 成長

thrilled 興奮的　agree that 同意～　potential 潛力　collaboration 合作　get down to 著手，開始進行～

✉ sample 512

Dear ［＿＿＿＿］

I'm so glad to hear that you're in agreement. A ❶cross promotion is just what we need to ❷spur sales. I'll call you later today to set up a meeting.

Thanks,

- - - - - - -

Try It！可以替換的字詞
❶joint 聯合的
mutual 相互的
dual 雙重的
shared 共同的
united 聯合的
❷encourage 有助於
increase 增加
urge 促進
stimulate 刺激
drive 驅動

我很高興聽到您已經同意了。交叉推廣正是我們刺激銷售的方式。我今天晚點會打電話給您，以安排一場會議。謝謝。

in agreement 同意　promotion 促銷，推廣　need to 需要～　spur 刺激　later 稍後　set up 設置，安排

✉ sample 513

Dear [_____]

I can't tell you how happy I am to hear that you've accepted our proposal. Hopefully we can really keep costs down and profits up with this plan. I'll contact you soon so we can enact the plan.

Thank you.

- - - - - - - -

當我聽到您接受我們的提案時，我不知如何向您表達我的喜悅。希望我們能夠透過此計畫確實壓低成本以及提升獲利。我會盡快與您聯繫，然後我們可以將這計畫付諸實行。謝謝您。

hopefully 懷抱希望地　keep costs down 降低成本　keep profits up 保持獲利增加　enact 實施

✉ sample 514

Dear [_____]

I'm very happy to hear that you have chosen to accept. I knew from the start that your company was the perfect one for us to pitch this idea to. I'm sure that we will be quite happy with the results.

Sincerely,

- - - - - - - -

我很高興聽到您選擇接受。我從一開始就知道，貴公司是我們竭力告知這個想法的最佳對象。我相信我們會對結果感到相當滿意。謹啟。

from the start 從一開始　perfect 完美的　pitch 竭力推廣　quite 相當地　results 結果，成效

✉ sample 515

Dear _____

It's great to hear that you like the idea. I'm excited about working with you. A Monday meeting works out quite well for me. I'll call you to work out a time.

Thank you,

- - - - - - - -

很高興聽到您喜歡這個想法。我也很興奮能夠與您合作。星期一的會議對我來說沒有問題。我會打電話給您敲定一個時間。謝謝。

it's great to hear that 很高興聽到～　work out 完成，擬定（計畫等）

招待客戶 Buyer Arrangement

Case 01 迎接客戶 Greeting the Buyer ▲

✉ sample 516

Dear ⌐⌐⌐⌐⌐

Greetings from Seoul! I just wanted to drop you a line and say hello. I hope we can get together soon to go over some of our new products.

Talk to you soon,

- - - - - - -

我來自首爾，向您問候！我寫這封信是想跟您打個招呼。希望我們能見面討論我們的新產品。到時候再聊。

Try It! 可以替換的字詞

Hello 打招呼
Compliments 問候
Good wishes 祝福
Respects 問候
Ciao 您好

greeting 問候 drop a line 給某人寫封短信 say hello 打個招呼 get together 聚在一起 go over 討論～

✉ sample 517

Dear ⌐⌐⌐⌐⌐

I hope everything is going well for you. I'm writing to say hello and touch base with you. I'm looking forward to showing you some of our new 2019 products the next time you're in town.

I hope to speak to you soon.

- - - - - - -

展信愉快。我寫這封信是想跟您打個招呼並和您取得聯繫。我期待您下次來鎮上時，向您展示我們2019 年的新產品。希望盡快和您商談。

Try It! 可以替換的字詞

line 產品系列
inventory 存貨
stock 存貨
goods 商品
merchandise 商品

go well 進展順利 touch base 取得聯繫 show 展示 next time 下次

✉ sample 518

Dear ....

It's been a while since we last spoke, so I thought I'd drop you a line and say hello. I'm going to be traveling in your area next week, so if you have a chance, maybe we can get together.

I hope you are doing well.

- - - - - - - -

自我們上次通話以來已經有一段時間了，所以我想寫這封信跟您打個招呼。我將在下週前往您所在地區，所以您可能的話，也許我們可以聚聚。願您一切順利。

while 一段時間　travel 旅行，差旅　area 地區　chance 可能性，機會

✉ sample 519

Dear ....

I thought I'd fire you an email and say hello. I was looking over a few of our new products and I thought of you. I'd love to get together with you sometime and discuss them. I hope everything is going well with you.

Regards,

- - - - - - - -

我想發一封電子郵件給您並打聲招呼。我正在檢視我們的一些新產品，然後就想到您了。我想跟您約個時間並討論這些產品。願您一切順利。感謝。

look over 查看～　get together 聚在一起　sometime 改天　discuss 討論

✉ **sample 520**

Dear ⌐- - - - - - - - ⌐

This is just an email to say hello and see how things are going. I haven't spoken to you in a couple of weeks and I wanted to remind you that our newest catalogue is going to be available soon. I look forward to talking to you about it.

Regards,

- - - - - - - -

brochure 小冊子

product line 產品系列

index 索引

directory 工商人名目錄

list of goods 商品清單

這封電子郵件只是想打個招呼，並跟您問候一下。我們已經有幾週沒有聯繫了，而我想提醒您，我們最新的產品目錄就要完成了。我期待著和您商談這件事。致上問候。

a couple of 幾個　remind 提醒　newest 最新的　available 可得到的

向客戶推薦韓國料理 Recommending Korean Food to Buyers ▲

✉ sample 521

Dear _____

We are looking forward to **hosting** you in Korea. I wondered if you would be interested in trying Bulgogi while you are here. It really is quite delicious. Let me know and I'll make reservations for us to go out to eat on Friday evening.

Sincerely,

- - - - - - - -

我們期待您來韓國時招待您。我想知道您到時候是否會想試試韓國烤肉。它的味道挺不錯的。到時候請通知我，好讓我預訂周五晚上外食的餐廳。感謝。

> host 招待 wonder if... 想知道是否～ delicious 美味的 make a reservation 預訂
> go out to eat 外出用餐

Try It！可以替換的字詞

feting 宴請（某人）
having 招待
receiving 接待
making you feel at home
讓您有賓至如歸的感覺
welcoming 歡迎

✉ sample 522

Dear _____

Your visit to Korea is almost upon us. I wanted to ask if you would like to try some authentic kimchee while you are in Seoul. There are many great restaurants that ❶ **specialize in** different styles of kimchee here, and I think you would find it very ❷**interesting**. Let me know and I will make reservations.

Kind regards,

- - - - - - - -

我們終於盼到您訪韓了。我想請問您到時候您是否願意嘗試一些正宗的泡菜。這裡有很多很棒的餐廳，擅長做不同風味的泡菜，我想您會很有興趣嚐嚐看的。請讓我知道，然後我會安排預訂。敬請台安。

> visit 訪問 want to ask 想問 authentic 真正的 specialize in 專精於～

Try It！可以替換的字詞

❶ concentrate on 專賣～
focus on 專賣～
excel at 擅長於～
make an art form of 專精於～
are wonderful at 在～方面令人讚嘆

❷ fascinating 迷人的
novel 新奇的
unusual 獨特的
out of the ordinary 與眾不同的
remarkable 出眾的

✉ sample 523

Dear _____

I'm excited about showing you around our offices next week. I was wondering if you would be interested in trying some Korean food while you are in town. If you want, we could go out on Friday night and try some traditional cooking. Let me know if you are interested.

I'll talk to you soon.

- - - - - - - -

我很高興下週可以帶您逛逛我們的辦公室。我想知道您過來這邊時，是否有興趣嚐些韓式料理。如果要的話，我們可以在週五晚上出去吃些傳統美食。請讓我知道您是否有興趣。到時候再聊。

excited 感到興奮的　interested in... 對～感興趣　try 嘗試　traditional cooking 傳統飯菜

✉ sample 524

Hi _____

I really enjoyed the dinner we had in New York last year. Those steaks were so big! Would you like to see what traditional Korean food is like? I can arrange for us to have dinner on Tuesday at a really great place near our offices. Email me if you want me to make a reservation.

Ciao,

- - - - - - - -

去年在紐約我們一起共進晚餐時，我真的很開心。那些牛排真是大！您想不想試試韓式料理的味道呢？我可以安排週二在我們公司附近一家非常好的地方一起吃晚餐。如果需要我訂餐廳的話，請發電子郵件給我。再見。

Would you like to...? 您想要～嗎？　arrange 安排　near 在～附近　last year 去年

✉ sample 525

Try It! 可以替換的字詞

delicious 美味的
savory 可口的
scrumptious 美味的
delectable 好吃的
tasty 美味的

I know this will be your first time in Korea, so I wanted to suggest that you eat in a Bulgogi restaurant. It's a style of barbecue that is absolutely mouth-watering. If you are interested, I can recommend a good restaurant.

Regards,

- - - - - - - -

我知道這會是您第一次來到韓國，所以我想推薦您去一家烤肉餐廳吃飯。那是燒烤的一種，保證令您垂涎欲滴。如果您有興趣，我可以推薦一家很好的餐廳，感謝。

first time 第一次　suggest 推薦　barbecue 烤肉　absolutely 絕對地　mouth-watering 令人垂涎欲滴的

推薦餐廳 Recommending a Restaurant ▲

✉ **sample 526**

Dear ┄┄┄┄┄┄

I'm looking forward to seeing you here in Seoul next week. I wanted to recommend that you go to Peter Luger's in Itaewon for dinner on Friday night. It really is the best steak house in Seoul and a great representation of American cuisine. If you'd like I can make reservations for you.

Regards,

Try It！可以替換的字詞
food 食物
dining 餐食
eating out 外食
fare 飲食
victuals 飲食

- - - - - - - -

我很期待下週在首爾這裡見到您。我想推薦您周五晚上去位於 Itaewon 的 Peter Luger's 吃晚餐。它真的是首爾最好的牛排館，也有很棒的美式料理。如果您願意，我可以為您安排預約。致上問候。

recommend 推薦　representation 代表　cuisine 菜餚　make a reservation 預約

✉ **sample 527**

Dear ┄┄┄┄┄┄

I'm excited about next week's meeting here. I know you'll be here for a few days, so I thought I'd recommend a restaurant you should try. The Pump Room is very famous here and you really should try it out. It's one of our best restaurants. Let me know if you want me to make reservations for you.

Regards,

Try It！可以替換的字詞
well-known 眾所周知的
celebrated 有名的
renowned 有名的
legendary 著名的
esteemed 廣受好評的

- - - - - - -

我很期待下週的會議。我知道您會過來這裡幾天，所以我想推薦您去一家餐館嚐嚐。Pump Room 在這裡非常有名，您真的應該試試。這是我們最好的餐廳之一。如果您希望我為您預訂，請告訴我。謹此。

for a few days 幾天的時間　restaurant 餐廳　really 真正地　try... out 嘗試～

✉ sample 528

Dear ....

I don't think you've been to Busan before, so I'd like to recommend a restaurant for you to try while you're here for the meeting. The Union Oyster house has really good seafood. I think you'd like it a lot.

See you next week,

我想您之前從沒來過釜山，所以您來這裡開會議時，我想推薦您一家餐館可去吃看看。Union Oyster 餐廳的海鮮非常棒。我想您會很喜歡的。下週見。

have been to... before 以前去過～　while... 當～的時候　seafood 海鮮　a lot 非常

✉ sample 529

Dear ....

I'm looking forward to the conference next week. I know you are going to be doing some sightseeing and enjoying the city in addition to doing business, so I wanted to recommend a restaurant to you. Chester's is a great Italian restaurant. It's one of the city's best, so you should definitely eat there while you're here.

Regards,

我期待下週的會議。我知道您除了公事之外，還有觀光行程，以及在這座城市裡找樂子，所以我想向您推薦一家餐廳。Chester's 是一家很棒的義大利餐廳。它是本市最佳餐廳之一，所以您過來這裡時，一定要過去吃看看。謹此。

conference（正式的）會議　do sightseeing 觀光　in addition to... 除了～之外　definitely 一定

✉ sample 530

Dear _____

We're all set for you to come next week. If I remember correctly, you're quite a gourmand. I'd like to recommend a restaurant that I think you'd really enjoy. It's called Chez Pierre, and it has some of the best French cooking I've ever had. You should really check it out while you're in town.

Regards,

- - - - - - - -

food lover 美食愛好者
foodie 美食主義者
gourmet 美食家
connoisseur 鑑賞家
food expert 美食專家

我們都準備好您下週的來訪了。如果我沒記錯的話，您是一位十足的饕客。我想推薦一家我認為您真的會很喜歡的餐廳。它叫作 Chez Pierre，那裡有一些我曾經吃過最好的法國菜。當您過來市區時，應該過去嚐看看。謹此。

be all set 一切都準備好了　remember 記得　correctly 正確地　gourmand 美食家　enjoy 喜歡　cooking 飯菜　check... out 去看看～

詢問客戶是否對韓國旅遊感興趣
Inquiring If Buyers Have Korean Touring Interests ▲

✉ sample 531

Dear _____

I'm looking forward to seeing you next month in Korea. I wanted to know if you'd be interested in doing some sightseeing while you are here. In particular, I thought you might enjoy visiting Gyeongbokgung Palace. It is a very interesting historical site and I think you would find it fascinating. Let me know if you are interested.

Regards,

- - - - - - - -

Try It！可以替換的字詞

attractive 吸引人的
appealing 動人的
exciting 令人興奮的
fascinating 迷人的
remarkable 很有名的

我很期待下個月在韓國見到您。我想知道您來這裡時，是否有興趣四處觀光一下。尤其是，您可能會喜歡到景福宮看看。這是一個非常令人感興趣的歷史遺址，我想您會發覺它的迷人之處。如果您有興趣，請告訴我。謹此。

do sightseeing 觀光　in particular 尤其是　palace 皇宮

✉ sample 532

Dear _____

I think all of the arrangements have been made for your visit. One last thing I wanted to know was whether or not there were any sights you would like to see while in Korea. I'd be happy to show you around. Are there any particular places you are interested in? Let me know if you want me to arrange anything.

I'll talk to you soon.

- - - - - - - -

Try It！可以替換的字詞

attractions 名勝景點
places of interest 旅遊勝地
things 景物
highlights 亮點
monuments 紀念館，歷史遺跡

我想，關於您到訪的所有安排事宜都已準備就緒。最後我想知道的是，您在韓國期間是否有任何想參觀的景點。我很樂意帶您四處看看。您有什麼的地方是特別感興趣的嗎？如果您想讓我安排任何事情，請告訴我。到時候再聊。

arrangement 安排　visit 參觀　whether... 是否～　sights 景點　while 當～的時候　particular 特別的

✉ sample 533

Dear _____

When we last spoke, I meant to ask you if you were planning on doing any sightseeing on your trip here. One place I'd like to recommend is Insa-dong. It is a historical district with a lot of art galleries and cafes. If you are interested, I can arrange for us to spend an afternoon there. Let me know if you'd like that.

Sincerely

- - - - - - -

我們上次交談時，我問過您過來這裡參訪時，是否有觀光行程的計畫。我想推薦仁寺洞這個地方。這是一個歷史悠久的地區，還有許多畫廊和咖啡館。如果您有興趣，我可以安排，我們可以在那裡度過一個下午。如果您願意，請告訴我。謹此。

meant to 有意要～　recommend 推薦　historical 歷史的　district 區域　spend 花時間

✉ sample 534

Dear _____

I think we have the schedule worked out for all of the meetings during your trip here next week. What we haven't discussed is what you'd like to do after hours. I'm sure you'd like to enjoy a little sightseeing while you're here. Is there any particular place you'd like to see? If not, I can recommend several interesting tours you might take. Let me know if you'd like me to do that.

Regards,

- - - - - - -

我想我們已在您下週參訪期間制定了所有會議的時間表。我們還沒有討論的是您想在工作時間結束後做的事情。我想您一定會在這裡享受些觀光行程。您有什麼特別想去看看的地方嗎？如果沒有，我可以推薦一些您可能會感興趣的旅程。請讓我知道您是否希望我這麼做。謹此。

trip 旅程，行程　work out 完成（計畫等）　after hours 下班後　several 一些

Dear ....

I wanted to see if you were planning on doing any sightseeing while you are here. Seoul is a very interesting city with a large number of historical sites. I could put together some recommendations for you if you'd like. Let me know and I'll send you some information.

Kind regards,

- - - - - - - -

我想詢問一下您到這裡時是否有任何觀光的計畫。首爾是一個非常好玩的城市，這裡有許多的歷史遺跡。如果您願意，我可以為您彙整一些。讓我知道，我會發一些資訊給您。敬請籌安。

plan on 打算～　while 當～的時候　recommendation 推薦

✉ sample 536

Dear ⌐ ⌐

I'm trying to put together a golf excursion for next weekend. Would you be interested in playing? I've invited a few people from Smith Tech and Jones Inc., so there should be plenty of business to do while we play. Let me know if you're interested.

Thanks,

- - - - - - - -

我想在下週末安排一次高爾夫之旅。您有興趣一起打球嗎？我邀請了一些來自史密斯科技和瓊斯公司的人，所以在我們打球的時候應該有很多生意可以談。如果您有興趣，請聯繫我。謝謝。

put together 安排，彙整　excursion 短途旅行　interested 感興趣的　plenty of 很多的～

Try It！可以替換的字詞

asked 邀請

called 號召

requested 請求

bid 邀請

offered an invitation to 向～提出邀請

✉ sample 537

Dear ⌐ ⌐

How would you feel about a round of golf this weekend? I'd like to talk over a few things with you away from our offices, and I thought playing golf would give us an opportunity to do that. Give me a call if you'd like, and we'll arrange everything.

Thanks,

- - - - - - - -

您覺得這個週來打一場高爾夫球如何？我想遠離我們的辦公室，並與您談談一些事情，我認為打高爾夫會讓我們有機會這樣做。如果您願意，可以打電話給我，我們會安排好一切。謝謝。

a round 一輪　a few 一些　away from 遠離～　play golf 打高爾夫球　arrange 安排，準備

Try It！可以替換的字詞

time 時間

an opening 一個開端

an occasion 一個場合

a break 一個空檔

a moment 一會兒

✉ sample 538

Dear ⬚⬚⬚⬚⬚⬚

I'm putting together a group to go golfing this weekend and I wondered if you'd be interested. Jerry Howard and Percy Johnson will both be there. I think the weather is going to be great. Let me know if you're up for it.

Talk to you soon,

- - - - - - - -

這個週末我找了一羣人要去打高爾夫球，我想知道您是否對此感興趣。Jerry Howard 和 Percy Johnson 兩人到時候都會到。我想天氣會很好。如果您願意參加，請告訴我。見面再聊。

> go golfing 去打高爾夫球　wonder if 想知道是否～　both 兩者都　weather 天氣
> be up for... 願意～（做某事）

Try It ! 可以替換的字詞

reorganizing 重新籌備

setting up 籌備

making arrangements for 為～作安排

making a plan for 為～制定計劃

placing 組成

✉ sample 539

Dear ⬚⬚⬚⬚⬚⬚

Would you be interested in getting together to play some golf next week? Jack Donahue told me that you play, and I thought it would be a good chance for us to get to know each other a little better. Let me know if you have a free afternoon and we can arrange it.

I look forward to hearing from you.

- - - - - - - -

您有興趣下週一起去打高爾夫嗎？Jack Donahue 告訴我您有在打球，我認為這是一個讓我們更能相互了解的好機會。如果您某個下午有時間，請告訴我，我們可以做安排。我期待您的回音。

> get together 聚在一起　get to know each other 進一步相互了解　a little 稍微地　free 閒暇的，空閒的

Try It ! 可以替換的字詞

a well-timed meeting
一個合時宜的見面機會

seasonable 適宜的

handy 有利的

ideal 理想的

an opportune time 一個合適的時機

✉ sample 540

Dear ⌈_____⌉

I'm writing to see if you'd be up for a game of golf some time in the next couple of weeks. I'd love to catch up with you and talk over some business. If you've got a free Saturday, let me know.

Regards,

- - - - - - - -

我寫這封信是想看看您未來數周之內是否有時間一起打一場高爾夫球賽。我很樂意跟您見面並談談一些事情。如果您某個週六有空，請跟我說。謹此。

Try It！可以替換的字詞

commerce 商務

dealings 交易

production 生產

broadcasting industry 廣播業

trade 買賣，交易

game 比賽　next 接下來的　couple of 幾個　catch up with 與～（某人）敘舊

出差 Business Trip

✉ sample 541

Dear _____

I'll be out of the office on business for the rest of the week. If you need anything, please ❶email Jerry Davis at 234-9852. He's another ❷account manager. He can answer most questions you might have.

Thanks,

- - - - - - - -

Try It ! 可以替換的字詞

❶call 打電話給
corresponds with 與～通信
speak to 與～談話
get a hold of 聯繫到～
contact 聯絡

❷business manager 業務經理
sales contact 銷售聯繫窗口
associate 同事
business professional 商務專業人士
business director 業務主任

我這個星期會去出差。如果您需要任何協助，請以電子郵件位址 234-9852 與 Jerry Davis 聯繫。他是另一位業務經理。他可以回答您可能遇到的大多數問題。謝謝。

on business 出差　for the rest of 剩下的～　anything 任何事情　another 另一個　account 客戶
most 大多數

✉ sample 542

Dear _____

I wanted to let you know that I'll be traveling for the next few days, so Bob Jackson will be covering for me. Just call him at extension 23 if you have any issues that need to be resolved. I should be back by Thursday.

Thanks,

- - - - - - - -

Try It ! 可以替換的字詞

handled 處理
dealt with 處理
finalized 定案
solved 解決
determined 決定

我想告訴您我將在接下來的幾天去出差，而 Bob Jackson 將代理我的職務。如果您有任何需要解決的問題，請致電分機 23。我將在周四前回來。謝謝。

let you know 讓您知道　travel 旅行，差旅　next 接下來的　cover 代理～職務　extension 分機
issue 問題

✉ sample 543

Dear [_____]

I'm going to be away for the next two days. In my
❶absence you can get in touch with Sarah Jones if you
need any information. She has ❷access to all of my
account information, so she should be able to help you
out with anything you might need to know.

Thanks,

- - - - - - - -

接下來的兩天我不在公司。我不在的時候，如果您需要任何資訊，可以與 Sarah Jones 聯繫。她將擁有我所有客戶資訊的使用權，因此對於您可能必須知道的任何事情，她應該可以協助您。謝謝。

be away 離開，不在　absence 不在，缺席　get in touch with 與～取得聯繫

✉ sample 544

Dear [_____]

I'll be out of the office next week for a symposium in
Florida. If you have any emergencies, you can talk to Pat
Mills. He'll be able to handle most issues, and he'll get in
touch with me if there's something he can't figure out.

Thanks,

- - - - - - - -

下週我將在佛羅里達州參加一個研討會。如果您有任何緊急情況，可以與帕特米爾斯聯繫。他能夠處理大多數問題，如果有什麼他無法解決的問題，他會和我聯繫。謝謝。

symposium 座談會，研討會　emergency 緊急情況　handle 處理　figure out 解決～（問題）

✉ sample 545

Dear _____

I'm going to be traveling for the next few days, so should any problems arise, Hugh Thomson will be your contact. He's up to speed on your account with us, so he'll be able to answer any questions you have.

Thanks,

- - - - - - - -

我將在接下來的幾天去出差，所以如果有任何問題，Hugh Thomson 將成為您的聯繫窗口。他已經取得我們客戶間往來的最新資訊。因此他可以回答您的任何問題。謝謝。

arise 出現　contact 聯繫人　up to speed on 獲得～的最新或必要資訊

要求幫忙預約飯店 Asking for a Hotel Reservation ▲

✉ sample 546

Dear [_____]

I'm looking forward to meeting with you next week. I was wondering if you could help me out by securing a hotel reservation for me. I don't know London very well, so I'm not sure what the best location would be.

I appreciate any help you can give me.

- - - - - - - -

我很期待下週與您見面。我想知道您是否可以幫我預訂酒店。我不太熟悉倫敦，所以我不確定最好的住宿地點在哪裡。我感謝您能給我的任何幫助。

> look forward to... 期待～　wonder 想知道　secure 確定，確認　reservation 預訂　very well 非常好
> location 位置，所在地

Try It! 可以替換的字詞

site 地點
place 地方
spot 地點
locality 地點
scene 景點

✉ sample 547

Dear [_____]

I'm having trouble ❶booking a hotel for the meetings next week. Would you be able to help me out with that? I need a room near the conference center for Monday, Tuesday, and Wednesday. Let me know if this is ❷ possible.

Thanks,

- - - - - - - -

我在為下週會議預訂酒店時遇到了困難。您能幫我解決這個問題嗎？我要在會議中心附近訂一間房，時間是週一、週二、週三。請讓我知道這是否可行。謝謝。

> have trouble... 在... ～有困難　book 預訂　room 房間　conference center 會議中心
> let me know 讓我知道

Try It! 可以替換的字詞

❶ reserving 預訂
obtaining 取得
procuring 取得
getting 取得
finding 找到

❷ doable 可行的
feasible 行得通的
realistic 確實可行的
practical 可實施的
reasonable 合理的，

✉ sample 548

Dear [_____]

Would it be possible for you to get hotel reservations for my stay in New York? I'll be arriving on Monday evening, so I'll need a room for three nights. I'd appreciate the assistance.

Thank you in advance.

- - - - - - - -

您可以預訂我在紐約停留時的酒店嗎？我將在周一晚上抵達，所以我需要一個房間，住三晚。我很感激您的幫助。先說聲謝謝您了。

stay 停留，留宿 arrive 抵達 need 需要 for three nights 三個晚上 assistance 幫助 in advance 預先

✉ sample 549

Dear [_____]

I'm trying to arrange my trip to meet with you next week. I was wondering if it would be possible for you to reserve a hotel room for me. I'd like to get a room near your offices if that is at all possible. Let me know if you can help me with this.

Thank you.

- - - - - - - -

我正試著安排下週與您見面的旅程。我想知道您是否可以為我預訂酒店房間。如果沒什麼問題的話，我想在您辦公室附近訂房。請讓我知道您是否可以協助我這件事。

try to 試圖～ arrange 安排 reserve 預訂 at all 完全地

✉ sample 550

Dear [_____]

I'm looking forward to next week's meetings. I wanted to find out if you could make my accommodation arrangements for me. I'm sure you know the local hotels much better than I do. It would really help a lot if you could do this for me.

Thanks,

- - - - - - - -

我期待下週的會議。我想知道您是否可以為我安排住宿。我相信您比我更了解當地的酒店。如果您能為我做這件事，那真的會有很大幫助。謝謝，

meeting 會議　accommodation 膳宿，住宿　arrangement 安排，準備工作　local hotel 當地的酒店
much better 比～多出更多　a lot 很多

Try It！可以替換的字詞

lodging 住宿
housing 住房
hotel 旅館
room 房間
overnight 過夜的

要求幫忙預約租車 Asking for a Rental Car Reservation ▲

✉ sample 551

Dear [_____]

I'm looking forward to coming to Sydney next month. Would it be possible for you to arrange a rental car for me? I'll be doing some sightseeing in my off-hours and I think it would be more convenient with a car.

Thanks for all of your help.

- - - - - - - -

我很期待下個月的雪梨之行。您可以幫我安排租車嗎？我會在下班時間四處觀光一下，而我覺得有車的話會比較方便。謝謝您一切的協助。

Try It！可以替換的字詞
shopping 購物
visiting of family and friends 拜訪家人和朋友
traveling to villages 到鄉下走走
touring 觀光
exploring 探險

look forward to 期待～　arrange 安排～　rental car 租車　off-hour 下班時間，非工作時間

✉ sample 552

Dear [_____]

I'm trying to get all of the details nailed down for my trip to your fine city next month. Would you be able to arrange a rental car for me? I'm going to be going back and forth between the hotel and your offices quite a bit, so I think having a car would be very convenient. Let me know if this is possible.

Thanks,

- - - - - - - -

為了下個月到訪您這座美好的城市，我正試圖要敲定我這趟旅程的所有細節。您能為我安排租車嗎？我會非常頻繁地往來於酒店和您的辦公室之間，所以我覺得有車會很方便。請讓我知道這是否可行。謝謝。

Try It！可以替換的字詞
arranged 安排好的
clarified 清晰明瞭的
set in stone 安排妥當的
set 規劃好的
approved 批准通過的

nail down 敲定　fine 美好的　go back and forth 往返　quite a bit 相當多　convenient 方便的

✉ sample 553

Dear [_____]

I have a favor to ask. Could you secure a rental car for the duration of my stay in Los Angeles? I'm going to need to be able to get around after hours, and I've heard that L.A. doesn't have much in the way of public transportation. Let me know if you can help me out with this.

Thanks in advance,

我想請您幫個忙。在我停留洛杉磯的期間，您可以幫我租一輛車子嗎？我想在辦公以外的時間四處逛逛，而且我聽說洛杉磯沒有很多大眾交通工具。請讓我知道您是否能夠幫我這件事。先跟您說聲謝謝。

favor 恩惠，幫忙　secure 取得　duration 期間　stay 停留　get around 到處走走　after hours 下班後 in the way of... 以～方式～　public transportation 大眾運輸工具

Try It！可以替換的字詞

extent 期間
period 期間
length 期間
time 時間
week 一週

✉ sample 554

[_____]

I'm about ready to pack my bags for next week's trip! I had one final request. Could you arrange for me to have a rental car while I'm in Chicago? I would really prefer to be able to drive myself to the meetings.

Thanks for your help.

我正準備要整理我下週出差的行李了！我有一項最後的請求。我到了芝加哥時，能否幫我安排租車？我真的比較喜歡自己開車去開會。謝謝您的幫助。

about 就要　pack 打包，整理　final 最後的　prefer 較喜歡　drive myself 自己開車

Try It！可以替換的字詞

appeal 請求
application 請求
favor 請求
plea 懇求
petition 懇求

✉ sample 555

Dear [_____]

Thank you so much for all of the work you've done arranging my trip next month. I do have one more request. Could you rent a car for my use during the week I'm there? I think I would be more comfortable if I were able to drive instead of relying on public transportation.

Thanks again for your help.

- - - - - - - -

非常感謝您為我下個月出差做的所有安排。我還有一個請求。您可以幫我租輛車，供我在那週期間使用嗎？如果我能自己開車，不是依賴大眾交通工具，我想我會覺得舒適些。再次謝謝您的幫忙。

request 請求　rent 租借　drive 駕駛　instead of... 而不是～　rely on... 依賴～

Try It！可以替換的字詞

more at ease 更輕鬆自在

more content 更滿意

calmer 更鎮靜

happier 更快樂點

more relaxed 更放鬆

✉ sample 556

Dear _____

Next week is the big meeting! I'm really excited about getting to work face-to-face with you. Would it be possible for you to arrange for someone to pick me up at the airport? My flight arrives at 10pm, so I'd rather not have to worry about finding a taxi. Let me know if you can do this for me.

Thanks,

- - - - - - - -

Try It! 可以替換的字詞

in person 親自
side by side 肩並肩地
together 一起
in the same office 在同一間辦公室
jointly 共同地

下週就要開這場大型會議了！我真的很期待可以和您面對面交流。您是否可能幫我安排機場接送呢？我的班機晚上 10 點抵達，所以我不想還要為叫計程車的事情擔心。請讓我知道您是否能為我做這件事。謝謝。

excited 感到興奮的 face-to-face 面對面地 possible 有可能的 pick... up 接送～（某人） arrive 抵達 I'd rather 我寧願

✉ sample 557

Dear _____

I'm trying to attend to all of the details for my trip to Paris next week. I was wondering if you could arrange an airport pickup service for me. My flight gets in at noon, and I have reservations at the Marriot. I appreciate the help.

Thanks,

- - - - - - - -

Try It! 可以替換的字詞

organize 安排
nail down 敲定
sort out 整頓好
manage 處理
arrange 安排

我正要整理下週前往巴黎出差的所有細節事情。我想知道您是否可以為我安排機場接送服務。我的班機在中午抵達，而且我在 Marriot 有訂房。我很感激您的幫助。謝謝。

attend to... 照料，整理～ detail 細節 wonder 想知道 get in 抵達 reservation 預訂

✉ sample 558

Dear _____

My trip to New York is coming up ❶quickly. I have my plane tickets and I've arranged for a hotel. The only thing left is to secure airport pickup. Could you take care of that for me? I'm ❷not familiar with any services of that nature in New York. I would greatly appreciate it.

Thank you.

- - - - - - - -

Try It！可以替換的字詞

❶ speedily 迅速地
soon 很快地
rapidly 很快地
fast 很快地
swiftly 很快地

❷ unaware of 對～不知情
a stranger to 對～一無所知
not sure how to identify
不確定如何識別～
not used to finding 不習慣去找尋～
ignorant of 不懂～

我的紐約之行很快就要到了。我已買好了機票，也預訂了酒店。唯一剩下的就是要確定機場接送的服務。您可以幫我處理這件事嗎？我不太熟悉在紐約的任何這類的服務。我將不勝感激。謝謝您。

plane ticket 機票　arrange for 為～做安排，為～做準備　secure 取得，確定　take care of... 處理～ familiar with... 熟悉～

✉ sample 559

Dear _____

I have a request regarding my trip to Houston next month. Would it be possible for you to arrange to have me picked up at the airport? I don't know the city well, so it would be a relief to know that someone is there to take me to the hotel.

Thanks for all of your help.

- - - - - - - -

Try It！可以替換的字詞

help 幫助
load off my mind 讓我放心
assistance 協助
liberation 放心
aid 協助

關於我下個月前往休斯頓出差一事，我有一項請求。您可以幫我安排機場接送嗎？我對這城市不太熟，所以如果知道到時候有人會帶我去酒店，那我就放心了。感謝您所有的幫助。

regarding 關於～　relief 安心，放心　take A to B 把 A 帶到 B 處

✉ sample 560

Dear [_____]

I'm writing about my trip to San Francisco next week. I would like to have someone pick me up at the airport when I arrive. My flight gets in at 7:30pm on Monday evening. Could you arrange for my pickup?

I appreciate your assistance.

- - - - - - - -

我寫這封信是關於我下週的舊金山之行。我抵達的時候，想要有人前來機場接我。我的班機抵達時間是週一晚上 7:30。您可以安排為我接機嗎？感謝您的協助。

> I would like to... 我想要～　have A pick B up 請 A 去接 B　assistance 幫助，協助

Try It！可以替換的字詞

escort me 陪同我

meet me 跟我會面

greet me 迎接我

wait for me 等候我

come and get me 前來接我

調整機場接送行程 Rearranging the Airport Pickup Schedule ▲

✉ sample 561

Dear [.............]

As you know, I will be arriving at the airport tomorrow. I'm writing to change the pickup time. It turns out the flight I'm on doesn't get in until 8:00. Could you arrange for me to be picked up then?

I appreciate your assistance.

- - - - - - - -

如您所知，我將於明日抵達機場。我寫這封信是要變更接送的時間。其實我搭的班機要一直到 8:00 才會抵達機場。到時候您可以幫我安排接機嗎？感謝您的協助。

arrive 抵達　airport 機場　change 變更 pickup 接送，接機　turn out (that) 結果是～ pick up 迎接，接送～（某人）	

Try It！可以替換的字詞

meeting 見面
rendezvous 會合
coming together 碰面
contact 聯絡
appointment 約定，約會

✉ sample 562

Dear [.............]

I've had a last-minute change in my schedule, so I'm going to be getting on a later flight tomorrow. Do you think you could change my pickup from 10:30 to 11:30? I'd appreciate it.

Thanks in advance,

- - - - - - - -

我的行程表在最後一刻出現變化，因此我明日將搭乘晚一點的班機。您可否幫我更改接送時間，從 10:30 改至 11:30 呢？辛苦您了。先跟您說聲感謝。

last-minute 最後一刻的　get on... 搭乘　flight 班機　in advance 預先

Try It！可以替換的字詞

catching 趕上，搭上
leaving on 搭～離開
booked on 預定～
traveling on 搭～旅行
coming in on 搭乘～過來

✉ sample 563

Dear ┄┄┄┄┄┄

I mistakenly gave you the wrong time for my airport pickup on Monday. I told you my flight got in at 8:00, but it's actually 7:00. Could you arrange for my ride to arrive an hour earlier?

Thank you.

- - - - - - - -

我之前給您週一在機場的接送時間是錯誤的。我原本跟您說的班機抵達時間是 8:00，但實際上是 7:00。您可以安排將我的接送時間提前一個小時嗎？謝謝您。

wrong time 錯誤的時間　get in 抵達　actually 實際上　arrange 安排　ride 搭乘，乘坐，搭載

✉ sample 564

Dear ┄┄┄┄┄┄

I'm going to need to change my schedule a little bit. I'm on a different flight now, and it doesn't get in until 11:00. I'll need my airport pickup service to come at that time, rather than at 10:00, as we previously planned.

Thank you for taking care of this for me.

- - - - - - - -

我得將我的行程表做一點修改。我現在搭乘的班機改了，要到 11:00 才會抵達。到時候我會需要機場接送服務，而非我們先前預定的 10:00。感謝您為我處理這件事。

schedule 行程表　a little bit 一點點　pickup service 接送服務　rather than 而不是～　previously 先前

✉ sample 565

Dear _____

I hate to **bother** you with this, but would you mind changing my airport pickup time from 12:00 to 1:30. I've had to change my flight, so I won't be getting in so early.

I appreciate your help.

Try It!可以替換的字詞

trouble 造成～的麻煩

annoy 煩擾

inconvenience 造成～的不便

bug 打擾

hassle 找～的麻煩

- - - - - - - -

我也不想拿這件事打擾您，只是可以請您將我的機場接送時間，從 12:00 改到 1:30 嗎？我必須更改我的班機，所以我不會那麼早抵達。感謝您的協助。

hate to 討厭，厭惡～　bother 打擾，麻煩　mind 介意

✉ sample 566

Try It！可以替換的字詞

Dear 〔_____〕

I'm going to go out to dinner on Thursday night and I'd like to try some **❶authentic** Korean food. Could you please make reservations for me at a **❷suitable** restaurant near my hotel? I would really appreciate it.

Thank you for your help.

- - - - - - - -

❶ bona fide 真實的
genuine 正真的
real 真實的
reliable 可靠的
legitimate 正統的

❷ apt 恰當的
proper 適當的
right 對的
appropriate 合適的
fitting 恰到好處的

我週四晚上會外出吃晚餐，且我想試試一些道地的韓式料理。可以請您在我住的酒店附近幫我訂一家適合的餐廳嗎？我會非常感激。感謝您的協助。

go out 外出　would like to... 想要～　authentic 真實的　make a reservation 預訂，預約　suitable 合適的

✉ sample 567

Try It！可以替換的字詞

Dear 〔_____〕

I'm looking forward to meeting with you in New York next week. Do you think you could do me a favor and make reservations at a restaurant for me? I'd like to have a good meal with my wife on Saturday night before we fly home on Sunday.

Thanks,

- - - - - - -

a bistro 小酒館
a café 小餐館
an eating place 吃飯的地方
a buffet restaurant 自助式餐廳
an eatery 飯館

我期待下週在紐約和您見面。您可否幫我個忙，幫我訂一家餐廳的位子呢？在週日搭機返回之前，我想和我太太在週六晚上好好吃一頓。感謝。

do a favor 幫個忙，提供協助　meal 一餐

✉ sample 568

Dear [_____]

Could I trouble you to make reservations at a restaurant for me on Tuesday evening? I'd like to eat somewhere close to my hotel. If I could get a table at 8:00, I'd really appreciate it.

Thanks,

- - - - - - - -

我可以麻煩您幫我在週四晚上預訂一家餐廳的位子嗎？我想在我住的酒店附近吃飯。麻煩您幫我訂8:00的位子，非常感激。謝謝。

✉ sample 569

Dear [_____]

Would it be possible for you to make restaurant reservations for my coworker and I for Friday evening? Neither of us has eaten Korean food before here, so we'd like to try it.

I appreciate all of your help.

- - - - - - - -

您是否可以幫我和我同事訂週五晚上的餐廳位子呢？我們都沒吃過韓式料理，所以想試試看。感謝您一切的協助。

✉ sample 570

Dear [_____]

I want to go out for dinner on Friday evening before I fly back home on Saturday morning. Do you think you could get reservations for me at a good restaurant that is near my hotel? I'd really appreciate it.

Thank you in advance.

- - - - - - - -

在週六早上搭機返家之前，我想在週五晚上外出吃晚餐。您認為您可否幫我在我住的酒店附近，訂一家好的餐廳的位子呢？感謝您的辛勞。先跟您說聲謝謝了。

fly back home 搭機返家，回家　near 在～附近

Try It！可以替換的字詞

head 前往

dash 急奔

hurry 趕時間

wing 搭機

soar 搭飛機

與合作夥伴的溝通 Communication With Partners

Case 01　通知公司的一項活動 Informing of a Company Event ▲

✉ sample 571

Dear _____

It's time again for our annual company celebration. We will be hosting a party for our employees and our partner companies. If you can make it to Korea next month, we would be happy to host you and your employees. Please let me know if you can make it.

Thanks,

我們年度的公司慶祝會又要到了。我們將為我們的員工與夥伴企業們辦一場派對。如果您下個月可以來韓國，我們會很樂於招待您與您的員工。請讓我知道您是否可前來參加。

annual 年度的　celebration 慶祝，慶祝活動　host 主辦，作東　employee 員工
partner company 夥伴企業　make it 前來參加

✉ sample 572

Dear _____

My company will be holding its annual shareholder's meeting next week, so I may be a little slower than usual to respond to phone calls and email. Normal business will resume the following week.

Thank you.

本公司將於下週舉辦年度股東大會，因此我也許會慢一點回覆電話及電子郵件。下週起將恢復正常作業。感謝您。

shareholder 股東　slower than usual 比平時慢些　respond 回覆　normal 平時的　resume 恢復

✉ sample 573

Dear [_____]

I'm writing to tell you about a conference my company is hosting next month. Import-export specialists from around the world will be meeting in Seoul to share ideas, network, and do business. If you are able to send a representative, please let me know.

Thanks,

我寫這封信是要告訴您本公司下個月將舉辦一場會議。來自全球的進出口專業人士將於首爾會面，並分享意見、交流及合作生意。如果您能派代表前來，請讓我知道。謝謝。

conference 會議　import 進口　export 出口　specialist 專家　from around the world 來自世界各地
share 分享　representative 代表

✉ sample 574

Dear [_____]

I just wanted to let you know that we will be holding a press conference on the 19th to unveil our latest product. We expect to get strong press coverage and the accompanying surge in orders such P.R. usually generates. This email is just a heads-up so that you can get your orders ready early.

Thanks,

我只是想通知您，我們將於 19 號召開一場記者會，以發表我們的最新產品。我們預期媒體將大幅報導，而且這樣的公關作用通常會產生伴隨而來的大量訂購。這封電子郵件就是要提醒您一下，讓您能夠提早將訂單準備好。謝謝。

press conference 記者會　unveil 發表，揭示　coverage 媒體報導　accompanying 伴隨著～
surge 激增，高漲　generate 產生　heads-up 提醒

✉ sample 575

Dear [_____]

I'm writing to tell you about my company's annual charity drive. Each year, our employees raise money for African famine relief. Last year we raised $20,000, which was donated to an organization that teaches sustainable agricultural techniques to villagers. If you would like to donate, please let me know.

Thank you.

- - - - - - - -

我寫這封信是要告訴您本公司的年度慈善活動。每年，我們的員工都會為拯救非洲飢荒而募資。去年我們募得兩萬美元，這筆錢捐給一個傳授村民永續性農業技術的組織。如果您想要捐款，請讓我知道。謝謝您。

charity 慈善　drive 運動，宣傳活動　raise money 募款　famine 飢荒　relief 救援　organization 組織　sustainable 永續性的

Try It！可以替換的字詞

generated 產出
gathered 募集
accumulated 累積
made 取得
collected 募集

✉ sample 576

Dear [............]

Because of a change in computer systems, all employees of Smith Tech have received new email addresses. From now on you can reach me at tjones@smithtechnology.com. Emails to my old address will not make it to me, so please update your address book accordingly.

Thank you for your attention.

Try It！可以替換的字詞

records 紀錄
notes 筆記
files 檔案
communications 聯絡資料
books 聯絡簿

- - - - - - - -

由於電腦系統的變更，史密斯科技所有員工都已收到新的電子郵件地址。從現在起，您可以將郵件寄至 tjones@smithtechnology.com. 給我。若寄到舊的郵件位址，我會收不到，因此，請更新您的郵件聯絡簿。感謝您的關注。

> because of 因為～　system 系統　receive 收到　from now on 從現在起　reach 連絡上
> accordingly 因此，相應地

✉ sample 577

Dear [............]

I just wanted to let you know that my email address has changed. I'm now jkim@hyundai.com. Please update your records.

Thanks,

Try It！可以替換的字詞

presently 現在
currently 目前
nowadays 當今
at this point 此刻
these days 最近

- - - - - - - -

我只是想讓您知道我的電子郵件地址已更改。我的現在是 jkim@hyundai.com. 請更新您的聯繫人紀錄表。謝謝。

> want to 想要～　let you know 讓您知道　change 更改，變更　update 更新

✉ sample 578

Dear [............]

My email address has changed. It is now plee@kia.com.
I would appreciate it if you could update your address
book. Sorry for any inconvenience.

Thanks,

- - - - - - - -

我的電子郵件地址已變更。現在是 plee@kia.com.。煩請更新您的郵件聯絡簿，不勝感激。如造成任何
不便，深表歉意。謝謝。

> any 任何，任一　inconvenience 不便

Try It！可以替換的字詞

bring... up-to-date 將～更新
revise 修正
amend 修正
alter 更改
change 改變

✉ sample 579

Dear [............]

I'm just writing to let you know that I've got a new email
address. I can now be reached at jkim@titanhardware.
com. Please disregard my previous address.

Thanks,

- - - - - - - -

我寫這封信的目的是要讓您知道我新的電子郵件地址。您現在可以寄到 jkim@titanhardware.com.。請
忽略我先前的郵件地址。謝謝。

> be reached at 在～被聯絡到　disregard 忽略，忽視　previous 先前的

Try It！可以替換的字詞

ignore 忽視
delete 刪除
forget about 忘記～
pay no attention to 不用再理會～
take no notice of 不必再注意～

✉ sample **580**

Dear _____

Due to our company's recent name change, I now have a new email address. You can reach me at byoung@smithtechnology.com, instead of smithtech.com. Email from my old address will be forwarded to my new account for the next ten days only, so please change my entry in your address book.

Thanks,

- - - - - - - -

由於我們公司最近名稱變更，我現在已經有新的電子郵件地址。您可以將信件寄到 byoung@smithtechnology.com 來給我，而不是 smithtech.com.。來自舊位址的郵件將轉送至我的新帳號，但僅於未來十天之內，因此請變更您聯絡簿中我的項目。謝謝。

forward 轉寄，轉送至（新的位址）　account 帳號　change 變更　entry 項目，條目，帳目

✉ sample 581

Dear ⌐ ⌐

I just wanted to let you know that my cell phone number has changed. You can now reach me at (917) 543-2345. Please disregard my previous number.

Thanks,

- - - - - - - -

我只是想讓您知道我的行動電話號碼已經更改。您現在可以撥打 (917) 543-2345 的號碼聯繫我。請不必理會先前的電話號碼。謝謝。

Try It！可以替換的字詞
contact 聯絡～
get in touch with 與～取得聯繫
access 聯絡到～
get hold of 聯絡到～
connect with 與～聯繫

cell phone number 行動電話號碼 change 更改 reach 聯繫到～（某人） disregard 不理會 previous 先前的

✉ sample 582

Dear ⌐ ⌐

I'm writing to give you my new cell phone number. We changed company plans, so I had to give up my old number. The new one is (347) 555-2387.

Thanks,

- - - - - - - -

我寫這封信的目的是要給您我新的行動電話號碼。我們改變公司計畫了，所以我必須放棄舊的號碼。新的號碼是 (347) 555-2387。謝謝。

Try It！可以替換的字詞
erase 刪除
update 更新
throw out 丟棄
do away with 去除
exchange this one with 用～換取這個

plan 計畫，方案 give up 放棄

✉ sample 583

Dear _____

I'm writing regarding a quick update of my contact information. My cell phone number has changed. It's now (973) 543 1345. Please update your records accordingly.

Thanks,

- - - - - - - -

我寫這封信是關於我聯絡資訊更新的簡短告知。我的行動電話號碼已經變更。現在號碼是 (973) 543 1345。所以請您更新您的聯絡人紀錄。謝謝。

quick 簡短的　update 最新的情況，更新（的訊息）　contact 聯絡　information 資訊　records 紀錄　accordingly 相應地，因此

Try It！可以替換的字詞

for that reason 基於那個理由
as a result 因此
in view of that 就那樣的觀點而言
fittingly 相應地
appropriately 適當地

✉ sample 584

Dear _____

Due to my company's recent decision to change cell phone providers, it has become necessary for me to change my cell phone number. Below is my new number. Please disregard my old number.

(405) 256 – 2837

Thank you.

- - - - - - - -

由於本公司最近決定更換行動電話電信業者，因此我必須變更我的行動電話號碼。以下是我的新號碼。請不必理會我的舊號碼。(405) 256-2837。謝謝您。

recent 最近的　decision 決定　provider 提供者　become necessary 變成是必需的　below 以下

Try It！可以替換的字詞

system 系統
policy 政策
vendors 供應商
services 服務
suppliers 廠商

✉ sample 585

Dear ╭┄┄┄┄┄┄╮

I think that the cell phone number you have for me is my old one. I've recently changed numbers and I want to make sure that you have the correct one should you need to contact me. Here it is: (646) 353 2534.

Thank you,

- - - - - - - -

我想您所保有的我的行動電話號碼應該是舊的。我最近變更號碼了，而我想確認，萬一您有需要連絡我，您擁有的是正確的號碼。我的電話號碼是：(646) 353 2534。謝謝您。

recently 最近　make sure 確認，確定～　correct 正確的，有效的　contact 連絡
should you need to 萬一您有需要～時

休假通知 Informing that I'm on Vacation ▲

✉ sample **586**

Dear ⸤⸍⸍⸍⸍⸍⸍⸍⸎

I'll be out of the office for the next week. I'm going on vacation. John Jones will be fielding my calls if you have any urgent problems. Otherwise, I'll talk to you when I return.

Thanks,

我下週都不在辦公室。我要去度假了。如果您有任何急迫的問題，約翰・瓊斯會幫我接電話。否則，我們可以在我回來的時候再聊。謝謝。

> be out of the office 不在辦公室　on vacation 度假中　field 接取；接或截（球）　urgent 急迫的
> otherwise 除此以外，否則

Try It！可以替換的字詞

handling 處理
tackling 追蹤
returning 回覆
taking 代接
accepting 接受，接收

✉ sample **587**

Dear ⸤⸍⸍⸍⸍⸍⸍⸍⸎

I'm writing to let you know that I'll be on vacation for the next two weeks. If you have any issues you need resolved, you can contact Mike Duncan. He'll be handling my accounts until I'm back.

Thanks,

我寫這封信是要讓您知道，接下來兩週時間，我會去度假。如果您有任何必須解決的問題，您可以與 Mike Duncan 聯繫。他將處理我的事務，直到我回來為止。

> issue 問題　resolve 解決　contact 聯繫　handle 處理　account 客戶，事務

Try It！可以替換的字詞

while I'm gone 當我不在的時候
for me 為我
in the interim 在這過渡期間
on my behalf 代表我
over the next couple of weeks
在未來幾個禮拜中

✉ sample 588

Dear ....

I will be away from the office for the next week, so please speak to me before Friday with any urgent business. After that, you can leave me a message or send me an email and I'll get back to you upon my return.

Thanks,

我下個星期都不在辦公室，所以如果您有任何急迫的事務，請於週五之前告訴我。在那之後，您可以留下訊息或發電子郵件給我，我回來的時候會回覆您。謝謝。

> be away from 離開，不在～　business 事務　message 訊息　get back to 回覆～；再連絡～
> upon my return 在我回來的時候

Try It ! 可以替換的字詞

call 打電話給～

phone 打電話給～

contact 聯絡～

write to 寫信給～

drop a line to 寫信給～

✉ sample 589

Dear ....

I am heading out on vacation after work tomorrow, and I'll be gone for the next two weeks. I'm long overdue for a break. If you have any problems while I'm away, you can call the main number at my office and they'll connect you with someone who can help.

I'll talk to you when I get back.

我在明天下班之後就要出發去度假了。未來兩週的時間我都不在。我太久沒有休息了。我不在的時候，如果您有任何問題，可以撥打我公司總機的電話，然後他們會將您的電話轉接給可以協助的人員。等我回來的時候，我們再聊吧。

> head out 出發　overdue 遲來的，到期未付的，逾期未還的　while 當～時候　main 總機
> connect A with B 將 A 的電話轉接給 B

Try It ! 可以替換的字詞

vacation 假期

trip 旅行

breather 喘息，休息

rest 休息

holiday 假日

✉ sample 590

Dear ⸂＿＿＿＿⸃

I'll be out of town starting next week, so we should talk before I leave. I want to get any issues settled before I go on vacation. Give me a call and we can go over everything.

Thanks,

- - - - - - - -

我下週要出遠門了，所以在我離開之前，我們應該有事情要談。我想在我去度假之前將任何問題處理好。請打個電話給我，讓我們一起來處理所有問題。謝謝。

Try It! 可以替換的字詞
completed 完成的
resolved 解決了的
determined 決定了的
firmed up 不會再更動的
decided 決定好了的

out of town 來開本地　starting 開始～　before 在～之前　settle 解決　call 打電話　go over 查看，檢視

✉ sample 591

Dear ⌐‥‥‥‥‥⌐

I just wanted to let you know that I received your email. All of the attached files were there, so that's all I need from you for now. Thanks for getting the figures to me so quickly.

Regards,

- - - - - - - -

我只是想讓您知道我收到您的電子郵件了。所有附加檔案都在，所以我需要您給我的東西現在都已經有了。感謝您如此迅速地給我這些數字。謝謝。

Try It！可以替換的字詞

connected 連結的
additional 附加的
affixed 附屬的
joined 加入的
added 新增的

receive 收到　attached 附加的　that's all I need 那就是我所需要的　for now 目前　figures 數字，金額

✉ sample 592

Dear ⌐‥‥‥‥‥⌐

Your email came through just fine. Now that I've got that list of contacts, I'll be able to start talking to people about joining our venture. If you need me to send anything to you, just let me know.

Thanks,

- - - - - - - -

我收到您發送的電子郵件了。既然我已經拿到連絡人清單，我可以開始找人商談合夥事業了。如果需要我寄什麼過去給您，儘管讓我知道。謝謝。

Try It！可以替換的字詞

prospects 預期目標
phone numbers 電話號碼
names 名稱，名字
clients 客戶
people 人員

come through 成功送達　fine 沒事的　now that 既然～　be able to 能夠～　join 加入，參與　venture 生意，事業　anything 任何事情

✉ sample 593

Dear ┆_____┆

I wanted to tell you that I got your email, and everything looks great. I'll show your proposal to my boss and get back to you when I have **an answer**.

Thank you for all of your hard work.

- - - - - - - -

我想告知您，我收到您的電子郵件了，且一切看來還不錯。我會將您的提案給我老闆看，當我有了答案時，我會回覆您。感謝您一切的辛勞。

proposal 提議，提案　boss 老闆　get back to 回覆，回電話給〜

✉ sample 594

Dear ┆_____┆

I received your email. I'm still **thinking over** some of your suggestions. I'll get back to you when I've given them some thought.

Thanks,

- - - - - - - -

我收到您的電子郵件了。我還在考慮您的一些建議。等我有了一些想法時，我會回覆您。謝謝。

think over 考慮，思考著　suggestion 建議　thought 想法

✉ sample 595

Dear ⌐⌐⌐⌐⌐⌐⌐

I got your email this morning along with the attached files. It looks like the contracts are in order, so we should be moving forward pretty quickly with this deal. I'll let you know if I need anything else from you.

Thanks,

- - - - - - - -

我今天早上收到您連同附加檔案一起的電子郵件了。這些合約看起來是沒有問題的，因此我們應該可以很快地進行這項交易的後續。如果我還需要您提供其他資訊，我會讓您知道。謝謝。

along with 連同～一起　attached files 附加檔案　contract 契約，合同
in order 井然有序的，狀況良好的

Try It! 可以替換的字詞

papers 文件

files 檔案

deals 協約

treaties 協議

pacts 合約

✉ sample 596

Dear ⸢_____⸥

I'm writing to let you know that we've got some excess inventory and we're looking to ❶liquidate. That means we'll be ❷flexible with pricing, so now is a great time to buy. If you have a chance, give me a call and we can discuss what I have available.

I hope to talk to you soon.

- - - - - - - -

Try It！可以替換的字詞

❶ slash prices 砍價
move goods quickly 盡速出貨
settle 處理掉
clear up 清除乾淨
pay a debt 支付債務～

❷ negotiable 可協商的
open to discussion 有議價空間的
bendy 易彎曲的，彈性的
unfixed 非固定的
open to offers 可供議價的

我寫這封信是要讓您知道我們的庫存過剩，且我們正打算清盤變現。意思是說，我們在價格方面會很有彈性，因此現在是購買的好時機。您有空的話，給我個電話，我們可以討論可提供給您的東西。希望很快與您再聊。

> excess 過多　inventory 庫存　look to... 尋求，打算～　liquidate 清盤，清算，變現
> that means 那意味著～　flexible 有彈性的　pricing 定價，價格　discuss 討論
> available 可行的，現有的

✉ sample 597

Dear ⸢_____⸥

I'm writing to set up a meeting with you. I'd like to show you a few samples of our new product line. I think you'll be very interested in what we're producing this season. Let me know when would be a good time for you.

I'll talk to you soon.

- - - - - - - -

Try It！可以替換的字詞

involved in 參與～其中
engrossed in 投入～其中
fascinated by 被～所著迷
captivated by 被～所著迷
attracted to 被～所吸引

我寫這封信的目的是想跟您約個時間見面。我想給您看看我們最新系列產品的幾個試樣。我想您對於我們這一季生產的東西會有興趣。讓我知道您方便的時間。我們再聊。

> set up 安排（會面等）　product line 產品系列　season 季節

✉ sample **598**

Dear ⌐‥‥‥‥‥¬

I wanted to get in touch with you to discuss your last order. I'd be interested to know if you were satisfied with the products you chose. We're trying to gauge response so that we can adjust our product line accordingly. If you have a chance, give me a call.

Thank you.

- - - - - - - -

我與您聯繫的目的是想討論一下您上次的訂貨。我會想知道您是否滿意您選擇的產品。我們正試著要檢視顧客回應情況，以便我們能夠相應地調整我們的產品系列。您有空的話，請給我打個電話。謝謝您。

get in touch 與～取得聯繫　gauge 量測，判斷　adjust 調整　accordingly 因此，相應地

✉ sample **599**

Dear ⌐‥‥‥‥‥¬

I hope you are doing well. I'm writing to ask you a few questions about what kind of orders you might be making this month. We have some new additions to our catalogue, so I wanted to point out some of them.

Regards,

- - - - - - - -

展信愉快。我寫這封信的目的是想請問您一些問題 ── 關於您這個月可能會下的訂單種類。我們的產品目錄上已新增了一些品項，因此我想指出一些給您看看。謹此。

a few 些許的　kind 種類　month 月　addition 新增（物品）　point out 指出～

✉ sample 600

Dear [_____]

I'm writing to find out what your schedule is like while you're in town next week. I'm sure you're quite busy, but I'd like to find a time to discuss some of our products with you. Let me know if you'd be interested.

I look forward to hearing from you.

- - - - - - - -

我寫這封信是想了解您下週過來市區這邊時的行程安排。我知道您一定非常忙碌，但我想和您談談我們的一些產品。請讓我知道您是否有興趣。期待得到您的回覆。

find out 找出，了解～ while 當～時候 town 城鎮 quite 十分地

Try It！可以替換的字詞

visiting this city 到訪本市

here 在這裡

at the Seoul office 在首爾的辦公室

in the factory 在工廠裡

touring our facilities 巡視我們的設備

解釋太晚回覆的原因 Making an Excuse for a Delayed Answer ▲

✉ sample 601

Dear [_____]

I'm ❶sorry I haven't been able to get back to you before now. We've had some issues to deal with here at the office, and they've prevented me from ❷keeping up with my email. I hope you understand.

Regards,

- - - - - - - -

❶apologetic 致歉的
afraid 恐怕，遺憾的
remorseful 後悔的
repentant 後悔的
ashamed 羞愧的

❷staying on top of 掌握～的最新狀況
responding to 回覆
giving time to 花時間處理～
replying to 回應～
answering 回答～

我很抱歉在這之前都還未能回覆您。我們公司內部有一些問題需要處理，因此造成我無法同時處理我的電子郵件。希望您能理解。謹此。

get back to 回覆，回電給～ before 在～之前 issue 問題 prevent 避免
keep up with... 趕上～的進度

✉ sample 602

Dear [_____]

I know it's been some time since you emailed me with your question. I kept intending to get back to you, but every time I sat down to email you, my phone would ring. You know how it is. Anyway, I've attached some price lists that I think will answer all of your questions.

Kind regards,

- - - - - - -

meaning 想要
trying 試圖
aiming 意圖要
planning 計畫要
preparing 準備要

我知道自您發電子郵件給我要詢問事情以來，已經過了一段時間。我一直都有想要回信給您，但每當我坐下來準備發信給您時，我的電話就響了。您知道是什麼狀況的。無論如何，我的附件中有一些價格的列表，我想是可以回答您的問題的。敬請籌安。

since 自從～ intend to... 意圖要，想要～ email 發送電子郵件給～ ring 電話響起 attach 附上
price list 價格清單 answer 대답하다

✉ sample 603

Dear ⌷‥‥‥‥‥⌷

I'm sorry I'm only just now getting back to you. We had a pretty severe problem with our email server, so the whole office was locked out of our inboxes! It's been a real problem as you can imagine. Anyway, I'm available now, so we can communicate more reliably.

Thanks for your patience.

- - - - - - - -

我很抱歉現在才回覆您。我們的電子郵件伺服器出現相當嚴重的問題，所以全公司人員的收件箱都被鎖住了。您可以想像這問題多嚴重。無論如何，我現在可以收件了，所以我們可以更可靠地進行溝通。感謝您的耐心。

> severe 嚴重的，棘手的　email server 電子郵件伺服器　lock 鎖住，封鎖　inbox 收件箱
> real 真的　available 有空的　reliably 可靠地；確實地

Try It! 可以替換的字詞

drastic 棘手的
serious 嚴重的
brutal 難處理的
extreme 極端的
far-reaching 影響深遠的

✉ sample 604

Dear ⌷‥‥‥‥‥⌷

I know it's taken me a while to respond, and I ❶apologize. I've had to be out of the office quite a bit this week. We have some clients visiting from out of the country and I was ❷delegated to show them around the city. I'm sorry if I've inconvenienced you.

Regards,

- - - - - - - -

Try It! 可以替換的字詞

❶ ask forgiveness 請求原諒
express regret 表示後悔
beg for excuse 請求寬恕
say sorry 說聲抱歉
ask for mercy 請求寬恕

❷ chosen 被選擇
selected 被選擇
asked 被要求
elected 被選出
preferred 寧可

我知道等我回覆已過了一段時間，在此表示歉意。這一週以來，很多時候我都必須離開辦公室。我們有一些來自國外的客戶到訪，而我被派去引領他們參觀這座城市。倘若已造成您不便，我致上歉意。謹此。

> a while 一段時間　respond 回覆　out of... 不在～　client 客戶　delegate 委派～為代表
> inconvenience 造成～不便

✉ sample 605

Try It！可以替換的字詞

Dear ⬚

I'm terribly sorry for the delay in getting back to you. I came down with the flu, so I've been in bed for the last four days. I'm finally back on my feet and ready to work. Why don't you give me a call and we can discuss your problem.

Thanks,

- - - - - - - -

contracted 罹患～

caught 染上～

developed 罹患～

got sick with 因～生病了

fell ill with 因～生病了

這麼晚才回覆您，我真的非常抱歉。我感冒了，所以在床上躺了四天。我現在終於恢復健康了，也準備繼續工作。您可否打個電話給我，我們可以討論您的問題。謝謝。

> terribly 非常地　come down with 罹患～（疾病等）　in bed 臥床　finally 最後
> on one's feet（患病或遭受挫折後）完全復原

承諾晚點會回信 Promising a Follow-up Email ▲

✉ sample 606

Dear _____

I will be out of the office for the rest of the day, so I won't be able to respond to your questions. I'll email you tomorrow morning when I get a moment to look over your concerns.

Thanks for your patience.

- - - - - - - -

我等一下會離開辦公室，所以今天我沒辦法回覆您的問題。等我明天抽空看過您的問題之後，會發電子郵件給您。感謝您的耐心等候。

> for the rest of the day 當日剩餘的時間　respond to 回覆～　moment（短暫的）時間，片刻
> look over 查看，檢視～　concerns 關切事項，問題

Try It！可以替換的字詞
an opportunity 機會
a chance 機會
a second 一點時間
a minute 一點時間
a break 休息時間

✉ sample 607

Dear _____

I have meetings scheduled back to back all afternoon, so I'll have to email you tomorrow about the project. I have a lot to tell you, and I just don't have time to get into it right now. Expect an email from me early tomorrow.

Thanks,

- - - - - - - -

我一整個下午排定了一場又一場的會議，所以關於這項專案，我只能等明天再寄發電子郵件給您。我有許多事情要跟您談，只是我現在抽不出時間。明天一早您會收到我的電子郵件。謝謝。

> back to back 一個接一個的，擁擠的　a lot 許多　get into... 開始從事，進入～（某種狀態）
> early 早的

Try It！可以替換的字詞
plan 計畫
development 發展
assignment 任務，作業
job 工作
task 任務

✉ sample **608**

Dear _____

Could I get back to you tomorrow about the Jones account? I've got a deadline for a report at the end of the day, so I've got to buckle down and finish it. I appreciate your patience.

Regards,

- - - - - - - -

關於瓊斯帳戶一事，我可以明天再回覆您嗎？我有一份報告的期限是在當日結束前，所以我得努力趕工來完成它。感謝您的耐心配合。祝安。

get back to ～再回覆～　account 帳戶，帳目，説明　deadline 截止期限　report 報告
buckle down 開始努力工作

✉ sample **609**

Dear _____

I'm going to have to email you later with the figures you've requested. It will take a while to get the numbers together, and I've got meetings with clients scheduled for the afternoon. I'll get everything together for you the day after tomorrow.

Thanks,

- - - - - - - -

我會晚一點將您要求的數字用電子郵件寄給您。整理這些數字需要花點時間，而且我預計下午還得跟客戶開會。我會在後天為您把所有資料整理好。感謝。

be going to... 將要～　figures 數字，數量，金額　request 要求　take a while 花一些時間
numbers 數字，價格，數據　client 客戶　scheduled for... 預定在～

✉ sample 610

Try It！可以替換的字詞

Dear _____

I got your email, but I haven't had a chance to look at it very closely. I'm very busy in the office at the moment, so I'll have to get back to you tomorrow.

Thanks for understanding.

read 閱讀

consider 考慮

examine 檢視

scan 掃視

glance at（粗略地）看一下

- - - - - - - -

我收到您的電子郵件了，但我還沒有機會很仔細地看一下。我目前正忙於公司的事情，所以我得明日再回覆您。感謝您的理解。

closely 仔細地　busy 忙碌的　at the moment 在這時候

✉ sample 611

Dear _____

How are things going? I'm writing because I still haven't received a reply to the email I sent you on Monday. I'm trying to make my **①final** decision, and your answer is a **②large** factor. Please let me know as soon as possible.

Thanks,

- - - - - - - -

近來可好？寫這封信給您是因為我週一寄了一封電子郵件給您，但我尚未收到您的回覆。我已準備要做最終決定了，而您的答案會是個關鍵因素。請盡速讓我知道。謝謝。

receive 收到　try to... 試圖要～　decision 決定　answer 答案　factor（會產生某種結果的）要素，因素　as soon as possible 盡速

✉ sample 612

Dear _____

I hope this email finds you well. I'm writing to see if you have made a decision on the proposal we discussed last week. We would like to know **one way or the other** so that we can pursue other options.

Thank you in advance.

- - - - - - - -

展信愉快。我寫這封信的目的是想問您是否已對於我們上周討論的提案有了決定。不管怎樣，我們想要知道一個結果，以便我們能夠做其它的選擇。先跟您說聲謝謝。

see if... 看是否，詢問～　proposal 提案　one way or the other 以某種方式，無論如何　pursue 尋求，追求

✉ sample 613

Dear _____

I'm writing to see when you will be able to give me an answer about the project. We are waiting for your reply before going forward. If you could let me know as soon as possible, I would really appreciate it.

Thank you.

- - - - - - - -

我寫這封信的目的是想詢問您，關於這個專案，您何時能夠給我一個答案。我們正在等待您的回覆，才能繼續進行下去。如果您能盡快讓我知道，我會非常感激的。謝謝您。

be able to 能夠～　give me an answer 給我一個答案　wait for 等待～　go forward 繼續前進

Try It！可以替換的字詞

quickly 快地
shortly 短暫地
presently 一會兒
fast 快速地
promptly 快速地

✉ sample 614

Dear _____

I hope everything is going well with you. I'm getting a little concerned because I haven't received an answer from you yet. Could you let me know as soon as possible what you want to do? The deadline is looming, so please contact me.

Thanks,

- - - - - - - -

願您一切安好。因為我尚未收到您給的答案，所以我點擔心。您可否盡快讓我知道您想要怎麼做。期限就要到了，麻煩您與我聯繫。謝謝。

everything 一切　a little 一點點　concerned 關切的，擔憂的　looming 即將到來，就在眼前的
contact 聯絡

Try It！可以替換的字詞

coming 要到了
approaching 接近了
imminent 就在眼前
pending 即將來到
near-term 所剩時間不多

✉ sample 615

Dear [_____]

Have you had a chance to think about what I asked you? It would help a lot if you could give me an answer fairly quickly. I have to make arrangements for purchasing the products, so I need to know if you're interested in partnering with me.

Thanks,

您有機會可以考慮我問您的事情了嗎？要是您可以非常迅速地給我一個答案，這會很有幫助的。我必須安排購買這些產品，所以我必須知道您是否有興趣與我合夥。謝謝。

chance 機會　ask 詢問，要求～　a lot 許多　fairly 非常地　make arrangements 做安排　purchase 購買 partner with 與～合夥

✉ sample **616**

Dear _____

Attached is the proposal we discussed previously. Please give careful attention to it, **❶as I believe** it is a way for us to benefit each other greatly. If you should have any questions at all, **❷don't hesitate to** contact me.

I look forward to hearing from you.

- - - - - - - -

Try It! 可以替換的字詞

❶ in that 因為～
because 因為～
since 因為～
as I'm sure 因為我確信
given that 由於～

❷ please 請
I hope you will 我希望您會～
by all means 務必一定要～
you know you can 您知道您可以～
you're welcome 歡迎您隨時～

附件是先前我們討論過的提案。請仔細查看，因為我相信那是我們彼此可以獲益良多的方法。無論您會遇到什麼樣的問題，請盡管與我聯繫。期待得到您的消息。

attach 附上　previously 先前　careful 小心的　attention 注意　each other 彼此　at all 根本，完全

✉ sample **617**

Dear _____

It was good to speak with you the other day. I hope that you give careful consideration to my proposal. I think that it is a good move for both of our companies. With your **specific expertise** and our expansive distribution network, we both stand to profit greatly.

I hope to hear from you soon.

- - - - - - - -

Try It! 可以替換的字詞

great production facilities
優良的生產設備
know-how 專業技能
talent 才能
strong suit 特長，優點
knowledge 知識

那天和您的交談非常愉快。我希望您已仔細考慮過我的提案。我想那對於我們雙方公司來說都是明智之舉。有您的特定專才及我們廣闊的經銷網絡，我們雙方皆能夠大大地獲利。希望很快有您的消息。

specific 特定的　expertise 專門知識，專門技術　expansive 廣闊的　distribution network 經銷網絡

✉ sample 618

Dear _____

I just wanted to **touch base with** you and ask you if you've had a chance to look over the proposal I sent you. I hope you give serious consideration to it. I think it's a winner for both of our companies. Let me know if you have any questions or concerns.

Thanks.

- - - - - - - -

我跟您連絡的目的是想問您，您是否有空看一下我寄給您的提案。我希望您可以認真考慮一下它。我想它對於我們雙方都是有利的。請讓我知道您是否有任何問題或疑問。謝謝。

Try It！可以替換的字詞

verify with 找～（某人）查證
discuss with 與～討論
explain to 解釋給～（某人聽）
converse with 與～（某人）對話
point out to 指出給～（某人看）

touch base 連絡，商討事情　serious 認真的　consideration 考慮　winner 有利情況，贏家

✉ sample 619

Dear _____

It was good to meet with you yesterday. I'm just writing to urge you to **consider** my proposal carefully. I really think that it offers a way for us both to profit greatly. If you need clarification on any part of the proposal, please let me know.

I look forward to hearing from you.

- - - - - - - -

昨天和您見面相當愉快。我寫這封信是想催促您仔細考慮一下我的提案。我真的認為它可以讓我們雙方大大地獲益。如果您需要我說明這項提案任何部分，請讓我知道。我期待有您的消息。

Try It！可以替換的字詞

think about 考慮，思考
ponder 思考
deliberate 仔細思考
mull over 仔細思考
contemplate 思量，仔細考慮

urge 催促，力勸　carefully 仔細地　offer 提供　both 兩者都 profit 獲益　clarification 澄清，說明清楚

✉ **sample 620**

Dear ....

I hope that you received the proposal I emailed you last week. I urge you to seriously consider it. Not only does it practically guarantee a profit for both our companies, but it also acts as a first step in a closer working relationship. I can foresee many situations in which we could benefit each other.

I hope to hear from you soon.

- - - - - - - -

希望您已經收到我上週以電子郵件寄給您的提案。我想請您認真考慮一下。它不只可以保證我們雙方實質上的獲益，且有助於我們彼此關係更密切的第一步。我可以預見在許多情況下，我們可以彼此互惠。希望可以很快有您的佳音。

seriously 認真地　not only... but also... 不僅～而且～　closer relationship 更密切的關係　foresee 預見

Try It！可以替換的字詞

obviously 明顯地
clearly 清楚地
basically 基本上
virtually 實際上
literally 實在地

通知重新考慮提案 Informing about Reconsideration of a Proposal ▲

✉ sample **621**

Dear [_____]

I'm writing to inform you that we are currently reconsidering the offer you made last month. At that time, we felt that it would not be profitable for us to accept, but we are now in the process of re-evaluating your proposal. I will contact you if we chose to go forward.

Thank you.

sensed 感覺到
believed 認為
deemed 認為
concluded 最終認為
thought 認為

- - - - - - - -

我寫這封信的目的是要通知您,目前我們正重新考慮您上個月提出的報價。當時,我們覺得接受的話,應無法獲利,不過我們現在正在重新評估您的提案。如果我們選擇接受的話,我會和您聯繫。謝謝您。

inform 通知　currently 目前　reconsider 重新考慮　profitable 可以獲利的　re-evaluete 重新評估

✉ sample **622**

Dear [_____]

I wanted to let you know that I've been thinking about your proposal, and there may be a way that we could accept it. I'm running the numbers, and I'll let you know if we decide to change our mind.

I'll talk to you soon.

point of view 觀點
thoughts 想法
opinion 意見
view 看法
way of thinking 思考方式

- - - - - - - -

我想讓您知道,我一直在考慮您的提案,且也許會有我們可以接受的可能。我正在計算這些數字,且我會讓您知道我們是否決定改變心意。

way 方式　accept 接受　number 數字,金額　decide 決定

✉ sample 623

Dear _____

The offer you made last month is starting to sound better than we initially thought. We are reconsidering our rejection, and may decide to talk you up on it after all. Would your offer still stand if we wanted to accept? When you get a chance, give me a call and let me know.

Thank you.

- - - - - - - -

我們已經開始認為您上個月的提案比我們原先所想的還要好。我們正重新審視我們拒絕的原因，且最後可能會同意您的說法。如果我們想要接受的話，您的提案是否還有效？如果您有空的話，給我個電話，並讓我知道。謝謝您。

better 更好的　initially 最初地　rejection 拒絕　talk... up 同意〜（某人）的說法　after all 畢竟，最終
stand 保持

✉ sample 624

Dear _____

I wanted to tell you that it looks like my boss has finally come around to my way of thinking. He's decided to reconsider your offer. I've been trying to convince him all week, and he's finally asked to look over the details again. Keep your fingers crossed, and hopefully he'll change his mind.

I'll talk to you soon.

- - - - - - - -

我想告訴您，我老闆似乎最後會根據我的想法而做出讓步。他已決定重新考慮您的提案。一整個禮拜以來，我一直試圖要說服他，而最後他願意再仔細審視細節部分。祈求好運吧，希望他可以改變心意。我們再聊。

look like... 似乎，看來〜　finally 最後　come around 讓步，改變立場　reconsider 重新考慮
convince 使〜相信　look over... 仔細審視〜

✉ sample 625

Dear _____

I'm writing to ask whether your offer of last month still stands. I know we refused this offer, but we have been having second thoughts. We are currently reconsidering. Would you be able to meet with us to discuss the offer again?

I look forward to hearing from you.

- - - - - - - -

我寫這封信的目的是想詢問您上個月的提案是否還有效。我知道我們拒絕過這項提案，不過我們已再三思考了一番。目前我們正在重新考慮。您可以與我碰個面再討論一次這項提案嗎？期待您的佳音。

refuse 拒絕　second thought 再三思考

Try It！可以替換的字詞

declined 委婉拒絕
turned down 拒絕
had to send back 必須退回
sent regrets to 對～抱以遺珠之憾
said no to 對～說不

sample 626

Dear _____

Could you possibly resend the fax? I have received it, but it isn't legible. I'll let you know when I've received it.

Thank you.

- - - - - - - -

可以麻煩您再傳真一次嗎？我已經收到了，但字跡並不清楚。我收到的時候會再通知您。謝謝您。

Try It！可以替換的字詞
readable 可閱讀的
intelligible 看得懂的
decipherable 可辨認的
understandable 可了解的
clear 清楚的

possibly 可能地 resend 重新傳送 fax 傳真 receive 收到 legible 字跡清晰的，可辨認的

✉ **sample 627**

Dear _____

I'm having a little trouble reading the fax you sent. It has lots of lines. I think it must have jammed when it was going through the machine. Could you please send it one more time?

Thank you.

- - - - - - - -

我沒有辦法閱讀您發送過來的傳真。我想它一定是在經過機器時有卡紙現象，可以請您再傳送一次嗎？謝謝您。

Try It！可以替換的字詞
got stuck 被卡住
got wedged 被卡住
got lodged 被卡住
got blocked 卡紙
got caught 卡紙

have trouble -ing 做～有困難 jam 塞進，擠進，卡住，發生故障 go through... 穿過，經過
machine 機器 one more time 再一次

✉ sample 628

Dear _____

I received the fax you ❶sent, but I'm afraid I can't read it. Could you please send it again? ❷It would be much appreciated.

Thank you.

- - - - - - -

❶ submitted 提交

transmitted 傳送

forwarded 傳遞

communicated 傳遞

passed on 傳過來

❷ I would be grateful 我會感激的。

It would help me a lot
那會幫我個大忙的。

Thanks for your help
感謝您的協助。

Many thanks 多謝了。

I will let you know when it's arrived
收到的時候，我會讓您知道。

我收到您發送過來的傳真了，但恐怕我沒辦法看得清楚。可以請您再傳送一次嗎？非常感激您的辛勞。謝謝您。

I'm afraid (that...) 恐怕我～

✉ sample 629

Dear _____

The fax you sent did not come through clearly. Could you be so kind as to send it again? I will email you if I have any problems this time.

Thank you very much.

- - - - - - -

was not comprehensible 無法辨識

was not able to be read 無法閱讀

was not printed properly
印得不太清楚

was not all here 沒有全部傳送到

was not the best quality
印刷品質不是很好

您發送過來的傳真內容不是很清楚。可以麻煩您再傳一次嗎？如果這次再有任何問題，我會用電子郵件通知您。非常感謝您。

come through 顯露，出現 clearly 清楚地 so... as to... 如此地～以致於～ kind 好心的 this time 這次

✉ sample 630

Dear [_____]

I'm afraid that the fax you sent look blurry. Do you think you could give it another try? I'd really appreciate it.

Thanks,

- - - - - - - -

抱歉，您發送過來的傳真內容看起來很模糊。您可以再試著傳一次嗎？非常感謝您的辛勞。謝謝。

blurry 模糊的　another 另一個的　try 試著

Try It！可以替換的字詞

fully 完全地

truly 真實地

genuinely 真正地

sincerely 誠摯地

thoroughly 全然地

✉ sample **631**

Dear _____

I'm afraid I'm having a little trouble with the file you sent in your last email. I'm getting a formatting error when I open it. Is there any chance you could send it to me as an .xls file?

Thanks,

- - - - - - - -

不好意思，我無法開啟您上一封電子郵件裡的檔案。我開啟檔案時出現格式錯誤的訊息。您是否可能以 .xls 的檔案寄給我呢？謝謝。

file 檔案　format 格式　error 錯誤　chance 機會，可能

Try It！可以替換的字詞

strange error message
奇怪的錯誤訊息

blank screen 螢幕一片空白

request to reboot 重新開機的要求

scrambled message 雜亂訊息；亂碼

series of beeps 一連串嗶聲

✉ sample **632**

Dear _____

I wasn't able to open the file related to your last email. I'm not sure what the problem is. Could you try resending it? I'll let you know if that doesn't work.

Thanks,

- - - - - - - -

我無法開啟附在您上一封電子郵件的檔案。我不確定問題在哪。您可以再傳一次嗎？如果還是無法使用，我會讓您知道。謝謝。

be able to... 能夠〜　related 有關的　sure 確地的　resend 重新傳送　work 有效，可用

Try It！可以替換的字詞

linked 連結的

associated 有關的

attached 附加的

coupled 成對的

tied 繫在一起的

✉ sample 633

Dear ⌐ _ _ _ _ _ _ _ ⌐

The file you sent me wouldn't download. I'm not sure if the problem is at my end or your end. Would you be so kind as to try resending it? If it still doesn't **work**, I'll have one of our IT guys look at it.

Thanks,

- - - - - - - -

您寄給我的檔案無法下載。我不確定問題是在我這邊還是您那一方。可以麻煩您再傳送一次嗎？如果還是無法作用，我會請我們一位 IT 人員查看一下。謝謝。

✉ sample 634

Dear ⌐ _ _ _ _ _ _ _ ⌐

I'm having a bit of a problem with the files you attached to your email. Do you happen to know of any reason why I wouldn't be able to open them? Is there any software I **need** to download? Please let me know so I can take a look at what you've sent me.

Thank you.

- - - - - - - -

對於您電子郵件上的附加檔案，我這邊出現了一點問題。您是否剛好知道我無法開啟這些檔案的原因呢？是否有任何我必須去下載的軟體呢？煩請告知，好讓我可以看看您寄了什麼給我。謝謝。

✉ sample 635

Dear _____

This file you sent me won't open. What format is it? I tried opening it with Word, but it didn't recognize the format. Could you check the format and resend it?

Thanks,

Try It! 可以替換的字詞
attempted opening 試圖開啟
struggled to open 努力要開啟
made an effort at opening 努力要開啟
took a crack at opening 試圖開啟
took a stab at opening 試圖開啟

- - - - - - - -

您寄給我的檔案無法開啟。它是什麼格式的？我試圖以 Word 開啟，但它無法辨識格式。您可以確認一下格式並重新再傳一次嗎？謝謝。

format 格式，版式　recognize 辨認，辨識　check 檢查，確認

索取行程表 Requesting the Schedule ▲

✉ **sample 636**

Dear ....

I'm looking forward to seeing you next week. Could I get the schedule for the meetings? I'd like to know exactly when I'll be meeting with various members of your team.

Thanks,

Try It！可以替換的字詞
committee 委員會
group 團體
cohort 同夥，一輩人
organization 組織
band 樂隊，一輩人

我期待下週能夠見到您。可以給我會議的行程表嗎？我想知道我將與您團隊中多位成員開會的確切時間。謝謝。

> look forward to 期待～ next week 下週 schedule 行程表 exactly 確切地 various 各種各樣的

✉ **sample 637**

....

I'm trying to ❶organize my plans for the week and I was wondering if I could get your schedule. I'm not sure when you are available. If I have a better ❷sense of what you'll be doing, I'll be able to meet with you more easily.

Thanks,

Try It！可以替換的字詞
❶ **put in order** 整理
sort out 整理出
arrange 安排
categorize 分類
systematize 將～系統化
❷ **feeling** 感覺
idea 想法
impression 印象
sensation 知覺
awareness 認知

我正試著彙整我這一週的計畫，而我想知道是否可以拿到您的行程表。我不確定您何時有空。如果我可以更加了解您將做的事情，我們的會面將更加順利。謝謝。

> organize 彙整 plan 計畫 wonder 想知道 sure 確定的 available 有空的，可以聯繫得到的
> easily 容易地

✉ sample 638

Dear [.............]

Could you put together a schedule for when each part of the project will be completed? I'd like to get some idea of when to expect delivery of the final package. There's no rush, so whenever you get a chance is fine.

Thanks,

- - - - - - - -

您可以彙整本專案中各部分須完成的行程表嗎？我想大致了解一下預計什麼時候可以收到最後的工作包。還不急，所以您準備好時再寄給我吧。謝謝。

put together 彙整	each 每一個	delivery 遞送	final 最終的	package（專案計畫中的）工作包
rush 急迫	whenever 無論何時

Try It！可以替換的字詞

You can take your time 您可以慢慢來

I can wait 我可以等

I'm just curious 我只是好奇

I'm not in a rush 我不急／不趕時間

This isn't critical 不要緊

✉ sample 639

Dear [.............]

I'm eager to see you in Seoul next week. I know you're going to be meeting with a lot of different people, so I'd like to get your schedule. Is there any way you could send it to me so that I can organize a meeting with you?

Thanks,

- - - - - - - -

我很渴望下週可以在首爾見到您。我知道您將與許多不同的人會面，所以我想拿到您的行程表。您是否可能將行程表寄給我，以便我可以安排跟您會面？感謝。

be eager to 渴望，很想要～　a lot of 許多的　so that... 以便～

Try It！可以替換的字詞

dissimilar 不同的

diverse 各樣的

unique 獨特的

distinctive 顯要的

atypical 非典型的

✉ sample 640

Dear _____

We're trying to figure out when to expect manufacturing to begin on the new product. Do you think you could send us a production schedule showing when each stage should be finished? It will help us get ready for the marketing phase.

Thanks a lot.

我們正試圖了解這項新產品開始製造的時間。您可否寄給我們一份生產時程表，可以看到每個階段應該完成的時間點？這對於我們行銷階段的準備工作很有幫助。非常感謝。

> try to... 試圖，試著要～　figure out... 了解，想出～　manufacturing 製造　production 生產
> stage 階段（phase）　finish 完成

✉ sample 641

Dear _____

I'm writing because I'd like to invite you to inspect our factory. I think seeing our production facilities would really give you a sense of the scale of our operation as well as its efficiency. If you would like to come and tour the factory, let me know and we will schedule a visit.

I look forward to hearing from you.

Try It！可以替換的字詞
size 大小
extent 程度
degree 程度
amount 規模
magnitude 規模

我寫這封信的目的是想邀請您來參觀我們的工廠。我想，看過我們的生產設施之後，您會真正了解我們運作的規模及其效率。如果您想過來參觀我們的工廠，請讓我知道，我們會安排訪視的行程。期待您的回覆。

> invite 邀請　inspect 參觀，視察　factory 工廠　facility 設施　operation 運作，操作，營運
> as well as 以及，和～　efficiency 效率　tour 參觀，巡視

✉ sample 642

Dear _____

I hope everything is going well on your end. I'd like to propose a visit to our factory in Korea. I think it would set aside some of your fears about our production capacity if you saw our operation with your own eyes. Let me know if you think this is a good idea.

Thanks,

Try It！可以替換的字詞
worries 擔憂
concerns 關切
doubts 疑問
reservations 保留態度
uncertainties 不確定性

願貴公司營運一切順利。我想建議您來看看我們位於首爾的工廠。我想，如果您親眼看到我們的運作狀況，這會消除您對於我們工廠產能的憂慮。請讓我知道您是否也認為這是個不錯的想法。感謝。

> on your end 在您那邊　set aside 將～擱置一邊　capacity 能力，產能　with your own eyes 親眼，親身

✉ sample 643

Dear _____

What would you think about coming out to see our factory? Whenever we engage in a new partnership with another company, we always like to open our factory to inspection. We can walk you through the production process and give you a good sense of how things work. Let me know if you'd like to do this and we'll schedule a time in the next week or so.

I look forward to hearing from you.

- - - - - - - -

您要不要過來看一下我們的工廠呢？每當我們與另一家公司成立新的合夥關係時，我們都會開放我們的工廠讓他們參觀一下。我們可以伴您走過生產過程，並讓您更加了解運作方式。請讓我知道您是否想要這麼做，我們會安排時間大約下個星期左右的時間。期待您的佳音。

engage in 投入，從事～ partnership（生意上的）夥伴關係 inspection 視察，參觀
walk 陪伴～（某人）走路 process 過程，程序 or so 諸如此類

✉ sample 644

Dear _____

I'm really excited about the new distribution deal. I think we are really going to benefit each other. I'd like to extend an invitation to come and visit our factory. When you see our production process, it really gives you a good sense of how orders will be filled. It will also give you a good view of our quality assurance system. Let me know if you would be up for a visit.

Thanks,

- - - - - - - -

我真的對於這份新的經銷合約相當興奮。我想我們確實可以互惠互利。在此我想向您提出邀請，前來參觀我們的工廠。當您見過我們的生產過程時，您才會真正了解您的貨是如何交付的。您也會清楚看到我們的品保系統。請讓我知道您是否願意過來一趟。謝謝。

distribution 經銷，分銷 deal 合約，交易 benefit 獲得利益 extend an invitation 提出邀請
fill an order 交付訂貨 view 觀察，觀點，觀看 quality assurance 品質保證

✉ sample 645

Dear [　　　　　]

Would you be interested in coming out to see our factory next month? I'd like to give you a chance to tour our facilities and see firsthand how our production process flows. If you have a free afternoon, let me know and we'll work out the details.

I look forward to hearing from you.

Try It！可以替換的字詞

arrangements 安排事項

plans 計畫

strategy 策略

little things 小事情

preparations 準備事項

您是否有興趣下個月過來看一下我們的工廠？我想給您一個參觀我們設備的機會，預先看看我們的生產過程是如何運行的。如果您有下午空閒的時間，請讓我知道，我們可以先處理好細節事項。期待您的佳音。

give A B 給予 A（人）B（物）　chance 機會　firsthand 預先　flow 運行，運作

通知職位變更 Informing of a Change in Position ▲

✉ sample 646

Dear _____

How are things going on your end? I've had a bit of a change here at my company. I've moved from the sales department to the marketing department. I'll now be managing our marketing efforts outside of Korea. From now on if you have any question about marketing, I'm the one to contact.

Thanks,

- - - - - - - -

您最近可好？我在我公司這邊有點變化。我已經從業務部門轉調至行銷部門。我現在掌管的是韓國以外的行銷業務。現在起，如果您有任何行銷上的問題，我是您聯繫的窗口。謝謝。

Try It！可以替換的字詞
running 營運
administering 管理
supervising 監管
overseeing 監督
leading 帶領

on your end 在您那一方　a bit of 一點點的～　department 部門　manage 管理
effort 努力的成果，任務　outside of 在～以外　from now on 從現在起

✉ sample 647

Dear _____

I'm writing to let you know that I've changed positions within the company. I'm now Vice President of Sales. Any questions you have concerning our sales initiatives can be directed to me from now on. I look forward to working with you in this new capacity.

Thanks,

- - - - - - - -

我寫這封信的目的是要讓您知道，我在公司的職位已經更換了。我現在是業務副理。現在起，如您有任何業務運作上的問題，可以直接找我。我期待在我新的職務上與您合作。感謝。

Try It！可以替換的字詞
jobs 工作
responsibilities 職責
titles 頭銜
duties 職責，職務
designations 指派之任務

position 職務，職位　within 在～之內　concerning 有關於～　initiatives 運作，活動　direct 指引
capacity 資格，地位，職位

✉ sample 648

Dear _____

I just wanted to let you know that I've moved out of the IT development department and am now in charge of promotions. I'm excited about the new position and I'm looking forward to working more closely with you. I'll contact you soon about some new projects I'm going to be overseeing.

Talk to you soon,

- - - - - - - -

在此我想讓您知道，我已經離開 IT 研發部門，現在負責產品推廣。我非常滿意新的職務，且我期待與您更密切合作。對於我即將負責的一些新專案，我會盡快與您聯繫。到時候再聊。

development 發展，研發　in charge of 負責～　promotion 推廣，促銷　closely 密切地
oversee 監督，管理

Try It！可以替換的字詞

transferred 轉調
shifted 轉調
jumped 跳槽
stepped 跨步，步行
pulled 拉拖，移動

✉ sample 649

Dear _____

I'm writing to inform you that I've changed positions within the company. I will now be working under Jim Davis in the marketing department. I'll be overseeing the new marketing plan for the G32, so you can expect to be hearing from me a lot concerning promotional events and advertising. I look forward to the new challenges.

Regards,

- - - - - - - -

我寫這封信的目的是要通知您，我在公司的職位已經更換了。我現在在行銷部門，在 Jim Davis 旗下做事。我將管理 G32 的新行銷計畫，所以您可預期將收到許多我給您的、關於推廣與廣告活動的消息。我期待新的挑戰來臨。敬請籌安。

inform A that... 通知 A～（某事）　work under... 隸屬於～（某人）　promotional events 促銷活動
advertising 廣告　challenge 挑戰，任務

Try It！可以替換的字詞

tests 考驗
opportunities 機會
trials 試煉
chances 機會
possibilities 可能性

✉ sample 650

Hi, ┈┈┈┈┈

I hope everything is going well with you. I just wanted to drop you a line to let you know that there's been a bit of restructuring in our office. I'll no longer be working in the sales department. Instead I'm going to be starting a new business development department. We'll be working on **expanding** our current initiatives, and forging new relationships with other companies. I'll be contacting you soon to discuss some of those initiatives with you.

I look forward to speaking with you.

Try It！可以替換的字詞

increasing 增加
growing 使成長
intensifying 強化
escalating 加強
developing 發展

願您一切安好。在此我想寫封信讓您知道，我們公司已進行些微的改組。我現在沒有在業務部工作了。我將開始負責一個新的事業發展部門。我們將拓展目前的業務，並與其他公司發展新的關係。我很快會再跟您聯繫，討論一些運作方案。我期待與您交談。

go well 進行順利　drop a line 寫封信；（藉由電話或書信）留下訊息　restructuring 改組，重組　expand 拓展　current 目前的　forge 打造，培養（關係等）

✉ sample 651

Dear 〔_____〕

I'm sure you've heard by now that I've moved from the sales department to the IT division. That means that from now on you'll be working with Joe King. He's joined the company a couple of years ago and he's really good at what he does. I've cc'd him on this email so that you two can get in contact.

Thanks,

- - - - - - - -

Try It！可以替換的字詞

skilled 熟練的

excellent 擅長的

skillful 具備技術的

proficient 精明的

talented 有天賦的

我相信您現在已經得知我已從業務部轉調至 IT 部門的消息。也就是說，現在起，您將與 Joe King 一起合作。他加入公司已經好幾年了，他也確實對於自己負責的工作表現良好。我已把這封電子郵件副本寄給他，以便您二位可以取得聯繫。謝謝。

by now 目前為止 division 部門 That means 那意思是說～ several years 幾年
get in contact 取得聯繫

✉ sample 652

Dear 〔_____〕

I'm writing to introduce Tim Bradstreet to you. He'll be filling my old position now that I am changing roles at the company. He has been brought up to speed on all of my accounts, so he'll be able to answer any questions you have. I've cc'd him on this email, so you cancontact him whenever you want.

Thank you,

- - - - - - - -

Try It！可以替換的字詞

reply to 回覆，回答～

respond to 回應～

resolve 解決

take action to 對～採取行動

help with 協助～

我寫這封信的目的是要將 Tim Bradstreet 介紹給您認識。他將取代我的職位，因為我在公司已經轉任至其他職位。他已經取得我所有客戶的最新資訊。所以他也能夠回答您任何提出的問題。我有把這封電子郵件副本寄給他。所以您可以隨時與他聯絡。感謝您。

fill 就任，填充 position 職務，職位 role 角色，職位
bring... up to speed 給予～最新或必要資訊；使～了解狀況 accounts 客戶

✉ sample 653

Dear _____

As you know, I've recently been made head of the IT development division, so I won't be working with the tech support office anymore. From now on Jason Lee will be the point man for any problems that might arise. You can reach Jason with the same phone number, but use x22. His email is jlee@smithtech.com. He's very capable and I'm sure he'll be able to help you with whatever issues you may have.

Thanks,

- - - - - - - -

如您所知，我最近已被調任 IT 部門的主管，所以已經不在技術支援處工作了。現在起，Jason Lee 將會是負責處理任何問題的重點人物。您可以用相同的電話號碼連絡到 Jason，但分機改為 22。他的電子郵件 jlee@smithtech.com.。他能力很強，我確信無論您有任何問題，他都可以處理。感謝。

head 主管　point man 重點人物，關鍵人物，要角　arise 出現，升起　reach 連絡到
capable 有能力的

✉ sample 654

Dear _____

This is just a quick note to let you know that Jeff Taylor will be taking over my old position and that I've been reassigned to the communications department. Jeff will now cover all of the work I did on your account. He has received all the information required, so I'm sure he's ready to field any questions you might have. His email adress is jtaylor@ jonesinc.net.

Thanks,

- - - - - - - -

這封信只是個簡短通知，讓您知道 Jeff Taylor 將接管我的舊職務，以及我將轉調至通訊部門。現在 Jeff 將負責所有我先前與您業務往來相關的工作。他已經得知所有必要資訊，所以我確定他已準備好回應您所有可能的問題。他的電子郵件是 jtaylor@ jonesinc.net.。感謝。

quick note 簡短通知　reassign 重新指派　cover 應付，負責
field 明智地應付（問題等）；將～（問題等）處理好

✉ sample 655

Dear [_____]

I'm writing to let you know that Sam Smith will be ❶ taking over my old duties now that I've been transferred to the quality assurance department. Sam ❷has been with the company for quite a while and he knows our products very well. If you have any concerns, Sam will be your contact in the company.

Thank you, and I look forward to working with you in my new capacity.

- - - - - - - -

我寫這封信的目的是要讓您知道 Sam Smith 將接任我的舊職務，因為我將被調派至品保部門。Sam 已經在這家公司有好長一段時間了，他非常了解我們的產品。如果您有任何問題，Sam 將會是您在公司中的窗口聯繫人。感謝您，而我也期待在我新的職位上能夠與您合作。

take over 接任，接管～　transfer 轉調　assurance 保證　quite a while 一段長時間
concerns 關切之事，問題　contact 窗口聯繫人，媒介

✉ sample 656

Dear [ ]

I heard that your old partner Jerry has been made director of the sales department. Will you still be working closely with him? I was wondering if you'd pass on my congratulations. I'd appreciate it.

Thanks,

----

praise 稱讚
best wishes 最好的祝福
pride 自豪
compliments 敬意
commendation 問候

我聽說您的老搭檔 Jerry 已獲晉升為業務部主管。您在工作上還跟他關係密切嗎？不知您可否幫我致上恭賀之意。感謝您的協助。謝謝。

partner 搭檔，夥伴　director 主管，經理，執行長　closely 密切地　pass on... 傳遞～

✉ sample 657

Dear [ ]

How is everything going? I wanted to drop you a line and ask you to give my regards to your CEO. He may not remember me, but we met several years ago at a seminar in New York. Could you tell him that Don says hello? I'd appreciate it.

Thanks,

----

thanks 謝謝
appreciation 謝意
gratitude 感激之意
respect 敬意
well wishes 問候

一切都還好嗎？我寫這封信是想拜託您為我向您的執行長致上問候之意。他也許不記得我了，不過我們數年前曾在紐約的一場座談會上碰面。您可以告訴他 Don 向他打聲招呼嗎？感謝您的協助。謝謝。

drop a line（以書信或電話）聯繫　give my regards to... 代我向～致上問候　remember 記得
several 數個的　ago 以前　seminar 座談會　say hello 打聲招呼

✉ sample 658

Dear [_____]

Please give my regards to your family. I know you've recently **relocated** to New York, so I've been thinking about you. I hope your family is settling in well. Let me know if there's anything I can do for any of you.

Regards,

- - - - - - - -

Try It! 可以替換的字詞

moved 搬家
changed location 搬遷
transferred 轉調
been displaced 搬遷
shifted 遷移

請為我向您的家人們致上問候之意。我知道您最近搬至紐約了,所以我一直掛念著您們。但願您的家人們都已安頓妥當。請讓我知道您是否有什麼需要我幫忙的。在此請安。

family 家人 recently 最近 relocate 轉調,搬遷 think about... 掛念著~ settle in 安頓下來

✉ sample 659

Dear [_____]

I hope you are doing well. I was writing to ask you to send my regards along to your new boss. I haven't had a chance to meet her yet, but I was happy to hear you'd be working with her. I look forward to talking to her about some **initiatives**.

Thanks,

- - - - - - - -

Try It! 可以替換的字詞

programs 計畫
proposals 提案
plans 計畫
projects 專案
thoughts 想法

願您一切順利。我寫這封信的目的是想拜託您代我向您的新老闆致上問候之意。我還沒有機會遇到她,但我很高興聽見您與她一起工作。我期待能夠與她談談一些行動方案。感謝。

do well 過得好 look forward to 期待~ initiative 先機,行動方案

✉ sample 660

Dear [_____]

Please give my regards to your brother. I just saw from the business **directory** that he's now working in the sales department at Smith Tech. Tell him I say hello and that I'd love to get together with him and talk about some sales initiatives we'd like to do with Smith Tech.

Thanks,

- - - - - - - -

請代我向您的哥哥致上問候之意。我剛在工商名錄中看到，他現在服務於 Smith Tech 的業務部門。請代我打聲招呼，以及我希望可以與他一起商談一些我們希望與 Smith Tech 合作的業務計畫。謝謝。

directory 工商名錄，電話簿　get together 在一起

Try It！可以替換的字詞

catalogue 產品目錄
reference 推薦函
handbook 手冊
register 登記簿
list 清單

✉ sample 661

Dear _____

I'm afraid I'm going to have to ❶delay my visit to your company. I've overextended myself a little on my business trip, so I'm having to rearrange my schedule a bit. I'll let you know when I'm ❷available as soon as I settle a few issues.

Thanks for understanding.

- - - - - - - -

Try It！可以替換的字詞

❶ postpone 延遲
set back 延後
defer 推遲
suspend 暫停
shelve 擱置

❷ around 有空的
on hand 準備好的
there 到那裡，有空的
close by 在一旁；有空的
close at hand 就在附近；有空的

我恐怕必須延後拜訪貴公司了。我出差時稍微過度承擔了一些工作，所以我的行程必須做一點更動。等我解決了一些問題，能夠抽出時間時，我會讓您知道。謝謝您的理解。

visit 拜訪　delay 延後　overextend oneself 過分擴展，使自己承擔過多的工作　business trip 出差
rearrange 重新安排　settle 解決

✉ sample 662

Dear _____

I'm going to have to delay the visit we have scheduled for next week. I apologize for the inconvenience, but we've had a minor crisis here at the office that I have to tend to. Would the following week be okay for you?

Thanks for your understanding.

- - - - - - - -

Try It！可以替換的字詞

financial 財務上的
slight 些微的
systematic 系統上的
little 小小的
miniature 微小的

我將得延後我們預計下周進行的訪問。造成不便，在此致上歉意，只是我們公司這邊出現了一點我必須去處理的小危機。再下週您是否方便？謝謝您的理解。

scheduled for... 預定在～　inconvenience 不便　crisis 危機　tend to... 照料，處理 ～
following 下一個的

✉ sample 663

Dear [_____]

Unfortunately, I'm going to have to put off visiting your offices until next month. It turns out that our schedule is just too ❶full this month. I'll get in touch with you next week to reschedule.

Thank you for your ❷tolerance.

- - - - - - - -

Try It！可以替換的字詞

❶ busy 忙碌的
packed 行程滿的
hectic 忙碌的
eventful 多事的
demanding 令人吃力的

❷ understanding 理解
patience 耐心
lack of complaint 不抱怨
leniencey 仁慈
charity 善心

很抱歉，我必須將拜訪貴公司的行程延後至下個月。事實上，我們這個月的行程太滿了。我下週會和您聯繫，重新安排時間。感謝您的包容。

put off 延後　turn out that... 結果是～　get in touch with... 與～聯繫　tolerance 包容

✉ sample 664

Dear [_____]

It looks like it's going to be necessary to postpone my visit to your offices. I've had several deals in the planning stages for the last few weeks, and it looks like two of them are going to happen. Therefore, I've got to be in the office to put the finishing touches on everything. I'll get in touch with you about rescheduling once I'm through with these projects.

I apologize for the inconvenience.

- - - - - - - -

Try It！可以替換的字詞

after I've completed 在我完成了～之後
at the end of 在～結束後
when we've done with 當我們完成～時
following 在～之後
as soon as I've finished 一旦我完成～時

目前情況看來我必須延後參訪貴公司的行程了。我有幾件交易案還在計畫階段，還需要最後幾週的處理時間，而其中兩件看來是會實現的。因此，我必須待在公司將所有事情做最後的了結。一旦我將這些計畫完成時，我會和您聯繫，以重新安排時間。造成不便，深表歉意。

postpone 延後　happen 發生，實現　put the finishing touch on... 對於～做最後的了結　once 一旦～　through 完成的

✉ sample **665**

Dear (.............)

I'm sorry to inconvenience you, but I'm going to have to delay my scheduled **visit** to your offices. It turns out that I have a scheduling conflict, so I'll have to be in New York for the rest of the week. I hope to find time next month to reschedule. Please accept my apologies.

Thank you for understanding.

- - - - - - - -

造成您的不便，真是抱歉，只是我必須延後我預定參訪貴公司的行程。事實上，我的行程出現衝突，所以我這個星期內還必須待在紐約。我希望下個月可以找到時間重新排定時間。請接受我的道歉。感謝您的理解。

Part 2

商務以外場合

 感謝 Thanks

Case 01 寄感謝函 Sending a Thank-you Card ▲

✉ sample 666

Dear _____

Thank you so much for the kind gift you sent. It was nice of you to ❶remember that I play tennis. The new racquet is really ❷terrific. What a great birthday present!

Thanks again,

- - - - - - - -

Try It! 可以替換的字詞

❶recall 回想起
consider 考慮
keep in mind 記在心裡
recollect 回想起
bear in mind 記在心裡

❷super 超棒的
wonderful 太好了
thoughtful 考慮周到的
great 太棒了
marvelous 令人驚歎的

非常感謝您送來的禮物。您人真好,還記得我會打網球。這支新球拍真的很棒。真是個很好的生日禮物。再次感謝。

> gift 禮物 sent 送,寄 nice 好心的,仁慈的 play tennis 打網球 racquet 球拍
> birthday present 生日禮物

✉ sample 667

Dear _____

Thank you for coming to the presentation last week. It was great to see you there. I hope you found it useful. I look forward to seeing you again soon.

Regards,

- - - - - - - -

Try It! 可以替換的字詞

showing 展示會
meeting 會議
production 成果發表會
staging 演出
annual event 年度盛事

感謝您上周前來參加這場發表會。很高興看到你來。我希望您有所收穫。我期待很快可以再見到您。謹致問候。

> presentation 簡報,發表會 It was great to... ～是很棒的 useful 有用的

✉ sample 668

Dear ⌞_____⌟

Thank you for the kind card you sent. I was having a
❶rough day and your card really brightened it for me.
And what a funny joke! It really ❷cracked me up.

I'll talk to you soon.

- - - - - - - -

Try It！可以替換的字詞

❶ bad 糟糕的
horrible 可怕的
crabby 不順遂的
irritating 令人煩躁的
long 漫長的

❷ made me laugh 讓我笑了
tickled me 取悅我
gave me a smile 讓我會心一笑
lightened my day 讓我開懷
lightened my load 釋放我的壓力

感謝您寄來的善心卡片。我過了很糟的一天，而您的卡片真的讓我豁然開朗了一下。那真是好笑呢！
那真的讓我笑開了。我們再聊。

rough 糟糕的　brighten 使明亮，使開顏　funny 有趣的　crack... up 讓～開懷大笑

✉ sample 669

Dear ⌞_____⌟

Thanks so much for inviting me over for dinner. I had
a great time meeting your husband and son. Next
time, we'll have to have you over. And the chicken was
delicious!

Regards,

- - - - - - - -

Try It！可以替換的字詞

tasty 美味的
flavorful 味道不錯的
mouth-watering 令人垂涎的
appetizing 開胃的
yummy 可口的

非常感謝您邀請我共進晚餐。我和您先生與兒子玩得很開心。下次，得換我們邀請您了。對了，雞肉
很好吃喔！謹致問候。

invite 邀請　had a great time -ing 在～玩得很開心　over 過來，在這邊　chicken 雞肉　delicious 美味的

✉ **sample 670**

Dear _____

Thank you for inviting me to your party last weekend. I had a very good time. I met a lot of people in the industry and made some really great contacts. I hope I can return the favor for you some time.

Thanks again,

- - - - - - - -

感謝您上周末邀請我來參加您的派對。我玩得非常開心。我遇見許多這個產業中的人，還有一些真的還不錯的人，我之後可以和他們聯絡。我希望日後我能夠報答您這份人情。再次感謝。

weekend 周末 a lot of 許多的 industry 產業 make contact 取得聯絡方式 return 歸還 favor 恩情

✉ sample **671**

Dear ⸢⸥

I'm writing to express my appreciation for the time you spent solving my computer problem yesterday. I know you had a lot to do. I could never have figured it out without your help. Please let me know if there's ever anything I can do for you.

Thanks,

- - - - - - - -

Try It！可以替換的字詞

fixed it 解決這件事
understood it 了解這事
rationalized it 將這事合理化
made it out 了解這事的始末
repaired it 修復它

我寫這封信的目的是對於您昨天花時間解決了我電腦的問題，表達感激之意。我知道您有許多事情要做。沒有您的一臂之力，我可能永遠都無法解決這問題。如果有任何我能夠為您效勞的地方，請讓我知道。謝謝。

express 表達　appreciation 感激之意　spend -ing 花時間～（做某事）
figure... out 想出～解決辦法，解決～　without... 沒有～的話

✉ sample **672**

Dear ⸢⸥

Thanks so much for all of your hard work lately. I know you've been putting in extra hours on this new account. It's not going ❶unnoticed. The partners and I all see how much you're doing to ❷ensure the success of our company.

Keep up the good work.

- - - - - - -

Try It！可以替換的字詞

❶ unappreciated 未獲賞識的
disregarded 不受重視的
unseen 沒有被看見的
ignored 被忽視的
overlooked 被忽視的

❷ promise 允諾
guarantee 保證
make certain 確定
obtain 獲得
acquire 取得

非常感謝您最近的一切辛勞。我知道您投入額外的時間處理新客戶的事情。這不會被埋沒的。夥伴們和我都看到您為了確保本公司的成功，付出了多大的努力。請繼續努力下去。

lately 最近　put in 投入，付出（努力或時間等）　extra 額外的　unnoticed 沒有被發現的
ensure 確保

✉ sample 673

Dear ⸛⸛⸛⸛⸛⸛⸛

Thank you for taking time to explain the new recordkeeping **procedures** to me yesterday. I would have been lost without you. I hope I can do something for you in return down the line. Let me know if I can!

Sincerely,

感謝您昨天花時間向我解說新的簿記程序。沒有您的話，我可能還是一片茫然。我希望來日我能夠為您做些什麼作為回報。如果有機會的話，請讓我知道。謹啟。

take time to 花時間～（去做某事）　recordkeeping 簿記的　procedure 程序　lost 茫然的
in return 作為回報　down the line 未來，往後日子裡

✉ sample 674

Dear ⸛⸛⸛⸛⸛⸛⸛

Thank you for working so hard to get the new ❶ **inventory** system up and running. I know it has meant some late nights for you. It'll be over soon, and you can rest assured that we won't forget your hard work when we are ❷**calculating** annual bonuses.

Regards,

感謝您如此地努力讓這新的財產目錄系統恢復運作。我知道您有幾個晚上加班到很晚。這事就快告一段落了，且您儘管放心，當我們在計算年度紅利時，不會忘記您付出的努力。謹此致謝。

hard 努力地　inventory 庫存　running 運作中　late 晚的　rest assured that... 放心～　calculate 計算

✉ sample 675

Dear _____

I'm writing to let you know how much I appreciate all of the time you've spent installing the new computer system. You work hard and never complain. Your work means a lot to the success of the company.

Thank you.

- - - - - - - -

我寫這封信的目的是要讓您知道，對於您安裝新電腦系統所付出的所有時間，我在此深表謝意。您很努力工作且從不抱怨。您的努力對於公司的成功具有相當大的意義。感謝您。

Try It！可以替換的字詞

gripe 訴苦
grumble 發牢騷
whine 嘀咕，發牢騷
criticize 批評
moan 悲歎，抱怨

install 安裝　computer system 電腦系統　complain 抱怨　success 成功

對於他人善意與指引表示謝意
Extending Thanks for Others' Kindness & Guidance

▲

✉ sample 676

Dear [_____]

Thank you so much for all of your help in finding a new administrative assistant. We were really in a bind, and your recommendation really worked out well. Let me know if there's anything I can do to help you down the line.

Thanks,

- - - - - - - -

Try It! 可以替換的字詞

secretary 秘書
professional assistant 專業助理
helper 幫手
office clerk 辦公室職員
office professional 辦公室專業人員

非常感謝您一切的協助，讓我們能夠找到一位新的行政助理。原本我們真的是一籌莫展，而您的推薦確實帶來很好的結果。如果未來我能夠為您做些什麼，請讓我知道。謝謝。

administrative 行政上的，管理的　assistant 助理，幫手　in a bind 陷入困境　work out 成功，有結果

✉ sample 677

Dear [_____]

Thank you for the advice you gave me yesterday. I've had a really hard time deciding the best way to deal with this difficult client, but your suggestions made me see things in a whole new light. I tried saying some of the things you recommended and it really helped. I really appreciate it.

Regards,

- - - - - - - -

Try It! 可以替換的字詞

advice 忠告
recommendation 建議
help 幫忙
asistance 協助
counsel 指示

感謝您昨天給我的忠告。我原本真的很苦惱，不知如何決定應付這位棘手客戶的最佳辦法，但您的建議讓我用一個全新的觀點去看待事情。我試著說些您建議該說的話，而確實很管用。我真的感激您的協助。謹致謝意。

advice 忠告　yesterday 昨天　best way 最佳辦法　whole 全部的　light 見解，觀點　recommend 建議

✉ sample 678

Dear ┌╌╌╌╌╌╌╌┐

I greatly appreciate the time you took to talk to me yesterday. You've had so much mo re experience than I have. It helps a lot to hear from someone who has gone through the same career difficulties I'm going through now. If there is anyway I can repay you, please let me know.

Thank you.

reward 獎勵
compensate 補償
give it back to 回饋給
settle up with 讓～感到滿足
return it to 回報～

- - - - - - - -

我非常感激昨天您花時間與我交談。您的經驗比我豐富多了。能夠聽到一個人訴說著與我目前正在經歷相同的職場辛酸，那會有很大的幫助。如果我有機會能夠回饋給您些什麼，請讓我知道。感謝您。

greatly 大大地　experience 經驗　go through 經歷～　career 職場　repay 償還

✉ sample 679

Dear ┌╌╌╌╌╌╌╌┐

Thank you for being so kind after the meeting on Friday. It was a very ❶stressful meeting, and your ❷sympathy meant a lot to me. It's nice to see a friendly face when tempers are running high. Let me know if there's ever anything I can do for you.

Regards,

Try It！可以替換的字詞

❶ difficult 艱困的
taxing 艱難的
hectic 忙亂的
tense 緊張的
nerve-wracking 極使人不安的

❷ friendliness 友善
caring 照料
hospitality 款待
empathy 同理心
kind-heartedness 好心腸

- - - - - - - -

感謝您在週五會議之後如此地善心。那是個令人很有壓力的會議，而您的關懷問候對我來說意義重大。當一個人快要發脾氣時，能夠看到一張友善的臉，是很棒的事。如果有任何我能會您做的事，請讓我知道。謹致謝意。

kind 善心的　stressful 令人很有壓力的　a lot 許多　friendly 友善的　face 面容
temper 情緒，脾氣，怒氣

✉ sample 680

Dear _____

Thank you for your wise words yesterday. I really needed some advice on how to repair my damaged relationship with our partner, and what you said was just the right idea. I hope I can repay you for your **valuable** friendship.

worthy 有價值的
priceless 無價的
precious 珍貴的
dear 摯愛的
important 重要的

- - - - - - - -

感謝您昨日說的至理名言。由於我與我們夥伴之間的關係已毀損，我確實需要一些能夠修復彼此關係的建議，而您說的話就是正確的想法。我希望我可以回報您所付出的珍貴友誼。

wise 明智的　advice 建議　repair 修復　damaged 毀損的　just 就是，正是　valuable 珍貴的

Case 04

對於本人能夠前往他公司拜訪表示感謝
Extending Thanks for Everything During My Visit of Others' Company ▲

✉ sample **681**

Dear ⸨⸨⸨⸨⸨⸨

It was a pleasure to visit your offices yesterday. Thank you so much for your hospitality. It was great to meet your staff and see how your operation works. I look forward to having you over to our offices soon.

Thank you.

- - - - - - - -

昨天有幸拜訪貴公司真是愉快。非常感謝您的款待。也很高興見到您的員工，以及看見貴公司的運作方式。我也期待很快能夠邀請您過來我們公司。謝謝您。

> pleasure 喜悅，榮幸　hospitality 款待　staff 員工　operation 運作　look forward to... 期待～
> office 辦公室

Try It！可以替換的字詞

kindness 善意
generosity 慷慨
warmth 溫暖
welcoming 款待
graciousness 親切招待

✉ sample **682**

Dear ⸨⸨⸨⸨⸨⸨

I greatly enjoyed my time at your offices yesterday. Everyone there was very warm and welcoming. I'm impressed with the way your company is run. Hopefully we will be able to host you at our offices soon.

Thank you.

- - - - - - - -

昨天到訪您公司真是相當愉快。那裏的每個人都很親切且熱情。我對於您公司的運作方式也有深刻的印象。希望我們能夠很快在我們公司招待您。感謝您。

> enjoy 過得愉快　welcoming 款待的　be impressed with... 對於～有深刻的印象　hopefully 但願
> host 以主人身分招待

Try It！可以替換的字詞

treat you 招待您
welcome you 歡迎您
meet you 與您見面
congregate you 與您相聚
enjoy your company
享受有您在一起的時光

✉ sample 683

Dear _____

Thank you so much for the hospitality you extended to me the other day. It was very useful to see your operation up close. I appreciate the time you spent showing me around.

I hope to see you again soon.

- - - - - - -

那天非常感謝您給我的招待。能夠就近看到貴公司運作方式是很有幫助的。我很感激您花時間帶我四處看看。希望很快能夠再見到您。

extend 給予，提供（幫助、招待等） useful 有用的 spend –ing 花費～（時間）做某事
show... around 帶～（某人）到各處看看

✉ sample 684

Dear _____

Thank you for your kind welcome to your headquarters yesterday. I found it very enlightening to see how your company operates. All of the staff members I met yesterday were courteous and pleasant. That speaks very well of your firm.

Sincerely,

- - - - - - -

感謝您昨日誠摯歡迎我到貴公司總部。看到您公司的運作狀況，讓我獲得不少啟發。昨天我遇見的所有員工都很有禮貌且親切。那證明您身在一家很好的公司。謹啟。

headquarters 總部，總公司 enlightening 受啟發的，擺脫矇昧的 operate 營運，運作
courteous 有禮貌的，殷勤的 pleasant 令人愉快的，親切的 speak well of... 表示對～好的意見
firm 公司

✉ sample 685

Dear [............]

I'm writing to express my gratitude for your hospitality. I greatly enjoyed visiting your company and seeing your efficient procedures. I'm excited about doing business with such a well-run company. I hope I can return the favor and host you here soon.

Thank you very much.

- - - - - - - -

我寫這封信的目的是要感激您的招待。我在參訪貴公司當中收益良多，也觀摩了很有效率的生產過程。我很期待能夠與這樣一家運作良好的公司合作。我希望我能夠回報這份善意，並盡快能夠在我們這邊招待您。非常感謝您。

Try It！可以替換的字詞

prosperous 蓬勃發展的
competitive 有競爭力的
established 有制度的
professional 專業的
functional 運作良好的

express 表達 gratitude 感激之意 visit 參訪 efficient 有效率的 return 歸還 favor 善意，恩惠

安慰 & 鼓勵 Consolation & Encouragement

Case 01 對他人職位變動表達安慰 Offering Consolation for Position Change ▲

✉ sample 686

Dear ⌐ ⌐

I'm sorry to hear that you're leaving the company. It's been a pleasure to work with you, and I hope that your future is bright. Good luck in all that you do.

Sincerely,

我很遺憾聽到您將離開這家公司。和您的合作相當愉快，也預祝您未來前途一片光明。祝您一切順利。謹啟。

> leave the company 離開這家公司 It's been a pleasure to... ～相當愉快 future 未來 bright 光明的

Try It！可以替換的字詞

departing 離開
going away from 離開
exiting 離開
resigning from 從～離職
parting 與～分開

✉ sample 687

Dear ⌐ ⌐

I'm sad to hear that you've decided to step down as Sales Director. I have the utmost respect for the work you've done. The sales department won't be the same without you. Good luck with whatever comes next for you.

Regards,

聽到您已決定卸任業務處主任，我感到相當遺憾。我相當重視您所付出的一切。業務處沒有您在會變得不太一樣。祝您往後一切順利。謹致問候。

> step down 卸任，下台 utmost 終極的 respect 重視 without 沒有～的話 whatever 無論什麼

Try It！可以替換的字詞

admiration 景仰
esteem 尊敬
high regards 高度尊敬
good opinion 好的評價
pride 驕傲

✉ sample **688**

Dear [_____]

I was saddened to hear of the recent downsizing at your company and that your position has been eliminated. I know that this is a harsh economic climate and even hard working loyal employees like you can sometimes suffer from a downturn. Let me know if there is anything I can do.

Kind regards,

聽到貴公司最近的縮編以及您遭去職一事，我感到有些傷感。我可以了解目前經濟不景氣，而且像您這樣努力工作且忠誠度高的員工，有時也會受到不景氣的波及。請讓我知道是否有什麼事我能做的。敬請台安。

sadden 使傷心　downsizing 規模縮小，縮編　position 職位　eliminate 移除　harsh 艱困的
economic climate 經濟景氣　loyal 忠心的　suffer from... 承受著～　downturn（經濟）衰退，下降

✉ sample **689**

Dear [_____]

I was sorry to hear about your departure from the company. If there is anything I can do to help with your transition, please feel free to contact me. I know moments of uncertainty can be difficult, but often things happen for a reason.

Regards,

我很遺憾聽到您離開這家公司的消息。在您這過渡期中，若有任何我可以幫上忙的地方，請儘管與我聯繫。我知道充滿不確定的時刻可能很難熬，但往往一切事情的發生，都會是最好的安排。謹致問候。

departure 離開　transition 轉換，過渡期　feel free 感到自在，儘管　contact 聯繫
uncertainty 不確定性　for a reason 有個原因

✉ sample 690

Dear ┌┄┄┄┄┄┄┐

I just heard that your ❶department is being ❷eliminated. I don't know what to say. I'm sorry that this has happened after all of the hard work you put in. Please know that I'll do everything I can to help you transit to a new job.

Best of luck,

- - - - - - -

Try It！可以替換的字詞

❶ job 工作
   division 部門
   sector 部門
   branch 分店
   unit 單位

❷ removed 移除
   done away with 移除
   abolished 根除
   purged 去除
   got rid of 移除

我剛聽說您的部門被裁撤掉了。我不知道該說什麼。我只是覺得遺憾，在您付出一切努力之後竟發生這樣的事情。但請您了解，我會盡我所能幫助您轉換至一份新的工作。祝幸運。

what to say 說些什麼　happen 發生　put in 付出，投入～（努力，時間等）　everything 一切
transit to 轉換（工作跑道等）

✉ sample 691

Dear ....

Words can't ❶**convey** how sad I was to hear of your ❷ **recent loss.** I want you to know that I am thinking of you during this time of need. If there's anything I can do for you, please feel free to get in touch with me.

Sincerely,

- - - - - - -

Try It！可以替換的字詞

❶tell 告訴
relay 傳達
show 顯示
state 陳述
express 表達

❷bereavement 喪親之痛
recent death 近日喪事
grief 悲痛
recent passing 近日家故
sadness 悲傷

當我聽到您最近的損失時，我無法以言語來傳達我有多麼傷心。我想要您知道，我正想到您處於這低潮時期。如果有任何我可以為您做的事，請儘管與我聯繫。謹啟。

convey 傳達　sad 傷心的　loss 損失，失敗，喪失　time of need 需要的時刻　feel free 感到自在
get in touch with 與～聯繫

✉ sample 692

Dear ....

I'm writing to offer my **condolences** for the loss of your mother. I know that this must be a terribly painful time for you. If you need anything at all, please let me know.

- - - - - - -

Try It！可以替換的字詞

sympathies 慰問
pity 憐惜
understanding 善解人意
compassion 同情
kindness 善意

我寫這封信的目的是要致上我對您喪母之痛的慰問。我知道這對您來說肯定是相當痛苦的時刻。如您需要任何協助，請讓我知道。

offer one's condolences 致上某人的慰問　must be... 一定是～　terribly 相當地　painful 痛苦的
at all 絲毫，根本

✉ sample 693

Dear _____

I'm so sorry to hear about the loss of your father. He was such a kind and genuine man, and I really enjoyed working with him these past few years. Please know that my thoughts and prayers go out to you and your family during this difficult time.

- - - - - - - -

我很遺憾得知令尊過世的消息。他是如此一位仁心且實在的人,而過去數年來我跟他的共事也很愉快。在這艱苦的時期,我的思念與祈念與您及您的家人同在,請知悉。

genuine 實在的,真實的 past 過去的 prayers 祈念文,禱告文

✉ sample 694

Dear _____

I was so sorry to hear about your recent illness and hospitalization. I hope that your stay was okay and you're beginning to feel better. If you need anything during your recovery, please give me a call. I'd be happy to help out anyway I can.

- - - - - - - -

我很遺憾得知您最近生病且住院的消息。我希望您住院時一切順利,及復原狀況良好。在這康復期間,如果您需要任何協助,請打個電話給我。我會很樂意盡一切之力提供協助。

illness 生病 hospitalization 住院 stay 住院,留院觀察 recovery 康復

✉ sample 695

Dear ┄┄┄┄┄┄

I'd like to offer my sympathy for your injury. I experienced a similar accident years ago and I know you must be suffering greatly. I want to tell you that I'm here for you and available if you need anything.

I hope you get better soon.

對於您受傷一事，我想表達我的慰問之意。我數年前也曾經歷過類似的意外，我知道您一定承受著很大的苦。我想告訴您，我與您同在，且如果您需要任何協助可以找我。祝您早日康復。

sympathy 慰問 experience 經歷 similar 類似的 greatly 很大地 available 有空的

Try It！可以替換的字詞

hurting 受傷的
aching 感覺疼痛的
broken-hearted 感到心碎的
anguished 感到極大痛苦的
distressed 感到沮喪的

✉ sample 696

Dear ....

Thank you for your concern. While I'm sorry to be leaving under these circumstances, I'm keeping a positive outlook. Knowing that I have friends in the business community like you really helps a lot.

Thanks again,

- - - - - - - -

Try It！可以替換的字詞

neighborhood 近鄰
group 群體
society 社團
selection 菁英分子
area 地區

感謝您的關切。雖然我也很遺憾在這樣的情況下必須缺席，但我仍保持樂觀態度。當我得知在這商業團體中，我還有像您這樣的朋友，這真的給我很多幫助。
再次感謝。

concern 關切，關心 under... circumstances 在～狀況下 positive 正面的，積極的 outlook 觀點 business 商業 community 社團，團體

✉ sample 697

Dear ....

I appreciate your kind words. It was a hard decision to make, but I just feel like it's time to move on. Don't worry. You haven't seen the last of me. I have a few projects brewing for the future.

Thanks,

- - - - - - - -

Try It！可以替換的字詞

waiting 等待中
stewing 醞釀中
pausing 等候中
preparing 準備中
fermenting 醞釀中

我很感激您的祝福。那是個困難的決定，而我只是覺得該是繼續前進的時刻了。別擔心。您還沒見到最後的我（不到最後還不知道輸贏）。我還有一些未來的計畫在醞釀中。謝謝。

kind 善意的 feel like 感到好似～ move on 繼續前進 last 最後的 brewing 醞釀中

✉ sample 698

Dear [_____]

Thank you for your thoughtful email. This is a very difficult period for me, and I'll admit that it's easy to despair. Notes like the one you sent me really help me keep my spirits up. I appreciate your friendship.

- - - - - - - -

lose hope 失去希望
be in anguish 陷入痛苦
be tormented 感到痛苦
be in distress 陷入沮喪
be grief-stricken 感到極度悲傷

感謝您貼心的問候郵件。對我來說這是艱困時期,且我必須承認這很容易令人感到絕望。像您寄給我的短信真的有助於讓我提振精神。我珍惜您這份友誼。

> thoughtful 貼心的 period 時期 admit 承認 despair 絕望
> keep one's spirits up 讓某人提振精神,使某人精神飽滿

✉ sample 699

Dear [_____]

Thank you for your kind note. I'm looking at this difficult event as an opportunity. I'm looking into starting up my own operation, so I hope this cloud will have a silver lining.

Thanks again for your concern.

- - - - - - - -

a happy ending 一個快樂的結局
a good result 一個好的結果
an optimistic result 一個樂觀的結果
a positive ending 一個有建設性的結果
a productive finale 一個豐收的結局

感謝您善意的短信。我將這困難的事件視為一個機會。我正尋求開展自己的事業,所以我希望這是黑暗中的一絲曙光。再次感謝您的關心。

> note 便條,短信 event 事件,(可能的)情況 look into 深入研究,仔細查看～
> start up 展開,籌備(營運、公司等) own 自己的 operation 營運
> silver lining 一條銀邊;(不幸或失望中的)一線希望

✉ sample 700

Dear [_____]

This has been a painful time for me and my team, but the concern of colleagues like you have done a lot to lessen the blow. Thank you for your thoughtfulness and support.

Try It！可以替換的字詞

friends 朋友

business associates 企業夥伴

teammates 隊友

fellow workers 同事

contemporaries 同年齡的人

- - - - - - - -

這對我及我的團隊一直是一段痛苦的時期，不過像您這樣的同事關心，減輕了不少我們承受的打擊。謝謝您的善體人意與支持。

painful 痛苦的　colleague 同事　a lot 許多　lessen 減輕，減少　blow 強風，打擊，不預期的災難　support 支持

（一般情況下）試著鼓勵他人 Trying to Cheer Up Others ▲

✉ sample 701

Hi, [_____]

I know things have been pretty stressful around the office recently. I hope you know that I appreciate all the hard work you've been doing. I promise that it WILL pay off. Just keep your spirits up, and we'll get through this.

Thanks for your hard work.

Try It！可以替換的字詞

mood 心情
thoughts 思緒
morale 士氣
drive 活力
confidence 信心

- - - - - - - -

我知道最近辦公室氛圍一直相當緊繃。我希望讓您知道我很感激您付出的一切辛勞。我承諾一切都將獲得回報。保持振作吧，我們會度過這一關的。謝謝您的努力。

pretty 相當地　stressful 有壓力的　recently 最近　promise 承諾　pay off 獲得回報，值得
keep one's spirits up 保持振作　get through 度過～（困難，難關等）

✉ sample 702

Dear [_____]

I noticed that you were a little quiet at lunch today. I know it can sometimes be discouraging to work so hard and feel like we're not getting anywhere, but we ARE making progress. Just try to think about the future, and you'll get through this tough patch.

Keep your chin up!

Try It！可以替換的字詞

improvement 進步
steps forward 往前進
advancement 前進
growth 成長
headway 往前

- - - - - - - -

我注意到你今天午餐時有點沉默。我知道有時候辛苦工作會令人沮喪，且感覺我們不會有什麼成果，但是，我們「真的」正在進步。想想未來吧，你會度過這艱困時期的。振作點吧！

quiet 安靜的　sometimes 有時候　discouraging 令人沮喪的　get nowhere 沒有成果，沒有目標
progress 進步，前進　tough 艱困的　patch 時期，一段時間

✉ sample 703

Dear _____

I hope you're not too discouraged by the slow speed of our project. I know it sometimes seems like not much is happening, but believe me when I tell you that every little bit helps. Think about the payoff down the road and you'll feel much better.

Regards,

- - - - - - - -

我希望你對於我們專案進行緩慢不會感到挫折。我知道有時候似乎沒有太多進度，但相信我曾經告訴過你的：一點一滴都是進步。想想未來獲得的報酬，你會感覺好些。謝謝。

discouraged 受到挫折的　seem like... 似乎是～　believe me 相信我　payoff 報酬，回報
down the road 未來

✉ sample 704

Dear _____

Don't let all of the recent ❶difficulties get you down. You're doing great work, and the right people are noticing it. Everything you do now will pay off later, I'm sure.

❷Cheer up!

- - - - - - - -

別讓最近這所有難題把你給打敗了。你表現得很好，而且上面的人都有注意到。你現在所做的一切，日後都將獲得會報，相信我。振作起來吧！

recent 最近的　get... down 使～感到沮喪　right 有影響力的，上層階級的　notice 注意到
pay off 清償（債務等）；獲得會報　later 日後，晚些

✉ **sample 705**

Dear ⌐⋯⋯⋯⌐

Try not to feel too stressed out by all of the recent troubles. Everything is going to be fine. Once this deal is finished, things will relax a little around the office.

Regards,

- - - - - - - -

試著別因為最近這一堆麻煩事件而感到太大的壓力。一切都會沒事的。一旦這項交易結束後，公司內的氣氛就會緩和一點。

be slowing down 緩慢下來
get better 漸入佳境
unwind 解開來
be loosened up 被放鬆
be decreased 被減少

stressed out 感到有壓力的　once 一旦～就～　deal 交易，協議　relax 緩和，放寬，減輕

對於遭降薪、升職遭拒等的鼓勵
Cheering Up Others Following Salary Cut Or Promotion Denial ▲

✉ sample 706

Dear _____

I'm sorry about the recent round of salary cuts. Nobody likes to feel as if they aren't getting what they deserve. Just keep thinking positively and working hard and before you know it, we'll be through this difficult period.

Sincerely,

- - - - - - - -

Try It ! 可以替換的字詞

merit 值得，應受

earn 博得，贏得

warrant 斷言

are entitled to 有權應得～

ought to have 應該擁有～

對於近日的減薪，我感到相當遺憾。沒有人希望感受到自己不受重視。往好的方面想，繼續努力，你會豁然開朗的。我們一定會度過這艱困時期。謹啟。

round 一次，（工作等的）一段期間　salary cut 減薪　nobody 沒有人　like to 想要，喜歡～
as if... 就如同～　get 取得　deserve 應得～　positively 正面地　through 度過

✉ sample 707

Dear _____

I'm sorry to hear that you didn't get the promotion. I know that you've worked hard for it. Don't let it get you down. I'm sure that next year there will be room for you at the top.

Keep up the good work.

- - - - - - - -

Try It ! 可以替換的字詞

in the management 在管理階層

higher up 晉升

in a better position 在更好的職位上

in a more qualified position
在一個需要更高資格的位置上

in a more esteemed position
在一個更受尊敬的位置上

我很遺憾得知你沒有獲得晉升的消息。我知道你一直很努力在爭取。別因為這件事而沮喪。我相信明年會有你晉升高位的空間。繼續努力吧！

promotion 晉升　get... down 使～沮喪　room 空間，位子　keep up 保持

✉ sample **708**

Dear [_____]

I know this round of salary cuts has been particularly difficult on you. Your work here is valued very much. Please don't see this unfortunate business as a judgment on your competence. As soon as we get out of this difficult period, you'll be rewarded for your fortitude and hard work.

Keep up the good work.

- - - - - - - -

我知道這一波降薪對你來說可能特別難受。你在這裡的工作非常受到重視。請勿將這不幸的營運狀況視為對你個人能力的判斷。一旦我們脫離此艱難困境之後,你的堅忍毅力與努力都將獲得回報。繼續努力吧!

Try It! 可以替換的字詞

tolerance 容忍
patience 耐心
staying power 持久力
forbearance 耐力
open-mindedness 心胸開放

particularly 特別地　value 重視,珍惜　judgement 判斷　competence 能力　fortitude 堅忍

✉ sample **709**

Dear [_____]

I'm sorry that there wasn't a place for you in this most recent round of promotions. Rest assured that I am aware of your hard work. You will be rewarded soon.

Regards,

- - - - - - - -

我很遺憾最近這一波晉升名單中沒有你。請放心,我知道你很努力工作。你會很快獲得獎勵的。謹啟。

Try It! 可以替換的字詞

a space 空間
a vacancy 空位
a position 位置
an area 區域
room 餘地

recent 最近的　rest assured that... 放心～　aware of... 知道,了解～

✉ sample 710

Dear _____

I'm sorry we were not able to provide you with **①a bonus that matched your hard work this year.** Sometimes the market simply affects the company in a way that doesn't allow us to reward even our hardest working employees. However, 2019 is shaping up to be a strong year for us, so you can expect ample **②compensation** at the end of the year.

Thanks for your patience.

- - - - - - - -

Try It! 可以替換的字詞

① an additional monetary reward 額外的獎金

a windfall 意外之財

a boon 利益

extra pay 額外的薪資

a premium 酬金

② wages 工資

salary 薪資

payback 薪資

reimbursement 報酬

payment 薪酬

我很遺憾我們今年無法依照您的辛勞給您獎勵金。有時候純粹就是市況不佳，使得公司甚至無法對於最辛勤努力的員工給予獎勵。不過，2019 年對於我們來說可預期是需求強勁的一年，所以你可以預期這一年年底時會有豐厚的補償。感謝你的耐心。

able to 能夠～　provide 提供　affect 影響　allow 允許　shape up 成形，具可能性　expect 預期　ample 豐厚的

祝賀 Congratulation

✉ sample 711

Dear [_____]

Congratulations on the new position! I was thrilled to hear that you've been moved up to a job that matches your experience and knowledge.

Best of luck to you!

- - - - - - -

Try It！可以替換的字詞

background 背景
skills 技術
insight 洞察力
qualifications 資格
grasp 能力

恭喜獲得新職務。我非常開心聽到您獲晉升至一個符合您經驗與知識的職位。致上最大的祝福。

> congratulation on 恭喜～　position 職位，位置　thrilled 感到興奮的　move up 高升，晉升
> match 配合　luck 好運

✉ sample 712

Dear [_____]

Congratulations! I just heard about your ❶promotion. It's ❷long overdue. I know you're going to do a terrific job as Advertising Director.

Good luck!

- - - - - - -

Try It！可以替換的字詞

❶step-up 晉升
upgrade 高升
advancement 升職
raise 加薪
expansion 進展

❷very late 非常晚
very tardy 非常遲了
in arrears 延遲了
behind schedule 進度落後了
past due 過時了

恭喜！我剛得知您獲得晉升的消息。真是等太久了。我知道您即將就任廣告處處長這麼棒的職位。祝幸運！

> promotion 晉升　overdue 過期了的，久等了的　terrific 非常好的　advertising 廣告
> director 主任，處長

✉ sample 713

Dear _____

I hear congratulations are in order. I'm so pleased that you've been promoted. I've been saying for months that it was time to move you up. I know we're going to be seeing some great work from you in the coming year.

Congratulations!

- - - - - - - -

我聽說有值得慶祝的事情。我很高興你能夠獲得晉升。幾個月來我一直說過，該是輪到你晉升的時候了。我也知道我們來年將可看見你的一些好表現。恭喜了！

be in order（在特定住況、行動中）適當的　pleased 高興的　promote 晉升　for months 幾個月以來
in the coming year 在來年裡

Try It！可以替換的字詞

it's well done 有好事降臨
of a nice job 有好的成果
thumbs up 有令人讚許的事
something good for you 你有好表現
best wishes 最佳祝福

✉ sample 714

Dear _____

Congratulations on your promotion! It's great to hear that you're moving up the corporate ladder. You've put in a lot of hours and I know you've earned this spot.

Best of luck!

- - - - - - - -

恭喜你獲得晉升！很高興聽到你在這家公司一路升官。你付出很多時間，且我知道你會拿下這個位子的。祝幸運！

move up the ladder 平步青雲　corporate 企業的　put in 投入，花費～（時間等）　earn 賺取，贏得
spot 位置，地位

Try It！可以替換的字詞

business 公司
professional 專業的
company 公司
commercial 商業上的
trade 貿易的

✉ sample 715

Dear _____

Congratulations on the new position. I think you're going to make a fine Sales Manager. You know this market better than anyone in the department and I'm sure you'll bring your expertise with you to this senior position.

Good luck!

- - - - - - - -

恭喜獲得新職務！我想您會是一位優秀的業務經理。您對於市場的了解比部門內任何人更甚，且我相信您會將您的專業知識帶入這個更高的職位。祝幸運！

fine 優秀的　better更佳的　expertise 專業知識，專門技術　senior 地位較高的

Try It！可以替換的字詞

part 部分

industry 產業

device 設備

domaine 領域

field of work 領域的工作

✉ sample 716

Dear [_____]

Congratulations! It's about time you tied the knot. I wish you and Sarah years of happiness . . . and lots of babies!

Best wishes,

- - - - - - - -

Try It！可以替換的字詞

married 結婚

took a vow 立下誓言，成婚

walked down the aisle 步入紅毯

pledged your love 宣示你的愛（結婚）

preformed nuptials 舉辦婚禮

恭喜！該是您結婚的時候了。我預祝您和 Sarah 永浴愛河……多子多孫！獻上最深的祝福。

It's about time 該是～的時候了　tie the knot 結婚　wish A happiness 祝 A 幸福快樂　lots of 許多的～

✉ sample 717

Dear [_____]

Congratulations on your wedding! I'm so happy for you and Jessica. You two are made for each other and I'm sure you have many happy years ahead of you.

Good luck!

- - - - - - - -

Try It！可以替換的字詞

compatible 相容的

well suited 非常速配的

like-minded 同心的

attuned 音感好的，相配的

in step 一致的，匹配的

新婚誌慶！我為您和 Jessica 感到高興。您二位是天作之合，且我深信您們未來的日子裡會是幸福快樂的。祝順心！

wedding 婚禮　happy for 為～感到高興　made for... 為～而設，～天造地設的　ahead of... 在～的前面

✉ sample 718

Dear [_____]

Congratulations on your big news! I'm excited to hear that you're getting married. Life is more than the import-export business! Here's to a bright future!

Best Wishes,

- - - - - - - -

promising 充滿希望的
happy 快樂的
prosperous 興旺的
good 美好的
wonderful 完美的

真是好消息，恭喜！我很開心得知您就要結婚了。生活不是只有進出口的生意！ 在此預祝未來一片光明！致上最深祝福。

> big news 好消息　get married 結婚　more than 不只是～　import-export 進出口
> Here's to ~!（準備乾杯時）祝您～，預祝～

✉ sample 719

Dear [_____]

Congratulations on the birth of your first son! I can't say how happy I am for you. I remember when my son was born. It was one of the happiest days of my life. I wish you and your family enjoy this precious moment. They grow up before you know it!

Best wishes!

- - - - - - - -

greatest 最棒的
most memorable 最難忘的
magnificent 極好的
terrific 極佳的
unforgettable 令人難忘的

恭喜您首度喜獲麟兒！我無法表達我多麼地為你高興。我記得我兒子出世時的那一刻。那是我人生當中最快樂的日子之一。我祝福您和您的家人好好享受這珍貴的時刻。小孩會在不知不覺中長大。獻上最深的祝福。

> birth 出生　remember 記得　born 出世　precious 珍貴的　grow up 長大

✉ **sample 720**

Dear [＿＿＿＿＿]

I'm **very** thrilled to hear about the birth of your daughter.
I know you're going to be as good of a father as you are
a sales manager. I hope you'll tell your wife how happy I
am for her too.

Congratulations!

- - - - - - - -

得知您的女兒出生時，我感到萬分喜悅。我知道您會成為一位很好的父親，就如同您是一位很好的業務經理一樣。請轉達尊夫人，我也為她感到喜悅。恭喜！

very 非常　thrilled 非常高興的　as... as... 像～一樣　sales 業務　manager 經理

Try It！可以替換的字詞

positively 肯定地，確實

surely 當然

absolutely 絕對地

completely 完全地

utterly 非常

寄送賀卡 Greeting Cards

Case 01 | 寄賀年卡 Sending New Year's Greeting Card ▲

✉ sample 721

Dear [_____]

Happy New Year! I wish you **all the best** in the coming year. I look forward to doing business with you!

Regards,

- - - - - - - -

新年快樂！我祝福您來年一切順利圓滿。我也期待與您一起在商場上合作！在此致上問候。

wish... all the best 祝福～一切順利圓滿　coming year 來年　look forward to... 期待～
do business 做生意　regards（書信結尾）致上問候

Try It！可以替換的字詞

good things 好事
happiness 快樂
prosperity 興旺
good luck 好運
best wishes 最好的祝福

✉ sample 722

Dear [_____]

Happy New Year! Another year is **under our belt**, and now we can look forward to what 2019 will bring. I hope we get to do some new projects this year.

Best Wishes,

- - - - - - - -

新年快樂！舊的一年已經過去，而現在我們可以期待 2019 年將帶來的一切。我希望我們今年可以完成一些新的計畫。獻上最深的祝福。

another 另一個　under one's belt 已經過去了的　bring 帶來　get to 開始進行，展開～
best wishes（書信結尾）致上最深的祝福

Try It！可以替換的字詞

over with 結束
out of the way 結束
finished 結束
past 過去了
done 結束

Sending New Year's Greeting Card case **01** 📄 **449**

✉ sample 723

Dear [_____]

I hope the New Year brings you success and ❶happiness.
I also hope yourbusiness andyour family both❷prosper.

Happy New Year,

- - - - - - - -

Try It！可以替換的字詞

❶pleasure 快樂
joy 喜悅
delights 高興
contentment 滿足
merriment 愉悅

❷do well 過得好
move forward 繼續前進
thrive 興旺
grow 成長
flourish 健壯有力

希望新的一年為您帶來成功與幸福。我也祝福您的公司與家人們興旺與和諧。新年快樂。

success 成功　happiness 幸福　family 家人

✉ sample 724

Dear [_____]

Here's to a great New Year! I wish you the best in the coming year. 2018 was a successful time for both of our firms, and I hope that 2019 will be even better!

Happy New Year,

- - - - - - - -

Try It！可以替換的字詞

abundant 豐收的
prosperous 繁盛的
victorious 勝利的
triumphant 得意洋洋的
winning 獲勝的

新年快樂！我祝福您來年一切順利。2018 年對於我們兩家公司而言都是成功的一年，而我希望 2019 年還會再更好！新年快樂！

Here's to（準備乾杯時）祝您～，預祝～　successful 成功的　both 兩者都　firm 公司　even 甚至

✉ sample 725

Dear ⌐‑‑‑‑‑‑‑¬

Happy New Year! I look forward to working with you in 2019, and I hope you and your family find success and happiness.

Best Wishes,

‑ ‑ ‑ ‑ ‑ ‑ ‑ ‑

新年快樂！我期待與您在 2019 年能夠合作，並希望您和您的家人們成功與快樂。獻上最深的祝福。

work with 與～合作　find 獲得，找到

Try It！可以替換的字詞

laboring 努力工作

toiling 辛勤地工作

striving 努力

cooperating 合作

operating 運作

sample 726

Dear [............]

Happy Holidays! I hope you are enjoying time with your family and friends. I'm enjoying a little time off myself.

Best Wishes,

- - - - - - -

假日愉快！我希望您和家人與朋友們玩得愉快。我也正偷得浮生半日閒。致上最深祝福。

> holiday 假日，假期　a little 一點點　time off （工作上的）休假，休息　myself 我自己，獨自
> best wishes 最深的祝福

Try It！可以替換的字詞

rest 休息
recess 休息
break 休息
lull 暫時的平靜
respite 喘息的機會

sample 727

Dear [............]

Merry Christmas! I hope you're having fine holidays this year. Say hello to your wife and kids for me! I'm excited to be spending some time off with mine. I hope you are too.

Regards,

- - - - - - -

聖誕快樂！我希望您今年的假期玩得愉快。代我向尊夫人及孩子們致上問候！我也很開心可以和我家人一起放假。我希望您也是。謹致問候。

> say hello to... 向～打聲招呼　for... 為了～　excited 開心的，興奮的

Try It！可以替換的字詞

celebration 慶祝活動
vacation 假期
festivals 佳節
galas 節日
events 盛事

✉ sample 728

Dear [ ]

Season's greetings! I hope this card finds you happy and healthy. I also hope you're taking some time off to be with your family.

Merry Christmas!

Try It！可以替換的字詞

Happy holidays 假日愉快
Merry Christmas 聖誕節快樂
Happy new year 新年快樂
Happy festivities 佳節愉快
Happy Yule time 聖誕佳節快樂

- - - - - - -

聖誕節快樂！我希望您收到這張卡片時是快樂且健康的。我也希望您挪出一些時間來陪伴您的家人。聖誕快樂！

season's greetings 聖誕節快樂　healthy 健康的

✉ sample 729

Dear [ ]

Happy Holidays! Here's to a great Christmas. I'm taking a few days off to enjoy the holidays with my family. I hope you're doing the same. Enjoy!

Merry Christmas!

Try It！可以替換的字詞

celebrate 慶祝
party 在～時舉辦派對
rejoice 歡慶
take pleasure in 以～為樂
delight in 以～為樂

- - - - - - -

假期愉快！聖誕節快樂。我放了幾天假，準備在假日期間享受天倫之樂。我希望您也是。玩得開心！聖誕快樂！

Here's to... （準備乾杯時）祝您～，預祝～　take a few days off 放幾天假　the same 同樣的

✉ sample 730

Dear _____

Merry Christmas! I'm sending best wishes your way. I hope Santa is good to you this year! Give your family my best.

Happy Holidays,

聖誕快樂！我祝福您未來一切美好。我希望聖誕老人今年為你帶來好東西。代我向您家人請安。假日愉快。

send 送出　give 給予　best（書信場合）最深的祝福

Try It！可以替換的字詞

my regards 我的問候

well wishes 誠摯的祝福

my thoughts 我的問候

best wishes 最深的祝福

good thoughts 真摯問候之意

寄感恩節卡片 Sending a Thanksgiving Card ▲

✉ sample 731

Dear ⸽_____⸽

Happy Thanksgiving! I know I'm thankful for the business we've done together this past year. I hope you have a restful holiday with your family.

Regards,

- - - - - - - -

Try It！可以替換的字詞
peaceful 平靜的
serene 安詳的
calm 平靜的
relaxing 放鬆的
quiet 安靜的

感恩節快樂！過去這一年來，我知道我很感激我們一起付出的辛勞。我祝福您與您的家人有一個放鬆的假日。在此請安。

thankful 感謝的　business 事業　past 過去的　restful 放鬆的

✉ sample 732

Dear ⸽_____⸽

Happy Thanksgiving! I hope you have a nice time with your family over the long weekend. And let's hope we've got more to be thankful for coming up in the future!

Best Wishes,

- - - - - - - -

Try It！可以替換的字詞
upcoming year 來年
forthcoming year 未來這一年
year to come 即將來到的這一年
coming year 明年
impending year 即將來到的這年

感恩節快樂！但願您與您的家人在這長長的周末假期中度過一段美好時光。也讓我們期待未來能有更多值得我們感恩的事情。

over the long weekend 在這長長的周末假期中　let's... 讓我們　coming up 出現

✉ sample 733

Dear _____

I hope you have a wonderful Thanksgiving. Give my best to your family. I'm thankful for the business we've been able to do together this year. May there be more in the future!

Happy Thanksgiving,

- - - - - - - -

Try It！可以替換的字詞

Please tell your family "hello".
請代為向您家人問候。

Send my best wishes to your family.
請代為向您家人致上最深的祝福。

I wish you and your family a joyous holiday.
我祝福您與您家人們假期愉快。

Please extend good wishes to your family. 請代為向您家人請安。

Say hello to your family for me.
請代為向您家人打聲招呼。

但願您的感恩節過得愉快。請代為向您家人致上我的問候之意。我很感恩我們今年能夠一起合作生意。但願未來我們會有更多合作機會。感恩節快樂。

wonderful 美好的　give one's best to... 向～致上我的問候之意　able to... 能夠～　May there be 但願～ in the future 在未來

✉ sample 734

Dear _____

Happy Thanksgiving! I hope this card finds you well. I'm thankful that we got a chance to work together this year, and I hope that we will have more opportunities to do so in the future.

Regards,

- - - - - - - -

Try It！可以替換的字詞

Respectfully 敬請道安
Sincerely 耑此，謹啟
Best wishes 並候近安
Affectionately 您親愛的
With honor 敬上

感恩節快樂！我希望您收到這張卡片時一切安好。我很感激我們今年有機會能夠一起合作，而且我希望我們未來能有更多機會合作。謹啟。

chance 機會　more 更多的　opportunity 機會

✉ **sample 735**

Dear ┌ ┄ ┄ ┄ ┄ ┐

I hope you spend a nice Thanksgiving with your family. Don't eat too much Turkey! I'm thankful for what a successful year we've had, and I hope we can continue to thrive into the coming year.

Best Wishes,

- - - - - - -

但願您與家人們一起度過了美好的感恩節。別吃太多火雞！我很感激我們一起度過成功的一年，而我希望我們能夠在未來這一年繼續發達下去。獻上最深的祝福。

spend 花費　what a successful year we've had 我們一起度過成功的一年　thrive 發達，興旺
coming year 未來這一年

Try It ! 可以替換的字詞

carry on 持續
move on 繼續
move forward 前進
persist 堅持
proceed 前進

✉ sample 736

Dear _____

Happy Easter! I hope you have a nice time with your family this weekend. Spring is in the air!

Regards,

- - - - - - - -

復活節快樂！但願您和您的家人在這周末共度了美好時光。春天的氣息洋溢著！謹致問候。

> Easter 復活節　weekend 周末　spring 春天　in the air 即將來臨

Try It！可以替換的字詞

finally here 終於來臨
such a beautiful season 如此美好的季節
my favorite time of year
我一年中最愛的時光
blooming all around us 在我們四周綻放
right around the corner 即將到來

✉ sample 737

Dear _____

I hope you have a pleasant Easter holiday with your family. I'm spending this weekend with my relatives in the country and I'm looking forward to getting away. Have a great weekend!

Best Wishes,

- - - - - - - -

但願您和您的家人度過一個愉快的復活節假期。我這個周末將和我鄉下的親友們一起度過，且我期待可以好好放鬆一下。周末愉快！獻上最深的祝福。

> pleasant 愉快的　relative 親戚　country 鄉下　get away 遠離塵囂，放鬆心情

Try It！可以替換的字詞

resting 休息一下
relaxing 放輕鬆
departing 出發
unwinding 放鬆心情
letting go 放下（煩惱）

✉ sample 738

Dear _____

Happy Easter! Have a good time with your family this weekend. Spring is here, and I'm already feeling re-energized!

Best Wishes,

- - - - - - - -

復活節快樂！祝您本周末與您的家人度過美好時光。春意盎然，而我也已經再次感受到一股活力了！致上最深祝福。

> already 已經　re-energized 重新感受一股活力

Try It！可以替換的字詞

refreshed 煥然一新的
renewed 翻新的
stress free 毫無壓力的
invigorated 精力充沛的
recharged 再次充電的

✉ sample 739

Dear _____

Ihope you have a nice Easter weekend withyourfamily. This is a great time of year. Enjoy yourself!

Regards,

- - - - - - - -

但願您和您的家人度過了一個愉快的復活節周末假期。這是一年當中的美好時光。盡情享受吧！謹致問候。

> enjoy yourself 盡情享受，玩得愉快

Try It！可以替換的字詞

terrific 很棒的
wonderful 美好的
fantastic 絕佳的
special 特別的
superb 超棒的

✉ sample 740

Dear [_____]

Happy Easter! I hope the Easter Bunny brings you lots of chocolate and candy! Have a great weekend with your family.

Best Wishes,

- - - - - - - -

Try It！可以替換的字詞

Sincerely yours
（收信人有名字）謹啟

Yours faithfully
（收信人沒有名字）謹啟

Yours truly
（收信人有無名字皆可）謹啟

Salutations （對上級或長者）敬上

Genuinely （正式、公務用）誠懇祝福

復活節快樂！但願復活節兔為您帶來許多巧克力和糖果！祝您和您的家人周末愉快。並候近安。

Easter Bunny 復活節兔（象徵著春天的復甦和新生命的誕生） bring 帶來 lots of 許多的 chocolate 巧克力

✉ sample 741

Happy Birthday Sam!

I hope you're having a great day! We really appreciate the work you do, and we hope you'll keep on doing it!

Have a great day!

- - - - - - - -

Try It！可以替換的字詞

Your work is highly valued 您的工作是很有價值的（別小看自己）

We love your work 我們肯定您的工作

The work you do is among the best 您的工作表現是數一數二的

Your work is terrific 您的表現很棒

You're doing a great job 您做得很好

生日快樂，Sam！希望您今天過得很好！我們非常感激您付出的辛勞，我們也希望您會持續有好的表現。祝您有美好的一天。

really 真正地　keep on -ing 持續著～

✉ sample 742

Happy Birthday Jim!

Here's to a great day for a great guy! You should go out tonight and have a good time. Remember that you need to stay young at heart!

Cheers!

- - - - - - - -

Try It！可以替換的字詞

feel youthful 感覺還年輕

have a youthful attitude 擁有年輕的心態

be forever young 永遠年輕

be optimistic 樂觀開朗的

stay positive 保持正面積極的

生日快樂，Jim！預祝您這位優秀的人擁有美好的一天。您今晚應該出去好好玩樂一下。記住，您必須保持有一顆年輕的心。玩得愉快！

guy 男子　go out 外出　remember 記得　stay young 保持年輕

✉ sample 743

Dear _____

On your birthday, we wanted to let you know how much we value the great work you do and your commitment to this company. We wouldn't have been nearly as successful as we were this past year without you. We hope your day is wonderful.

Happy Birthday!

- - - - - - - -

在您生日這一天，我們想讓您知道，我們多麼看重您在工作上的好表現，以及您對公司的全心投入。過去這一年如果沒有您的話，我們幾乎無法達到目前如此成功的地步。我們祝您有美好的一天。生日快樂！

value 珍惜，看重，重視　commitment 奉獻，投入　not nearly 幾乎無法～

Try It！可以替換的字詞

your dedication 您的奉獻
your loyalty 您的忠誠
your devotion 您投入的努力
your faithfulness 您的忠心
how dependable you are
我們有多依賴您

✉ sample 744

Dear _____

Happy Birthday! I wish you health and happiness and many more good years! Have a terrific day today.

Best Wishes,

- - - - - - - -

生日快樂！我祝福您身體健康、幸福快樂，且歲歲有今朝！祝您今日有美好的一天。致上最深祝福。

wish 祝福　many 許多的　years 年　terrific 美好的

Try It！可以替換的字詞

well-being 身體健康
strength 強健
vigor 精神飽滿
energy 活力十足
fitness 身心健康

✉ sample 745

Dear [.............]

I hope you're having a great Birthday! You're really important to this whole organization, and we're all happy you're working with us. Enjoy your big day!

Happy Birthday!

department 部門
company 公司
establishment 機構
association 協會
group 團體

- - - - - - - -

祝福您生日大快樂！您對於這整個組織來說確實相當重要，我們都很開心有您和我們在一起工作。好好慶祝您的大日子吧！生日快樂！

important 重要的　whole 整個的　organization 組織　big day 大日子

✉ sample 746

Dear _____

Thank you very much for the bonus yesterday. It is ❶ wonderful working for such a ❷responsive boss. Please enjoy your weekend.

- - - - - - - -

❶magnificent 美好的
super 超棒的
amazing 令人驚奇的
astonishing 令人驚奇的
brilliant 極好的

❷receptive 樂於接受的
alert 謹慎的
family-oriented 以家庭為導向的
understanding 善解人意的
reactive 有問必答的

非常感謝您昨日發放的獎勵金。我們有這麼一位積極回應的老闆，能夠為他做事是很幸福的。祝您周末愉快。

bonus 獎勵金　responsive 有回應的　boss 老闆，主人

✉ sample 747

Dear _____

Thank you for the birthday cake yesterday. I was not expecting it at all. It is nice having great coworkers. Let's do dinner sometime, shall we?

- - - - - - - -

ice cream 冰淇淋
gifts 禮物
party 派對
surprises 驚喜
card 卡片

感謝您昨日的生日卡片。那真是出乎我意料之外。能有這麼棒的同事真好。我們找個時間一起吃晚餐，好嗎？

expect 預期　not at all 一點也不～　coworker 同事

✉ sample **748**

Dear ....

Please accept my thanks for everything you did yesterday. You really stepped up and took charge of the meeting. It was a job well done.

對於昨日您所做的一切，請接受我的道謝。您果然挺身而出，主持了這場會議。您做得很好。

accept 接受　step up 向前進，挺身而出　take charge of... 負責

✉ sample **749**

Dear ....

Thank you for working late last night. We wouldn't have finished this project without your extra effort. The company owes you a very large thank you. Please look for it in your paycheck next week!

感謝您昨晚不辭勞苦地加班。沒有您多付出的努力，我們無法完成這項專案。公司要好好答謝您一番。請在下週發放的薪津中留意您的報酬！

finish 完成　project 專案　extra 額外的，另外的　owe 虧欠～，因～而感謝
paycheck（支票支付的）薪資

Dear [ ]

I wanted to thank you for the extra help last week. Our committee really valued your work. We would not have been successful without you.

- - - - - - - -

對於您上週額外的協助，我想表達謝意。我們委員會真的非常重視您的工作。沒有您的話，我們是無法成功的。

---

committee 委員會　value 重視，珍視，珍惜　successful 成功的

executives 主管們
board 董事會
team 團隊
commission 委員會
agency 代理商

推薦 Recommendation

推薦特定職位給某人 **Recommending Someone for a Position** ▲

✉ sample 751

Dear ⌐ ¬

I'm writing to recommend Nicole Rosen for the position of Sales Manager. I've worked with Ms. Rosen a number of times in the past and always found her to be responsible and highly capable. I believe she has the knowledge, experience and connections to get you the results you're looking for.

If you have any questions, feel free to contact me.

- - - - - - - -

我寫這封信是想推薦 Nicole Rosen 擔任銷售經理。我過去曾與 Rosen 女士多次合作，我始終認為她有責任心而且能力很好。我相信她擁有這方面的知識、經驗和人脈，可以帶給您預期的結果。如果您有任何疑問，請隨時與我聯繫。

> recommend 推薦 position 職位，職務 responsible 有責任的 capable 有能力的
> connection 人際關係，人脈 results 結果，績效 look for 找尋～

Try It！可以替換的字詞

relations 人際關係
associates 人脈
prospects 潛力，前景
acquaintances 認識的人
contacts 門路

✉ sample 752

Dear ⌐ ¬

I've heard that you're looking for a new IT manager, and I thought I'd make a recommendation. I worked with Chris Gaston at Smith Tech for many years and I know that he is a very capable specialist with a strong management background. You could definitely use someone like that on your team.

Let me know if you have any questions about Mr. Gaston.

- - - - - - - -

我聽說您正在尋找一位新的 IT 經理，我想我這邊有推薦人選。我和史密斯科技的 Chris Gaston 共事多年，我知道他是一位非常有能力的專業人士，且擁有出色的管理背景。您絕對可以在您的團隊中雇用這樣的人。如果您對 Gaston 先生有任何疑問，請與我聯繫。

> recommendation 推薦 specialist 專家 management 管理，經營 background 背景 definitely 絕對地

Try It！可以替換的字詞

expert 專家
authority 權威
whiz 能手
professional 專業人士
consultant 顧問

✉ sample 753

Dear _____

I'm writing to recommend a former colleague of mine, Julia Frasier, for the position of Sales Coordinator. I've known Ms. Frasier for several years. She has climbed through the ranks at Giant Motors, and definitely has the experience for the position you are seeking to fill. If you have any questions, I'd be happy to talk to you about Ms. Frasier in more detail.

Try It！可以替換的字詞

progressed 前進
ascended 高升
excelled 表現突出
risen 晉升
advanced 晉升

- - - - - - - -

我寫這封信的目的是要推薦我的一位前同事 Julia Frasier 擔任跟單員。我認識 Frasier 女士多年。她從 Giant Motors 一路晉升上來，且對於您想填補的這個職缺，她絕對有相當的資歷。如果您有任何疑問，我很樂意更詳盡地與您討論 Frasier 女士。

former 先前的　colleague 同事　coordinator （對於計劃、發展等的）協調員　several years 數年　climb （付出努力）向上爬，晉升　rank 層級，高地位　be happy to... 很樂意～　detail 詳細說明

✉ sample 754

Dear _____

I've thought a little about the position you're trying to fill, and it occurs to me that I might know someone who fits the bill. Sean Thompson is a young database specialist I worked with last year. He was really able to get the job done efficiently and accurately. I can give you his contact information if you'd like.

I'll talk to you soon.

Try It！可以替換的字詞

is experienced 經驗豐富的
is qualified 具備資格的
is capable 有能力的
is competent 稱職的
is able 有能力的

- - - - - - - -

我稍微想過您要填補的職位，因此我突然想到一位我認識且符合資格的人。Sean Thompson 是我去年一起合作過的年輕資料管理師。他確實能夠有效率且準確地完成工作。如果您願意，我可以給您他的聯絡咨詢。到時候再聊。

a little 稍微地　it occurs to me that... 我突然想到～　fit the bill 符合資格要求　specialist 專家　efficiently 有效率地　accurately 準確地

✉ **sample 755**

Dear ⌈............⌋

I know you're looking for someone to fill the Executive Assistant position, and I wondered if you had thought about **promoting** from within. I think Jeff Sims would be a terrific fit for that position. He's got the experience, and I think he's ready to move up from the receptionist desk. What do you think?

- - - - - - - -

Try It！可以替換的字詞

moving up 升遷
raising 晉升
upgrading 晉升
elevating 晉升
supporting 支援

我知道您正在找人填補行政助理這個職位，我想知道您是否想過從內部晉升。我認為 Jeff Sims 非常適合這個職位。他有經驗，我認為他已準備好從接待處升上了。您覺得如何呢？

fill 填補～　executive 行政上的，執行的　assistant 助理，助手　move up 晉升

✉ sample 756

Dear _____

Thank you for taking time to get in touch with us. I've arranged to interview Ms. Rosen on the 21st. She sounds like a terrific candidate. I'll let you know how it goes. We are always happy to have recommendations.

Thank you.

- - - - - - - -

感謝您抽出時間來聯繫我們。我已經安排在 21 日和 Rosen 女士面談。她似乎是一位很優秀的候選人。我會告訴您結果如何。我們一直都很樂意接受推薦。謝謝您。

Try It! 可以替換的字詞

applicant 求職者，申請人
contender 競爭者
interviewee 接受面試者
nominee 被提名人
entrant 競試者

take time 花時間　get in touch with 與～取得聯繫　arrange 安排　terrific 非常好的　candidate 候選人

✉ sample 757

Dear _____

Thank you for your recommendation of Mr. Gaston. Unfortunately, we have already filled the IT manager position. We will keep Mr. Gaston's information on file should a position open up further down the line.

Thanks again for your help.

- - - - - - - -

感謝您推薦 Gaston 先生。遺憾的是，我們已經找到人填補 IT 經理的職位了。我們會保留 Gaston 先生的資料，也許未來會有其適當的職缺。再次感謝您的幫助。

Try It! 可以替換的字詞

later 日後
later on 後來
shortly 不久之後
in the future 未來
someday 有朝一日

unfortunately 遺憾地　fill the position 填補這個職位　on file（文件等）存檔，記錄下來備查
open up 開放

✉ sample 758

Dear [＿＿＿＿]

Thank you so much for forwarding Ms. Fraiser's name to us. She turned out to be exactly whom we needed. We interviewed her last week and immediately offered her the position. The hiring process is always streamlined when we have good recommendations.

Thank you again for your help.

- - - - - - - -

Try It！可以替換的字詞

shortened 縮短的
simplified 簡化的
cut down 縮短
easy 簡單化的
unproblematic 不成問題的

非常感謝您將 Fraiser 女士的名字轉寄給我們。而她竟然就是我們所需要的人選。我們上週與她面試，並立即給了她這個職位。當我們有好的推薦人選時，總是會精簡聘顧流程。再次感謝您的幫助。

> forward 轉發，轉寄　turn out 結果是～　interview 面試　immediately 立即，立刻　hiring 僱用，聘用　streamline 提高效率，簡化流程

✉ sample 759

Dear [＿＿＿＿]

I appreciate you forwarding us Mr. Thompson's name. He sounds like a strong candidate. Could you tell us a little more about exactly what kind of database work he did for you? We're looking for a pretty specific skill set, so I'd like to know as much as possible.

Thanks for your help on this.

- - - - - - - -

Try It！可以替換的字詞

exact 精確的
precise 確切的
definite 確定的
clear-cut 明確的
distinct 顯著的

我很感謝您轉發 Thompson 先生的名單給我們。聽起來他是個非常優秀的候選人。您能告訴我們更多關於他為您做了什麼樣的資料庫嗎？我們正在找的人須具備相當特定的技能，所以我想盡可能了解。感謝您對於此事的幫助。

> database 資料庫　specific 特定的　skill set 技能　as much as possible 盡可能多的

✉ sample 760

Dear _____

Thanks for the recommendation. We had been considering Sims for a promotion, but we heard from a couple of other people in the office that they had had some problems with him in the past. We're a little ❶wary of putting someone with a history of conflict in such a ❷ sensitive position. Thanks for the idea though.

Regards,

– – – – – – – –

Try It！可以替換的字詞

❶ cautious 謹慎的

suspicious 有疑慮的

leery 猜疑的

careful 小心的

guarded 戒備的

❷ touchy 棘手的

vulnerable 敏感的，脆弱的

susceptible 敏感的

fragile 敏感的，脆弱的

frail 敏感的

謝謝推薦。我們一直在考慮讓 Sims 晉升，但我們從辦公室其他同仁那裡得知，他們過去和他有一些問題。對於將一個過去曾與同仁發生過衝突的人，擺在這樣一個敏感的職位上，我們會有些不放心。不過還是謝謝您的意見。祝福您。致上問候。

consider 考慮 a couple of... 一些 past 過去的 wary 謹慎的 conflict 衝突，矛盾

邀請、招待 Invitation

Case
01 | **邀請某人共進晚餐 Inviting Someone over for Dinner** ▲

✉ sample 761

Dear [............]

I'm glad the meeting went so well yesterday. I meant to ask you if you'd like to come over for dinner next weekend. It would be nice to spend some time together outside the **confines** of the office. Let me know if you're up for it.

I'll talk to you soon.

- - - - - - - -

我很高興昨天的會議進展順利。我想問您下週末是否願意過來吃個晚飯。在公司外面一起度過一段時光還不錯。請讓我知道您是否有意願。我們再聊。

> glad 高興的　come over 過來　spend time together 共度時光　confine 邊界，限制，範圍
> up for... 願意～

Try It!可以替換的字詞

walls 圍牆
borders 邊界
perimeters 邊緣
restrictions 邊界
limits 邊界

✉ sample 762

Dear [............]

I hope **everything is going well** in your office. I'm writing to invite you to dinner. My wife and I are going to have a few people over for a little get-together on Saturday at 7:00. If you're free, we'd love to have you. Let me know.

Kind regards,

- - - - - - - -

但願您公司一切順利。我寫這封信是想邀請您一起去吃晚飯。我太太和我想在週六晚上七點邀請大家小聚一下。如果您有空，我們希望您能加入。請讓我知道。謹致問候。

> go well 進行順利　have... come over 叫某人來　get-together 相聚　free 空閒的

Try It!可以替換的字詞

all is well 一切順利
things are fine 一切都沒事
everyone is doing well 大家都順利
the week has been pleasant
過去這一週過得愉快
everything is working out well
一切進行順利

✉ sample 763

Dear ⌐ ⌐

I was wondering if you'd be interested in dinner at my place this weekend. It would give us a chance to unwind a little after **hectic** schedule of the past few weeks. Let me know if you can make it Saturday evening.

I look forward to hearing from you.

- - - - - - -

crazy 狂亂的
chaotic 混亂的
hairy 可怕的
wild 忙亂的
frantic 狂亂的

我想知道您這週末是否有興趣來我家吃飯。在過去幾週忙碌的行程結束之後，這會讓我們有機會放鬆一下。請讓我知道您是否週六晚上能來。我期待您的回覆。

wonder 想知道　interested 對～感興趣的　my place 我家　weekend 週末　schedule 行程（表）

✉ sample 764

Dear ⌐ ⌐

I'm looking forward to working with you on the upcoming project. Would you like to come over to my house for dinner this weekend? We could get to know each other a little better before we get started on the deal. Let me know if you'd be interested.

Thanks,

- - - - - - -

Try It! 可以替換的字詞

get acquainted 認識一下
chat a little 聊天一下
have a drink or two 喝一兩杯
enjoy a little downtime
享受一點休息時光
learn about each other 互相學習

我期待在即將進行的專案中與您合作。您這個週末可以來我家吃晚飯嗎？在我們開始進行這項交易之前，我們可以稍微更加認識彼此。請讓我知道您是否願意過來。謝謝。

look forward to 期待～　upcoming 即將到來的　get started on 開始做～

✉ sample 765

Dear ⸬⸬⸬⸬⸬⸬⸬

I'm having a few people from the office over for dinner Saturday night. If you can make it, we'd love to see you there. I think it's good for the staff to see each other outside the office every once in a while. Let me know if you can make it.

I'll talk to you soon.

- - - - - - - -

personnel 人員
employees 員工
work force 僱員
team 團隊
workers 工人

我將在週六晚間請公司幾位同仁共進晚餐。如果您可以，我們很希望看到您來。我認為員工們偶爾在辦公室以外的地方相聚是件好事。請讓我知道您是否能來。我們再聊。

would love to 很願意～ staff 員工 each other 彼此，互相 once in a while 有時候，不定期地

✉ sample 766

Dear (.............)

We will be holding a party next Friday evening to celebrate our latest client implementation. I hope you'll be able to ❶attend the event, as you have been a key player on this project and we wouldn't have been nearly as successful without you. Please see the attached ❷ memo for details on the party.

Regards,

- - - - - - - -

Try It! 可以替換的字詞

❶ make it to 前來參加
make an appearance at 出席
be present at 出席
be available for 可以參加
join us at 加入我們的～

❷ guides 指南
maps 地圖
directions 指示
instructions 説明
information 資訊

我們將在下週五晚上舉辦一場派對，以慶祝我們最近在經營客戶上的成就。我希望您能參加這個活動，因為您一直是這個專案的關鍵人物，沒有您我們不會如此接近成功。有關聚會的詳細資訊，請參閱隨附的備忘錄。謹致問候。

hold a party 舉辦一場派對　implementation 表現，實現　attend 參加　key 關鍵的
not nearly 不會這麼接近～

✉ sample 767

Dear (.............)

I'm having a little get-together at my place on Saturday. I'm inviting a few people from the office. It'll be a pretty informal affair. Let me know if you'd like to come.

I'll talk to you soon.

- - - - - - - -

Try It! 可以替換的字詞

casual 非正式的
relaxed 放鬆的
comfortable 舒適的
easygoing 悠閒的
laid back 休閒的

我週六將在我的住處舉辦一場小聚會。我將邀請公司幾位同事。這是一個非正式的活動。讓我知道您是否願意過來。我們見面再聊。

my place 我的住處　people from the office 公司的同事　informal 非正式的　affair 活動，事件
would like to... 想要～

✉ sample 768

Dear ⌐‾‾‾‾‾‾‾¬

As you know, John Smith, CEO, has recently published a book on the habits of effective management in a corporate setting. To celebrate his accomplishment, we will be holding a dinner party with our acquaintances on July 15th in his honor. You will be receiving an invitation in the near future with the event details. Please save the date.

Thanks.

- - - - - - - -

如您所知，首席執行長 John Smith 最近出了一本關於企業環境中有效管理習慣養成的書。為慶祝他的成就，我們將於7月15日與我們熟識的一些人舉行晚宴以表恭賀之意。您不久之後會收到邀請函，內含活動的細節。請記住此日期，謝謝。

habit 習慣，習性　corporate 企業的　accomplishment 成就，成績　acquaintance 熟識的人
in one's honor 向某人致意　save保留

✉ sample 769

Dear ⌐‾‾‾‾‾‾‾¬

To celebrate the closing of the Crawford deal, I'm throwing a little party at my house on Friday. We'll have drinks and hors d'oeuvres at around 6:00. I'd love to see you there. Let me know if you can attend.

Regards,

- - - - - - - -

為了慶祝拿到 Crawford 交易案，我周五將在我家裡舉辦了一場小型派對。我們將在6:00左右開始供應飲料和開胃小菜。我很希望可以見到您來。請讓我知道您是否能參加。致上問候。

deal 交易，買賣　throw a party 舉辦一場派對　around 大約～

✉ **sample 770**

Dear [＿＿＿＿＿]

Congratulations on landing the contract. You and your team did a terrific job. I'd like to celebrate with you by throwing a party this weekend at my place. I was considering Friday evening after work. Let me know if that would be a good night for you.

Thanks again,

- - - - - - - -

恭喜拿下這份合約。您和您的團隊表現得非常好。這個週末在我住家舉辦一場派對，我想和您一起慶祝。我正考慮週五下班後的晚上舉行。請讓我知道這是否對您來說會是個美好的夜晚。再次感謝。

congratulation 恭喜　land 取得　contract 合約　terrific 極好的　after work 下班後

台灣廣廈 國際出版集團
Taiwan Mansion International Group

國家圖書館出版品預行編目資料

外國人天天在用上班族萬用E-mail大全 / 白善燁著；游辰云、Joung譯
-- 新北市：國際學村，2018.10
面；　公分 . --（英文隨身學系列；14）
ISBN 978-986-454-086-0　（平裝）
1.語言學習 2.英語學習

805.179　　　　　　　　　　　　　　　107012901

 國際學村

外國人天天在用上班族萬用 E-mail 大全

作　　者／白善燁　　　　　　編輯中心／第六編輯室
翻　　譯／游辰云・Joung　　編輯長／伍俊宏・編輯／許加慶
　　　　　　　　　　　　　　封面設計／曾詩涵・內頁排版／菩薩蠻數位文化有限公司
　　　　　　　　　　　　　　製版・印刷・裝訂／皇甫・秉成

行企研發中心總監／陳冠蒨　　整合行銷組／陳宜鈴
媒體公關組／徐毓庭　　　　　綜合業務組／何欣穎

發　行　人／江媛珍
法律顧問／第一國際法律事務所 余淑杏律師・北辰著作權事務所 蕭雄淋律師
出　　版／台灣廣廈有聲圖書有限公司
　　　　　　地址：新北市235中和區中山路二段359巷7號2樓
　　　　　　電話：（886）2-2225-5777・傳真：（886）2-2225-8052

代理印務・全球總經銷／知遠文化事業有限公司
　　　　　　地址：新北市222深坑區北深路三段155巷25號5樓
　　　　　　電話：（886）2-2664-8800・傳真：（886）2-2664-8801
　　　　　　網址：www.booknews.com.tw（博訊書網）
郵政劃撥／劃撥帳號：18836722
　　　　　　劃撥戶名：知遠文化事業有限公司（※單次購書金額未達500元，請另付60元郵資。）

■出版日期：2018年10月　　　■初版8刷：2022年12月
ISBN：978-986-454-086-0　　版權所有，未經同意不得重製、轉載、翻印。